Old Dog, New Tricks

The Lycan Files: Book 6

JP Cameron

To Madi and Nyah
Night and day
Sisters, nieces and trouble twice over.

No matter the path the future takes,
You'll always have each other.
Treasure that —
Let the small stuff slide as life is
Too darn short.

Copyright © 2021 JP Cameron

All rights reserved

ISBN: 9798492513986

Imprint: Independently published

Books in the Series:

Dog Days

Puppy Love

The Furry and the Furious

Barking Mad

Let Sleeping ~~Dogs~~ Gods Lie

Old Dog, New Tricks

Dogs of War

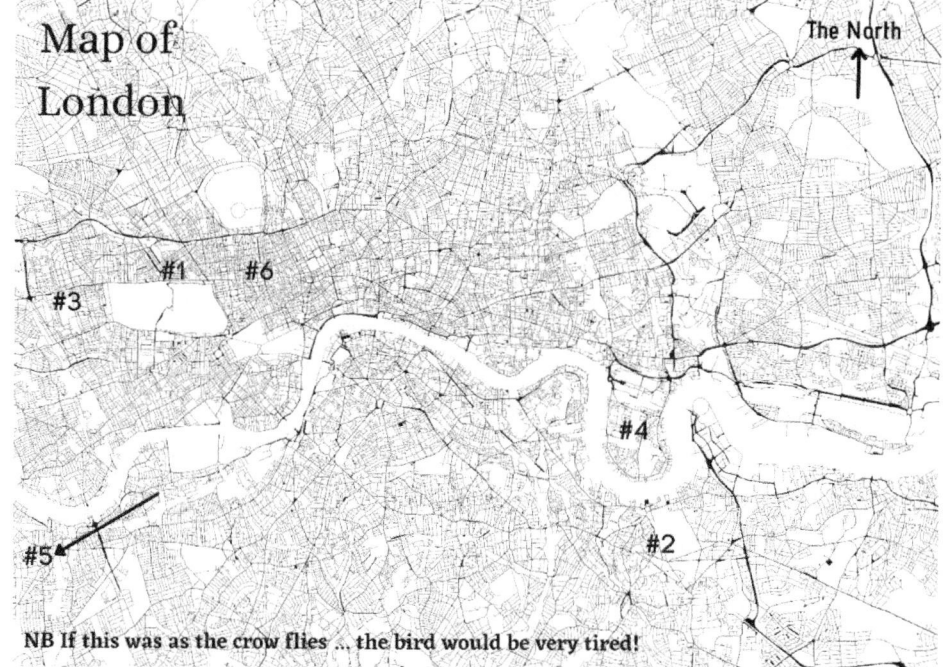

Sites you might find of interest

#1 Pet Cemetery, Hyde Park

The Hyde Park pet cemetery (originally the London Hyde Park Dog Cemetery and advertised as The Secret Pet Cemetery of Hyde Park) is a disused burial ground for animals in Hyde Park, London. It was established in the early 1880s in the garden of Victoria Lodge, home of one of the park keepers.

The cemetery became popular after the burial of a dog belonging to Sarah Fairbrother, wife of Prince George, Duke of Cambridge. Some 1,000 burials were carried out before the cemetery was generally closed in 1903; sporadic burials were carried out thereafter until 1976. Most of the animals are dogs, though some cats, monkeys and birds were also buried. The site is owned by the charity The Royal Parks and not open to the public except as part of occasional tours.

#2 Greenwich Park

Greenwich Park is a former hunting park in Greenwich and one of the largest single green spaces in south-east London. One of the Royal Parks of London, and the first to be enclosed (in 1433), it covers 74 hectares (180 acres), and is part of the Greenwich World Heritage Site. It commands fine views over the River Thames, the Isle of Dogs and the City of London (Simon Jenkins rated the view of the Royal Hospital with Canary Wharf in the distance as one of the top ten in England).

The park is open year-round. It is listed Grade I on the Register of Historic Parks and Gardens. In 2020, it was awarded a National Lottery grant to restore its historic features, build a learning centre, enhance the park's biodiversity, and provide better access for people with disabilities.

#3 Holland Park

Holland Park is an area of Kensington, on the western edge of Central London, that contains a street and public park of the same name. It has no official boundaries but is roughly bounded by Kensington High Street to the south, Holland Road to the west, Holland Park Avenue to the north, and Kensington Church Street to the east. Adjacent districts are Notting Hill to the north, Earl's Court to the south, and Shepherd's Bush to the northwest.

The area is principally composed of tree-lined streets with large Victorian townhouses, and contains many shops, cultural tourist attractions such as the Design Museum, luxury spas, hotels, and restaurants, as well as the embassies of several countries. The street of Holland Park is formed from three linked roads constructed between 1860 and 1880 in projects of master builders William and Francis Radford, who were contracted to build and built over 200 houses in the area. Notable nineteenth-century residential developments in the area include the Royal Crescent and Aubrey House.

#4 Lotus floating restaurant - Isle of Dogs

London's worldly-wise diners may have seen it all, but even the most jaded of customers would need a heart of stone not to be at least a little bit excited about dining aboard a flamboyant Chinese boat in the middle of futuristic Docklands.

The regular menu is less out of the ordinary, but there's a wide choice of dim sum seafood dishes including the fabulously hyperbolic 'gargantuan prawns'. If you're 'feeling brave' (their words), staff will happily guide you through some 'weird & wonderful' specialities from the separate Chinese menu: brace yourself for plates of sea slug, fish lips & duck's feet hotpot. There's a function room on the top deck, with the bonus of firework displays, dragon-boat racing & lion dances by arrangement.

#5 Glastonbury Tor

Glastonbury Tor is a hill near Glastonbury in the English county of Somerset, topped by the roofless St Michael's Tower, a Grade I listed building. The entire site is managed by the National Trust and has been designated a scheduled monument. The Tor is mentioned in Celtic mythology, particularly in myths linked to King Arthur, and has several other enduring mythological and spiritual associations.

The conical hill of clay and Blue Lias rises from the Somerset Levels. It was formed when surrounding softer deposits were eroded, leaving the hard cap of sandstone exposed. The slopes of the hill are terraced, but the method by which they were formed remains unexplained.

#6 All Saints Church, Margaret Street

All Saints, Margaret Street, is a Grade I listed Anglo-Catholic church in London. The church was designed by the architect William Butterfield and built between 1850 and 1859. It has been hailed as Butterfield's masterpiece and a pioneering building of the High Victorian Gothic style that would characterize British architecture from around 1850 to 1870.

The church is situated on the north side of Margaret Street in Fitzrovia, near Oxford Street, within a small courtyard. Two other buildings face onto this courtyard: one is the vicarage and the other (formerly a choir school) now houses the parish room and flats for assistant priests.

All Saints is noted for its architecture, style of worship, and musical tradition.

Contents

Sites you might find of interest

Contents

Prologue

Chapter 1

Chapter 2

Chapter 3

Chapter 4

Chapter 5

Chapter 6

Chapter 7

Chapter 8

Chapter 9

Chapter 10

Chapter 11

Chapter 12

Chapter 13

Chapter 14

Chapter 15

Chapter 16

Chapter 17

Chapter 18

Chapter 19

Chapter 20

Chapter 21

Chapter 22

Chapter 23
Chapter 24
Chapter 25
Chapter 26
Chapter 27
Chapter 28
Chapter 29
Chapter 30
Chapter 31
Chapter 32
Chapter 33
Chapter 34
Chapter 35
Chapter 36
Chapter 37
Chapter 38
Chapter 39
Chapter 40
Chapter 41
Chapter 42
Chapter 43
Chapter 44
Chapter 45
Chapter 46
Chapter 47
Chapter 48
Chapter 49
Chapter 50

Chapter 51
Chapter 52
Chapter 53
Chapter 54
Chapter 55
Chapter 56
Chapter 57
Chapter 58
Chapter 59
Chapter 60
About the Author

Prologue

So we've covered a lot of ground. What the Realms are like, what creatures there are who call them their home. Why mortals and immortals tend to have problems co-existing. And what happens when things inevitably go wrong between them … like neighbours renewing a decades old grudge because *our Darren heard Ethel from next door say we were too loud the other night*, or some such excuse for weapons to be taken down from the wall and armour donned.

I guess one thing we haven't really spoken about is the Law of the Real. What rules do the immortals have to abide by in their own Realm, compared to the often thoroughly complicated, sometimes conflicting and most usually annoying regulations and laws that mortals think up to complicate their lives and offer another avenue of corruption and abuse to be explored.

Mortals, given a simple rule to follow, will often expend far more energy in efforts to avoid sticking to it *without it being noted* than actually following it would have required … or find a way to either use the rule to demean and make their fellow mortals suffer because of the rule, or decide that the rule is actually against their rights, beliefs or general existence and spend further energies trying to have the rule revoked, changed or those that have to implement the rule castigated for their part in the suffering it causes.

Immortals are a lot simpler, on the whole, yet at the same time can be just as convoluted and stress inducing when it comes to laws.

The Courts typically set the statutes for the lands where Ivory, Shadow and Wyld hold strong. Wherever Oberon, Madb and to a lesser degree Herne rule, the laws are medieval in their structure. To obey, without question, the Lords and Ladies of the Courts. And to not in any way seek to breach the Accords written between the Realms. That tends to be the simplest interpretation of what passes as laws that change depending on the

Courts' current moods ... in times of peace, and oft-time boredom, Oberon and Titania were known to pass random stipulations very much based on their latest whim. Down to changing dress codes of the Courts, the types of drinks that were to be served at any formal gathering and to whom, even who was allowed to dance with whom at the Beltane fayre or All Hallows Eve. Duels had been fought and lives lost over matters as simple as who had whose favour when it was decided that they were instead meant to for another. Much like the old mortal Royal Courts, before people rose up in revolution and started cutting off Royal heads to prove that they might be invested by God, but they were still only mortal and as vulnerable to an axe-swing or guillotine blade as the most common peasant.

In times of war, which given many mortals' mistaken assumption that what lay beyond the Veil was paradise, happened more often than you would think ... the laws were much simpler. Obey one's Lord and Lady, defend one's Court and use any and all means to bring down their enemies. You can wear what you like, sleep with who you like and generally do what you like as long as it is in defence of the Lord and Lady. Far less complicated than how mortals fare at times of conflict when their own laws confound and befuddle the simplest soldier on the battlefield. Are you treating your enemies fairly? Are your actions honourable and noble, when your enemy is trying their very best to end the lives of you and your blade brothers, your shield sisters? Will anyone have cause to come back after the battle is won, to point a finger and say *you may have fought well but I think you should have instead done this or that*, from the safety of their desks.

And whilst there are times that it is right and proper to ask these questions, and hold those in power to task for how they acted, it is also often true that the foot soldier on the ground doesn't care about anything but keeping alive, them and their brethren, when faced by a bunch of murderous sods also seeking to come out on top. Perspectives are based on who is holding the weapon and where they are pointing it.

Of course, there are many places beyond the Courts' immediate control. Whilst the Verdance is the Wyld's hunting ground, even Herne is not able to say that his will and law is obeyed throughout all the far reaches of that vast forest. And deep within the mountains, high up in the cloud cities and out on the shimmering oceans that are to be found in the Real, immortal creatures pay only lip service to the laws passed at the far-away

Courts ... safe in the knowledge that unless they seriously fuck up, no-one is going to bother wasting their energies hunting them down to stand trial for their wrongdoings.

And that's where their greatest mistake lies. For whilst the Courts might not be bothered what the dwarrow of the Deeps get up to, or the Naga out on the far distant Isles, we Redcloaks are tasked with tracking down lawbreakers like bounty hunters of the old Wild West in the Mortal Realm. More than one miscreant, thinking themselves safe sat within their fortress far beyond the reach of Oberon, has wakened to find one or more of the packs smiling back at them, usually at the end of something sharp.

We don't make friends for the work we do in the Real, but we do earn grudging respect and a tidy income for our efforts, since like most of the Uppers of society, the Courts are willing to pay well to save their energies and make trouble go away. We definitely *could* have a quieter life if we just stuck to patrolling the Mortal Realm, keeping the Ways secure and ass-kicking any Accord-breakers from here to the Furies' tender care ... but we echo the words of many bounty hunters who could have retired and lived simpler, easier lives with those they love but instead chose the open road, the dirt and muck, the shed blood and pained wounds.

Where'd the fun in that be?

Chapter 1

Mortals always seem to be at a significant disadvantage against the magical creatures they face in folklore and mythology. Thankfully, Nature has provided a variety of substances and tools to even the balance and make the mightiest fairy sorcerer feel faint and weak, or the most horrible ogre suddenly cowed and craven.

Just the sort of thing any plucky hero or heroine needs to vanquish their foe.

Somewhere far from London.

Thick greenery clung to him, as he crashed headlong through the lush undergrowth, shoving aside broad leaves that sprouted from every bough and branch, snapping vines that sought to snare and catch at him. The heat was oppressive, the air saturated with a cloying dampness that invaded every gasping breath he took as he ran. Too afraid to stop, too terrified to think of what lay behind him.

And what might be following him.

As he stumbled and sobbed, his mind leapt from the present to the recent past like some badly narrated movie. The excavation of the newly discovered Mayan site had been a crowning glory, a mud-smeared and vine wrapped jewel untouched by thieves or members of his chosen profession. A unique find - somehow missed when the larger settlements had already been unearthed and claimed. Let the world have their *Chichen Itza, Tulum* and *Teotihuacan*, crowded with tourists and made over into cheap attractions for screaming brats and overweight oglers.

No, this find was more akin to *Calakmul*. Far from the beaten track and lying deep in the heart of the Amazonian jungle. Discovered purely by chance when photos from a private aircraft identified too-regular shaped structures peeking from the foliage of the forest. The images had been recovered after the aircraft in question was impounded for running drugs across South America, cutting through the undiscovered expanse of the Amazon rainforest to avoid the eyes of the authorities.

Certain societies, with enough funding and key contacts at the highest levels, were always on the watch for such evidence, the merest chance of a new discovery worth the payments made, the promises kept. And this had been one such find.

The archaeological expedition was a joint effort between the United States and the United Kingdom, with experts from various fields of study coming together in a show of solidarity amongst rising political unrest between the two countries. Initial mapping of the location revealed artefacts of unsurpassed beauty and in pristine condition, untouched by the ravages of time. And the pictographs … oh the images found detailed the lives, and deaths, of so many at this site … it had been like opening a window in time and stepping through.

With guides recruited from natives of the region, always ready to earn dollars and spend days away from their fishing nets and huts, and with armed soldiers to deter any bandits or locals from stealing the wealth of history this site looked to contain, the thirty strong company had traversed through swamp and forest, river and mud hole, to secure their foothold at the location as quickly as possible.

And what a find! Like *Calakmul*, twin pyramids surrounded by lower lying buildings enscribed with pictograms of exquisite detail, structures filled with ancient pottery and tools, clothing and even foodstuffs somehow preserved. The first pyramid temple was familiar territory, mirroring a site found at *Edzna* and praising the twin Gods of Sunrise and Sunset with a temple of Masks in honour of their divinity.

But the second? This was unlike anything found before.

A pyramid *inverted*, leading down into the depths of the dark forbidding earth. Away from the sunlight and warmth, far from the faces of their benevolent gods. The bottom chamber had been sealed, passages leading down adorned with fearsome masks and further images of torture and death. The whole structure had an oppressive feel to it, weighing down on every member of the team as they explored and recorded their findings. Statues of men and beasts, some familiar like the Jaguar Gods but some more fantastical that even their palaeozoologist from the UK could attest to ever seeing, and had seemed struck by their likeness to creatures of myth and legend.

He slapped a leaf from his face at the memory of her. Something he recalled as the woman had stared at the stone statues. As a prominent archaeologist himself, he knew well the feelings of awe and wonder when finding such relics of the past, gazing upon them and thinking back to the hands that had crafted them. The images they sought to freeze forever in their art. But she ... she had seemed off somehow, even afraid as she first looked on them. And that had made no sense.

He stopped, dragging a ragged gulp of moist air into his lungs. Ahead, somewhere, he knew lay civilisation. A road they had discovered on their sojourns of the area, made by loggers or drug cartels to facilitate transport through this vastness of jungle. If he could just reach that, follow it wherever it led, he had a chance.

More than those who remained behind.

The day they broke the seals on the final chamber had been one they felt would be recorded in the annuls of history, like the first pyramids of Egypt. The team had noted the room was locked from the outside with dire warnings set in stone tablets awaiting anyone foolish enough to approach. Their translators had struggled with the full meaning of the message, but were sure of one thing. A dire warning against *Ba'alche' ku xíimbal bey juntúul máak*.

'*The beast that walks as man*'.

Typical tribal superstition, they had all agreed, as the workers finally broke through the sacred seals and opened the solid stone door.

It had been a murder pit, much like found at *Teotihuacan*'s pyramid of the Moon. But far larger, with easily identifiable remains of men and beasts that had been torn apart in the most barbaric of ways. An altar, directly below the heart of the pyramid, deepest within the earth, and upon it a stone-flaked knife and bowl. Stained with the lives of countless sacrifices.

Oh, if they had only stopped then. Left things well enough alone!

The disappearances had started soon after. Firstly, guides and workers vanishing into the night without a trace. The guards were not troubled, and the research team accepted that such things invariably happened. Then Professor Lain Brookes was taken. The soldiers with them had scouted around, fearing bandits were operating in the area ... but when they found his body, they knew no bandit could have been responsible for his death.

No man, even.

A crack of something breaking underfoot echoed in the undergrowth behind him, and he jerked, realising he'd stood still for too long. Shooting a quick look around him for any sign of his pursuer, he sobbed a prayer to God to see him safe and kept from harm, then staggered into a run again as he thrust foliage out of his way.

Too many dead, all their faces staring back at him, filling his mind till he wanted to scream and beg for their mercy. And behind, that feeling, that presence, looming with death in its wake.

He slipped, skidding in wet mud and tangling in a mass of knotted vines. Sobbing, he tore at the greenery, pushing himself up into a crouch. Wincing at a stabbing pain that tore through his ankle. Twisted, maybe worse. But he couldn't stop ...

Breath fell on his neck, hot and fetid, stinking with the tang of coppery metal. Unmistakable, even in the depths of the jungle.

"Oh god, no!" He cried out as he scrambled back, seeking to escape what stalked him. "Leave me alone!"

But still it came on.

"NO! NO! Please, leave me alone! We didn't know what we were doing! No! *Please!*" He screamed, raising his arms to beg at the other, a last attempt to save himself. "Take anything you want, just leave me alone!"

He jerked his passport and wallet from his shirt pocket, tossing them down along with his phone. Anything of value, an offering to save his life.

"Just take them! Please!" He begged, eyes staring up at the other, disbelief and fear pounding in his head. "Why are you doing this?!"

Amber eyes blazed, and a guttural snarl echoed in the suddenly silent forest as the only answer to his pleas.

Savage screams rent the air, causing birds to shriek and burst into flight, escaping what was happening beneath them. The sounds guttered, fading to gasps torn from bloodied lips, then finally stilled.

Amber burned bright in the shadows, as sounds echoed around the forest floor. All too familiar for both predator and prey, those animals which watched from their hiding places. The crack of bone, the tearing of flesh. The tang of blood spilled to soak the ground and darken the earth, as the creature fed.

Until finally, silence settled once more upon the scene. The presence faded, vanishing back into the dark undergrowth. Leaving behind the ruins of a life, the scraps for smaller predators to fight over. Yet something of itself lingered, causing those animals brave enough to approach to stop … sniff the air … then turn away. Their hunger overruled by the taste of what had filled the air only a short while before.

Fear.

And death.

Chapter 2

Cold Iron

Cold Iron is iron taken from meteoric iron - hence nearly pure, then smelted into form. This was not unheard of in ancient days - Tutenkhamen had an iron dagger in his tomb, and it was made from meteoric iron, and hence one of the most valuable items in the hoard. The fact of cold-forging the meteorite metal is thought to retain the purity of the metal, whilst other 'hot forged' iron picks up impurities in the smelting.

Whatever the reason, Cold Iron is an effective deterrent to fae of all kinds. It breaks their glamour, interrupts their natural healing abilities and inflicts a wasting sickness on them that robs them of much of their strength and magic.

More bloody missing cats.

I groaned as I slipped open the file on my desk, left there by Jacob earlier that morning and sat waiting for me to make my way into the office. A coffee mug steamed by my elbow and a half-eaten pastrami and pickle sandwich kept it company as I read the brief details.

Six months had passed since *'the event'*. When a chunk of London had vanished behind rolling walls of mist that enclosed the four-borough segment from all sides as well as above and below. The mortal residents left outside had initially been warned of some sort of chemical leak, possibly a terrorist attack, and kept from attempting to enter the mists through barricades, blockades and as much man- and woman-power that could be thrown at the problem.

Conspiracy theories had blossomed like fungi on rotten wood across the internet as time ticked by, whilst the authorities dealt with a never-ending stream of requests, pleas and demands to free those trapped inside the mists, allow access for business owners to their premises and for researchers and concerned citizens to be granted rights to investigate the phenomena.

All, of course, flatly denied.

There had been small scale riots, with mortals demanding to be allowed to enter the mists and find those that had disappeared. These had been curtailed after those involved were made to bear witness to the effects of the mists on biological matter. A pig's corpse, if I remember rightly, was forced into contact with the mists whilst wrapped in protective layers meant to simulate clothing. The result had *not* been pretty, and apart from an outcry from the animal rights' sector about wilful misuse of a deceased porcus, the attempts by civilians to breach the barricades and enter the mists had dropped off significantly.

There were still those who would not be deterred, convinced some grand conspiracy was afoot, or that riches to be plundered lay just beyond the mists. Despite all the efforts of the mortal authorities, and the extra help we lent as quietly and discreetly as possible, some idiots got through.

Posts on the web showed the last footage of the doomed, as they ventured where they really shouldn't. Nothing grabbed them … the horror enthusiasts disappointed when beasts didn't appear and rip the intruders limb from limb.

They simply … vaporised. Mostly with a scream, or at least some noise to suggest their passing had not been easy or pleasant. Leaving just enough physical evidence behind to be swept up into a jar and returned to any loved ones, to bury or do whatever they wished with the mortal remains of their kith and kin.

Six months on, we were down to maybe one event a week, if not longer. Usually a case of someone demanding their missing friend be rescued, after admitting they had stupidly attempted to cross the mists. Pilots had stopped trying to fly over the barrier and drop in from above, when their machinery failed, and they were forced to make emergency landings or simply crash. So many drones had been lost in the first few weeks that way as well, insurers had started adding clauses to accident-coverage – *any and all reference to being lost in the mists of London* meaning automatic denial of repayment.

The rest of the world watched and waited, the news feeds still entertaining all the running theories on the *'localised event in London, UK'*. From experimental research gone horribly wrong, to a biological event of unknown origins. Aliens were mentioned a lot, whilst a host of fake mystics and prophets crawled out of the woodwork, to reveal they were in touch with the lost. To pass on messages of good health and reassurance for a simple donation of however many dollars or pounds or euros, or currency of whatever denomination you had to spare …

The mortals, on the whole, seemed to have no real idea what was going on, and what had landed on their very doorstep.

Which is how we wanted it to stay, for as long as possible.

I picked up the case file and waved it in the air, looking around the room.

"Cheers you'se all!" I told my fellow packmates, as they looked up from where they lounged and worked their way through their own breakfasts. "It makes me all warm and fuzzy-like, knowing you care as much as I do about mortals and their missing pets. This must have taken, what, all night to scrounge up all these pamphlets? Nice job!"

Chuckles greeted me, as well as the odd meow, but I shrugged the jibes off, lowering the file and taking another bite of my sandwich. A little bit of normality, compared to the shitstorm we'd fielded just before all things Twilight-y went to hell in a handbag … well, I could live with that.

Well, maybe not *all* of it, as my mind waltzed immediately back to the missing person in the room, and the debt I owed one particular Goddess.

"Find the one who is lost. Find. My. Daughter."

Yeah, no pressure there at all.

"How many does that make now?" Emma asked as she stopped by my desk, mug of steaming jasmine tea filling the air around her with a fresh, floral bite. She and Jacob had been running covert support teams, keeping the boundaries of Twilight clear of mortals. A task assigned to the packs by Cormac Smith in the week after things went so badly wrong.

The OPS operative seemed to be in charge of managing the phenomena, acting as PoC (point of contact I'd been informed) for the packs as well as overseeing the mortal police and other emergency services keeping things as calm as possible. I was still bound by my oath not to reveal anything about King Brann and their specialist operations, but Cormac had seen the need to bring more of us into the group of *accepted third party contractors*. As such, all the Alphas were now on OPS's books and Jessica, by de facto, was in almost constant communication with the mortal.

I didn't feel like they were cheating on me, or anything. I wouldn't say Cormac and I had any sort of special relationship … in fact, it made my life a whole lot easier with him bugging someone else rather than me when the shit hit the fan.

"Uh, let me check." I riffled through the other cases on my desk, and grabbed out a sheet of paper where I'd been scribbling my notes. "With this little batch of beauties, that makes, ah, well over twenty-five pets posted as missing in the last week. Mostly cats, a few small lap dogs but nothing larger. And no one has said anything about break-ins, sightings of dodgy vans lingering in the vicinity or the like."

I laid the piece of paper on the table, and my packmate leant over to inspect it.

"I haven't added in this lot yet, but so far these pets are all going missing from these two locations. Which is kinda hinky, even for London." I tapped the two areas I'd scribbled down taken from the missing pet ads.

Gloucester Road, South Kensington

Holland Park

"And yeah, the fact those two places are just a hop, skip and a jump from here *really* doesn't have me suspicious as fuck at all." I told her before she made the obvious connection.

Emma raised an eyebrow, obviously seeing the link but remaining doubtful.

"You think someone's out to get at you by kidnapping a load of mortals' pets? To, what, prove you're a crap kitten-finder?" She shook her head and I had to agree, it did seem a weird-ass way of getting at me. "More likely, you pissed off someone by *not* saving their pet maybe, and this is their way of getting even. But even that doesn't make much sense."

"Since when has sense and me ever gone hand in hand?" I shot back at her, and she answered with a grin and a nod.

"How're things on No Man's Land?" I queried, changing the subject from my baffling but somewhat inconsequential case compared to what she and Jacob were handling.

We'd named the border between the Mortal Realm and the newly born shard of Twilight, somewhat ominously, No Man's Land for several justifiable reasons. One, the barriers erected at every conceivable route into the mists had been set a good twenty feet back to ward off anything from inside snatching a guard or unwary mortal who strayed too close. This left the space between a barren, empty land … much like the expanse seen in old World War One documentaries between the Allies and the Germans' trenches.

Secondly, for the simple fact that no man, or woman or child for that matter, was allowed beyond the barriers without express permission from the security forces manning the perimeter. And to date, that number could be counted on a blind butcher's hand.

And finally, well, it suited the place. We'd lost kin, from our pack and the others, fighting to stop the bloody place being created. Fought and lost, so the mists were a constant memory of how much we'd failed.

"Same old, same old." She replied with a shrug, stepping away from the desk and taking a swig from her tea before continuing. "Idiot mortals still trying to sneak over for dares, or to get into the mists for looting or shits and giggles. We're keeping score of the number of arses kicked. I'm up by ten but I reckon Jacob's probably closing the count. Mornings are normally the worst."

Despite the fact there was televised and eyeballed-evidence of a pig's carcass flaking away to ash as it sat in the mists, and the numerous last recordings of mortals trying to be heroes and be the first through the mists, there were still enough idiots to keep both OPS and us lycan busy.

Well, almost all of us lycan.

"Any chance…?" I started to ask, but Emma shook her head, smiling grimly as she guessed what I was going to ask next.

"No way, Morgan. Jessica's made it clear you're to stay as far away from No Man's Land as possible." My packmate told me in no uncertain terms. "Or did you forget dumping the Harrowing into Queen-bitch's face? You get close, who knows what shit she'll throw at you, and anyone else near?"

I sighed, nodding to show I agreed. Not with the decision but with the simple fact.

That was the rub. I thought I'd been doing the right thing. One last-ditch attempt to save Elspeth, and by dint of association the man she loved, when I used Robert Knox's corrupted version of the killer of immortals on Morgana. It hadn't quite gone as planned, given how she had survived the initial exposure, and I'd been booted through a Way before finding out if she managed to defeat the bloody thing. Given the walls of mist were still up, and Elspeth had not miraculously reappeared, we'd all agreed the newly crowned Queen of Twilight was probably still alive.

And that meant she had a major grudge to settle with me, the sort of thing that, given her immortal nature and powers, could very well level the rest of London to ruins as a backlash whilst she dealt with me.

Hence Jessica had slapped me with a restraining order on venturing anywhere near the mists, just so I didn't tempt fate and have something big and nasty come looking for payback.

Instead, I was on desk duty. Handling any cases of a normal nature, whilst Jacob, Emma and most of the other pack – as well as members of the three remaining lycan packs in London – supported OPS and kept the barricades patrolled and arses firmly kicked, of whatever drew too close.

If it were only a matter of deterring mortals from trying to cross into the mists, I wouldn't have minded so much. However, things were never that simple.

Another possible sign that Morgana still lived was the fact Real creatures were being drawn to the site of Twilight's rebirth as well. Not from beyond the Veil, as it seemed the Ways were closed for traffic whilst the Courts sorted out the shitstorm she had released as a civil war on their turf. No, these were creatures who'd moved across and had, up until now, lived quietly alongside their neighbours without causing more trouble than the odd prank.

They weren't appearing in enough numbers to be more than a nuisance at the moment, with the odd troll or goblin appearing in the Lows or after dark, approaching the barricades around the mists. But when stopped, they all said the same thing.

She is calling us.

Yet here I sat, being handed lost kitten flyers. Knight Errant of the Courts, son of the Lord of the Wyld, twiddling my pinkies whilst things slowly but surely went to hell.

You couldn't make this shit up.

Chapter 3

With me effectively benched, I decided there was fuck all use me hanging around the office apart from drinking coffee and fielding sarcastic quips from my packmates. If pets were going missing and Jess felt this was a good use of my time to find them, then that's what I'd do. Sitting at a desk wasn't getting that done.

So, I decided it was time I went and checked out the locations where the little critters were vanishing from. Do some old-fashioned footwork.

One thing more surprising than their ability to blithely waltz into extreme danger with the innocence of lambs dancing in front of hungry wolves, when it comes to mortals, is their knack for being able to ignore something truly life-changing in front of their very eyes. Make it common-place. Boring even.

Being launched through the air in a metal tube with flimsy non-flapping wings, strapped to explosive fuel with no control over their speed and direction, and no way to escape safely mid-air? Let's serve food and alcohol, and show movies to make the whole thing common-place and boring. Or powering across the oceans of the Mortal Realm, on contraptions made of a substance *inherently non-buoyant* and again filled with very flammable fuel and piloted by devices susceptible to all manner of virus, hacks and technical failures? Let's convert them into floating palaces, add a few swimming pools and water slides to the mix, and pack in the mortals like tinned sardines for weeks at a time.

Utter madness.

It had been six months since massive walls of mist had risen around four districts of London, seemingly impenetrable and obviously of other than natural origin. Yes, the conspiracy theories were crawling out of the cracks like ants after spilled sugar, but after a few weeks of traffic congestion and maps being hastily re-drawn via GPS to avoid the London districts, life had returned to normal for mostly everyone living in the city itself.

The London Underground stations affected had been closed, and lines re aligned to prevent the general public accessing them. The mortals were still getting over what they thought had been a terrorist attack on the Circle line, where a dozen or so tube trains had gone dark and over a hundred passengers had been killed by some sort of chemical agent. Or that was the cover story, given those unfortunate enough to be travelling at that time had either been changed to vicious killing machines called the Harrowed or had died at the monsters' hands before my packmates and OPS strike squads had dealt with them.

We'd lost packmates in those dark tunnels, and an Alpha who had sacrificed himself to stop the Harrowed escaping above ground and causing more carnage. No one had walked away from that mess unscathed.

Summer had been and gone, the energy sapping heat now draining away to a chillier and greyer October. Given I'd left the office after rush hour was over, the streets were mostly empty. Adults were at work, children were back in school, and universities had re-opened their hallowed doors to gather back in the in-betweeners looking to either secure the next step forward in their life plan, or avoid nagging parents telling them they needed to get a job.

As I walked the London streets, I passed newsagent shops with billboards sat outside, papers filled with today's news filling every shelf. And whilst more than a few headlines were along the lines of *"London Mists – Government asks for calm"*, *"The Mists took my son but no-one cares!"* or even *"The Mists – A Sign From God?"* these were joined by more than a few more mundane topics: *"Brexit – When will the UK leave the EU?"*, *"US President: His Tweets today."* And even *"Brexit: Where will we get our wine now?"*

I had to chuckle over the simple truth that mortals, when faced with a scary and confusing situation, could still worry about the smaller and less important matters affecting them. Like where their favourite alcohol was going to come from now that borders and the rules had changed.

The day was slowly losing its chill as I turned from Hyde Park and headed off the main throughway, wending my way towards Holland Park. I'd chosen this direction to investigate given Gloucester Road was probably busier and filled with more tourists. The last thing I wanted were nosey mortals staring over my shoulder when I started poking around. Especially if I found something.

My surroundings slowly began to change as I walked steadily westwards. Large Victorian town houses appeared on each side of the street as I tramped along them, trees turning every shade other than green interspersed along the pavements to break up the concrete paths. There was a feeling of openness about the place, a marked difference from the cramped and narrow streets that were commonplace around the centre of the city.

And yet, as I walked in a slow, uncommitted wander, I couldn't help but sense an oddness to my surroundings. A feeling of discord jarring my senses like a bad smell.

Something wasn't right.

I've learned to trust my spider-senses when they start tingling, from past experiences of ignoring that old *danger-danger* alarm in my head and ending with me in pain. Lots of it.

So right about now, I *should* be reaching for any one of the several little items I had stashed in my pockets. To ward off any supernatural attack, or at least give whatever I was picking up on an unpleasant experience when it showed its mug. A face-full of salt crystals had proven plenty effective when bursting the Morrigan's tracker many weeks ago, and I'd scaled things up since then.

But there was one small fact that had me doubting myself. Thinking I was not picking up on a sense of imminent trouble, but just dealing with echoes of my own fucked-up mess I carried around with me permanently.

The thing was, I *knew* I was on edge and thinking something was wrong because … well, because I was walking the backstreets less than a short hop skip and a jump from where I knew No. 73 Abbotsbury Road stood.

A solid Edwardian style boxed townhouse of redbrick, blue front door and a white pillared porch on the side. A small brick flower bed out front filled with wildflowers, and ivy trailing up the wall and white painted drainpipe. With bedroom windows that looked out onto Holland Park.

The home of Dr Sarah Maria Conner.

My ex.

She had moved into the house shortly after confirming her position at the Natural History Museum, seeing the location not such a vast distance to travel to work each morning and home to afterwards, but giving her some green space as well. Something she loved, the feeling of nature close by, breaking up the concrete jungle of London. She'd bought the place outright, using funds supplied by her family, I'd been told over wine one night. They were big back in Spain, owning numerous farms, vineyards, wineries and olive groves. The biggest suppliers to Europe and the US for all things authentically tapas, both the produce for the recipes and the wine to match the dishes.

Which was why she was sort of a respected black sheep of the clan, having walked away from a lifelong link to olives and grapes, instead focusing on the origins of much-dead species in the dirt and stone underfoot. That hadn't meant her family had cut her off entirely, and had generously helped pay for a roof over her head whilst she explored this strange *hobby* of hers. But Sarah admitted on more than one occasion the sense of isolation and loneliness she sometimes felt that separated her from those she loved and cared for.

And after all that, I'd gone and forced her to be ripped from the life she'd created here in London. Bundled off halfway round the world, even further from her family, from her friends and colleagues. With nightmares plaguing her from what she had been exposed to, forced to witness.

The truth about me, and my kin.

So yeah, I was sort of suspicious that my *hinky* feeling was plain and simple guilt.

Rather than confront my demons and go stand outside her empty home, I decided I'd duck down through Melbury Road and head into Holland Park itself. If anyone were stealing household pets, there were bound to be flyers up and the odd dog-walker I could stop to chat to. Get some more information from. Plus, there was always the chance whoever was to blame was using the park to spot potential victims. There were small dogs on the list of missing pets that would need short walks, and be perfect to watch for from a bench or such. And my lycan senses were great for spotting mortals or other types loitering with intent.

However, any plans I had for checking out the green space were scuppered as I neared the park gates … to find them chained up and firmly locked. I checked my phone for the time, but we were well into the morning, when the park should be open for any and all locals and passers-by to use as they wished.

A note had been tagged to the gates, and I stepped up to read the brief apology.

Holland Park will be closed … foreseeable future … reported incidents requiring our staff to investigate … police are involved … apologies for any inconvenience but the safety of people and animals …

"You won't be getting in there, mate." A voice spoke up behind me, and I turned to see a middle-aged man approaching. A squat, solid-looking bulldog was on a leash, panting from its morning walk. Taking advantage of the stop, the dog slumped down on the ground near my feet, tongue lolling out of its mouth and its eyes closing in a prelude to imminent sleep. "Been locked up all week, it has."

"What happened?" I wasn't getting any weird vibes from the man, any hint he was anything other than a local out for a walk with his dog. The mutt itself cracked open an eye and gave a snort, obviously sensing my odd nature but thoroughly unimpressed with any effort beyond blowing bubbles from its nose.

"Right weird it was. Probably kids or foreigners, mucking around." The man growled, as his dog started a slow but solid build up to a deep sonorous snore. "You from round 'ere?"

I shrugged, nodding in the direction of Sarah's house.

"No, but a good friend of mine lives round here. On Abbotsbury Road. I used to come down here a lot to visit her, and we'd sit in the park when it was sunny." I told him the truth, remembering some good times just camping out on the grass and chatting about unimportant stuff. The stab of pain was nothing new now, familiar and something I could choose to ignore. At least a little. "Haven't been back for almost a year now."

"Yeah, well, you won't be doing that anytime soon." The man answered, nodding to the closed gates. "Started finding bits of dead animal, didn't they? Squirrels, birds, even a bloody fox. Ripped apart like something outta a horror movie. Park staff thought maybe a feral 'ousecat was doing the killin', but then we started losing pets. Cats mostly, but a few of the smaller dogs. Nuffink like Albert 'ere but still ...."

He held out his hand, and I shook it, sensing his simple mortal nature through the contact.

"Frank Appleby. And this 'ere's Albert."

"Morgan Black. Pleased to meet you both."

The bulldog, hearing its name, cracked open one eye and gave a grunt, rolling onto his back and offering up his belly for a rub. I obliged, leaning down, hearing the dog's deep and sonorous snuffles of delight.

"Got a way wiv dogs, Morgan, ain't you? Albert normally won't let no stranger near 'im." Frank told me, and I shrugged, rising to my feet again.

"I've got one of my own, so I guess they must smell him and think I'm ok." I lied, knowing Albert wasn't rolling over and acting playful because I smelt of Bear. He sensed how different I was from his mortal owner, and was hedging his bets to avoid any confusion around pack ranking.

For his part, the bulldog seemed to realise that he could go back to sleep again, which he did with surprising rapidity. Snores soon echoed out of his wide, toothy mouth.

Frank gestured at his dog, lying on his back, a leg stretched out and twitching, lost in his dreams of chasing cats and munching prime steak dinners, if the drool from his mouth was anything to go by.

"People started saying they felt some'at watching them. Nuffink they could prove, but you know how people are." He continued, shaking his head. "Dead animals kept turning up, and someone started saying wot happens if it's a child next? Next thing we know, park's all locked up, the plod's on patrol at night and we're told to only take out our pets *if necessary*. Like Albert can tell me if it's necessary for him to go pee or shit."

The dog grunted in his sleep, and the man gave one last shrug, obviously having said his piece.

"No one found anything? No paw marks, prints, anything like that?" I asked but the man just shot me a dubious look.

"You 'ain't one of those nutters who thinks it's the bloody Beast of Bodmin, or werewolves or shit, right?" Frank laughed, and shook the lead vigorously. Albert cracked open his eyes and gave a deep sigh at being disturbed, rolling over ponderously and pushing himself up before letting loose a loud fart. "It's kids, or foreigners, I tell you. Mucking around and wanting to scare us locals for bloody laughs, is all. Still, best you find some other park to get cosy with your missus coz I reckon this one's gonna be shut for a while. Come on, Albert. Home."

With that, he started walking off again, half dragging his bulldog along and shooting me the odd look over his shoulder. No doubt the police would get a report of someone matching my description asking odd questions in the area, but I wasn't too worried. The only police officer I had had any experience with, who was jaded enough about me to warrant questioning my motives, was currently somewhere behind the mists of Twilight, with Elspeth.

Instead, I stepped up to the locked gates and looked over them, into the green space. I let my senses search for anything untoward, anything that might give me a clue as to what the hell was going on here.

Frank had been right. I couldn't sense a single living thing beyond the gates. Not just mortals, but no rabbits, birds or any of the usual fauna that lived in the park. It was like it had been cleared out, methodically. Or else anything that hadn't been killed had taken the hint and run for cover elsewhere.

And it was silent. With the hubbub of London swirling around me, the park itself was still. Silent.

Like the grave.

And that prickling feeling was back, this time easier for me to identify. The sense of being watched, of being appraised. By something that had no good will toward me at all. But I could now get a better feel of whatever the hell it was too.

Something familiar somehow, a recognition of who I was. What I was. And somehow, a sense of belonging ... like it was local, but then *definitely* not at the same time. A weird-ass split sensation that I had never felt before, and had no clue what it meant.

I took a breath and pushed away from the gate, casually looking around but finding no physical threat beyond the nebulous presence. Nothing to ward against. Just that sense of ill ease, and the certain knowledge that something round here wanted to do me harm.

Whatever was going on here, it wasn't a simple case of pets being kidnapped. No. Something nasty was at work, something that had an appetite for fresh meat. I was now pretty sure those missing pets weren't simply stashed someplace, alive and well, stolen for ransom or onward trade. More likely, their remains were hidden away out of sight, somewhere where the smell of dead animal would be masked.

Something was hungry, and killing to appease its need for fresh meat and blood.

And lucky ol' me now had to find the bastard, and put an end to its killing.

Before it moved onto larger prey.

Chapter 4

Silver

Silver is known to be especially effective against werewolves, wendigos, shapechangers ... in fact most creatures that change their form are vulnerable to silver. A silver bullet, a silver sword, even a silver stake will effectively slay any of the creatures who would naturally shrug off mortal injury.

Interestingly, silver burns the fae as well, acting like sodium hitting water. An altogether unpleasant experience for the victim, and being a particularly good way to break fae-enchantments like warding circles or ensorclements. Sir Terry Pratchett once wrote of a wild, feral fae unicorn being tamed by having silver horseshoes fitted to it. In this instance, the unicorn suffered no ill effects, unlike other dark fae who have been known to erupt like a firework when silver was pressed to them.

Hanging round my ex-girlfriend's old stomping ground wasn't going to do much good for the case, apart from bringing back memories of what I'd lost. And make me even grumpier than I was already.

Normally, I'd have hauled my arse back to the office, to go speak to my resident expert on all things weird and spooky. But given the fact, like her once-policeman / now-guardian boyfriend, Ellie was locked up behind Morgana's mists, that option was no longer available to me.

However, the fact I didn't have *Ellie* around to ask, didn't mean I couldn't go check out her sources of information. That inexhaustible library which filled her home and covered pretty much every subject anyone had thought it worthwhile putting pen to paper about. And then some besides.

Now, if someone in London upped and vanished for six months without letting certain companies and people know they'd be back, there was a good chance they'd return home to find a tower block where their house had been and several families already with signed leases. London does not sit idly by and let good space go to waste. Especially with the almost criminal rental levels that can be charged for central locations.

However, whether from a certain sense of impending doom or just happy coincidence from the witch's recent decisions, Ellie had already made sure her house would not sit abandoned. It would in fact be looked after whilst she was not in residence. Not only did it offer the current caretaker a place all of her own, but it also was well grounded in magical experimentation, and so probably one of the few places a newly minted witch with unpredictable talents might practice without fearing of blowing up the toilet or setting fire to the kitchen.

Two events Felix was already well acquainted with.

Leaving behind whatever lurked in Holland Park, I dialled up a taxi and rode the short distance to Primrose Hill, mulling things over in my head. Walking round Sarah's home turf had stirred up memories and feelings I was slowly getting a handle on, but now added to them was the realisation something nasty had moved into the area and was treating the place like an all-you-can-eat- buffet table. There were lots of contenders in my head; anything from a hungry ogre to a tribe of goblins settling into the neighbourhood. But a couple of niggly things had me wanting a bit more research done before running off half-cocked.

Firstly, the fact this was happening now, when all manner of weirdos were being drawn to the mists of Twilight made me wonder if this wasn't something that had felt the call too, and just stopped for a bite or two to eat before continuing its journey. And secondly, the feel of it had been decidedly odd. That sense I'd gotten just outside the park. Like something I'd maybe come across before, something on its own turf. Which thoroughly threw the idea this was an out of towner.

Ogres and goblins never got too house-proud about their dens, moving on as and when it was appropriate. Normally when the remains of past meals were overflowing and too much trouble to shove to one side anymore. Those type of predators wouldn't give off that sense of belonging, let alone a feeling of ... *kinship* even.

But it did have me thinking. Maybe that weird connection was from my true nature. The fact I was a creature of the Wyld Court. What I might be sensing was my blood reacting to another like me. Nothing like the feeling I'd gotten from Jack, so I didn't think it was the Ripper watching me from the shadows. But the Court itself was filled with all manner of nasties, and

Ellie's library was sure to have something to help me understand what it could be.

Stopping off along the way to pick up provisions, and finding my tour round Holland Park and quick natter with bulldog-guy had eaten up most of the morning, I arrived outside the witch's cottage at just after eleven with two stacks of pizza boxes slowly cooling but fresh from the nearest Papa Johns' takeout. One decorated with pineapple, one kept true to the belief that all a decent pizza needs is cheese, pepperoni and more of the same.

The faint sounds of music echoed through to me as I walked up the narrow street in Primrose Hill, stopping at the gate to Ellie's home. The source of the music was definitely coming from the cottage, another sign that someone other than the witch was in residence given she had not kept any sort of sound system in the place. Not that she didn't like music, just the witch had said she preferred to have the soundtrack of life fill the space around her rather than anything manufactured.

Felix was definitely of a different wavelength.

She opened the door as I raised my hand to knock, and the volume escalated several notches.

… I must confess I still believe … still believe

When I'm not with you, I lose my mind

Give me a sign

Hit me baby one more time …

Peering over Felix's shoulder, I could see she had moved the sofas and chairs in the front room aside. Now an open space existed, fitted with half a dozen of those training dummies you see in martial arts gyms. At least one of them looked like someone had taken a flamethrower to it, whilst another had chunks missing from it in key places.

I looked down on my friend, as she stood in the doorway. Felix had pulled back her white dreadlocks with a band, and was wearing what I could only describe as multi layered and multi coloured gym gear. Two strappy tops one on top of the other, leggings that ended just below her knees and chunky trainers. She was sweating lightly, like she had been working out, but there was a suspicious aroma of burning plastic that made me guess she had been practising her skills instead.

"Yo! What's up? And one of those for me?" She asked with a grin, stepping back to let me into the cottage.

I ducked into the open living room, letting the scents of the place fill my nose. The slight tang of Felix's sweat, overscored by whatever antiperspirant she was using. The much stronger crackle of magic expended, with that virulent sharpness from the Veil still mingled with the Twilight essence I was beginning to get all too familiar with. The stench of melted rubber and plastic, as well as the dying scent trails of some sort of health drink, and what smelt like eggs and avocado from what I guessed was breakfast.

"You, uh, train to Britney Spears?" I queried, setting the pizza boxes down and stepping closer to the most badly damaged dummy. The thing had been repeatedly hit hard, denting the thick outer surface where its nose and central ribcage would be, but fire had done far worse damage. Bits had been melted off its shoulders and lower down, where any normal mortal man might wince and cross his legs in empathic pain.

"Surprised you recognise her. Don't you old people like jazz and stuff?" She snarked at me, as I noted the name tag scribbled on a white sticky note and set over the dummy's heart.

Gary.

Figured.

"Anyways, nothing wrong with a bit of Britney." She told me as she moved over to a compact sound system she had sitting near the farthest wall. This was set squarely in a small warding circle, a simple but effective tool to earth the machine and stop it from short-circuiting, what with all the magic she was throwing around. "Give me her and Christina Aguilera over the crap they call music these days."

I grunted, not wanting to get into an argument around musical tastes. Not that I had anything to hide, just that my preferences were kinda niche. Instead, I checked over the other dummies, seeing each had a name tag with a few lines scribbled on them.

Bully from primary school. Jerk from Costa Coffee. Men with bad breath. Fuckwits who hurt animals. Anyone calling me child. And …

"Uh, '*Morgan*'?" I looked back at Felix, eyebrow cocked. "Seriously, I'm on your punching list?"

Felix grinned at me, walking over to the punching dummy with my name on it. The thing was in better shape than Gary's … not melted, but with a few dents and scrapes to show that I'd been the focus of some effort. She threw an arm around it, hugging it.

"Sure. When I just think of all the free meals you scrounged off my dad and me, I definitely get the urge to hit you." She told me with a bright smile. "I figure better the dummy than the real thing, right?"

"Uh huh." I replied with a shake of my head.

"So what brings you round? Just checking I haven't burned the place to the ground or blown it to Oz and frightened the munchkins??" She asked with a wry smile. "Not that I'm complaining, since you always seem to bring pizza just when I'm feeling hungry."

I'd taken to dropping in on Felix irregularly, ever since she moved out of Danny's house and taken up residence in Elspeth's cottage. Nominally to make sure my friend was doing ok after the events at the Southbank centre, given how she had gone up against an all-powerful immortal and her cronies as her third-only real exposure to, well, the Real. First it had been Gary and the shit he had tried to pull on her, to bind them together in some sort of black magic and bad juju rite, then it had been Baba Yaga and The Ripper, where Felix had faced off against the hag and prevailed, with a little help from a rather worrying source.

And yeah, I knew Elspeth and she had become close, the witch nurturing the newbie with the powers Felix had gained from her immersion in Veil-magic. The young woman had helped bring Gregory Allen back to life, a feat that few of those skilled at magic at any level could boast about. But that had been one solitary positive amongst a shit-load of scary as fuck negatives.

No, I knew Felix had been dropped in the proverbial deep-end, and despite being a good swimmer, I wanted to make sure I was there if she needed anything. Free food, someone to talk to, a shoulder if wanted. Turns out I also doubled as a good punching dummy.

There was also the small fact, though I'd never admit it to the young woman, that Danny had asked me to keep an eye on her. Make sure she was ok since the things his daughter was going through were far beyond his ability as a run of the mill mortal to understand or help with. He didn't love her any less, just felt pretty useless after his over-protectiveness had led to Felix blowing up their toilet at home from frustration.

And finally, I knew I sometimes came round to the cottage as a simple reminder. A promise I'd made to get the witch out of the mess both she and I were to blame for her landing in. Elspeth, for breaking the oaths she'd made to her Goddess and turning instead to the mortal man she loved, doing anything and everything to keep them together. And me for opening my big mouth and summoning a Fury right where Morgana wanted it, alerting the immortal creature to the witch's broken oaths and painting a big fat target on my friend for eternal punishment.

Yeah, I wasn't *still* kicking myself for that fuck up. Much.

"Reckon the folks of Munchkin Land are the only ones who might understand your dress sense." I shot back at her with a grin, as she rolled her eyes at the barb. "No, something's come up and I reckoned Ellie's books are a good place to do some fact-finding."

"You, reading? Wonders never cease." She replied with a flick of her head, then freed her dreads from the simple wrap and shook them out to signify she was done with her workout. "We can read and eat, I'll grab the plates. What're you hunting?"

That was Felix all over. Always willing to help, get stuck in and be involved. Whether it was a simple matter of searching through books for some clues, or going up against a big bad thing from mythology. My friend, despite the changes going on in her life, had remained true to herself … something I found refreshing given all the crazy shit I'd been handling these past weeks.

Not that I'd tell her that. Even I could see the amount of piss-take I'd earn from such a gushy confession. I'm not *that* stupid.

Plates were grabbed, along with a couple of glasses of spring water to help wash the cheese down, as I manoeuvred the punching dummies into a corner and re-positioned the sofa and chairs back to their old position. I doubted Elspeth would mind Felix re-arranging things whilst she lived at the cottage, but she would never forgive me if I got cheese or tomato sauce on her precious books if I tried to balance food and them on my lap alone.

"So, what're we looking for?" Felix asked again, as I snagged a bite of slowly cooling but still delicious pepperoni and double cheese.

Finishing my mouthful, I lined up my thoughts from the little I'd put together this morning. It wasn't much.

"Something's been stealing pets. Small scale, cats and lapdogs mostly, but its managing to do it without being caught on anyone's home security or cameras on the streets." I let my eyes run over the floor to ceiling bookshelves that the witch had fitted to the inner room. "Never from a person walking them, so it's not a simple mugging or kidnapping for ransom. Then there's been some sort of incident at Holland Park. Lots of the local wildlife found dead and dismembered in the grounds. I haven't had a proper look round yet, but it sounds like a predator and a hungry one at that."

"Urgh, that sounds delightful." Felix scrunched her face, setting aside the slice of pizza she was about to eat. "So, you think this thing is, what, invisible? Walking through walls like a ghost to nick the pets? And it's then eating them? Aren't there enough trash bins around for it to steal from?"

"It likes fresh meat, another reason why I think it's something from my side of the woods." I answered. "I spotted enough trash bins to feed a fox for a lifetime, and the residents don't look like they keep the lids on all that regularly. No, this thing doesn't want processed chemical crap. There was a feeling I got around the place. Animalistic, raw. Definitely predatory and just that little bit familiar though I don't know why. But let's start with carnivores able to summon or somehow influence animals coz I don't think it's getting into the owners' homes itself but somehow getting the pets to get out themselves. Otherwise we'd be hearing about break-ins by now."

"Well, that narrows things down a bit. Not." Felix snorted, taking her pizza back up and biting off a chunk. "Anything else?"

"It's probably nocturnal, as I'm sure someone would have noticed something chowing down on a bunch of rabbits and birds in the park, let alone heard it happening. And it's smart, as its been able to avoid all the cameras in the streets." I added, thinking of the CCTV dotted around Holland Park.

I never got used to that ever-present feeling of being watched, even if I had to assume no-one ever really watched the taped footage … the digital copies just scanned by algorithms searching for specific criteria. Like mortals walking around with big knives or explosive devices strapped to them at one end of the spectrum, to the more absurd mortals running around butt naked at the other.

I'd gotten bored one evening, and delved into the logic behind having so much surveillance operating all the time, since no mortal could possibly sit through that feed and spot anything of worth. I'd found out they instead ran search patterns, keying in criteria for the latest threats the authorities were on the look-out for. And yes, even in the midst of a supernatural event where a big chunk of London had vanished behind impenetrable walls of mist, those in charge *were still* worried about nude people wandering their streets. Just goes to show.

"Smart, huh? Guess that rules out you." She smirked at me, then pushed herself up off the chair she'd collapsed into. "Ok, intelligent predator, nocturnal and with an affinity with small animals. And your tingly familiar feeling, whatever the hell that is. Let's see …"

Elspeth seemed to have no discernible logic to how she stored her books, as they crammed every shelf, nook and cranny. In fact, any possible place a volume might fit. However, Felix must have had the inside track on how they were organised, as she quickly focused on the section nearest to the kitchen, crouching down to scan the lower levels of the bookshelves. A few minutes of effort, and she had dragged off half a dozen volumes from different slots, setting them down on the table in front of me.

"Let's try these." She settled back into her chair, as I spread the books out over the wooden surface, checking their ornate covers. *"The Impossible Zoo* by Leo Ruickbie, Bulfinch's *Mythology,* Breverton's *Phantasmagoria: A Compendium of Monsters, Myths and Legends, Mysterious Creatures – a guide to Cryptozoology Volumes 1 and 2* by George E Eberhart and *A Witch's Bestiary:*

Visions of Supernatural Creatures by Maja D'Aoust. I figured you wanted the ones in English, and you didn't mention a specific mythology so I went kinda generalist. The ones in Old Germanic are a pain to read, and don't start me on the Latin!"

"Uh, yeah, these are good. Real good, thanks." I reassured Felix, grabbing the Witch's Bestiary as that one had me straight-off curious. "Ellie shared her index with you then? I figured the books were just wherever she could fit them."

"Um, nope. No index." Felix looked over at me, then shrugged. "It's more … I just ask the cottage what I want to find, and it sort of lets me know where to look. Ellie said it was something bound into the stones of the building, there to help whichever witch lives here. Like a magical *Alexa* or something."

"Sure. A magical invisible helper. What every up-and-coming witch needs." I grinned, then thought for a second. "Since when do you read Old Germanic and Latin? The first I *know* for a fact isn't taught in this country."

Felix laugh, shaking her head.

"No, that's just a little trick Elspeth taught me. All I need is a drop of elvish blood and a little chant, and whatever I look at, translates to English for me." She smiled, shrugging her shoulders. "I wish I'd known the bloody thing when I was trying to learn French in school."

Elven blood. As in from a fae. I knew from personal experience that the blood of creatures from the Courts could reveal obscured and hidden things, and had been a rich source of fuel for mortals dabbling in magic this side of the Veil before the Accords put a stop to that practice. I wasn't going to ask why Ellie of all people had access to the stuff, and whether Felix knew that 'elven blood' *wasn't* a quaint label for something natural and totally harmless. Like okra being called Ladies Fingers.

Silence settled between us, as I sensed the next question given it was so big and plain in the young woman's eyes as she watched me.

"You *are* going to get her back, aren't you Morgan?" She asked, that quiet catch in her voice making her seem a lot younger in years suddenly. "I like having my own space and all, but this is *her* home, not mine. And I really miss her …"

"Yeah, me too." I admitted, smiling reassuringly as I leant over and laid a hand over hers for a moment. "Trust me, just as soon as I'm able, I'm going into those mists and dragging her and Gregory back. And nothing, Morgana, Twilight fae, Norns or whatever, is going to stop me. That's my promise."

"Good." She grinned, turning her hand to grip my own for a moment. I got that flicker of power from her, the latent storm she held inside, sourced from Twilight and the Veil combined, before she slipped free and grabbed a book. "Let's get on with finding out what's eating people's pets so you can kick its arse and get on with saving her."

Chapter 5

Two hours later, both pizzas had been devoured and the plates shoved to one side. We'd chewed through the six books, then gone back to see if the cottage could suggest anything else that might help. All in all, a full score of tomes now were scattered on the table, whilst Felix and I both had pads of paper we'd found in a drawer, covered with pencilled scribbles from our research.

I settled back on the sofa, rubbing my neck and quietly admitting that whilst good research saved lives and such, it was tedious. Oh so bloody tedious. But necessary, so I didn't say anything out loud. Instead, I nodded to my companion as she chewed thoughtfully on the end of her pencil, closing up the volume she'd been leafing through.

"So, what've you got?"

Felix set her teeth-dented pencil down, picking up the pad she'd been writing on and scanning over her scrawl.

"Ok, so we're looking for a predator, singular, with an appetite for fresh meat and that can somehow call its prey to it or appear to be normal in some way so as not to alert the pets' owners to its intent. Probably works at night, to keep from being seen, and clever enough to know about CCTV and such. That about right?" She checked her notes, before adding. "Oh, and that weird feeling you got of something familiar. Let's not forget that helpful clue."

I nodded, knowing there was no rushing Felix.

"Good. I'd hate to have been looking for the wrong thing!" She smiled sarcastically, before continuing. "Taking all of them into account? I've got, well, fuck all."

I cocked an eyebrow, about to make a crack about all the time spent studying at university somehow not training her how to *research* but she raised a hand in her defence.

"Hold on. What I *have* got is a bunch of hunter gods and goddesses who were known to be able to charm or affect animals. But they didn't butcher or feed on their prey, the hunt was more symbolic than anything to do with appetite." Felix tapped one set of scribbles, then moved on. "Then I've got predators like the *Rakshasa* of India, *Black Dogs* of Europe, *Tanuki* of Japan ... all predator style hunters that would kill animals to feed on. But none of them seem to have any ability to call their prey to them, and instead tend to break into wherever the food lives and eat it there. Messily."

"I've got nocturnal monsters like vampires that could avoid being seen, but they don't butcher animals like you've described. Nothing that really ticks all the boxes you've given me." She shrugged, setting aside her pad and looking across at me. "You do any better?"

I looked down at my pad, and then decided honesty was the best policy here. Holding it up, I showed her the list of names I'd scribbled down ... then crossed through each time to show they didn't fit the brief.

"What's that one?" She nodded to one name I'd left uncrossed but ringed with a big question mark. "*Bayun Sith*? Sounds like a bad guy from Star Wars?"

"It's the original Cheshire Cat, a hunter of the Wyld Court and a right royal pain in my arse." I replied, before crossing the name through with my pencil. "And as much as I know it can get in and out of places unseen, and it's certainly a predator ... that's just not its MO. So, yeah, basically I've got fuck all too."

I sighed, placing my pad down and rubbing my forehead with two fingers. Elspeth made this sort of thing look so bloody easy. We'd find some spurious clue like a shred of fur or a blurry print that could be from a finger or possibly just a dirty smear, and she'd go back to her books then come to us with the name of the thing we were hunting. Its height, weight, favourite hangouts as well as other helpful details like whether it preferred coffee or tea in the morning, and whether it pronounced scone with an "on" or an "own". All from a quick read-through of the very books we'd been flicking through for the past couple of hours.

"We've got fuck all then. This thing could be anything?" I queried, just so I was clear.

Felix looked a little uncomfortable, and I rolled my eyes.

"What is it? C'mon, show me. I'm a big boy, I won't cry."

She shook her head, then picked her pad up again and flicked the page over.

"Well, there was *one* thing I found. One possible conclusion that might fit pretty much the entire brief. *Predator, smart enough to dodge the cameras, knows to operate at night to avoid being seen. Something familiar.* Like you said." She told me, and turned the pad so I could see what she had written.

Lycanthrope. Werewolf?

"You're definitely taking the piss now." I told her but it was my turn to hold up a hand to stop her instant response. "No, don't worry. The thought had crossed my mind too. But if this is one of my lot, one of the packs, then it means we've got a rogue out there somewhere, who's chosen to snack on mortals' pet furballs as well as the local wildlife instead of all the far easier prey that fills this city. Which is idiotic."

At that moment, the candles sat in the windows of the cottage suddenly flared a bright blue, a sure sign the warding had been activated.

Someone ... *something* was approaching the house.

Felix, with all the self-preservation of a lemming with an inflatable pool ring and a good run up to the cliff's edge, pushed herself up and almost hopped over to the window, peering out into the front garden.

"Uh, Morgan. Did you order an extra from *American Horror Story* today?" She prompted, looking back at me. "I'm not due any creepy ass nun-types, so I'm guessing she's after you and your immortal soul?"

Creepy nuns. I was on my feet in the next breath, motioning for Felix to step away from the window as I moved to the front door and drew it open.

Bright sunlight created a warm and almost mystical aura around the tall, thin figure that had stopped just outside the porch. Her dirty habit, for one moment, was transformed into clean cloth, the stains washed away in the bright light. Nothing, however, could change the fevered blood-stained eyes that stared at me from the depths of the habit's hood, the rest of the face hidden by the mask the Sister of the Arch wore.

"Morgan Black." She greeted me, her voice a dry rasp like reptile scales rubbing together. "You must come with me. A matter awaits you, and the Sisterhood wish your speediest attention."

"Uh, hi Sister." I greeted her, not knowing which of the Order she was. Sisters Wrath and Gluttony I'd known fairly well, but both were dead, at the hands of Baba Yaga and Jack the Ripper. This tall, looming menace in black and white attire was a stranger. "Is this urgent? Only coz we're trying to track down something right now …"

"The killer of pets and small animals. Yes, we Saw." She told me bluntly, those mad eyes of hers flaring in the shadows. "These two matters are linked."

The Sister brushed past me, stepping into the house without any difficulty. Sisters of the Arch were a law unto themselves, with a foot in both the Mortal Realm and the Real, Seers one and all with the ability to navigate the tricky paths of foresight without all the silly encumbrances and limitations other fortune-tellers were bound by. They also could breach any hearth or home without being unduly weakened, which is why nothing bad happened as she planted her feet inside Ellie's cottage.

A large proportion of Real creatures made up the flock of the Sisters, the creatures either running from their personal fuckups or seeking shelter from whatever horrors hunted them back the other side of the Veil. That made the Sisters excellent sources of information when we were hunting a particular offender, since all we needed to do was ask our questions and they would determine what answers we needed without unduly affecting their flock. Part of the bargain, however, meant that to keep the deal sweet with them, if they asked for our aid we were honour bound to answer.

Me especially, it turned out as the Sisters had been the ones to hand me over to Mark and Jessica Walker, after my father and grandmother had dumped me on the nuns to 'protect me'. I still had doubts about how much actual goodwill had been involved in that decision from my father, Herne the Horny, instead of a simple lack of parental skills and desires to raise me as his son after my mother died.

"Um, Morgan, who is she and what's she doing?" Felix piped up as the nun looked around the interior of the cottage. The nun's feelings were made quite clear as she let loose a distinctively judgy sniff, then walked over to the arch separating the living room from Elspeth's sanctum.

"Come, Morgan Black. Time passes, as does my patience." The Sister shot me a burning look then stepped up to the brick arch and laid one gaunt hand onto its surface. "Bring the child, for this should prove an education as to the seriousness of the matter."

"Child?" I heard Felix's indrawn breath, and shook my head as I saw where this was leading rapidly.

"Felix, don't even think about it!" I told my friend as I felt the familiar crackle of magic, the taint of the Veil, rising in the room. For her part, the nun simply looked over at me, her bright mad eyes conveying a very simple message. *Deal with the situation or I will.* "The Sisters of the Arch speak like that to everyone, me especially, so there's no use getting riled by them. It's a nun thing. Plus if you throw down in here, you're liable to leave Ellie's home a smoking ruin. And you wouldn't want that, right?"

My friend drew a sharp breath, closing her eyes for a moment before she unclenched her hands and looked across at me, nodding once.

"Good." I relaxed a notch, then turned back to the Sister. "Uh, Sister … what's your name by the way?"

"Sister Sloth." She replied, fingers caressing the bricks in the arch. The air between them began to move sluggishly back and forth, weaving together until it seemed the doorway was filled with pulsing mist, gently moved by some unseen breeze.

"Right. Sister Sloth." I squirreled that away, remembering the nuns of the Order all took names from the very long list of wrongdoings their flock suffered from. "You said this is linked to the pet stealing, the animal killings?"

The air in the arch darkened, falling in on itself so now instead of mist, the way was now an open portal leading elsewhere. Sisters of the Arch could travel anywhere an archway or such existed, helpful for them to visit the mortals and immortals wherever they hid. And it helped limit the level of horror they caused the normal people of the city to suffer, given their less than appealing demeanour and frankly frightening as fuck presence.

I motioned for Felix to join me, as I stepped up to the dark-filled archway. She shot me a questioning look, but I just shrugged, knowing this was most likely perfectly safe and no threat to either of us. The Sisters did not take sides in any conflict, and to my knowledge things were still ok between the Order and the lycans despite the deaths of the two nuns on our watch. That blame lay squarely at the feet of Robert Knox, Baba Yaga and Jack the Ripper … and two of the three had already met their grisly ends.

"Sister?" I prompted, as she stepped to the darkness. Sister Sloth turned, her bright orbs narrowing in the shade of her habit as she focused on me.

"That which you hunt? It no longer feeds on mortals' pets and small creatures of the glades." She replied archly, as she stepped into the darkness. It enfolded her, embracing her essence as she stepped elsewhere. "Now, it feeds on man flesh and blood."

Fuck. I grabbed Felix's hand, giving it a squeeze to show I was with her before I stepped into the darkness and followed the nun.

Chapter 6

Salt

Salt is renowned as being a deterrent against any vengeful spirit. Ghosts, ghasts, revenants, wraiths and apparitions all can be disrupted by passing pure salt through their corporeal form. Salt also provides an effective barrier if used to block entrance or the exit of these creatures in relation to a dwelling if it is lain along the doorways and window ledges.

Certain creatures like vampires and the more rural fae spirits like leprechauns, can be confounded by throwing salt at them. They will be forced to stop whatever aggressive actions they are performing, and count every single grain before returning to their vengeful ways.

We emerged from the arch in Elspeth's cottage, to find ourselves definitely elsewhere.

Lush greenness spread out before us, darkened by close set trees and what looked like decaying red brick walls and arches hidden amongst the scrub and foliage. The air was clear and sharp, October's chill adding a bite even at close to midday, full of outdoor scents.

I looked over at my companion as she steadied herself from moving in one step from the cottage to halfway across London, unless I missed my guess. She was still clad in her exercise gear, definitely not suited for the outdoors so I quickly shucked off my jacket and slipped it round her shoulders.

Felix pulled the material tight, shooting me a quick smile to show her thanks.

At least I could manage the simple gestures as a Knight, stopping my friend from catching a chill. That, and Gods knew what she'd be like with her newfound magic if she started sneezing and blowing shit up by accident.

"Greenwich Park, right?" I asked Sister Sloth, who stood waiting in the shade of the overgrown trees. When the nun nodded, I drew a breath. It figured shit would happen here, given my last visit to the beautiful parkland had been whilst dosed on wolfsbane and about to be buried by a pack of *hexen-wolfen* students I'd crossed paths with.

Life is circular, bringing you back to places for specific reasons. For me, it was normally to deal with whatever new trouble was taking place in the same old place, with the same old mess that needed cleaning up with fresh new idiots.

My indrawn breath also picked up the sharp coppery tang of spilled blood, my senses pricking at the echoes of violence done. Fear like acid still smeared the air of the place, staining it with a vicious tang despite it slowly fading as the fresh air leached it of its potency.

"Indeed, Morgan Black." The nun told me, and gestured towards the darker recesses behind her. "This is what I have brought you to witness. To explain."

Motioning for Felix to stay put, I carefully walked into the patch of shadows that clung to the remains of the wall. I guessed we were behind the Observatory, up on Greenwich Hill summit and within the dense trees that had been planted to help remove the starkness of the building on the skyline. The general public tended not to dwell in this part of the park, what with the main paths leading off to the left of the buildings and the unchecked green growth making it difficult to get to.

But there were always some who would want the seclusion, who would seek a place away from prying eyes and mockery.

A place of safety. Until now.

My eyes quickly adjusted as the smell of blood and rent flesh thickened like a soup in the air. And there, that weird sense I'd felt before as well, from Holland Park but different somehow. A familiarity, but this time much stronger, and more easily identified. Yet at the same time, confusing as fuck. No way could I be picking up on what my nose and other senses were telling me. Just couldn't be.

Under a broken brick arch, where rubbish had piled up amongst the rotting detritus from the trees and bushes, I marked out splashes of gore that stained the walls and floor. The lumpy objects scattered further than any body should allow, if all the parts had remained attached. There, a blood stained and filthy shoe, the ankle bone sticking from its hole, rent and splintered. Across from that, what looked like a ribcage, split wide with extreme force, the shoulders and lower body partially attached. Entrails had been severed and, unless I missed my guess, partially consumed given the ragged lengths of split links I saw lying in the dirt.

Whoever this body was, they had been brutally dismembered, ripped apart and fed on by something with monstrous strength and an insane hunger. Then my eyes finished cataloguing details, coming up with an anomaly. There were too many limbs for this to be one person only. Enough mangled feet and hands that I could pick out from the filth and gore for not one or two but three victims.

"Four gathered here last night, seeking solace and comfort in their own company. Three souls were sent to God." Sister Sloth confirmed from where she stood beneath the shade of the gnarled and twisted trees. "The fourth, brother Grubbins, is being tended to elsewhere. He stepped away to relieve himself, and returned to find his friends being savagely attacked."

I knelt down carefully, avoiding the gore spattered around the small clearing, and checked the dirt. It had been scuffed up from whatever little fight the three transients had managed to put up for their lives, and soaked with their lifeblood when they had invariably been torn apart. But amongst all the mess, I saw what I was looking for. I just wished I didn't.

"Did this Grubbins get a good look at what was attacking his friends?" I asked, as I shifted one piece of ruined flesh aside to get a clear look at the earth beside it. Definitely there, my eyes weren't playing tricks on me. But it made no sense.

"He did, before running for his life. The creature seemed maddened, not fully in control of itself, hence we believe the reason our brother still lives." Sister Sloth replied. "My Sisters were able to draw up a sketch from what the brother told them. Here."

I pushed myself up, wiping a small smear of blood I'd not been able to avoid on my trousers, before turning to find the nun holding out a clean sheet of paper.

Nodding my thanks, I took it and glanced at the drawing. Done in simple pencil, it wouldn't have won any awards but showed enough detail to confirm my fears.

"Uh, Morgan?" Felix called out from where she now crouched down in the grass, out of the shadows and in a patch of sunlight. "You might want to come look at this."

Gripping the paper carefully, not wanting to crease the drawing in any way, I walked over to join my companion. She was peering down at some flattened grass, stained with streaks of blood. A trail, obviously.

"What've you got?" I queried, as I crouched down beside her.

"So, there's this." She pointed to a scuffed and roughened patch of dirt, where an obvious pawprint indented the ground. Claws had ripped holes out of the grass, and the span was large enough for this not to be any normal dog or canine that might be running around the park. She pointed out another pawprint, crushing the grass with more weight as if the owner of the feet had stepped away from the carnage before stopping.

"Then there's ... well, this." Felix nodded to a point a short distance away. What could be a stride, maybe the distance of one simple step. The grass here was flattened too, but this time there were no claws, no pads indenting the dirt. Instead, a perfectly normal large-sized footprint. Five toes and heel easily identified from the shape left behind

"There's a couple more, then they change again." She crab-walked a short distance, not bothering to get up, and pointed down to a final set of prints. I guessed what she had found, and didn't bother following. "So, riddle me this. What had a paw, then a footprint, then a shoe print? Is the killer one of those *hexen-wolfen* students from my class, you think?"

It was a good guess, and for a moment I let myself believe that maybe, yes, it could be one of Robert Knox's little projects come back to bite me in the arse. But all three university students had been removed from the area, their hexed belts burned, and a watch set on them individually in case any of them started showing signs of withdrawal symptoms from the magic they'd used. And none of them had been advanced in lore enough to craft new hexed objects. They'd relied on their professor to provide the means for their change.

No, whilst I wanted to believe this wasn't what it looked like … sometimes, the fact was, if it looked like a duck, swam like a duck, and quacked like a duck, then it probably *was* a duck.

Or in this case …

"No, I don't think it's any of your old classmates come back to begin snacking on tramps." I told her, seeing that concern writ wide on her face. That was Felix … one of the small group had kidnapped her, assaulted her father and attempted to do horrible things to her whilst the other three covered up for him, but she still worried for them. Too good a heart, even if she did bury it at times with sarcasm and attitude.

"What then? You're not thinking…?" She started to ask, so I nodded, holding out the paper with the drawing on it before she could finish.

Felix took a quick look, her indrawn breath telling me she made the connection.

"Each one of us has a specific form, tailored to how we want to look when we Change." I answered quietly as she stared at the charcoal picture of a lycan wearing its man-beast suit. "There's differences, something very wrong about that one, but I'd know it … *him* anywhere."

"Who is it?" She asked, but I just shook my head, not believing what I was thinking. What the evidence was telling me, no matter how crazy it seemed.

It was Jacob Moon I was sensing. My packmate in the hand drawn image. Somehow, impossibly, mixed up in this mess. Maybe even the cause of it all.

It made no sense.

Chapter 7

Garlic

Garlic is renowned as a sure-fire protection against vampires, or any supernatural creature that feeds on its victims' vital fluids. But it is also thought to provide protection against evil spirits, both by warding the mortal who consumes the garlic from being infected by vampirism or any of the supernatural infections spread through the creatures' bite and by blocking any evil influence that the creature attempts to put over its victim by the substance's very nature.

Its ability to cleanse poisons and other malign infections from the mortal body also help combat many of the supernatural creatures that see mortals as simple sustenance, its smell and presence alone forcing the creatures to seek their prey elsewhere.

"I think … shit, it's Jacob. The lycan in the picture is my packmate." I told Felix quietly, not wanting to voice something so utterly stupid and *wrong*. But she deserved to know. "His scent is all over this place too."

My packmate was no rogue, no blood-mad lycan on a killing frenzy. Yes, he could easily butcher and dismember three vagrants … hell, I'd seen him bench-press a car before and smash through a solid brick wall when it got between him and his hunt. But a killer of innocents? And the fact he'd *chowed down* on them too? No, none of this added up except for a major *what the fuck* moment.

I *really* needed to talk to him. And Jessica.

"Are you going to inform the mortal police about these deaths?" I turned back to face Sister Sloth, nodding to the gory-strewn killing ground.

The nun shook her head, those mad eyes of hers glowing brightly.

"They are but fodder for the creature which slew our flock. There is little they can do, apart from complicate matters. Or appease its hunger."

She replied with a sharp edge to her words, a demand she was placing purely on my shoulders. "The Sisters of the Arch ask you to undertake this hunt. Find the thing which did this and stop it before it feeds upon any more innocent souls. Or we will take matters into our own hands."

There was the threat. Once crossed, the Sisterhood were less *turn the other cheek* and more Old Testament wrath and brimstone, and if there was any chance a lycan was involved … whether my friend and packmate or not … there was no way I wanted the Sisters on their case.

"Meanwhile, we will see to our fallen, and give them the blessings to ensure their onward journey is a peaceful one." She finished, and I realised our time was coming to an end.

"Any chance I can speak to this Grubbins? See if I can get some more details?" I queried, knowing it was going to be asking a lot for the victim, mortal or otherwise, to go through the events of the slaughter all over again. But something was *so* wrong with the picture I'd been painted, I needed to check all the details.

I didn't necessarily think the tramp was lying, or intentionally pointing the finger at my packmate. Why would he? But there were creatures of the Real who could mimic the appearance of another down to their cellular level. Hell, we'd fought one in the Natural History Museum. Anything like that could have taken Jacob's face, though most Shape-changers had to eat something of their prey to take its form, and I couldn't see my packmate letting that happen anytime soon.

Just as I didn't see him murdering a bunch of defenceless transients. Or stealing a load of household pets and chowing on them for appetisers.

And there was that wrongness about his Changed beast-man suit, the little things that didn't look right. But it was definitely still him.

This whole thing was just plain hinky.

Sister Sloth was silent for a long moment after my request, long enough for me to think she was in some sort of communication with the rest of her Sisters. Finally, she gave one sharp nod.

"Brother Grubbins will be made available when he is more settled, at a place of his choosing. He will be accompanied by either myself or one of my

Order." She told me. "We will pass the location of the meeting to you when it is right to do so, as well as the exact time to meet. Do not bring any other, and if any sort of coercion or duplicity is attempted, we will *not* be pleased."

"Didn't even cross my mind." I honestly told her, then nodded back at my companion. "Since we're done here, mind taking us back to where you found us? It's a long bloody walk, and I'd rather my friend here didn't catch her death of cold."

"Hm. Mortals, so fragile." The nun commented with a roll of those blood-hued orbs. "I recall the days when the river of London froze solid, and the temperature was so cold, tears were as ice on the cheeks of children. *That* was cold."

"Oh, the good old days." I snarked, earning a sharp look from the nun. "So, I'll expect to hear from you, soon?"

"You will hear from us, Morgan Black. Do not fear otherwise." She finally answered, as the air around us once more blurred and shifted. "Remember, we are counting on you to bring this thing to justice. One already remains at large, who has the blood of our Sisterhood on his hands. We will not suffer another."

The next breath, we were back in Ellie's cottage, standing just a step away from the brick archway. Felix slipped my coat from her shoulders, handing it over, as the warmth of the room dispelled any lingering chill from Greenwich Park.

"Are they always so … uh?" She asked, but I just shrugged, knowing the Sisters for what they were.

"The nuns tend to the lost, the broken. People from here as well as creatures from the Real that are shit out of luck, and still falling." I answered truthfully. "They spend their days up to their eyeballs in the muck of negative emotion that is all that their flock has left. Despair, anger, frustration, loathing … they deal with that day in, day out without a word of thanks, anyone offering to make their lives easier. So yeah, when something kicks the people they look after, they take it very seriously. And usually bite the foot off the idiot doing the kicking."

"You honestly think this time it's Jacob?" She asked again, and I shook my head, not sure of anything right there and then.

"This is the moment the facts say one thing, but the thing they are saying is impossible. And bloody idiotic." I sighed, wanting nothing more than to go vent my frustration on one of the nearest punching dummies Felix had to hand. Maybe even the one with my name on it, given how right now I really didn't want to be me, handling this mess. "Look, sorry I dragged you along to that little slaughter-fest. I've got to go speak to Jessica, and Jacob. Sort this shit out. But thanks for helping with the research."

"Yeah, what good it did us." She replied but then smiled. "There'll be a perfectly reasonable explanation as to why this guy Grubbins thinks he saw your friend. You'll find it, work out who the real bad guy is and go kick its butt before tea-time. I have faith in you."

"Shit, kid. When did you start getting so wise?" I mocked, but felt her words lighten my mood a little. "But thanks."

"Go on. I want to finish my work-out and burn off all the calories you brought round!" She grinned, nodding to the punching dummies. "Let me know how things go."

"Deal." I gave her shoulder a quick squeeze, then made for the front door.

Time to go check in with my Alpha, and drop this lovely bombshell on her lap. Fair's fair, if things were as crazy as they seemed and Jacob had gone wild, chowing down on innocents, I wanted our Alpha to decide what needed doing, and backing up any of us who had to bring him in. For his own good, and the mortals at risk.

It was just so *wrong* to be thinking this of my packmate.

An hour and a half later, I was seated on one of the sofas in Jessica's living room, cradling a foaming mug of coffee that was cooling slightly since I hadn't had much chance to take a drink since I arrived.

Opposite, Jessica faced me with one leg crossed over the other. She had her notepad on her lap, another mug of coffee near to hand, and a very sceptical look on her face.

"So that's pretty much where I've landed." I finished up, having run through everything that had happened that morning. From me leaving the office, the walk over to Holland Park and what I'd found there, to my jaunt over to see Felix and the shitstorm that had followed. Not bad going for half a day's effort. "I know how it sounds, but the facts …"

"Are what they are, but ah dinnae recall you ever being the sort tae take things at face value?" Jessica replied with an arched eyebrow. She had been making brief notes as I talked, and now she looked over them, mulling things through.

I took the chance to drink a mouthful of rich caffeine goodness. The pizza had been filling, but my energy levels were craving a shot of java from the surprise I'd just had. Just something to balance the *flight or fight* instinct that bloodshed always arouses in lycan. Well, *fight* mostly.

"The way ah see things, these are the facts we have." My Alpha looked back up, and I swallowed quickly. "Nay need tae rush yer drink. You've had a busy morning."

I nodded my thanks, and took another swig before setting the cup aside.

"All good." I told her, seeing her smile before she continued.

"As ah was saying. The facts are that *something* has been taking mortal pets from their owners, with nae arousing suspicion or seemingly interacting with the mortals involved. This something also has been killing the local wildlife in Holland Park, with less subtlety than it has used tae gain access tae the pets. And then this attack upon transients in Greenwich Park, all the way across London, which as you describe it was a scene of pure butchery. And this time, unlike all the other pet thefts and animal killings, the killer allowed itself tae be seen, its act witnessed. Giving us a description and drawing of our own packmate, Jacob."

She checked her facts, then looked across at me again.

"Did ah miss anything?"

"Only some weird-ass vibes I got at Holland Park," I reminded her. "There was a feeling like I was being watched whilst I was there, that something was keeping tabs on me, and it was something familiar but then also not. At Greenwich, it was sort of the same, but I could almost *taste* Jacob being there. More than his footprint or whatever, it was him. But also not. I honestly don't know what the fuck's going on."

"Dinnae feel bad, this is a mess and then some." She reproved me slightly, before sighing and setting the pad aside. "Ah will admit, ah trust yer senses more than some mere footprint or sketch made from a description given by a mortal or creature of the Real. One who had just seen his comrades butchered before his eyes. If it were only this transient's testimony, ah would feel better at doubting Jacob's involvement."

"Yeah, but he was there. I'd put money on it." I grimly admitted, not wanting my packmate to be involved any more than she did. But I knew what I had sensed. "Maybe, oh I don't know, maybe he had been there earlier? Gone on a hunt or something, and all I was sensing was him there during the day?"

Jessica shook her head, expression schooled as she marshalled her thoughts.

"Jacob has been on duty at Twilight's border fer every day this past week, and nae had any reason tae be venturing over tae Greenwich fer any hunt." She confirmed, picking up her pad again and tapping in some details. "He has an apartment on the Isle of Dogs, where ah believe he lives alone …"

"And you can get from that side of the river to Greenwich via the footbridge without too much effort." I finished up the thought. "He'd still need to get across Greenwich itself, and into the Park, but it's doable. But even if that's all true, it doesn't make *sense*."

"Nae much does these days." Jessica replied with uncharacteristic glibness. "But we soldier on, do we not?"

"Yeah. Soldier on. That's what we do, for sure." I snarked back with a sigh. "You know what would really be helpful right now? Ellie, doing one of her rituals to see what *actually* happened last night. Have we had any luck finding someone…?"

Jessica's sigh spoke volumes as she shook her head.

Before things had gone so drastically wrong at the Southbank Centre, Ellie had already prepared the way for her to step down as our consultant witch. Needing time to spend with a newly resurrected Greg, let alone to find out what life as a mere mortal without her witch talents looked like.

Plus there was the small fact she'd skirted the articles of the Accords by bringing Greg back from the dead, using lore she'd found whilst doing research on Robert Knox. The mortal ex police officer hadn't asked to be returned, though she had been convinced his spirit remained with her after his death, and she had had to make use of stolen life energy, drained from other victims of Knox's madness. None of which had made Jessica particularly pleased, and put their mutual friendship and working relationship at extreme odds.

So, Ellie presented us with a shortlist of other practitioners who might be interested in filling the role she provided the pack. Five witches, and one warlock, three from her own circle and the three others she had worked alongside over the years and learned to trust.

All well and good, but the whole thing had left a bad taste in more than just my mouth. It felt a little like we were giving up on Elspeth, letting her rot with Morgana behind the Twilight mists. Yeah, mistakes had been made, but that didn't mean we should just give up on her. Ellie had proven to be an invaluable member of the team, a pack-member despite not being lycan, and replacing her had felt wrong on more than one level.

Fate, it seemed, seemed to agree, since each and every person on the list she had provided had politely declined to enter into any sort of working relationship with us. Jessica had made the offers clear, that despite Ellie's habit of getting hands-on and involved, the role was purely for a professional consultant on matters of research and magic. That they wouldn't be expected to get in harm's way.

But still, they declined.

It made me wonder what sort of reputation we had in the magical circles, to be so obviously *not* a bunch of fun-loving lycanthropes to work with.

Then again, I privately had a sneaky suspicion that at least three of the names Ellie had given us had declined less over the type of work they'd be doing, and more over a tenuously related matter.

That being Felix.

Turned out, my young friend hadn't yet sworn vows to Tera, the Goddess of the Mortal Realm. Though Ellie had been a valued member of her witch's coven, Felix was still finding her feet and had stubbornly refused to rush into any such binding decisions. No bolt of lightning had struck her down, no earthquake had levelled her home, in fact no unexplainable natural event had occurred to her to indicate a Goddess's displeasure. But I couldn't help but wonder if the witches had their own agenda, and were snubbing us until they got their claws into Felix fully.

And yeah, whilst I knew our consultant was not the sort to think in those terms at all, I had plenty enough other examples of witches acting in less harmonious and charitable ways to be a suspicious bastard. Take Cerce, for instance.

"Whilst ah dinnae disagree that *Miss MacElvy* would prove invaluable right about now," My Alpha answered, the fact she referred to Ellie by her last name speaking volumes, "The fact is, we are without that resource at our disposal. So fer now, ah think it best we tackle this problem head on."

The sound of footsteps on the stairs, and a familiar scent in the air, preceded the entrance of Jacob Moon as he stomped onto the wooden floorboards. There was an odd sharpness to his scent, probably from spending too much time near the Twilight mists given their obvious kinship with the Veil, but I still wrinkled my nose at the faint burned bite.

He stopped, looking across at the pair of us, eyes hooded, the questions that must be springing to his mind stored away behind a façade of stone.

"You texted him?" I queried, and Jessica nodded. Head on, she'd said. That was our Alpha, not one to beat around the bush or waste time.

I braced myself as Jessica motioned for Jacob to join us.

Time to find out what the fuck was going on.

Chapter 8

"We've got a problem."

Those were Jacob's words of greeting, as he settled down on one of the other sofas, facing us both.

I was happy to let Jessica take the lead here, as I tried to guess what problem my packmate could be talking about. He couldn't be talking about Greenwich, surely?

"What's wrong?" Jessica asked without any trace of doubt or concern in her voice. No evidence to suggest she was in any way wary of the lycan sitting opposite her. Hell, I couldn't sense even the slightest waver in her demeanour, that solidness we all knew and relied on. If she had worries, she was keeping them locked down tight.

"Something's affecting the pack. The others as well." He settled into the sofa, laying his large hands on his knees as he spoke. "Headaches. Inability to sleep. Some of the pack are reporting they are feeling wired, hungover. Which we all know isn't possible. I don't know if it's to do with the mists, or whatever shit Morgana pulled in reforging this Twilight Court, but I've got two of my team not fit for patrol today, and the other Alphas are telling me there's another eight or more showing symptoms too. And that's from three mentioning *something* wasn't right last week."

Jessica remained focused on Jacob as I thought through this little revelation. None of the pack had mentioned feeling weird or sick to me, but then I wasn't part of the team set to patrol the mists, on order of our Alpha. So that meant I wasn't really crossing paths with the usual mutts as I chased down missing pets and tried *not* to feel too pissed at being benched.

It was quite possible this was a wider problem. But it still didn't explain the slaughter I'd been taken to see by Sister Sloth, and Jacob's scent being all over the scene.

"It cannae be a hex or curse, given our kin's immunity tae such things. Well, almost all of us, present company accepted." Jessica mused, whilst Jacob shot me an amused look. Yeah, remind me I was still tied into a blood-hex I'd let the mortal secret police bind to me, why not? It wasn't a cause of ongoing embarrassment, knowing that if I tried to talk about what I'd witnessed beneath the Tower of London, I'd collapse and suffer a fit, cue foaming of mouth and writhing of limbs.

Nope, not embarrassing *at all*.

"What about you, Jacob?" She enquired lightly, seeming to simply be concerned for her packmates, with no ulterior motive to her question whatsoever.

But Jacob was no fool, and obviously picked up on something in her voice or presence. He shot me a look, one eyebrow raised, so I just shrugged.

"What about me?" He asked bluntly, never one to mess around when the direct approach yielded best results. Whether that meant punching through a brick wall, or in this case being a right suspicious bastard.

"Just answer the question, Jacob. Are you afflicted, like yer packmates?" Jessica pressed, and this time her tone made it clear she wasn't going to be denied a response.

My packmate looked at us for a long moment, expression closed. Obviously weighing up his next words. Then, as if something had been decided in his head, he shook his head.

"Not like the others, no." He replied carefully, settling back into the sofa and letting loose a heavy sigh. "But yeah, I've been having problems sleeping since … well, since the Blooding. Since I … *we* lost Lucille. And then, what with the shit hitting the fan at the Southbank centre and the mists taking a chunk of London, I just started needing something to take the edge off. Get me to sleep, without all the crap popping into my head. Take me out of the game, just so I can recharge."

Now, us lycan are fairly proof against most substances that mortals use to ensure a good night's sleep. Our nature means we don't suffer hangovers, but we also don't get drunk from imbibing too much alcohol. The best we can hope for is a pleasant buzz and short-lasting high before the poisons are eradicated from our blood. It's the same for most pharmaceutical substances. Sleeping pills, pain killers like morphine or codeine, all are pretty useless to us. I may have mentioned, but Mother Nature likes a balance, so whilst we got the buffed-up healing skills of Wolverine or Deadpool, we also get the pain to go with it.

If Jacob had been suffering from insomnia and nightmares, and wanted something to knock him out, there was only a limited number of options he had to choose from. A nasty suspicion reared its ugly head, and I looked across at my packmate, guessing what the fuckwit had been doing.

"You've been dosing yourself with Wolfsbane, haven't you, you bloody idiot?" I asked, not caring how I sounded. "I thought we destroyed all that crap?!"

Jacob shook his head, as Jessica gave an exasperated hiss of breath, her eyes narrowing at what he was admitting to.

"Not all. I kept back some of the product Cerce handed over. Originally I thought we should keep some just in case any more showed up, so we could get Elspeth to compare them. See if she could prove it was from the same source." The lycan admitted, showing he'd been as practical as ever. At least to begin with. "I figured it was safe on the office premises. No-one could get their hands on it to use against us. But then I started not being able to sleep. I tried herbal tea, meditation, fuck it I tried pretty much everything. But nothing worked."

He looked at Jessica, the truth written on his craggy, hard face. He knew what he'd done, and the reasons behind it.

"You needed me in good shape, to manage the patrols of the mists. Keeping anything from creeping in, or getting out." He told us both, not an accusation, just a statement of fact. "I only took a little, just as a test to see if the stuff would work. I got enough sleep to get myself back in the game, keep anyone else from getting hurt. But then the nightmares started back up, so I took a little more. Just enough to knock me out, but not leave me unable to function."

"And now you're, what, dosing every night?" I asked, the slight flinch in his eyes answering me. Fuck, Jacob was damaged, bearing the pain of losing the lycan he'd partnered with. Had loved. And carrying the burden of keeping the pack together after our losses, needing to support Jessica in every way he could. All the while keeping his own shit hidden, locked away. I didn't know whether to punch the idiot, or give him a thoroughly brotherly hug. "Shit, mate, you *know* that stuff is poison to us. You don't get inoculated against it by taking a little at a time. It isn't snake venom or any shit like that. You're crippling yourself!"

"And last night? Did you dose yerself?" Jessica asked quietly, bringing the conversation right back to the reason we were talking. Oh yeah, the murders. And Jacob having been there.

My packmate nodded, once.

"I finished at the mists at maybe ten, half ten. Came back here to organise the shift for today, then headed home." He admitted, shoulders slumping a fraction with the pain of admitting what he'd done. "I was out by half eleven, and I didn't wake until seven this morning. Which is when I found out Daniel and Siobhan were too sick to take patrol. Why?"

Our Alpha looked over at me, nodding once to let me know this was my lead now, my responsibility to pick up. I took a breath, everything Jacob had said set against what I'd found at the slaughter scene.

"Because three homeless were killed in the early hours of this morning at Greenwich Park. They were butchered, torn apart. Fed on." I told him, watching for his immediate reactions. Any twitch to say this wasn't news to him. "And your scent was all over the scene, with other evidence to suggest a lycan was the killer. Kinda points a fairly big fucking finger at you."

Jacob stiffened at my words, eyes fixed on me as I talked. His expression was closed, the guilt and pain he'd just admitted to locked away again behind the granite that I knew was his default setting. Eyes cold, hooded.

"Three very messily dead members of the Arches' congregation. The Sisters are after blood, but have let me find out just what the fuck happened, before they take direct action." I rounded off, knowing he would understand just how bad an outcome it would be if the Sisters got involved. Between them and the Furies, I wasn't sure who scared me the most. "But you were out cold, sleeping off a Wolfsbane-induced trip so it couldn't have been you. Right?"

Jacob grunted, cracking his neck but not bothering to answer.

"Ok, this is what is going tae happen." Jessica interjected before I could frame a suitable response to his silence. Short on words, heavy on the *get a fucking grip*. "Jacob, you will surrender the remaining Wolfsbane tae me. Whatever is affecting you, this is nae the way tae face it."

Jacob nodded once, a sense of relief escaping his locked down emotions. His Alpha knew the truth, and she was still on his side. Of course, that still didn't help matters if he was responsible for killing innocents, even whilst under the influence of the malign substance.

"Ah want a full list of those of our pack, and those other lycan, who are similarly affected. Names, how long they have been patrolling the mists. Anything you can find that links them, nae matter if it is the smallest detail." She instructed him, picking up her tablet and tapping away on the screen. "Ah have sent an email tae the pack, instructing them tae give you any and all details on their well-being. Whatever is affecting mah lycan, ah want it found. Now."

"Uh, aren't we forgetting one little thing?" I queried, earning a sharp look from Jessica. But then she took a breath, nodding before continuing.

"Ah had nae forgotten, Morgan." She answered me with a small smile. "Jacob will be given one last dose of Wolfsbane tonight, and ah want you tae watch over him whilst he sleeps. If anything is affecting him, anything that might explain his connection tae the killings in the park, ah want you there tae witness it. And deal with it as you see fit."

Jacob exchanged a flat look with me, the usual witty banter we shared lost in the moment.

"Look, if you're worried I won't be able to handle you, tripping on Wolfsbane …" I offered, knowing that despite my *unique* heritage and additional gifts from the Courts, Jacob still saw himself as the stronger of us two. Or at least better trained in all-out combat, what with his military experience. "I can ask Emma along? I *know* she can kick your arse."

"No. You'll do." He replied after a moment, telling me he'd at least thought through the offer rather than replying based purely on his pride. Not wanting his packmate to know of his screw up. Then he switched his attention back to Jessica.

"I know you need to be sure." He told her, choosing his words carefully now. No matter his personal feelings, she was his Alpha and he owed her too much. "But I want you to remember this. I did my tours abroad, spent time in absolutely hell-holes. Utter bloodbaths, where bodies of both enemies and comrades were always within reach. If I *were* the sort to prey on mortals, I would have snapped then. I didn't. No matter what the evidence is, I didn't eat any defenceless transients in a drug-fuelled mess. Let alone the fact I would have woken covered in blood, tasting it. Smelling of it. I want us to be clear, is all."

"And we are." She answered truthfully. "But ah am also aware how capable you are. Tae commit a brutal murder, then clean up all evidence of the fact, ah dinnae think it would stretch yer talents beyond what ah know you can achieve when you put yer mind tae it. So we must be sure."

That seemed to be the end of the discussion, as Jacob gave a grunt and settled back on his seat whilst Jessica went back to typing on her pad. I suddenly felt like the spare wheel, the awkward third member of a party when the other two were not speaking to each other.

"So then, I guess I can go let the nuns know we're making progress?" I offered, getting a stony look from Jacob and a curt nod from Jessica. "Great. Well, then …"

I was saved from trying to make any more small-talk, by the thumping of feet on the stairs. Edward, tall and gangly, always looking like he was outgrowing his clothes with some adolescent growth-spurt despite him being an adult, poked his head over the low wall by the stairs.

"Uh, am I interrupting?" He asked, taking in the scene of us all sat together, but catching the conflicting vibes we were all throwing out.

"Dinnae worry yerself, Edward." Our Alpha told him, setting her pad aside, calm and collected. "How can ah help you?"

"Uh, it's Morgan I'm after?" He replied almost apologetically, as I pushed myself off the sofa, glad for the easy out. "You've got a, well, someone's asking for you downstairs."

I ran a very short list of potential people I knew might have dropped by the office to see me. Danny would've called ahead, and Felix would have charmed her way past the front desk and be greeting me herself. Cormac Smith seemed to have forgotten about me, now that he had a direct line to the lycan Alphas, and I was certain Cerce had fled back Real side when I let slip who had robbed her of her keepsake of Arthurian legend.

"It's not a towering red skinned immortal with tattoos and talons, wearing a freaky as fuck helmet over her eyes and telling me I need to return a gnome is it?" I queried almost as a joke.

Jessica tsked under her breath, as aware as I that Tisiphone had recovered from the attack Morgana had inflicted on the Fury to drain her of her immortal energy. Corporeal once more, the Fury had visited Jessica to make it clear that my debt to the sisters was still very much owed.

Thankfully, at least for my own skin, Jessica had convinced the enraged Fury that what had happened at the Southbank Centre lay for the most part at Morgana's feet. The immortal had planned, and indeed had needed a being of the Fury's power to fuel her rebirth of Twilight, and she had manipulated me easily enough to guarantee I summoned one of their kind to take her down.

Tisiphone had eventually agreed, telling my Alpha that no vengeance was sought on me. That she and her sisters would be taking to task the Queen of Twilight separately, and that matter was not for the lycans to be concerned with. Just my little missing gnome problem to be dealt with unless I wished to take Terrigyle's place under their cruel ministrations.

"Uh, no. Definitely not. It's …" Edward struggled with an explanation, finally giving up. "Oh, just come on down and see, will you?"

I looked over at Jessica, who gave me a nod to say I could leave. Jacob rose with me, obviously taking the interruption as a way of leaving too.

"I'll go get you that list." He growled to Jessica, who replied with a small smile. The sort that showed a hint of teeth, just to show things were not settled between them. He had held back a proscribed substance from destruction, and had been using it himself. No matter the fact he'd done it for all the right reasons, it still sat between them, marring the until now perfect working relationship they'd had. Even friendship.

The three of us tramped down the stairs, Jacob nodding to me once before heading off to start gathering the information Jessica wanted. I still was struggling with the shit that had landed on our laps ... on one hand, one of the toughest lycan I knew weakened by the loss of his partner and his own pain so much that he stupidly started messing with the one substance that seriously fucked us up. To knock himself out, allow him to sleep and function as Jessica needed him to.

But on the other hand, *something* had butchered three homeless mortals or creatures of the Real, and my senses had tagged Jacob all over that mess. I hadn't gotten the same sensation over at Holland Park, so I wasn't pinning the pet and wildlife killing on him.

Yet.

How did I reconcile my packmate and long-time friend possibly giving into his beast, and now a bloodthirsty butcher who fed on his prey in the early hours of the morning? Fact was ... I couldn't. There had to be a truth, and there had to be a lie. It was just matter of figuring out which was which.

Edward paced with me to the stairs leading to the ground floor. Then he stopped, motioning for me to head on down by myself.

"This is beginning to freak me out, mate." I told Edward. "Who the hell is it?"

My packmate just shook his head, motioning for me to head on down.

Shit, who the hell was down there? I started down the stairs, working through that list again in my head. Maybe it *was* Cormac Smith and a bunch of his governmental stooges, looking to complicate my life as he had a habit of doing. Or maybe it was the mortal police, having found out about Gregory Allen's mortal remains having been removed and somehow linking that mess to me. I still had Gary Weatherby's disappearance hanging over me, despite us cleaning the boathouse of any trace of my having been there. All the mortal police needed was a shred of evidence to begin digging into the story Felix and I had cooked up, to cover off the actual events and Gary's whereabouts.

Whoever it was, they had Edward lost for words and that was something I just wasn't used to. Normally he could talk the hindlegs off a donkey, and used vocalisation to deal with high stress situations. I'd known him to try carrying on a conversation with the actual targets of a hunt whilst rendering them immobile, which was normally quite one-sided.

Him being silent meant exactly what?

I stepped onto the ground floor, looking beyond the reception desk which stood momentarily empty. To where potential clients were seated, a comfortable nest of sofas and single chairs to park their butts. Left with coffees, teas or water. Alcoholic beverages to steady any shocked nerves. The latest glossy magazine to hide behind. Whatever they needed whilst we worked out who the lucky mutt taking their case was.

The sense of the person hit me even as I saw the back of their head. She was wearing a hat, the floppy sort in shades of maroon that I guessed was more for keeping the wearer's head warm than any conscious fashion statement. But underneath, lustrous dark hair hung down over her shoulders. So black, it had a blue sheen to it.

She turned in her seat, and my stomach lurched about a hundred miles straight up as if I'd fallen from a great height. It couldn't be. But my eyes were telling me what my fine-tuned lycan senses had already confirmed.

"Hello, Morgan."

Doctor Sarah Maria Conner greeted me, smiling hesitantly.

Chapter 9

Holy Water

Holy Water is thought to be effective against evil or demonic creatures, inflicting great pain on them when they are doused in it or to break curses and possessions if the afflicted is anointed with the substance. It is thought that the divinity linked to the blessing counteracts the malign influence, and causes demons and devils to feel the incandescence of the Divine, burning them like magnesium flares in open air.

The strength of the blessing, in fact the belief of the one doing the blessing, often is the deciding factor on whether the Water is strong enough to counter greater or lesser Evil. Should the priest or clergy be beset by doubts, unsure of their faith, then often the Holy Water is less effective which is often why devils and demons target these secular types so that they are unable to provide effective protection to the other mortals.

"Uh, what the fuck? I mean … hi?" I almost stammered, sucker-punched like never before.

Sarah slowly got to her feet. She was wearing a light coat against the cold weather, falling past her knees and with the collar turned up, jeans and a pale blouse with embroidered flowers on the material. Dark comfortable trainers finished the ensemble. A healthy tan only accented her Spanish ancestry, giving her a glow of healthiness and vitality that no amount of photo-shop software or sun-beds could replicate.

Her eyes were bright, a little too bright, deep brown against her tanned skin and dark hair. But it was *her*. My ex, who I had last seen in the underground parking lot beneath the Half Moon public house. At the Blooding, kidnapped by the Nighters, by fucking Talen and Sal Orben. And made to see us lycan for what we really were, at our most savage. Made to see me, in my true suit, wearing my true face.

"You're supposed to be in South America." I told her kind of stupidly, trying to work out how she could be standing in the reception of *Good Deeds*. What it meant for us, that she was here, talking to me. I mean, *what the hell?*

"I was. The Board sent me to look at some fossils dug up in Brazil, but I was pulled out of that pretty quickly. I ..." She began, then shook her head. "Look, can we go somewhere to talk? Somewhere private?"

The fact she wanted to talk to me at all, and wasn't screaming in recalled fear from that night or calling me a long list of swear words in Spanish had me thoroughly stumped. She should have been a gibbering wreck still, it had only been just over six months since she witnessed the truth. The least I could do was let her talk.

"Sure. I think I know someplace we can talk." I rallied my brain cells, knowing I should be getting a message to the Sisters. Let them know we were working on finding the killer of their congregants, and not to take any action themselves. Make sure Jacob was off the hook until we were sure what was going on.

But this was *Sarah*.

"Come on." I motioned for her to head out first, as I reached over the reception desk and grabbed out a post-It note and pen. Scribbling a message to Jessica, I followed after her.

Hyde Park is a well-known haunt for mortals any time of the year, its rolling grassland usually filled with the noise and physical presence of teenagers, families, strangers even. Crushing the grass underfoot, littering the open space with rubbish, generally leaving little chance of privacy.

However, if you know where to look, there are still a few secret places left tucked away that allow for a little breathing space. Somewhere set back from the all-consuming chaos that naturally occurred wherever mortals congregated.

The Pet Cemetery in Hyde Park was one such corner.

Located in the North-West section of the park, the Victorian cemetery was closed to the mortal public, and had been since the beginning of the 1900s for fear of vandalism and the sort of wanton damage mortals make without conscious thought. The Royal Parks look after the upkeep of the place, but the gardeners seem to think it atmospheric and in keeping with its character to let ferns and ivy grow almost unchecked over the thousand or so graves in the place.

With the place on our very doorstep, Jessica had arranged for the pack to have special access to visit whenever we liked. Perks of us making regular donations to another charitable body needing funds. It was a haven, a source of peace and tranquillity we could slip off to, to sit on a mausoleum and let the stresses of the day unwind when things got too much. Or just wander around the place, enjoying the idiocies of what mortals chose to call their beloved companions. I mean, what self-respecting descendant of wolves would want to be known as *Mr Fluffy*?

The gate creaked open with the sort of sound that movie special effects experts spend thousands of local currency trying to replicate, when all you really needed was rusted iron and time. Ahead of us, concrete paving had been set in the earth, carefully tended to keep grass and weeds from obscuring each flagstone, leading into the graveyard.

"You know, Morgan, when I said somewhere private, I didn't *exactly* have this in mind!" Sarah told me with that familiar tone of hers; half sarcastic, half intrigued. "Well, I can't say you don't take me to interesting places. A graveyard?"

"Pet Cemetery. Like Stephen King wrote about, but with less zombie pets. Zero to date, last time I checked." I replied, as I closed the gate behind us. "There are some benches a little further in."

She didn't say anything as we walked deeper into the grounds, surrounded by carefully cropped bushes of green and white, ivy and vines bound together to form natural barriers. And the gravestones.

Rows on rows of little headstones, peeking up from the ground in their hundreds. Like teeth, weathered by wind and rain. The writing on them still fairly legible, where their owners had left parting messages to their beloved pets.

Prince – Marine Commando of Anisor 11 Years. He asked so little, and gave so much.

In Loving Memory of Our Faithful Little Friend – Wobbles

Darling Dolly. My Sunbeam. My Consolation. My Joy.

On and on, the little messages enscribed in stone, capturing the joy, the pain, the loss each and every mortal felt at losing their companion and friend.

Near the centre several wooden benches had been set off the side of the concrete path to give grieving owners a chance to sit in peace and spend some time with their pets. Stephen King had done a wonderful job in turning a place of quiet sorrow and contemplation into a thing of horror and fear. The mortal was a genius for messing with the common everyday stuff, but I didn't really mind as the thought of *Mr Bimbles* or *Floppy* clawing their way out of their graves to exact vengeance just made me laugh.

However, it kept most of the homeless or teenage youths out of the place. Those individuals who normally were happy to ignore the rules to find a place to sleep at night or fool around under the influence of rampant hormones. Even these mortals didn't dare risk the chance Mr King was onto something with his writing.

I offered up the bench to Sarah, and she perched herself on the wooden seat, drawing her coat about her. Not wanting to presume, still trying to figure out what had brought my ex to my door again, I leant against the side of a larger stone mausoleum, a home for a whole family pack of beloved dogs that had all been interred together.

The silence stretched out, Sarah looking down at her hands whilst I tried not to stare at her. Finally, I gave a sigh, knowing one of us would have to start somewhere.

"So. I never expected I'd see you again." I admitted to her, seeing her flinch at my voice but then look up at me, and fix her eyes on my own. "Given, well, what happened, I mean."

I saw her flinch again, and mentally kicked myself. Yeah, nice going Morgan. Remind the fragile mortal about the horrific event she'd been exposed to, why don't you? That'll be a nice trip down memory lane to have …

But then, I had to know. Did she even remember? Or had OPS, Cormac Smith and his gang, had they somehow wiped her memories of the whole shitstorm? Ellie had told me the witches were taking care of the *Hexen-wolfen* university students, helping them with their craft to erase the damage done by the cursed artefacts Robert Knox had gifted them with. But I had no idea what OPS resources were like … hell, the bastards had drugged me through the blood-hex I still carried, and were versatile in using curses to keep their secrets. Wiping a mortal's memory wasn't a far stretch from that.

Sarah drew a breath, composing herself before answering.

"Look, Morgan. I know it's weird, me showing up at your office like this. But I needed to talk to you. About us. About what happened." Sarah began. She pushed out a breath, shaking her head. "I still remember that night … *ay Dios mio* … those *bastardos* who kidnapped me. They drugged me. Kept laughing at me, talking about the *truth*. How I was such a stupid, ignorant *mortal* who didn't know anything no matter my education, what I did for a living. I was just an ignorant bitch who couldn't even see the truth about the 'man' I was involved with. Oh, they laughed about that. About you."

I went to speak but she held up a hand, stopping me.

"No, please. Let me finish? This is hard enough already." She asked me, and after a moment, I nodded. It was the least I could do, after all she had gone through.

"And then I saw you. Saw all of you. In that place." Sarah went on after a moment. "I *saw* you change, become that other … creature. All of you become something horrible, something terrible. And yes, at first I just couldn't believe it. Like every nightmare and horror story suddenly come true. Everything my *nona* spoke about, the spooks in the night, the devils that would come devour me for disobeying my parents, for fooling around with boys. For doing *wrong*. And you were one of them. A monster."

It was pretty much what I'd expected, what I'd feared. Sarah had seen through the Looking Glass, the other side of the Veil. And it had been filled with horror; monstrous, terrible creatures from every myth and nightmare that the mortals had gathered since they first crawled out of their caves and braved the darkness.

And I was one of those things.

"It was all so crazy. None of it made sense. You were fighting each other, monsters attacking more monsters and I couldn't get away, couldn't stop seeing all the blood, all the horrible injuries … things were dying right in front of me but I couldn't stop seeing it all." Sarah shook her head, the images still so vivid in her mind, still haunting her. OPS had *definitely* not wiped them, and it looked like they'd done fuck all to help her deal with them either. "I kept expecting one of you to come at me, to hurt me. Kill me. But it never happened."

"And then suddenly there were other people. *Normal* people, soldiers with guns. Men and women in suits ordering everything to stop. Specialists, a subsection of the government who handle this sort of 'event', they told me. Making it sound so commonplace, so ordinary. They gave me something to counter the drugs I'd been given, but that just made me realise nothing had changed. It was all real, everything I'd seen was true." Sarah shook her head. "Then they gave me a bunch of forms to sign, legal agreements to say I wouldn't tell anyone what I'd seen. What had been done to me. They told me if I did try I'd face criminal proceedings, even a penal sentence at '*Her Majesty's leisure*'. My entire career discredited, and whoever I spoke to would face the same penalties. It was like a whole different nightmare, the sort where governments make people disappear just with a click of their fingers."

"Whilst they were telling me all this, someone went to my home and packed my clothes, personal items, anything they thought I might need. Someone else contacted the Museum to make arrangements for my transfer. The next thing I knew I was being told I was going to Brazil. To work on an expedition for the local government, assessing fossils of historical value. For an undetermined period of time."

"No one asked me what I wanted. No one gave me any choice. I was effectively kidnapped again, my phone and laptop only returned to me after they installed some sort of tracking software. To make sure I didn't try and break the rules I'd been told to stick to." She continued, and I had to fight a growl from breaking free. "I was escorted all the way to City airport and put on a private charter plane. Someone travelled with me all the way to Mexico, where I was handed over to more government types who were waiting for me. Like I was some sort of criminal. Not a victim."

Cormac Smith had told me, in the basement of the Half Moon, that they'd take care of Sarah. They were experienced in handling cases of mortals coming face to face with the Real, with the truth. That they'd look after her, help her deal with the experience so that she at least could have a normal life still.

Instead, it sounded like they'd put her through the wringer, making her sign agreements of secrecy before she was even properly herself again. Hell, Sarah probably had the same hex bound to her blood as me, forbidding her from mentioning any details of her experience. But without her knowledge. And they'd shipped her off, halfway around the world, without giving her time even to stop, to try and understand what had happened.

Cormac and I were due to have some harsh words, when next I had a chance to speak to the OPS operative. I might even use *adult* language.

"But that's the thing, Morgan. I didn't *feel* like a victim by that point. I was upset, *mio dios* was I angry and confused, but I wasn't afraid anymore. All I could think about, on the flight to Sao Paulo and then at the dig site, was … I needed to be back in London. Here." Sarah slapped the wooden bench beside her, kicking the grass underfoot. "Not side-lined, sent off like some naughty *chico* to bed without supper. All the way across the sea, away from what had happened. What I'd seen. When all I wanted to do was get some *answers*."

"The truth is I'm a doctor of Paleozoology because I *love* finding things out. Asking questions, digging up answers to problems." She explained, a little needlessly as I was painfully aware of her field of study. It had been one of the major problems Jessica and the pack had had about me seeing her. She was *invested* in finding out about us, putting clues together to learn the truth of how different we were from mortals. When that was the last thing we wanted. "I study the remains of animals that have been dead millions of years to try to build a picture of what they were like, what made them special. Different from all the other creatures that still exist with us now."

"And suddenly, I find that you aren't like us. None of you are. You are unique, totally different from *homo sapiens* or any other lifeform native to Earth. Maybe even a whole new divergent line we thought was extinct." She pointed a finger at me, forehead creased. "But you're alive, not some fossil or fragments I have to piece together and still make guesses about. You're able to speak, to answer me when I ask you questions. Real, so I can take samples and see what makes you different. Right there in front of me."

I kept quiet, knowing this was important for her to explain, and for me to understand. Mortals, when confronted with the reality of the Veil and beyond, of the truth behind all the myths and legends, tend to go one of two ways. Either they went stark raving mad, taking up religion like a fanatic or escaping what filled their head through drugs and alcohol, finding a nice, padded cell to spend the rest of their days hiding inside… either that or they rationalised it. Made sense of the craziness. Very few mortals had the capacity to handle the truth, but if anyone was going to, I'd put money on Dr Sarah Conner as strong-minded enough to handle the revelations.

"What I'm trying to say, Morgan, is … yes, it was horrible. I'd never seen anything so terrifying as all of you changing, becoming those *things*. Monsters. And all the blood, the sounds you made when you fought, *mio dios* they'll haunt me for a long while." She wrapped up, pushing herself up off the bench and coming to stand opposite me. Her scent swirled around me, the hint of sweat and an odd spiced perfume overlaying the actual smell of her skin, her breath. Her essence. "But the fact is, I got through the fear all by myself. And then I started to realise how all the little things began to add up. The times you never showed up when we'd arranged to meet. The calls you got when you had to run off to go help a friend. The small bruises and cuts you always said you got by being so clumsy, falling over or wrestling with Bear. So many little things, but enough to make me think you were hiding something. Maybe seeing someone else, maybe leading a double life."

I couldn't help myself, I let loose a bark of laughter. It was instinctive, a release of what I was feeling inside. The very idea I had been seeing someone else whilst with Sarah, after the mess I had made of that relationship was just insane. But she'd been spot on about me leading a double life, just not the sort of one she was suspicious about.

"What're you thinking?" She asked me, standing opposite me on the concrete path.

"Well, that's a nice easy one to answer!" I grinned ruefully as she smiled, acknowledging my point. "Where would you like me to begin?"

I drew a breath, marshalling my thoughts before I answered. This was very thin ice, and the last thing I needed to do was stomp all over the conversation with my usual tact and diplomacy.

"Is that why you're here? Why you came back?" I finally asked, bracing myself for the response I knew I might get. "To study me? To get answers?"

Sarah hugged herself as a gust of wind whipped through the cemetery, biting and sharp. Those dark brown eyes of hers fixed on me, full of intelligence, full of life.

"No." She answered, then shook her head and corrected herself. "Well, actually yes. I want answers, Morgan I *need* them. The scientist in me wants to do a complete analysis of you, when you are like this and when you're … well, that other thing. I want to find out what makes you special, but also what makes you the same as us. As me. You are a living, breathing culmination of everything I have ever wanted to discover in my work. A singular creature that no-one else has written about, ever proved existed alongside us."

I nodded, having expected that to be her reason. It hurt, but at least I was getting the truth. And it meant things could be settled between us once and for all.

Sarah saw my expression and smiled, shaking her head again.

"Oh Morgan, that's not all. Not even close." She told me, gesturing first to me then herself. "Just like you're more than what I see before me, I'm more than just a scientist. Much more. I asked myself a hundred times why I came back, why I looked you up again. After everything, what is it that made me come here when I could have just closed the door and walked away. And I realised something. I wanted … no, I *needed* to come see you because … *mio dios,* I missed you, you big idiot. I … You're going to make me say it, aren't you?"

I shrugged, not wanting to put words in her mouth, to assume I knew what she was suggesting. Even though a little part of me was jumping up and down to hear what I suddenly hoped she would say, like a puppy begging for the treat,

"Dammit, Morgan, I think I ... no, I know I *love* you. You understand?" Sarah stepped into my circle, reaching up to hesitantly lay a hand on my chest. Over my heart. "And I think you love me too. Unless shape-changers, werewolves or whatever the hell you are, you're all great at faking emotions too?"

At that moment, I really didn't have the words to answer her right there and then. All I could do was wrap my arms around her, and hug her tight against me.

It seemed enough.

Chapter 10

"Werewolves."

"What?" Sarah asked, as I carefully held her. I hadn't answered her question, both for the fact I was still getting over her telling me she loved me, but also for the fact I didn't want to lie to her face. Not right now.

Not about loving her. I knew that was a simple fact, one that had been messing up my life for longer than I cared to think about. No, I just didn't want to lie and tell Sarah we *didn't* pretend to be something we weren't. That we hadn't learned how to trick mortals on a day-to-day basis into believing us to be just like them. Because that was just one of the many basic lessons we'd learned to fit in.

To appear normal and not incite an angry mob looking to turn the poor lycan into so many furry mittens.

"Werewolves. Well, lycanthropes. Or just lycans coz that's easier." I replied, murmuring into her hair. It smelt good, just so fucking good, even if there was a strange scent to her that I only properly noticed up close. A sharpness, probably from a new washing powder or skin care treatment. Like burned spices. It smelt odd, was all, but I could happily ignore it and focus on the fact Sarah was back, in my arms and had admitted she loved me.

Three out of three really ain't bad, I mentally told Meatloaf. If you don't get the reference, look up his songs and lyrics. *Bat out of hell*, I think the album was.

"Yep, I really wouldn't go calling any of us shape-changers." I warned her, thinking back to the creature who had worked with the Mistress. The bastard who had almost beheaded me whilst trekking in Madb's backyard. Let alone the sneaky fucker who had helped Elspeth steal Gregory Allen's body, and run riot around London for shits and giggles, causing a distraction for Morgana after she busted him out of prison. "We're like dogs to their cats, and getting the two mixed up is one reason we've had so much bad press with the mortals."

"Mortals? That's what you call us? Anyone not a … a 'lycan' Or from wherever you come from?" She queried, pushing back a little to part us so she could look me in the eye. "Does that mean you're not, well, mortal?"

"We're not aliens. And it's just a word. I'm not immortal, if that's what you're thinking." I answered her with a sardonic grin. "Trust me, I aged like a bloody hundred years when I found out you'd been kidnapped. And then when I lost you."

"Idiot." She murmured, pressing back close and giving me a warm, hard hug.

We stood there for a long moment before she pushed herself away again. But this time she took a full step back, separating us. I didn't try to hold onto her, letting her have her space. It was enough that we'd been close.

"Um, Morgan?" Sarah spoke up, and my stomach did that little lurch. I picked up the solid warmth of her feelings for me, a core relief I had to assume was from her finding we were still good. But there was also a small spike, a nervousness that I remembered from sitting in my apartment, just before she asked me to help her find her colleague's daughter.

"I need your help."

Bingo.

"It's not another daughter gone missing, is it?" I quipped. "Coz that's a little careless parenting, if they keep misplacing their offspring like that."

The nervousness spiked again, and my smile slipped as she looked at me. Her expression said it all, but she replied anyway.

"No, not like that. You found her, after all." Sarah shook her head, then continued. "No, I need help finding someone else. Not a friend, but a colleague. From the expedition to the Amazon. Dr Julius Eduardo."

"The Amazon? I thought you said Sao Paulo? You know, Brazil?" I questioned, cocking my head at this new piece of information. "Isn't the Amazon a little bit up and to the left?"

"You don't listen, do you *mi amor*?" She chided me gently, that sharp smile of hers telling me she hadn't taken offence. "The government spooks shipped me off to a dig in Sao Paulo first, but I wasn't there for more than three weeks before I was suddenly informed I'd been reassigned. Someone had obtained evidence of an unmapped and unclaimed Mayan temple, photos taken from aerial surveillance. I was to be part of the secondary joint expedition funded by the Jeffersonian and the Natural History Museum. To identify and catalogue zoological findings the initial expedition had unearthed before they were forced to leave."

"Forced to leave? If the place was so 'undiscovered', who the hell was there to kick your lot out?" I know I was asking the wrong questions and focusing on the little things, but that's how my brain works sometimes. "It's not like the occupants could do much, given they're how old, and dead. They *were* dead, right?"

"*Banditos*, I was told. Drug runners operating in the region." She replied, shrugging herself. "The photos that led to the temple's discovery were found on an intercepted drug trafficker's plane. One of the men liked to take photos of the jungle from on high, and had a digital camera on him when they were caught."

"*Drugs. On high*. I see what you did there." I gestured for her to continue with the story. "What happened?"

"Very funny. But there's not much left to tell you. We spent weeks getting to the site through thick jungle, then several months mapping the ruins before we ventured inside each temple." Sarah explained, settling herself back onto the bench as she recalled what had led her back to my door. "The find was amazing, the ruins almost completely untouched by time. Morgan, there was so much to catalogue, so much we had to protect before the locals found the site and started stripping it to sell on the black market. It really was the discovery of the century."

"And then we had to pull out suddenly. The soldiers sent to guard us received word of increased activity by the *banditos* in the region, and they thought we were at risk of kidnapping or worse." She creased her brow, the memories not so pleasant now. "Before we could clear the site, the *bastardos* found us. I remember gunfire and screaming. Explosions, fire. The soldiers bundled me, Dr Eduardo and Dr Miles Cooper into one of the transports we had for emergencies, splitting us up into threes to make extraction easier. Dr George Stands, the head of the exhibition, stayed back with a unit of the soldiers to see if they could save the site, or at least as much of the treasures we'd identified as possible."

"Our guards got us back through the jungle somehow, got us onto a flight back to London. I … we haven't heard any word about the rest of the expedition, or Dr Stands. If they made it to safety or if they were captured. Or worse."

"And this Dr Eduardo? You reckon he's gone missing now?" I had a whole boatload of questions, enough to sail around the world with, but they could wait. For now, I'd stick with the obvious one "Why?"

"Miles and I, we've kept in touch since we got back. Reported what happened to the Museum and handed over the little data and artefacts we were able to bring with us." Sarah answered, scowling at the memory of what they had been forced to leave behind. "Julius was supposed to act as liaison with the Jeffersonian and Dr Stands, and he's the one who would know if our colleagues made it out ok. But no one has heard from him for a few days now. He's not answering his phone, and when Miles and I went round to his home, it looked empty and deserted from outside. So yes, I think he's missing, and definitely needs our help."

She looked at me with those deep eyes of hers, pushing back a lock of blue-black hair.

"Will you help me find him?"

And there was the question. The Twilight Court had returned, slap bang in downtown London. In my backyard. There was a killer on the loose, and some weird shit affecting my lycan brethren. And that didn't even touch on the fact I still had to find Terrigyle and get him back to the Furies otherwise my ass was theirs. Plus, I had to find a way to save Elspeth, and Gregory. Get them out of Morgana's grasp and somehow keep the witch safe from the Furies too.

Oh, and speaking of her Royal Pain In the Arse-ness, I had Morgana to worry about. The Queen of Twilight, if she had somehow survived me letting the Harrowing loose on her. Oh, she'd be looking for payback, and I had to work out how to survive that little wrinkle too.

And finally, I still had my silver-poisoned and definitely bat-shit crazy half-brother to locate and deal with. No way was I forgetting that Jack the Ripper still had it in for me, wherever the bastard was lurking. Licking his wounds, planning on making my life an utter ruin.

So, not much on my plate right now. At all.

I heaved a heavy sigh, looking her straight in the face. That gorgeous Spanish face that I spent far too much time thinking about.

And nodded.

"I'll need to speak to Jessica. Get her sign off for me taking the hunt." I answered, knowing I was on tricky ground as it was, what with Sarah being back in the picture and now asking me for help. Again. "Thing is, there's a lot going on right now so she may not give it the green light. Just so you know."

"Yeah, that whole thing with the walls of mists and South London disappearing. *Mia dios*, is that something to do with you lot?" Sarah asked, and I nodded, happy to leave it as a thing for 'us lot'. Too many details she didn't need to know. "Look, if you can help then great, but I don't want to get you into trouble."

"Ha. Don't worry. I do that all on my lonesome." I grinned, knowing the last thing I wanted was to give Sarah a reason to go cold on me. Not that I should be worried, now she knew my secret.

"Well, if I do get you into hot water, I promise to kiss whatever hurts better." She smiled warmly, and I felt things trip inside me. Knight Errant of the Courts, lycan kitten finder extraordinaire and son of Herne the mighty Hunter, I might be. But I was still just a simple mutt when it came to my love life. "I was thinking, now that I know your big bad secret, how about I come round later?"

"So we can play *Darwin finds a new species*? Start taking samples, figuring out what make me so unique?" I snarked, knowing how much Sarah must be jumping up and down inside to start running her tests, cataloguing all things lycan. "Thing is, I've got a job tonight. Prior party, already booked. But if you want, you can come round this afternoon. I know Bear will love to see you. It'll give me time to square things off with my boss."

Sarah smiled and got back up again. Stepping up to me, she leaned in close, hands reaching round to link behind my neck. Drawing me down for a soft, gentle kiss.

When we parted, she pulled out a mobile phone and flicked to her calendar.

"Four o'clock ok with you? I'll bring a good Merlot. And sausages." She asked me, knowing the two bribes needed to make both Bear and I very happy, as she tapped in the appointment.

"Yeah, just see if you can find the black pudding ones. He's fixated on them right now." I replied, working things out in my head. Four in the afternoon. That gave me two hours to speak to Jessica and square away not only taking a new hunt on top of proving Jacob wasn't this mystery murderer … but also the revelation that Sarah was back in town, and knew enough about us now to have one foot firmly in the Real. All that before I could head home and get the place ready for a visitor.

"Oh *madre maria!* Bear, he's not a, what did you say, a lycan?" Sarah asked me suddenly, and I grinned, shaking my head.

"No, Bear is one hundred percent hound, through and through." I reassured her without letting slip *what* sort of hound that was. "The only shape he has is the fluffy brick shit-house you know and love."

"Ok then. Black pudding sausages and a five-year-old Merlot." Sarah tapped the details into her phone, then returned it back to her pocket. "It's a date."

"Now, you don't need to rush back off to your boss just yet, right?" She asked, looking at me with lowered eyes and a hint of a smile. When I shook my head, that smile grew more wicked, more inviting. "Good. It looks like we've got the place to ourselves, and a woman likes to be told how much she's been missed these past months we were apart."

"Or better yet, *mia amor,* why don't you show me?"

Chapter 11

Herbs

Herbs are often seen as having special powers to ward off supernatural creatures, or weaken them. Wolfsbane is an obvious and well known deterrent to lycanthropes, but some of the more well known and common herbs are also useful barriers to fae and other occult creatures.

Sage can be burned within a home to cleanse any malign influence, and Dill was often considered an effective barrier to evil spirits if made into a wreath and hung from doorways. Oregano, Rosemary and Thyme are said to drive negativity from a dwelling, dispersing any tricksome fae or more malign intent by creatures wishing the occupants ill.

Jessica did *not* take the news well.

The last time my Alpha had been truly vexed with me, she knocked me halfway across her bedroom with a sucker punch, and that had been her pulling the punch enough so I didn't end up bouncing *through* the brick wall.

This time, she simply settled back on her sofa, fingers rubbing her temples and loosing a thoroughly fucked off sigh.

"Ah dinnae know anyone else this side of the Veil who can give me this number of headaches tae worry about. Ah really dinnae know." My Alpha shook her head, as I stood opposite her, having delivered her the good news. "Do you understand the position this puts us in? Puts me in?"

I nodded, not cockily but just the simple truth that I knew what she meant.

The Accords exist to safeguard the mortals and their Realm, keep them protected from a bloody history of the Real rampaging all over them like a bulldozer running over ants, causing pain and ruin as only immortals can. But agreements require something from both parties, and for the mortals to remain safe, they had to remain unknowing. Ignorant of the Real and the creatures who live there. This was what OPS and their fellow spooks under Her Majesty in the United Kingdom worked to achieve, alongside their counterparts in the other countries across the Mortal Realm. A blanket of ignorance achieved through misdirection, lies and the 'handling' of anyone who managed despite everything to glimpse the truth.

Sometimes the shadowy government forces simply recruited the mortals rather than locking them up and throwing away the key, as they had with Robert Knox. Which, let's be honest, had been a monumental disaster and indirectly led to the current shitshow we all were having to deal with. Sometimes compassion seriously bites one in the arse, when burying the bastard in the deepest hole they could find would've saved us all a lot of pain and misery.

And that was the problem I'd just handed Jessica. Sarah was now the one with forbidden knowledge, an insight into the Real. Well, at least in terms of us lycan. OPS had sent her off to either lose those memories or be indoctrinated into their ranks, but she'd slipped free and landed back in my lap. And she wanted to remain free, but also learn more about us.

She also seemed more grounded in her feelings towards me, and keen to move things on between us from the awkward confusion we'd shared to something more solid and stable. It helped that she now knew the secret I'd been keeping between us. And I was *firmly* invested in seeing that happen.

Jessica sighed again, fixing me with a stern, hard gaze of her cloud-grey eyes. She read me like a book, seeing all that was going through my head and heart, understanding me better maybe than I did myself. Which, given my ability to confuse myself on occasion, was not that surprising.

"Ah can see there is nae use telling you tae walk away from this mortal, this woman who has captured yer heart so obviously." She finally spoke, coming to a decision. "Nor will it aid us, ah reckon, if ah simply hand her back tae the mortal authorities tae do with as they will. Instead, ah will extend pack protection over Sarah Conner and speak tae the authorities on her behalf. You may take the hunt fer her missing colleague. *If* it does nae interfere with yer hunt fer the killer of the Sister's flock, and the missing animals."

I went to thank her, but shut my mouth as she held up a hand to stop me.

"Mark me, Morgan." She continued, tone and scent telling me just how serious she was in this moment. This made the time she threatened to kick me out of the pack positively jovial. "You swore tae abide by mah rules, and never again threaten the safety of the pack nor our brethren. Whatever you think tae share with the woman you love, make sure it puts neither us nor her in harm's way. Ah would think recent events are testament tae the trouble you draw tae yourself and those close tae you. And she is nae strong enough tae survive another run-in with those who seek tae do you harm."

I simply nodded, accepting the painful but fair point.

Felix was collateral damage from my friendship with her and Danny, and she at least had managed to acquire armour of her own to defend herself against anything of the Real. Sarah had been exposed to the truth, but was defenceless if anything decided to try to use her against me. Again. Or simply treat her as most Real creatures do with mortals … a cross between a pleasant snack and a punching bag.

"You are still due tae keep Jacob company this evening, and watch fer anything that might explain how his scent came tae be at the scene of slaughter." Jessica reminded me, moving on now that she had plucked that particularly painful splinter. "Ah would ask you tae focus on that with all yer energies, and set aside any *personal* matters with your mortal fer the day. The Sisters are due fer an update, so dinnae let that slip yer mind."

"Absolutely. Totally on the case there." I tried hard not to wince as I let slip the white lie, knowing I'd already agreed with Sarah for her to come over to the apartment in a short while. I wouldn't let it hinder my date with Jacob at his home in the evening, so I didn't feel too bad bending the truth *just* a little to her.

Jessica shook her head one last time, reading the truth so easily from me that I wondered why sometimes I bothered, then picked her tablet back up. A signal our meeting was at an end, and I should withdraw before she found something else to be pissed at me for. There was normally a long list, I had to admit.

With my Alpha's approval in the bag, no matter that it came with a bucketload of caveats, I got my arse into gear. Jacob had already left the office, hopefully getting Jessica the details she wanted and *not* stopping off to chow down on any luckless mortals or wildlife.

Now, it did strike me as a little, well, cavalier of our Alpha to have let Jacob out of sight, given what I'd discovered and the questions that loomed over his head like an anvil about to drop.

But I trusted Jessica, and knew she wouldn't be putting mortals' lives at risk. Well, at least unnecessarily. We'd used them as bait more times than I can count, to lure out our prey on hunts where the bastard was particularly clever, but never with their knowledge and never allowing them to come to harm. It's trickier than it sounds, but we've had lots and lots of practice.

The point was, if Jessica had let Jacob out without a leash, then she either trusted him explicitly and was disregarding the troubling evidence I'd found or … well, or she *had* a leash on him. Just not one he was aware of.

I may have mentioned but Alphas are a breed apart from us common lycan. Stronger, tougher, faster, just plain deadlier with a lifespan that, if not foreshortened by the things we hunted or that hunted us, could run to tens of centuries, maybe longer. They had sharper senses, including hearing which had gotten me into far too much trouble when I thought Jessica was out of earshot, and a sense of pack that was so strong they knew when one of their own was in trouble, hurt or in need. There was an unspoken communication between the pack leaders, so that when one needed aid, the rest just knew and would show up as soon as they could. It was why I'd mistakenly thought Talen Orben had been in our office that time, when instead the bastard was just scoping it out as a new pad for him and his partner, Sal.

Hadn't turned out that well for those two, I was still happy to admit.

Fact was, if Jessica had let Jacob go, it was only because she had some way of keeping an eye on him. And given us lycan are suspicious as hell, and can sense when someone was eyeballing us, she would have made sure whoever was watching was as discreet and subtle as could be. Hence her not even thinking to ask me.

Given how strong and different Alphas were to the common lycan, I'd more than once wondered where we all came from. Where the roots of lycanthropy first sprang to life from and how different we'd been then to how we were now. Having Elspeth around helped, when I'd asked her that question, losing me an afternoon as she gleefully dug into her library and other sources of knowledge to find me some answers.

It seemed werewolves, or man-beasts, had been kicking around maybe two thousand, two and a half thousand years B.C. when a man-beast showed up in *The Epic of Gilgamesh* in old Sumaria, whilst there was some dark and truly twisted mythology coming out of what is now known as South America that also pertained to men and beasts changing shape. Greek and Roman history had a lot to say about the transformations of men and women into wolf-like monsters, whilst a nomadic tribe from Russia – the Neuri from Scythia – well known for transforming into beasts for days on end.

There was one interesting line of enquiry, a demi-god and cult based on *Zeus Lycaean*. This had a particularly grisly story attached that showed just how stupid mortals can be, especially when messing with their Gods. But from that had sprung a myth around a cursed king doomed to take the form of a bestial wolf, never dying, ever ravenous for the flesh of other mortals. Sound familiar?

Ellie had tracked across Europe with the darker myths and legends, stories transformed in modern fairy tales like Red Riding Hood … the 'wolf' in this actually having been a man cursed to bestial form … before moving across the seas to the Americas. Both Native Americans and the South American Incan and Mayan myths were full of shape changers and tricksters taking on the forms of men and animals, with the *loop garou* making many a reference from French settlers.

Historically we'd been linked to various demi-Gods and monsters, and some utterly dark mythology and ritual practices of sacrifice by cults and tribes who also invented advanced architecture, indoor plumbing, astronomy, medicinal practices and, oh let's not forget their most famous invention … chocolate. Oh yeah, the Mayans invented that substance as a wholesome drink which was so good, it formed a basis of currency in their civilisation.

Just goes to show. Me, I reckon the story of Kaldi, the Ethiopian goatherd who noticed how his goats got excited and energised after eating beans from a particular plant and from there sprung coffee, needed much more airtime.

Basically, I had to hope Jessica had tabs on Jacob, that she'd be able to intervene if he went rogue before I got to babysit him that night. Coz otherwise I was in for a very different sort of *'bros at home'* kinda evening.

I wrapped up a few things in the office, checking in with Emma on any more reports of stolen pets beyond those my packmates had so helpfully collected for me already. Sister Sloth had intimated that the creature behind the missing animals was now feeding on mortals, which was on one hand good news for the pet owners of London, and at the same time, equal parts disturbing.

With that worrying thought, I decided I didn't need to be in the office, and in fact was better off heading home and getting the place ready for Sarah. And that included having a rather blunt and to the point conversation with my live-in security detail.

Goldspur, over the passage of the last six months, had definitely matured. As the Morrigan had warned me, she was evolving in line with the level of threat her father, the apple tree, faced being in my home. Which wasn't a reassuring thought, since most dryads take decades to grow into their adult selves, staying that way for as long as their tree remained healthy and hale. The one living with me had sprouted in all manner of troubling ways in just over half a year, telling me just how safe my home was.

Felix, for reasons she refused to disclose to me, had decided the dryad needed some good old fashioned womanly advice, after I simply asked my friend to explain to the fae why walking around mostly unclothed and jumping on me in bed was just not a good thing to do. Boundaries were needed, I had thought, but then Felix had helped create the sort of demilitarized No Man's Land you find sat between North and South Korea.

Sometimes, just sometimes, I think Felix doesn't have my best interests at heart. Just a suspicion.

Anyhow, Goldspur was a permanent resident at my home, given how she had defended it with deadly skill when OPS attempted to storm the place to recover stolen goods they thought I possessed. The fact I actually *did* have the items in question was not the point. Fact was, unless I wanted to remove the entire apple tree my fae grandmother had *gifted* me, then the dryad and I would be sharing my home. And that meant me making sure she in no way endangered whatever was happening between Sarah and me.

"Just so we're clear," I told the dryad, as I sat on my sofa and explained things as simply as I possibly could. To avoid any chance of confusion. "There'll be a woman coming over here in about, oh an hour. She is to be extended guest rights like you did for Danny and Felix, but you on no account are to show yourself whilst she is here. Just, I don't know, stay with your father and catch up on family stuff. Or take a nap. Just, please, no surprise entrances. Is that going to be a problem?"

I know I sounded like a bit of an arse, telling the dryad she had to hide away as if I was embarrassed about her or something. But the reality was, Goldspur was a very well endowed, physically fit and very attractive fae. No matter that she had green skin, green tattoos, amber eyes and two very large knives she refused to ever be separated from. There was simply *no* way I could see Sarah being comfortable and happy, finding out I was sharing the same living space with her.

It's not that I thought Sarah was the jealous sort. Hell, if I managed to explain where Goldspur came from, I reckon she would straight away stop seeing her as a potential romantic threat and more as an amazing being of creation that she needed to talk to, learn everything about and understand how she was alive.

But Goldspur was still naïve, child-like in terms of how to act around mortals. Of what to say, and what not to say. All she needed to do, to cause a major misunderstanding with Sarah was let slip she had thought it perfectly ok to try and join me in the shower one night, to enjoy the hot water and steam I had so helpfully provided ... before I added that to the list of things we just didn't do. Or the time she had spied on my tenants, and the guy in 12B had been as ever fixated on the Adult channel. She had come away from *that* experience with some very odd ideas, and far too many questions I really hadn't wanted to answer.

The tenant in 12B, by some happy coincidence, had vacated the apartment soon after. Turns out he had been using the rental as a place to escape to, from his family and normal life, to indulge his personal habits. A little word to the agency handling my building, and he had taken those habits elsewhere. And before anyone thinks I judged him too harshly, I *did* let him keep his deposit.

Goldspur eyed me from where she sat, perched on the edge of her seat, those big amber eyes of hers bright and filled with innocence. If I hadn't seen her carve almost a full Special Forces strike squad from OPS apart whilst giggling, I'd have believed the act whole-heartedly.

"Morgan Black. Are you embarrassed of me?" The dryad asked quietly, lowering her head so that she was looking at her lap. Where her hands were folded, almost but not quite touching the hilts of her knives.

"Uh, no. Not at all." I answered her truthfully whilst inwardly wincing. I just am not good with the whole *let's talk emotions* thing, and categorically knew from past experience that I was a master at putting my foot in my mouth and saying the wrong thing all too frequently. I'd earned enough *I'm fine*'s from Sarah to wear as proof of my ineptitude.

But Goldspur was here, looking like I'd kicked a puppy, so I couldn't just ignore her feelings. I had to explain.

Getting off the sofa, I stepped across the room and knelt down, clasping her slim hands in my own. I felt the tremor of the almost childlike fae's emotions, still too young to keep them locked down and hidden.

"Look, the woman I've got coming over, she's not part of our world. Well, only by accident." I tried to think of the simplest way to explain, so the young dryad would understand. "I care about her. A lot. But things are, well, tricky right now. Delicate, you could say. And I don't want to scare her or bring back some really bad memories for her. For now, just until she's ready, I'm asking if you'd be kind to her and remain hidden. Until she can get to know you like I know you. Like Bear knows you. Is that ok?"

Goldspur looked up, her eyes huge in her face, her green skin pale.

Then a smile quirked her lips.

"You wish to conjugate with this woman?" She asked, and I groaned at the sudden spike of childish humour I felt coming from her. Across the room, Bear lifted his head and chuffed a bark, cocking his head almost as a question. "My father has told me much of the mating rituals of mortals, and I witnessed many confusing and strange oddities in the magic box below us. Why do they need to complicate such a simple task, and give such odd names for so simple a thing? I still do not understand, what is *reverse cowgirl?*"

"And that's exactly why I'm asking you to stay hidden for now." I shook my head, pushing myself up to stand. "All Sarah is coming over for is to talk. Nothing else. Just talk and catch up. But if you show up, talking like that? Let's just not go there, ok?"

The dryad shrugged, rising as well and stepping close to me. She reached up and laid a hand on my cheek, as she looked me in the eye. Her skin was warm, pulsing with the life she shared with her father-tree.

"Downtown Abbey." She replied, and for the life of me, I had to take a moment to put those two words together and make sense.

"What? Like the tv series?" I asked, and she nodded.

"Felicity told me I should watch *Downtown Abbey*, as it will help me understand the mortals. Maybe even you." The dryad eyed me, chin set in a very definite line. Not one to be argued with. "If you will obtain for me the entire series, I will promise to remain hidden whilst this Sarah of yours is here."

I knew the promise she made was real, and that she would abide by its terms if I agreed. Goldspur was still too young to have learned the deviousness of her kin. It was a simple enough trade, and she could have asked for a lot more. I simply nodded.

"Then it is a deal." She told me, leaning up on her tiptoes to kiss my cheek. "I shall go speak to my father, and return once your guest has left."

The dryad stepped away, walking over to Bear and giving his massive head a final rub before she turned and laid a hand on her father-tree. The scent of fresh apples filled the air, fresh and fruity, as she slowly slipped into the trunk and was gone.

I heaved a sigh, shaking my head at the weirdness of my life. Even for a lycan, I was pushing the boundaries of what made sense, and what was just plain crazy.

"Ok then." I looked across at Bear, as the trollhound slowly pushed himself up off the floor and shook himself. "Time to get this place ready for company."

And that's when everything blurred, disappearing in a shrouding mist and stink of the Veil.

Then I was …

Elsewhere.

Chapter 12

"Oh, for fuck's sake. What now?" I snarled as I looked around me, taking in my surroundings.

Mists swirled thickly, cold and damp on my skin, the stench of death strong in my nose. Spilled guts, cooling puddles of blood. Bodies ripped apart, dismembered, scattered around me like broken dolls. Splashed with plenty of sticky redness.

"Why, grandmother, you do bring me to such interesting places." I growled as I felt the familiar presence close by. "You know, I had new wards put in place. Decent ones this time. You shouldn't be able to just bloody yank me to this sort of shit-hole whenever you fancy. Just saying."

The Morrigan gave a sharp laugh, as she slowly walked towards me through the field of corpses. She was in her battle armour, stained in silver and red blood, with her rune carved staff acting as a walking stick as she stepped over the dead bodies.

"You are blood of my blood, pup." The fae reminded me, her cold blue lips curling in a knowing smile. "Wherever you go, whatever you do, I will always be able to call on you."

"You know, someone really needs to write a rulebook with all this shit in it." I growled again, as I looked around the battlefield. "Where the hell are we, and why'd you drag me here?"

The Morrigan leant her staff over her shoulder, gazing across at me before looking back around the grounds soaked in blood.

"This? This is just one of many such sites across the Real, pup." She replied laconically. "With Morgana free and having declared herself, and Twilight once more risen, war has riven my home. Brethren of Ivory and

Shadow have ceded from their Lord and Ladies, and fight to make their way to their new Queen."

The Morrigan gestured at the bodies around her.

"That we cannot allow. Hence, these fields of the fallen."

I focused on the bodies, taking the time now to see details. They were a mixture of Ivory and Shadow fae and fae-kin, gold and ebony armour splattered with silver gore. Gnarled goblins, monstrous ogres, dour dwarrow. A mixture of Court creatures, but all with that red-stained mark on their armour. The inverted trident.

The mark of Morgana.

"And you brought me here to show me how bad it is? That's what you wanted me to know?" I guessed, waving a hand to the dead bodies. "Just so I understood you're busy and we're on our own in the Mortal Realm? I think I got that from the past six months of silence from you lot."

"Tch, pup." My grandmother replied, tapping the staff on her shoulder. "If I'd wanted you to know something that simple, I would have simply sent you a note. In blood and bone."

I hated to think what any message in blood and bone would look like, but given how most fae still wrote their letters on mortal or animal skin, I didn't have to imagine too hard.

"Fine, what then? I'm kinda busy right now." I told her, and caught her knowing expression. "What?"

"I am well aware of your *busy-ness*." The Morrigan replied, arching her eyebrow, tone cold. "Whilst war reaves the Real, whilst Morgana gains power and her Court strengthens in the Mortal Realm, I am truly heartened that you can find the time to make yet another foolish attempt to find a mate. Ignoring your previous failed attempts, having learned nothing."

It seemed not only was everyone aware of my bungled attempts at a love life, but that everyone was a critic as well. I ground my teeth, not even bothering to ask how she seemed to know about something that had literally just landed in my lap.

A lycan could get paranoid, dwelling on that too much.

"What's so important that you dragged me here to tell me?" I asked through gritted teeth, knowing the Morrigan was taking great delight in stringing this out.

The fae looked at me, her dark eyes shimmering with dark fire, her features stark in the gloom that surrounded us.

"You are hunted, pup." She told me, lips curling up with dark delight at her words. "I have told you that there are those of the Court seeking to join Twilight, hearing Morgana's call and answering it? Well, not all those she speaks to are in the Real. *Some* abide in your Mortal Realm, and it is one of these that now stalks you."

"Yeah, well. We've been dealing with anything trying to get into the mists without too much bother." I replied with a shrug of my shoulders. "What makes this anything I should worry about?"

"Because its nature is of yours, yet not. A thing of savage fury, animalistic lust and the need to rend flesh, shed blood." She smiled ghoulishly. "The Seers have read its dark desires in the ice, and seen the trail of death it leaves behind it. This thing, pup, is most definitely something to cause you worry."

"Hold on, so you're saying something big and bad has come into my backyard and started killing things?" I actually gave a short bark of relief, feeling one very specific worry start to unknot inside me. "That's actually good news! We were worried it was one of the pack gone rogue, doing the killings. If it's just some fucked up, bloodthirsty nasty, that's way better!"

The Morrigan shook her head, the carved runes bound into her braided hair clacking together like the snap of teeth.

"You find joy in the oddest of places, pup." She sighed, nodding to the corpse strewn field around us. "Do not mistake this thing for one of these fallen creatures you see here, nor any of those you have hunted beyond the Veil. This thing is death, a thing of dark desire."

I felt a cold shiver inside at her words. The Morrigan was actually worried, I could sense from the sliver she let me feel. And if this thing could make the Crow of Battle, Mistress of War, concerned then I'd probably better take it a little seriously.

"What is it? What have your Seers seen?" I queried, already guessing the answer, or lack of one, I'd get. This wasn't the first time I'd been told of visions from Shadow, and found the details somewhat lacking.

I wasn't disappointed.

"Age. This thing is old, of a time when mortals feared the dark and hid in houses of stone against the night." The Morrigan answered, eyes hooded now as she spoke. "It is a thing of blood and hunger, but the Seers could not sense much more. It is not native to your land, but something links it to you and all your kind. A bond of kinship, perhaps, or an echo of the beast you all carry inside you. Possibly a thing of the Wyld. Whatever this is, you must look to the past to understand it, to reveal your future and what must be done to face the creature."

Great. I lined up the little facts I could glean from what the Morrigan told me, biting back the frustration of never, ever getting a straight answer from the fae.

It was old, an immortal and obviously a predator. The thing about it being linked to us lycan was dubious as fuck, but that might explain some of the evidence I'd seen in Greenwich. The footprints of beast and man, the savagery unleashed on the corpses. Still didn't explain how Jacob's scent had gotten all over the crime scene, but I was used to things not adding up. If ever the clues all agreed and pointed a finger definitively at someone, in my opinion, then all that said was they were fake, that we were looking at the wrong person.

Life doesn't *do* obvious, at least in my experience.

"One thing more, as I have already mentioned." The Morrigan brought me back to the moment, as I closed off my musings and re-focused on her.

"Uh, and that is? For the forgetful amongst us?" I asked, seeing her dark eyes burn with fire. Whether from humour or ire, I never could tell.

"This thing *hunts*, and its prey is you and your pack." She told me, that smile so sharklike all she needed was a couple of fins and tail to look the part now. "Whether it serves Morgana and acts as her retribution for the wounds you caused her, or commands its own purposes, it matters not. It is coming for you. Now might not be the best of times to be involved once more with a defenceless mortal, with this thing stalking the shadows."

"Oh no." I growled. Whilst a little voice inside me did in fact agree with the fae's logic, the greater part of ganged up and squashed that voice back into its box and sat on it. "I'm not going to let some bloody bogeyman fuck with things, or threaten harm to *anyone* I care about. Sarah, Felix, hell, anyone. I had enough of that with that bastard Jack. If it's hunting me, then the bastard is in for a big shock coz I'm done with letting people around me get hurt."

"Admirable sentiments." She smiled coldly, waving a hand at the scattered corpses surrounding us. "I am sure there were those that felt the same way, who lie here cooling on the earth, their blood shed and life riven from them. But perhaps for you, it will be different. Maybe third time is indeed a charm."

The fae made *no* effort to hide her thoughts behind those words, letting me sense just how much she believed them. Zilch, nada, diddly fucking squat.

"Yeah well, we'll see. But point of fact, we won't if I'm stuck here when Sarah turns up. So if we are done?" I queried and the Morrigan nodded once. "Good. Mind sending me back the same way you brought me here? I've got stuff to do."

The Morrigan gestured with her free hand as the scent of Veil blossomed around me, the Way opening up to drag me back through and home.

"My last warning, pup." She told me, as the bodies began to fade away, leaving only darkness and the fae standing, facing me. Those dark eyes of hers burning bright in the shadows. "This thing that stalks you. It *knows* you. Whatever its purpose, it will hunt you as you hunt your marks. Trust no-one, doubt everything. For in this, you are the prey and must find a way to evades its jaws. For they are closing on you. Beware."

With that, the darkness shimmered and faded, and I found myself standing in my living room, Bear facing me with hackles raised and head cocked in question. Behind him, I caught the tell-tale shimmer of Goldspur's presence, lurking within the apple tree but ready to spring forth and deal out green-hued carnage.

"Stand down everyone, it's just me. Granny wanted a quick chat, is all." I told the room, seeing the dryad fade once more back into the tree trunk. For his part, Bear gave a massive yawn and a thoroughly disgruntled chuff, settling himself back down amongst the tree roots now that there was no prospect of violence.

The Morrigan's last words stuck with me, that coldness I'd felt before returning.

You are the hunted.

It's jaws are closing on you.

Beware.

Chapter 13

Mirrors

Reflective surfaces can be a particularly useful tool to detect supernatural creatures using glamour, as often the mirror will show the truth of the creature and not the magical image it is using to hide behind. They are known to reveal the truth of the vampire, as the supernatural creature has no reflection in any surface.

Mirrors have also been used to trap more insubstantial horrors within their reflective surface, trapping them if the wraith or revenant allows itself to be reflected when it becomes fully corporeal just before it attacks its victim. In this way, some mirrors are considered cursed, with the horrors locked inside them, always there at the corner of the eye but never truly seen.

I dealt with the ominous foreboding from my meeting with the Morrigan by soaking in a long hot shower to take my mind off her warning. And also to remove any lingering magics I might have picked up whilst being yanked into the Real.

You never could be too careful.

Washed, bundled up in a fresh set of clothes which didn't carry the reek of bloodshed and death, and having done a quick tidy up of the apartment to clear away empty bottles of wine and several pizza boxes from when Felix had come over to see Goldspur, I was in a far better frame of mind when the intercom announced I had a visitor.

Buzzing Sarah through the main entrance, I waited as patiently as possible for the lift to bring her to me. I could have gone downstairs and been waiting for her in the lobby like a gentleman, but I figured she was old enough and big enough to remember what floor I lived on and how to push the *up* button. Plus I was still slightly paranoid about Goldspur making a surprise appearance, so wanted to hang around just to make sure it didn't happen.

I opened the door just as she had her hand raised to knock, grinning as I caught her surprised expression. She had changed too, switching the jeans and blouse for a simple but elegant dress that cut off at mid-thigh, highlighting her tanned skin and natural Spanish features against its simple white linen. A long coat, hanging to her knees, staved off the autumnal weather and she'd switched her trainers for low slung boots, of the type that went with most outfits and had enough of a heel to bring her up almost to my height.

Sarah smiled warmly, and I breathed in her scent, that rich spiciness and clean floral aroma that to me was part and parcel to who she was. That faint odd scent was there still, a sharpness of burned spices but nothing off-putting. Just different.

She held up a large paper bag, with the neck of a bottle sticking out of it and a lumpish square at the bottom that I guessed were Bear's treats.

"I bring gifts. Am I welcome?" She asked with a faint laugh, and I mocked a formal bow.

"Most welcome. Come on in. The fluff monster is waiting for you."

Sarah stepped inside as I held the door open for her, but stopped as she brushed up against me. Before I knew it, she was rising up on her tiptoes and kissing me, warm and softly. Part of me sat up and began baying, blood thumping in my ears, but I calmed myself, parting from her after a long moment and taking a breath.

"I hope that's not the way you greet anyone who opens a door for you?" I snarked, and she stuck her tongue out at me but laughed the next moment.

We quickly headed upstairs, passing the first-floor guest accommodation and moved to the top level. Sarah had been here before, had seen the apple tree but I'd lied then and told her it was a prop made by a friend studying stage craft for movies. Now she knew at least a little of the truth, I guessed I might have to correct a few of the fibs I'd told her as and when they came up in conversation.

Thankfully, Bear was an attention-stealer all to himself, already up and awake when the pair of us came up the stairs. He chuffed a short bark on seeing me, obviously intrigued that we had visitors, and then he stopped as Sarah stepped onto the open plan floor.

"Hey, big guy!" She greeted him, opening her arms and lowering herself down to give him a huge hug. I'd taken the bottle of wine and sausages off her on the stairs, figuring she was due to get a friendly mauling from my hound as soon as he saw her.

Bear snarled.

His hackles spiked, lips drawing back to show the jagged teeth in his massive jaws. He tensed, eyes narrowed as he focused on Sarah, his stance shouting to me that he was a blink away from powering forward, but not in any friendly greeting kind of way. The trollhound was ready to attack, and hurl himself at and *through* the perceived threat.

"Woah! Bear, back down!" I stepped between them, blocking Sarah and reaching down with my free hand to press hard on his solid forehead. "Fucks' sake, dog! It's Sarah! Cool it!"

Bear pushed against my hand, jaws snapping shut but a rumbling growl still throbbing up from his chest. I shot a look back at Sarah, who had taken a step back to the top of the stairs. She was shocked, expression confused at the aggressive response she'd triggered from my dog.

"I'm sorry! I think it's my new perfume." She told me, hand brushing against her throat and holding it up. "I picked up in Sao Paulo, but it might be too much for Bear. I didn't think, sorry!"

I shook my head, focusing back on the snarling, growling trollhound. Setting the paper package aside, I crouched down, grabbing his furry jowls and bringing his head up to stare into my own. Given his size, it wasn't much of an effort, as I stared directly into his large brown orbs.

"Hey, enough! It's Sarah. She's come back so calm the fuck down." I told him, firmly, confused as to why he was acting up so badly. "It's *Sarah*! Remember?"

The rumbling growl throbbed in his chest, as Bear glared at me first, then tried to see past me. I held him, knowing he wasn't using his full strength to get past me as I was still on my own feet, seeing his hackles finally start to settle as I got through to him.

"Maybe I should go? I didn't mean to cause problems …" Sarah started to say, but I just waved a hand back at her.

"Sarah. Remember?" I growled back at Bear, shoving my face into his own and letting him scent me, feel the intent of what I was saying.

A thing people still get wrong about lycanthropes … well, apart from all the other things like full moons, silver bullets and it being a disease you can catch from a bite … is that we can talk to and understand animals. Fact is, we *can* understand animals, and make them understand us, but it's not strictly speaking to them. Most animals don't use words, they don't have a dictionary of language to tell them when to use farther or further. Their language is more feelings and thoughts, a mixture of emotion and intent.

Bear and I were a lot closer than most animals I came into contact with. I rescued him as a puppy, and he'd grown with me, gotten used to how I thought and acted. He could understand me, and I him, with the sort of ease that usually only was witnessed with old married couples. And we argued about the same, just with more teeth and hair.

"Sarah!" I growled, and he chuffed, snarls dying in his chest to a questioning rumble. I ruffled his massive head, and turned on my heel, showing Sarah behind me. "See? *Sarah*. Remember all the treats she gave you, and belly rubs too?"

She stepped forward, one step and then a second. Lowering herself again to a crouch, holding out her hands, spreading her arms.

"Hey, you. Remember me? You know me, it's Sarah." She spoke to him with a gentle voice, and the trollhound gave another questioning chuff before shaking himself and brushing past me. He paced toward her, head lowered, until he faced her almost eye to eye.

And then he licked her full in the face, lathering her with slobber.

I drew a breath, choking down a laugh as Sarah fell back on her backside, wrapping her arms around Bear as he nuzzled in, making happy rumbling noises. Whatever the hell that had been wrong, the trollhound was back to normal. Slobbering and lovable, just one massive King Kong sized puppy.

Grabbing the paper bag, I left the pair of them to wrestle and get reacquainted whilst I pulled out the pack of, Gods bless her, premium black pudding sausages. These went into a pan in the kitchen, gas flames turned to medium heat, and I pulled the cork out of the wine and set it to one side to breathe.

The sizzle of cooking sausages filled the air, and Bear finally stopped his friendly mauling of Sarah to shamble over in my direction. I poked my head out of the kitchen area and snorted a laugh, seeing the good doctor sat on the floor, hair a complete mess and wearing more of Bear than any make-up she had come with.

"He remembers me." She brushed her hair back and wiped some trollhound slobber off her cheek. "*Por mi santa abuela,* I had forgotten how much drool he has!"

"You know where to go, if you want to go de-Bear yourself!" I nodded at the open bottle of wine. "There'll be a full glass waiting, promise."

Pushing herself up off the floor, Sarah slipped her coat off and laid it over the arm of the nearest chair with the small bag she had had slung over a shoulder. Straightening her dress, she walked past the pair of us, me at the cooker with a pan of slowly darkening sausages and Bear sitting expectantly on the floor beside me with his stump of a tail thumping the floor. She smiled, the image so familiar from the many times before when she had visited my home, then carried on walking.

"Oh, Morgan?" She called out as she reached the door, leaning out to look back at me. I guessed she was going to ask for a towel or something, my brain scrambling to remember if I had set out fresh laundry.

"Yeah?" I queried as Bear leant against me hard, his massive jowls parted and his tongue hanging out as he inhaled the rich meaty aromas coming from the frying pan. A low rumbling throbbed up from his chest, the trollhound's version of a cat-like purr.

"You can always come help wash Bear off me." She smiled with a delicious curve of her lips, lowering her eyes to look at me under her long lashes. "I'm sure the food can wait a few minutes … ?"

"Uh …" I actually froze, hot pan in one hand as my brain tried to frantically think of the right words to say, whilst other parts of me leapt up and howled for me to quit thinking and just *go*. "Let me just … ah, hot sausages!"

Sarah laughed, an easy and familiar sound, as she winked at me.

"Ah, *chulo*. Don't worry, I was joking. Well, at least a little." She told me as I tried to juggle the pan, find a hot plate to transfer them to and somehow move Bear who was practically sitting on my feet as he awaited his bounty. "Let me freshen up, and I'll take that wine you offered. Then we can … talk. And, you know. Stuff."

My brain valiantly tried to untangle itself, as I warred between cursing at missing a longed-for opportunity, but also feeling just a little relieved. Don't get me wrong, I wanted Sarah in very physical ways, and had vivid dreams where she and I were together again. Especially after facing the Mistress of the Sewers when the immortal wore her face to mess my head up, and then seeing the real 'her' before things went so badly wrong at the Blooding.

But I'd also been single that whole time, and as everyone keeps reminding me, I wasn't all that experienced in the ways of love, relationships and handling the hot-wiring of my hormones that Sarah could cause simply by walking into the same room as me.

"Ah, it's *muy buena* I can still short-circuit that head of yours, Morgan." She told me with one last cheeky smile, before she ducked into the washroom. "A woman likes to know she has that effect on her man."

The door clicked behind her, and I looked down at Bear, who cocked his head and gave a deep throated huff.

"Yeah, I know. Weird, huh?" I shook my head, realising I needed a swig of that wine to calm things down just a little. "And what was with all that barking and snarling shit you pulled? You pretending to be a real guard dog for once?"

Bear huffed again, pawing at his face and snorting.

"Ok, fine. So she's a little different." I had to agree with the trollhound. Sarah *was* acting a *lot* more confident in her feelings towards me, with the little nicknames and hell, her telling me she loved me. That had been a complete surprise, and then some.

But then again, the woman been through hell. Her entire life turned upside down by my kith and kin. By lycans. And then shipped off to the other side of the world, with no chance to work things out … yeah, that could make a person act a little oddly, and maybe come to some fairly fundamental decisions in their life and feelings towards the people in it. Maybe. "Just, you know, chill. Ok? Give her some space, and try not to rush her. A lot's happened."

I wasn't sure if I was giving those instructions to my dog, or me. But one thing was for sure.

Sarah was here, right now. I'd be the biggest idiot ever if after everything she and I had been through, and she'd *still* walked back into my life, I managed to screw things up. This was my chance, my shot at happiness.

With that thought, I poured two glasses of wine, and set about sorting some food for both of us, and Bear. Least so I could stop him begging and slobbering all over Sarah a second time.

Chapter 14

"So, good news. I can take your case." I told Sarah, as we sat together.

She had washed most of Bear off her face and hair, freshening herself up whilst I sorted out some cold meats, pickles, fresh tomatoes and slices of black bread I knew she liked so much. Sarah was a picker when it came to food, preferring a little of everything rather than one main thing. I guess it was something she'd inherited from her Spanish family and their love of *tapas*, but whilst she wasn't a vegetarian, she definitely ate more salads and vegetables than lumps of meat.

Of course, she wasn't above stealing a slice of my steak when we ate out, *just to check it was cooked right* being the usual excuse.

Thus I was a little surprised when, having settled us down at the coffee table, she immediately speared two of the black pudding sausages Bear had gratuitously donated to our feast. These she settled back with, and the glass of wine, as I sorted myself out with some snacks and sank into the sofa beside her.

"That's great!" Sarah answered after deftly slicing up her sausages and devouring down several chunks of still-hot meat. "Miles and I are really worried about him, so if you can find him, or at least any idea where he is or how he is, it'd be amazing!"

I held up my hand, remembering we'd had this discussion the last time she asked me to find someone. But I felt it was important to remind her of a few salient points.

"I can't make any promises. There could be all manner of good reasons why he vanished, like he decided he needed a break after the expedition. Gone to see friends or relatives." I shrugged, knowing it was doubtful the man's disappearance after their recent misadventure in South America was entirely innocent, but there was always the chance. "The last thing I want happening is me knocking down doors only to find this colleague of yours chilling with his wife and family. Or friends. Or whatever. But you get my point."

"He's not married, and has no children." Sarah replied, nodding to show she understood but happy to indicate the flaws in my logic in the same breath. "Julius is what we call an *obsessive* when it comes to ancient South American culture. He's written multiple papers on how the Mayans changed the course of civilisation as we know it now, and their many astounding accomplishments given their resources and heritage. He has no time for starting a family, making friends or any of what he calls *that nonsense*. Unless you are one of a few people he considers deserving of his respect, he can be a little obnoxious, if I'm being honest with you."

"Oh well. Worth a shot." I sighed, munching on a fresh radish. Yes, I eat things other than pastrami sandwiches and pizza. I do my five a day. Just the five sometimes are a bulk intake when I remember to catch up at the end of a hard week. "So where do you suggest I start looking for him?"

"He has a house over in Greenwich." She told me, brow furrowing as she searched for the address. "67 Hyde Vale Road. We joked that he should be called Dr Jekyll for living there. But we've tried there already. He didn't answer the door and there was no sign of life. No twitching of curtains or lights suddenly turned off. I've seen the detective shows, *chulo*."

Greenwich. That little alarm bell in my head started clanging, the one I've named *suspicious bastard* too many times. For good reason.

"Uh, this might be a weird question, but did this colleague of yours go into the park at night? Maybe, I don't know, talk to any homeless people who might hang around there?" I asked guardedly, suspicions lining up in my head. I knew that Greenwich Park was officially closed at sundown, but enough locals and transients managed to sneak in to enjoy the one place that the keepers weren't too strict at policing. As long as the gates were locked, they'd done their job.

These days, I had less than pleasant memories associated with the place. A while before the Sister dragged Felix and I there to bear witness to a murder scene, I'd been manhandled into the park by three cursed university students, intent on killing me and burying my body in the grounds to hide the evidence. As much as I might have wanted the park keepers to have done their job and stopped anyone from accessing the site, if they *had* been around and tried, I'd have just had their blood on my hands as well.

Sarah gave me a look, her expression making it plain my attempt to ask an innocuous question had failed miserably. I just shrugged, giving her my best "*So?*" expression.

"Yes. I believe Julius mentioned before, he sometimes spends time with the homeless. It reminds him of where he comes from, his roots in South America. It's one of his redeeming qualities, spending time with those less fortunate than us." She told me, head cocked. "He also lectures at the university as a guest speaker often, mostly about Mayan culture and the amazing contributions that we take for granted these days. Why?"

I hadn't liked lying to Sarah at the best of times, when I'd had to do so to keep the pack's secret and my truth hidden. But right now, all I had were suspicions, and a need to speak to the Sisters and this brother Grubbins who survived the attack. Nothing concrete.

What better way to hide a body than amongst a bunch of other victims, all torn apart, to hide the actual number of people slain? But had the homeless been involved somehow in luring him to his death, or just been victims in the wrong place at the wrong time?

Hell, I didn't even know that he was dead. Just me being a suspicious bastard.

"It helps me narrow down where he could have gone to." I answered Sarah's question, mixing truth with the lie. "Knowing as much as I can about whomever I'm hunting. Where they might go, who they might mix with. Now I can check with some of the homeless who sleep in the park. See if they've seen him recently."

"Oh, ok. That makes sense." Sarah settled back, sipping her wine and munching on some more sliced meat. "Honestly, anything that you can do to find him would be such a relief to us."

I nodded, not wanting to promise anything further now that there was a slim chance he was mixed up in the horrific mess in Greenwich Park.

There wasn't anything else I needed to start my hunt for the missing professor, doctor or whatever he was. But that would have to wait until after

I'd spent the night babysitting Jacob to prove he was no brutal killer. Well. At least of innocent mortals and their pets.

Instead, we slipped into catching each other up, hesitantly at first but with each word exchanged, each laugh made, we strengthened the connection we'd shared before things went to hell in a handbasket just prior to the Blooding.

Sarah told me about the dig she'd been sent to look at first in Sao Paulo, where they'd uncovered evidence of a dinosaur called *Ubirajara jubatus*, called *Lord of the Spear* locally or *maned devil* in Latin for the spears of feathers it had displayed on its shoulders. There was some big hoo-ha between Germany and Brazil, where the original fossil discovered back in 1995 was taken from the site and housed in Stuttgart despite the local government's desire to retain their unique find. Discovering more of the dinosaur remains was huge for Brazil, and Sarah had spent days and nights confirming their authenticity before she got the news she was heading on to the next site. The Amazonian discovery.

For my part, I filled her in on the general happenings in London since she was bundled halfway across the world. The crazy stories of escaped animals from London zoo running amok through the City of London (*a jest played by Chimera to keep the mortal authorities occupied*), the bomb alert at a popular restaurant just outside the Tower of London (*called in by Gregory Allen on my request, to clear mortals away from Jack the Ripper and Baba Yaga*), a bright spear of light seen over the Southbank Centre on the night of a planetary alignment that had everyone mystified (*part of the ritual used by Morgana and the Norns to bring back the Twilight Realm*) as well as the strange mists that had swallowed several London districts and refused to disperse or let anyone or anything through (*raised by Morgana and the Norns to protect their fledging Court from reprisal by Ivory or Shadow, let alone the mortals*). Not forgetting all the other weird shit that had been part of Robert Knox and Morgana's plan to keep us distracted and chasing escaped prisoners and freshly created Harrowed whilst they went about their centuries-in-the-making ritual.

I didn't explain the actual details to Sarah, since this would have been exactly what Jessica had warned me against doing. Instead I gave her the crib notes that most mortals knew. What had filled the newspapers, and online reports on every channel and service, starting as miscellaneous stories but ending as front-page news.

Even mortals start to notice something is wrong when the weird shit literally explodes in their face for the umpteenth time.

"So, how much of that was… well, you know. *Supernatural?*" Sarah asked, wiggling her fingers in the age-old manner to describe anything spooky or magical. It's also been used to describe how witches, warlocks and anyone manipulating the energies of magic work, which always pissed Elspeth off.

"Ours is a calling entrenched in the cultures, beliefs and very spirit of the world we live in," The witch had told me when I asked her to wiggle her fingers and cast a spell one time. *"We do not wiggle digits, wrinkle our noses or flap our hands about as if we are swatting flies. We instead draw on the energies of the Goddess in precise forms, much like martial artists do so when they practice their kata. And much like those martial artists, I can and will still kick your backside across the room if you ask me that again."*

As an aside, I realised whoever had choreographed the Marvel movie, *Dr Strange*, was either a witch or warlock themselves or had done some very insightful research. The *Harry Potter* movies, not so much.

"Honestly? All of them." I told her, knowing I wasn't breaking any specific rules here. The Accords dictated that mortals were to remain unaware of the Real, of the immortals and creatures that lived there, and the occurrences when the Realms collided. But Sarah already knew more than the average bear, to quote the Great Yogi, so all I was doing was filling in some blanks. Nothing that could get me or the pack into trouble … or more trouble than I was already in I told myself.

And almost believed it.

"*Mi santa abuela!* How is that possible? Does no-one suspect?" She asked, taking another gulp of wine before setting her glass aside. "Surely, someone must see *something* that doesn't add up? What about all the conspiracy theorists? They *must* be questioning what is being told the public, coming up with other explanations no matter how crazy. It's what they do!"

"True." I nodded, on firm ground here. This was something we lycans learned very early on when dealing with mortals. "But the fact is, most people *don't want to know*. They long for a normal life, with normal things like getting a job, finding a husband or wife, starting a family and getting a home.

Growing old. Living a peaceful and undisturbed existence. Everything that sits outside of that, they pretty much ignore with as much effort as they can, until either it goes away or things get so bad they have to wake up and smell the shit they are in."

I held up a hand, stopping Sarah as she went to defend her fellow mortals against my very unsubtle and maybe a little unjust generalism.

"Look, I'm not trying to be insulting." I apologised, knowing that once again I was nearing a foot in mouth moment. "Fact is, there are some people who *do* notice inconsistencies, things that don't just add up. But they're few and very far between ... and you've met the people who handle their cases yourself. Why do you think you were shipped off to South America so quickly? Assigned a job when normally I'm guessing that sort of thing takes weeks to arrange? You were isolated, and the plan probably was for you to be gradually convinced you hadn't seen anything weird, hadn't really had anything bad happen. It was all a series of misunderstandings, or maybe something you ate giving you hallucinations. You work too hard, don't sleep enough and the stress made you see things that weren't real. That sort of thing."

Sarah shook her head, obviously wanting to say I was wrong. But this was a very important moment for me, for her and maybe for us. I had to make her understand.

"This is the truth, Sarah. You were either going to be convinced, with help, that everything that happened was in your imagination and not true. Or, if you stubbornly refused to go with that plan, then the authorities *might* have recruited you. Changed your name, erased your past. All that secret shit you read about or see in the movies. But for real." I told her bluntly, watching her eyes, looking for the understanding to settle there. "If you'd refused those two options, then behind door number three would be their final play. A padded room somewhere. Medications to fog your mind and wipe those memories clean away. Your entire life discredited so no-one would believe you if you tried to tell what you had seen. What had happened. That's what these people will do, to ensure the rest of humanity, the mortals ... everyone they are entrusted to keep safe *are* safe. At the expense of the odd one or two people, they ... *we* sometimes think it's worth the cost."

"This is what you need to realise. Understand." I told her, leaning forward, keeping my voice calm but letting her read the seriousness of what I was saying in my posture, my eyes. "You've not even scratched the surface of what *really* exists, what the world is *really* like. It's bigger, scarier and meaner than anything you can imagine, and it sure as hell isn't a picnic with the faeries whilst you watch the butterflies dance. The butterflies in this story are like the moths Godzilla has to fight."

"You have a choice. You can stop. Go back to the things that already fill your life, that give you so much satisfaction. Finding out about long dead species, recreating them and learning what they were like, how they lived. With no fear of them biting your face off or devouring you in your sleep. You'll be able to have friends without the constant secrecy, enjoy fun past times without keeping a weapon to hand. Live a life without worrying about the big things that go bump in the night. You have a chance at a *normal* life still."

"Ah, *chulo*, are you asking me to walk away?" She asked me softly, and I really did feel like an utter shit, sat there on my sofa basically reading her the riot act. But it was the right thing to do, and fuck it, I was a Knight of the Courts now. Seemed like the sort of thing I should be doing, even if it hurt like hell.

"No. You just need to know this is Pandora's box, and once you fully open it, the lid doesn't go back on. No returns, no refunds. Any warranty instantly expires." I replied and she nodded, throwing back her long black hair and picking up her glass. She smiled at me as I raised my own, and she chinked them carefully together.

"Then, *mi amor*, let us say *arriba, abajo, afuera, adentro*." She took a long drink of wine then put the glass down. I quickly followed, as she pushed herself up off the sofa and leaned over to give me a long, slow kiss.

When we broke, she smiled and took my hands, tugging me off the sofa.

"Now, you say I have not even scratched the surface? Then I would like very much to explore and learn some very intimate things about you, *Senor Werewolf*." Sarah laughed throatily, as she turned, still holding my hand and tugged me towards the bedroom. "Scratching may be involved."

To be fair, I didn't need much tugging.

"What did that toast mean?" I asked as I reached around and scooped her up easily, pulling her against me so that her feet dangled, and she looped her arms around my neck. The scent of her filled the air all around me, the slight weight of her was a familiar burden in my arms, and I felt her nuzzle at my neck. "Sarah?"

"Ah, it is a Spanish drinking toast. The literal translation is *Up, Down, Out* and *In*." She answered between kisses, looking up at me with those wonderful soulful eyes of hers, dark brown. The hue of rich oiled wood flecked with shards of gold. "Which is pretty much what I want to do with you, so it seemed fitting!"

I growled a laugh, nudging the door open and stepping into the bedroom. Bear chuffed a grumbling moan, but I shot him a *don't you dare* look and the trollhound sighed heavily, snaffled the last of the black pudding sausages from the coffee table and settled down amongst the roots of the tree with his prize.

Then I closed the door firmly on the rest of the world, and let it go hang for a while.

Chapter 15

Cursed Items – removal of

Many supernatural monsters seem to be invulnerable or unkillable, when in fact they are simply warded by an object they own that keeps them safe and secure. The cap that Redcap steeps in blood to guarantee its strength, the One Ring that Sauron has imbued with his magic and so is unkillable until it is destroyed. Dorian Grey, unkillable and never aging until he himself stabs the painting which contains his soul.

The object that ensures their immortality is most often cleverly hidden, quite often disguised as something unlike its true nature entirely. Yet supernatural entities often misjudge their prey's ingenuity and determination, and can be overcome by a hero or heroine with a little perseverance and familiarity with solving puzzles. That and by listening to any helpful hints offered by mysterious crones, hags or strangers met along the path of their quest.

Things happened.

If more details are needed, then either use your imagination or go ask someone for the *Birds and Bees* talk. I'm not particularly good at sharing intimate facts. Sorry.

One thing happened, though, that is worth mentioning.

After *events,* I rolled over and took a moment to slow my breathing. Sweat stuck to my skin, and my muscles ached pleasantly. I think I might even have felt *languid,* and that has never been a word I've associated with me in any way, shape or form.

Beside me, amongst the rumpled and thoroughly messed up bed sheets, Sarah settled back. The scent of her still wrapped around me like the most natural perfume, even with that slight odd tang that I now guessed was whatever she had brought back from Brazil.

I listened to her breathing for a long moment, then caught an all-together out of place sound that had *no* place in the bedroom right now.

"Sarah?" I queried, rolling over to gaze at the curve of her back as she lay on her side, away from me. "Are you *writing*?!"

The woman I loved rolled over, a pencil held to her lips as she nibbled the end. Totally naked, her dress tossed to the bedroom floor, her underwear lost amongst the pillows and sheets. She still wore an intricate bracelet, ethnic in design with beads, leather thongs and small charms that covered her wrist. That and a simple silver necklace that I had given her a while ago. Apart from those two items, wholly naked and looking gorgeous to my hungry eyes.

A small pad of paper was clasped in one hand, and she had managed an impressive set of notes already if the small, tight writing filling the paper was anything to go by.

"Where the hell did you stash that?" I joked, given I knew very intimately all the clothing she had worn to come see me and none of it looked like it had space for those items to sit comfortably.

She laughed, scribbling one last line then setting the pad aside, leaning in to lay a small hand on my chest.

"A girl has to have some secrets, Morgan. The day I cannot surprise you, is the day I've lost your heart." She told me with a wicked smile as she leaned in to kiss me.

When we broke, I nodded to the pad.

"Please don't tell me you were scoring me?" I told her with a grin of my own, running my hand over her skin and eliciting a shiver from her.

Sarah took a breath, closing her eyes for a moment and savouring the sensation before she opened them and met my gaze. That wicked smile of hers lit the room, as she let her hands drift over my body in reply.

"No, I was just making some observations. Strength, stamina, that sort of thing." She told me with a laugh. "I always like to record everything I learn about a new species!"

"Oh, and there was one last thing …" Sarah added, as I drew her to me, feeling my strength and stamina definitely returning. "I just wanted to confirm. Not just doggy-style, huh?"

I stopped her laugh with my mouth, and pulled the sheet back over us, putting an end to all conversation or note-taking for a while.

Chapter 16

Then the earth moved.

Literally.

Sarah was curled up against me, head on my chest and one leg wrapped around me, nestling in and slowing her breath as she listened to my heartbeat. It was something I knew she did, but I hadn't asked where the habit came from. Partly to avoid hearing it was a thing she used to do with an ex, partly because I didn't really need to know. It was just nice when she did it with me.

As the apartment shook, she jerked upright, sheet clinging to her as she stared around the room, eyes wide.

"Are we having an earthquake?" She asked, just a little stupidly, but it was ok. Both our heads were more than a little fuzzy from all the *catching up* we'd just done. "*Mi dio*, this is the wrong country for that shit?"

"Hey, the UK gets tremors. Just teeny-weeny ones that break plant pots, not buildings." I told her reassuringly, reaching up to gently pull her down to me again. "See, it's already done with."

It was true, the shaking had quit almost as soon as it started. Nothing had jumped off the walls, no vases had fallen and shattered … not that I had any … and generally everything remained standing as the motion subsided.

Whilst Sarah slowly calmed, I cleared my head of the pleasant fog that had fallen over everything but my most basic thoughts, and let my senses roam. Because the fact was, this hadn't been a simple earthquake. Not even close.

When I'd invested in having my wards re-written, the previous ones having proven monumentally ineffective at doing their job, I'd decided to change them up a little. Time for an upgrade.

Where before I'd had the basic package, which simply stopped anything unfriendly coming in, and provided shielding from most supernatural attacks against those inside, I felt I needed more of a heads up when things were looking to do me or my friends harm. Whilst still subtle enough not to scare the living daylights out of the mortals living in the building, or outside. The last thing I needed was for my home to be reported as a health hazard, or to get a reputation as haunted or the like.

So now, the wards I had in place were twinned. The first constantly scanned the immediate vicinity of my apartment block, reacting to any perceived threat by natural or supernatural entities. If anyone even looked at my home with a bad thought in mind, the place would shake, the strength of the tremor denoting the intensity of the desire to do harm.

In this case, given how it had felt like an actual full-on earthquake, it meant something with a serious problem with me was approaching. I snuck a glance at Sarah, as she lay back down on the sheet and closed her eyes a moment.

Why the fuck does this always happen? I've been single for months, sleeping alone ... but the moment I get Sarah back and we're together? The big bad comes a'calling. My life was, in a nutshell, fucking cursed.

"I'm just going to go get some water. You want any?" I asked, but Sarah just stretched in a gloriously sexy way and shook her head.

"I'm fine. Just don't stray too far. I've got lots more things to make notes on." She grinned wolfishly at me. "We haven't even gotten to important stuff like how long a werewolf can hold its breath!"

"Funny." I snarked but grabbed a pair of jogging pants and pulled them on. Then I walked across the room to the bedroom door.

Too late.

"Morgan Black? And the female companion with you?" Goldspur's voice piped up from outside. Clear and tinkling with her inhuman tones. "You will be glad to hear that the one who sought entry to our home has been put to flight. The threat is over."

I slapped a hand over my eyes and hung my head, groaning, as Sarah shot back up again, clutching the sheet to her.

"Morgan, who the hell is that?" She asked loudly, fixing me with a hard, bright stare. The furrow in her brow and the way her chin formed a perfect V with her lips tightening above them told me I had better answer quick, and have the *right* answer first time.

"Uh, ok. I can promise you this is *not* what it sounds like." I turned back to Sarah, holding up my hands in case she had found anything within reach to throw at me. There were a few weapons hidden around the bedroom, but I was hoping the only thing she'd have to hand was a pillow.

"What it *sounds* like is another woman living in the apartment of the man I have professed to love, and have just bounced bones with, *chulo*." Sarah replied, eyebrow arched, lips definitely set in a thin line. "Otherwise, why did she say *our home*? And I ask again, who the hell is she?"

I'll give Sarah this, she picked up on Goldspur's poor choice of words with laser-like precision whilst I was still shoving the dregs of raw emotion down to try and think straight.

Now, I've read in books and seen in films, where the hero of the story is in this sort of tight spot. With two women present, when there should only be one. And of course, the hero is able to pass the second woman off as his niece, mother, aunt or visiting pen pal from another country, just stopping for a brief stay before returning back to her native country and husband, fiancé, large family of children and the like. All the right things to calm jealously down and allay any suspicion.

I suck at that sort of thing, so decided to go with the honest truth. What harm could it do?

"I'm going to open the door, and show you who is outside." I told Sarah, even as I reached for the door. "Goldspur, would you mind stepping in here a second?"

I slid the door open, and the dryad stepped into the bedroom. Thankfully, she was dressed, wearing a long t-shirt adorned with distinctive tribal tangled knotwork, and leggings that had been laced up each leg. She still wore the two knives, snugly sat on her hips, and her braided hair had been pulled back with the use of what I thought looked like a tanned leather strip.

"Sarah, this is Goldspur." I introduced the dryad, who slipped into a very simple curtsey. "Goldspur, this is Sarah Conner."

"Your mate. Yes." The dryad replied, even as Sarah looked at her slowly, taking in the green skin, the green tattoos, the overlarge amber eyes. The general inhumanness that no simple clothing could hide. "As requested, I remained with my father for the duration of your courtship, and did not listen to your coupling as that would be rude. However, I *did* have to sing quiet loudly with my father to do so, so you may wish to be less voluble next time."

"*Dios mio!* You have her father living here too? How many people were listening to us?!" Sarah clutched the sheet to her body, looking around frantically as if expecting a horde of lecherous weirdos to spring from the cupboards and wardrobes.

I shook my head, realising I was not making things any better.

"Sarah, listen to me." I spoke gently, calmly, capturing her attention without further infuriating her. "Here's the truth. Goldspur is a dryad. Like in Greek mythology. A spirit of the trees. She lives in her father, the apple tree. Which is real. Because he has grown in my living room, she's a de facto guardian of the apartment and it kinda makes it their home too. Hence her saying *our home*."

"The apple tree is real? But you said … And how …?" Sarah retorted, obviously trying to get her head around the facts I was unloading on her. It was a lot, but I figured she'd at least get the point I was trying to make. That nothing dubious was going on, nothing for her to worry about in terms of us.

"Long, long story." I shrugged, walking back to sit on the edge of the bed. I didn't try to hold her or anything. Just wanted to be close. "The point is, there is nothing going on with Goldspur and me. Just don't even think that. She protects this apartment, and trust me, she does a bloody good job. See those knives she wears?"

Sarah nodded, once, and I carried on.

"She's *really* good with them. But that's it." I tried to reassure her with the truth, with my voice and presence. Simple stuff, but hostage negotiators would have applauded me for the efforts I was making, to avoid everything exploding in my face. "Nothing to worry about."

Sarah's brow furrowed, the angry lines to her face slowly fading, replaced with bemusement and just a little bit of awe if I was reading her right. Here she was, in the same breathing space as something straight out of myth, a creature wholly inhuman. Alien even, except with less tentacles, acid blood or spring-loaded sets of teeth to worry about. In fact, Goldspur was positively girl-next-door compared to the sort of creatures Sarah *could* have met as an introduction to the Real.

"So, she's like ... your house elf?" She asked finally, but I shook my head, wincing. Thankfully the dryad was not familiar with the works of JK Rowling, otherwise those words would have been like the old-style glove to the face before a nasty fight.

"Fuck, no. She's not my servant." I answered truthfully. "Goldspur is like a live-in security system. Probably better at protecting this place than my resident guard dog in fact."

Hearing my words, the dryad stepped forward, eyes on Sarah.

"I do no cleaning, nor mending of torn garments or broken shoes. If there were one, I would not milk his cow, nor would I feed any of Morgan Black's farmyard stock." She listed off, referring back to the old duties undertaken by other fae when they lived with mortals. "I do not desire to share his bed to sport or sleep, nor do I wish to raise a family with him if that were possible. I am ward of this hearth and home, bound to protect my father for all his days. And so I also protect where we live. Against *all* threats."

I chose to ignore that last little jibe, not wanting to start off down that rabbit hole. Instead, I watched as Sarah took in Goldspur's words, thought on what I'd told her, and came to a decision.

"It's a pleasure to meet you ... Goldspur." She shuffled under the sheet until she was at the edge of the bed, and held out a hand to shake. "I am sorry if we were too loud. I will see that we keep things more quiet next time."

Goldspur carefully took her hand, clasping it with her own green digits. I heard Sarah give a small gasp, realising she probably wasn't used to shaking hands with a creature whose body pulsed with the energy of her parent. Forget warm skin. The dryad had her father's sap running through her, and that would feel mighty weird to a mortal.

With the introductions concluded, and me still in one piece, I motioned for Goldspur to head back out of the bedroom. She complied, and I stepped over to Sarah.

"So, we good then?" I enquired carefully, seeing the other look at me, thoughts bouncing around behind her deep brown eyes.

Sarah took a breath, then nodded. In the next moment, she pulled me down and kissed me hard.

"That's to remind you who's in your bed, and who's fixing to be the only one here." She told me, then with the next breath, she punched me hard in the shoulder. "And that's for not telling me about your housemate and the truth before I had to find out *naked*. You need to learn better timing, *hombre*."

I grinned foolishly, not even wincing from the punch. Sarah had grown up with brothers and knew how to swing her fists, but I was a big tough lycan so could shrug it off.

"I just need to go check with Goldspur about the thing. That ok?" I asked, and she nodded.

"Go find out what rang your doorbell, then come back to bed." Sarah rolled back, pulling the sheet with her but letting it slide to reveal a slice of naked thigh. "I might get lonely and start thinking you like your women *green*."

"Har bloody har." I growled at, then ducked out of the bedroom.

Time to see what sort of trouble had, indeed, come knocking.

Chapter 17

Sunlight

Sunlight is a natural bane to many supernatural entities linked to darkness and shadow. Vampires, for all that they are terrifying predators, are afflicted by any number of weaknesses. The light of the sun will turn them to dust, from which they can only recover if their remains are then offered life-restoring blood. Troll-kin, living mountains or the more feral bridge trolls, will be turned to stone by the touch of sunlight. Shades of the dead are known to be rendered powerless under the rays of the sun, reduced to harmless apparitions or forced to flee entirely.

Mortals have learned to harness the sun's light through crystals and clever mechanisms. Darkness is easily banished, and effective weapons against those vulnerable to solar energy should be considered mandatory for any hero or heroine venturing into the shadows.

Goldspur and Bear were both waiting for me in the living room, as I slid the bedroom door shut behind me.

"Ok. Whatever triggered the alarm?" I asked as I made a beeline for the kitchen. I hadn't been joking when I said I needed water. Catching up with Sarah was thirsty work, so I cracked open a bottle of chilled spring water and drank down half the contents as I walked back to join the other two.

"This entity, it came wishing violence upon you. Its emotions were strong and filled with the desire, nay, the lust to inflict pain and suffering." The dryad told me as she settled onto the arm of the sofa. Bear huffed for attention, settling beside me so I could give his head a scratch.

"The list of things that *wish violence upon me* is long and not exactly exclusive." I admitted, as I set the bottle of water aside for a moment. "Was there anything more? And I'm guessing the second wards did their job?

"I felt the touch of Wyld about the intruder, strongly so. And great personal pain. Fear and weakness, despite its desire to harm you." Goldspur thought for a moment, then added. "Its mind felt … not well, fractured into pieces and filled with anger, hate, pain and fear. This thing was not sane, I would say. But yes, your wards are much improved. They dealt with its efforts to break in most effectively."

As noted, I'd had new wards fitted to my home, to the entire block actually. It had been done under the guise of workmen updating the cladding on the apartment block, the residents wholly unaware that the 'workmen' who hung from cradles in front of their windows were actually a cadre of dwarrow under glamour. Loaned to me by Madb and the Morrigan, to get my home in order.

It seemed that my grandmother, whilst recovering from wounds received from fighting her own elite cadre of Crow guard, had found my protections wanting. The Queen of Shadow and her Herald had conferred, and decided as a reward for my services to their Court, I was to be gifted a castle befitting a Knight. With the proverbial drawbridge and murder holes to see off any pesky invaders.

The first wards triggered when anyone with ill intent approached my building. If they left at that point, no harm no foul. But if they continued to act on their feelings, and tried to breach my threshold, then the second ones tripped.

Fireworks, loud explosions and the like tended to attract attention, and had the danger of damaging innocent bystanders caught in the ward's blast radius. Instead, I went for subtlety. Whomever came at me, be it mortal or creature of the Real, they would find themselves subjected to something akin to five hundred thousand volts of electricity. About half a fairly decent lightning bolt, and ten times the strength of the standard police tasers used by mortals.

If, say, a bunch of OPS heavies now decided to break into my home, they'd find the experience much less pleasant. Whilst non-lethal, that level of current was guaranteed to leave them twitching on the floor no matter how good their insulation was, and also fry any and all electrical equipment they carried. They'd be right as rain after an hour or so, their brains only slightly scrambled …with the added bonus they could probably light a bulb just by holding it.

If the intruder were something far nastier, and Real-er, then the ward would wreak havoc with any glamour they might be hiding behind and give them a long, hard shock. Hurling them hopefully into the Thames, which as a fast-flowing river would fuck up any craftings they might use to try and save themselves. If not, then they'd still be sent packing with scorch marks at the very least, possibly on fire if they were stupid enough to try and push through the warding.

I said I'd gone for subtle, and to be fair, the chance of explosions from anything tripping the wards was fairly low. Compared to the sort of protection the dwarrow *had* offered to install, I reckon I had been the soul of practicality and sensibility.

In this instance, whatever … whomever had tried to break in had been dealt with efficiently and without causing any panic amongst the mortals. And after hearing Goldspur describe the bastard, I had a decent suspicion who it had been. And with this bastard, panic and mortals went hand in hand.

"Jack's back." I swore. Loudly. And with feeling.

Jack the Ripper. My half-brother by Herne, and a genuine and utter bastard. He'd been bound in the Ivory Court's Burning Halls after his … our father hunted him down and bound him for his crimes against mortals. But then Morgana had arranged his release with the rest of the lunatics she'd wanted free and this side of the Veil, causing chaos and mayhem in their wake.

My half-brother had taken my existence as a personal insult, and made a spirited attempt at shortening the Wyld Court's Christmas Card list, after tag-teaming with Baba Yaga. Between them, they had killed a bunch of homeless transients and two Sisters of the Arch. When we'd finally crossed claws, Gregory Allen had gotten in the way and paid for the mistake with his life … but not before shoving one of my silver and cold-iron forged swords through Jack's side, seriously wounding him. Felix had added insult to injury by then dumping his arse in the Thames, sending him downstream at speed, poisoned by my sword and unable to deal with the damage done to him due to the grounding effect of the river.

Later, Ellie had fashioned a tracker for him, and before we lost her to the Twilight Court, she told Jessica and me that whilst the bastard was still kicking around, he was thoroughly messed up and a shadow of his former self. They'd downgraded his threat level, against my wishes, given what trouble could a lone, poisoned and crippled fae cause us when we weighed against Morgana, Queen of Twilight?

And now he'd popped up again. Outside my door, on the same day Sarah had come over. Coincidence? That could go fuck itself.

"You sure he's gone?" I asked Goldspur, knowing how much he liked to lie in wait and ambush his victims. An echo of his former persona, *Spring Heeled Jack*, who used to hide on the rooftops of London and jump down on victims to scare them shitless. This was before he grew to enjoy the taste of mortal flesh and blood, and he switched his *modus operandi* to something far more deadly.

"My father has tapped into the earth of this place. His roots now travel through the whole of the abode and down into the land about." She replied, shaking her head once. "He is sure this creature, Jack you call him, departed at speed. He has marked its nature, and will track it through the earth but there are many places he cannot travel. Places mortals have bound with unnatural stone."

"They call it concrete." I answered her with half my mind, as the rest of it started working out what the hell the immediate future looked like.

I'd need to let Jessica know that the Ripper, even in his weakened state, was back. If we were lucky, we could hunt the bastard down and have him bound up either to the Burning Halls or off to the tender mercies of the Furies without too much of a problem. Then I remembered Jacob's warning … the weird affliction affecting the packs, leaving pack members weakened. Could that be something Jack had done? Payback for his wounding? It seemed a stretch, but it definitely affected our ability to hunt and face him head on, if we weren't at full strength.

And what about Sarah? We'd just gotten together, and suddenly my homicidal half-brother was on the scene. He wouldn't think twice of harming or killing her to pay me back. I'd painted a target on her forehead, just when we were making steps to actually be together.

Why the fuck can't things go right for once? I wanted to punch something, repeatedly, but forced the rage down until I could use it to deal with the problems in front of me.

There really was only one option I could think of, to keep her safe. It kind of made sense, but I had *no* idea how she'd take it. Whether she'd work out my motives, or just freak out.

Fuck it. I *had* to make her see the sense of it.

The door to the bedroom slid open, Sarah stepping into the living room. She'd thrown on one of my t-shirts and her panties, obviously grown a little bored of waiting for me to come back to join her.

No time like the present.

"Thought I could grab some of that water…?" She began, but I cut her off, taking her gently by the arm and guiding her to the sofa. I sat her down, joining her as I held her hands in my own and faced her.

"Why do I feel like you're about to give me some very bad news, *chulo*?" She asked me, freeing one hand to cup my chin and look me in the eyes. "If you are going to ask me to break up with you all of a sudden, after what we just did, I won't be responsible for my reply and actions. Just so you know."

"Uh, hell, no! Nothing that stupid. Well, maybe a little stupid …" I began, seeing her forehead furrow in a frown as I fumbled the words. "Ah, fuck it, look. Would you consider moving in here with me for a few days? I know I'm going too fast and rushing things, but it's the only way I can think of keeping you safe …"

I was rabbiting, the words tumbling out of my lips until Sarah laid a finger on my mouth, shushing me.

"*Chula*, what's wrong? Why do I need to be kept safe?" She asked, putting aside any humour as she read how serious I was right then. "Talk to me."

So I did. Not all the details, but as many facts as I thought she was ready for. That someone was after me, looking for payback. They'd hurt my friends once already, putting their lives at risk, until we'd 'handled' him. But he was back, and the sort of crazed, rabid dog that would burn down a building he was in if it meant he got me too. He was beyond the police to deal with, involving them would only get more people hurt, but my friends and I would be able to track and find him now I knew he was lurking nearby.

"You just need me to stay inside. Not talk to any strangers?" Sarah asked after a moment, thinking on what I had said. I rolled my eyeballs, heaving a sigh but she smiled and shook her head, forestalling my reply. "Ah *chulo*, I am sorry. That was a joke. I understand you are just worried about me, and do not want to see me hurt. I also don't want that, so of course I'll try to stay safe whilst you hunt this *bastardo* down and deal with him."

"But," She continued, as I breathed a sigh of relief. "I cannot simply sit here, hiding behind your door and twiddling my thumbs. I have a job, commitments. People I need to see. So unless you are able to accompany me when I go outside, we have a small problem, no?"

There was no way Jessica was going to sign off on me ditching everything I had on to keep Sarah company, even though she had granted the woman pack protection. My Alpha already had concerns over my being able to focus on the tasks at hand, with my love life knocking on my door. For good reason.

I could just tell Sarah the whole truth, who it was *exactly* after me. She'd have to take it seriously if she knew Jack the bloody Ripper was the problem ... but I didn't want to terrify her either. Finding out he was my half-brother might push her past the point of belief, and make her start thinking I just wasn't worth the hassle.

For purely selfish reasons, I really didn't like that option.

"I have a solution, Morgan's mate." Goldspur spoke up, having stayed quiet whilst Sarah and I talked. I hadn't forgotten about the dryad, but was a little surprised to hear her volunteering a solution. And also slightly concerned *what* sort of help she was offering.

"Ok, I'm game. What's your suggestion?" I asked, hoping she wasn't about to suggest some elaborate trap where we lured Jack back to the apartment, and she dealt with him as she had done the OPS security team. My half-brother was injured, sickened by silver and cold-iron poisoning, but I still didn't want to corner the bastard in my home. I knew far too well just how nasty Jack could be, and him being wounded just made him desperate and crazed.

Pardon me for caring, but I really didn't want World War Three going down in my living room. I was emotionally attached to my home, and it hurt to see the shit kicked out of it. Even if Goldspur was able to repair the damage afterwards.

"Simple. If Morgan's mate desires to leave the protection of this hearth, then I can accompany her and so extend its warding against any that might seek to do her ill." The dryad replied brightly. "I cannot be away from my father for too long, but I trust you will deal with the malcontent speedily so that should not present a problem."

"Uh, you can leave here?" I asked a little stupidly, and Goldspur smiled, motioning to her attire. "Since when?"

"How do you think I obtained new clothing, after your instructions that I should wear such clothing whilst my father and I live here?" She asked, and I refused to look at Sarah, guessing she would once again pick up on the nuances of what the dryad said. Questions about what she *hadn't* been wearing were coming my way, I was sure. "Felicity kindly offered to take me to places where we exchanged paper and plastic for garments to clothe me. It was ... fun."

I honestly had to stop for a moment as a vision of Goldspur out on the streets of London with her knives, green skin and striking resemblance to something straight out of Lord of the Rings filled my head. Most mortals would think she was part of a photo-shoot or event in the city, but surely the police would've stepped in when reports of a *green-skinned woman with knives wandering around the shops of central London* reached them? They tended to be hot on anyone these days even suspected of carrying a toy weapon, be it real or not. Let alone two Shadow-forged knives.

Then my brain kicked in.

"Glamour, right?" I figured and the dryad nodded. Of course, she'd hide her true self, appearing as just another mortal on the streets, clothes shopping with her friend. I had no idea who had paid for the purchases, but Goldspur's mention of *paper and plastic* made me wonder if any of my credit cards were missing ...

But her suggestion actually made sense, and was an option I hadn't considered. I looked over at Sarah, seeing her eyeing the dryad a little warily. I couldn't blame her. Up until a short while ago, Goldspur was a thing of myth and fantasy. Now, she was my house-mate and guardian, and was offering to play bodyguard to her. Asking a *lot* of trust.

Finally, Sarah shrugged, stepping up and enfolding Goldspur in a warm hug. The dryad flinched for a second, hands twitching to the knives at her belt, but when Sarah simply held her, the younger fae instead raised her arms and awkwardly embraced her back.

When Sarah loosened hold of her and stepped away, the mortal woman smiled warmly.

"Then if it will not be too much of a burden for you, I accept your kind offer to keep me safe." She told the dryad, who let a small smile light her face in response. "Besides, I'd love a chance to chat with you and find out how *terrible* it must be, having to live with this big-footed oaf. Us girls need to stick together, and if he's being difficult in any way, you can tell me."

I suddenly wondered if putting these two together for any length of time was really in my own best interests. Felix had been bad enough, but now Sarah too?

"Now, if you don't mind *señora* Goldspur?" Sarah turned back to me and took me by the hand. She snagged the half-drunk bottle of water I had set to one side, and started walking back to the bedroom, pulling me with her. "My man has a date later this evening, so I'd like to spend as much time as I can with him before he goes off to save the world or whatever it is he does. I promise we'll keep the noise down, even if I have to gag him. Or sit on him!"

Goldspur giggled, and I sighed theatrically, before shoving the worry that Jack's reappearance had kindled in me to the back of my mind. Time to deal with him later, to speak to Jessica and handle Jacob's problem, let alone deal with whatever had happened to Sarah's colleague, and whatever was snacking on rodents and homeless people.

For now, I had my hands full.

Literally.

Chapter 18

It was nearing eight that evening when I shut the bedroom door behind me. I left Sarah curled up in the sheet and pillows, thoroughly worn out and sound asleep. And snoring quietly.

We all make funny noises when we sleep. It's a fact. Anyone who says different is either lying or one of the undead, as they are the only freaks that are wholly silent when not conscious. Something to do with having died once already, and the *silence of the grave* never really leaving them. Find yourself sleeping beside one of them … you'd best have a stake close to hand.

Bear shifted and stretched as I appeared out of the bedroom, washed and fully clothed. He gave me a hopeful huff, making a beeline for the kitchen and his walking lead and harness.

Jacob had texted me a short while ago, and we'd agreed to meet at his home in the Isle of Dogs as close to nine as possible. He'd spent the day patrolling the mists and checking in with the packs, getting an update on who was showing signs of this mysterious malady. As Jessica had asked. I'll give him this, my packmate might be pissed at us for thinking him to blame for the murders in Greenwich Park but he wasn't letting that get in the way of doing his job. Professional, even if he was an utter sod at times.

Given the time, I was able to walk Bear and get him bedded down with enough food to last the night. It was easier on the kitchen white goods if I provided him his food in easy to reach places, unless I wanted a complete refit on my hands again. There were only so many fridges I could order before the suppliers and insurers started asking pointed questions like how I was wrecking them so quickly, and why I needed a clause in my contract covering canine drool.

We did a quick patrol of the area, me keeping an eye out for Jack just in case he'd doubled back and was lurking anywhere nearby, and Bear dousing the plant-life with the contents of his bladder. I'd been worried his uncommon breed would mean he'd kill off all the trees and flowers around my home, but turns out trollhound pee wasn't per se toxic, just *different*. Which was why the plants had grown to about three times their normal size, and the trees around the apartment block had started blossoming with purple and blue leaves and fruit. Who knew?

With no sign of my half-brother, and my companion's tank emptied, I bundled him back inside. Setting out several bowls of fresh water, I scribbled a quick note for Sarah on a spare pad. Just letting her know where things were, in case she'd forgotten, and that I'd hopefully be back first thing in the morning when the job was done. That, and a reminder not to step outside for any reason or let anyone into the apartment.

Goldspur appeared from her tree as I finished writing, her amber eyes glowing in the dimmed light.

"Fear not, Morgan Black. I shall ward our home, and your mate." She told me with a bright smile, fingers settling on the knife hilts at her waist. "But do not forget our bargain struck. The full set of Downton Abbey, including the specials and feature movie. Felicity is going to watch them with me."

"I'll order it for delivery tonight." I promised, receiving a nod in thanks before she melted back into her father's trunk. A dryad, wanting to watch period drama. Weird didn't even begin to cover it.

Rather than grab a taxi and incur further criticism from Jessica over my expense claims, I decided to use London's great public transport system for a change. It would give me the chance to get a feel of the mortals' mood. How they were coping with the mists, the strangeness that had dropped on them from on high like a Gods almighty birdshit. Whilst there was little I could learn cooped up in the back of a private cab, all I needed to do was simply step into any of the Tube stations around London. For any lycan, that was like turning on the radio and bouncing through the endless channels of noise.

By the time I walked down the staircase at South Quay, I'd heard enough to restore my faith in the reality of mortals. Whilst Morgana hadn't exactly announced the return of the Twilight Court with blaring trumpets and dancing elephants, I still wouldn't say erecting huge impassable walls of mist around four suburbs of London after sending a spear of burning light into the heavens had been subtle. As I'd seen on the streets when walking to Holland Park, the tabloids were still churning out headline news months after the event, from the serious ... *Growing concerns over missing Londoners lost to the mist* ... to the ridiculous ... *Women gives birth to quadruplets: says the mists is the father!* ...

But listening to the mortals on the London tube-trains, and standing near them in the stations, all I heard were the day-to-day stresses of life this side of the Veil. Jobs sucked, taxes were too high and who the hell could afford to buy a house in this current market? Men and women were still going out drinking and partying, dancing in clubs and hooking up for quick flings or the start of something more serious. Parents were still moaning about their children, gossiping about them and sharing their latest antics in the very same breath. This all mixed with a healthy dose of gripes and moans about government, gossip about the latest celebrity drama or favourite tv show, and just a splash of intellectual discourse on Brexit, and what insanity the new President of the United States was to blame for.

Basically, like nothing had changed.

Mortals might find the dark a thing to fear, might jump at shadows or shiver at the creaking of tree branches in the wind. But when faced with the actual terror of the Real knocking on their front door and ringing the bell, they could blithely ignore the looming threat and bounce around like little lambs in the meadow. Chewing grass, headbutting each other and without a care in the world. Whilst the wolves circled with bared teeth, their attack momentarily blunted whilst they watched with more than a little disbelief.

It did make me wonder sometimes. Whether the signatories of the Accords, those who had promised to keep the mortals in the dark as long as the immortals of the Real kept to their side of the Veil and behaved themselves, if they had understood just how easy the common folk would make the task. They must have known how strong the power of disbelief was with their charges, just how much the average man or woman could turn a blind eye to if it meant a peaceful life. Even if said life was dangerously shortened.

It certainly made hunting in the Mortal Realm a lot easier, when mortals were writing news articles about man-beasts ravaging their flocks and terrorising villages in the deep countryside. Whilst we stuck to the cities and left the poor sheep alone.

Jacob was a typical lycan in that he never felt truly at ease indoors. Something about the permanence of a building, the walls and ceiling weighing down and smothering his senses. Wolves might use caves and dens to hide their pups, but they are always happiest outside in the fresh air.

True to this need, this inborn rebellion against a solid home, the ex-soldier and pack enforcer had spent a considerable amount of his wages from both sides of the Veil on a suitable place to rest his head. One that didn't feel like it was a prison, rooted to the ground. Far from it, in actual fact.

It had once been called the Lotus, a floating houseboat converted into a Chinese restaurant. Its mooring was at one of the inner docks, making it exclusive for the locals living in the neighbourhood, cut off from the hordes who descended on Canary Wharf proper. Eventually, it had closed, and Jacob had managed to purchase it and obtain planning permission to reconfigure it as a living residence without too much hassle. It's funny how a little money greases the wheels of mortal due process.

My packmate was waiting for me as I walked down Oakland Quay, enjoying the fresh smell of the Thames, the harsh shriek of gulls that had evaded any hungry troll's cooking pot and the cold sting of winter on the breeze. It brought a freshness to the normally muggy and heavy air of the city, a balm against the usual discomfort we all put up with when living in the concrete jungle.

"Get anyone asking for a *number 21 and egg fried rice* lately?" I snarked, as Jacob watched me approach. His arms were crossed, expression stolid and stone-like. Betraying nothing, a blank wall upon which sarcasm and wit broke like waves on a cliff.

"Hnh. Funny." He replied when I reached him. "Still wake up thinking you have a real job, not just chasing little kitties and finding lost puppies for spoilt children?"

It was going to be one of *those* fun evenings.

The original floating restaurant had been modelled to look a lot like a Chinese pagoda from the outside. Red painted fencing around the exterior, a slanted green tiled roof and windows on every level for the patrons to enjoy the view of the dock and water. It had been moored right outside a large block of flats, meaning any and all locals could hang out of their windows and see what was going on below or enjoy the fragrant scents of Chinese fast food wafting up from the kitchens below.

Jacob had done away with a lot of the faux cultural trappings, replacing them with more modern touches. The roof had been stripped back, a massive weight removed and instead was open to the fresh air and reached via interior stairs. He'd still built an awning over the top, so that he could sit out in the fresh air without feeling like a hundred people were watching his every move, but it was open to the sides to reduce the *hemmed in* feeling he hated so much. The windows had been replaced, some walled up but most just fitted with smoked glass to reduce any visibility from the outside into his home. The fake oriental fencing had been replaced by sturdier railing, allowing anyone to walk around the exterior without risking a fall into the water by accident.

One nice touch was the large number of large planters he's added to the deck outside, filled with climbing vines and large leafed plants. These covered a lot of the outer walls, carefully nurtured to grow where needed without reducing sunlight to any windows. I hadn't thought a hardened ex-soldier and one of the hardest lycan I knew would have a green thumb, but it turned out Jacob seemed to have a knack at nurturing flora.

Whilst they provided a nice contrast to the plain outer walls, I also noted the cleverly hidden wards enscribed beneath the vines and leaves, etched into every surface. Jacob, like me, had made his home a fortress against anything that came looking for trouble. I also knew he'd added special anti-climb paint and a number of other tricks to the exterior of the boat to make it as difficult as possible for an intruder to gain access.

As a final measure, my packmate had also moved the mooring of his floating home, shifting it from directly outside the apartment block to further down the quay. With some careful manoeuvring, he had taken advantage of existing structures along the inner dock to leave his home as little overlooked as possible. Securing a fair degree of privacy. He'd also extended the ramp and moored the boat further out into the water, given that no other traffic passed through the dock on a regular basis, and fitted a secure gate and tunnel to ward the entrance to his home.

All in all, Jacob had done a decent job converting the restaurant into a spacious habitat for him and anyone he invited over. The interior was fitted out with extra bedrooms, two spacious lounges, multiple washrooms and an industrial sized kitchen that he had simply upgraded when he moved in.

He'd even added a wet room that allowed access directly to the dock's water, if ever he fancied a swim or needed to get into or out of the house unseen. Something we lycan needed on the odd occasion, to avoid prying eyes and scaring the locals.

"Should I have called ahead for a reservation?" I asked with a grin, as Jacob swung the gate open and motioned for me to head on through.

His stony silence just made me smile even more, so he sighed and just gave me a *gentle* shove to keep walking.

Chapter 19

Water, fast flowing

Water is well known as an earthing agent, disrupting magic and cleansing away hexes and charms that the bearer might be suffering from. The stronger the flow of the water, the greater its power to counter and negate harmful magic. Some fae creatures, especially those directly opposed to water, will find its touch to be like acid, burning them like silver – but the water must be moving, and at pace. Simple stagnant or slow turgid water ways pose little or no threat to any supernatural creature, even witches who are mistakenly believed to melt at its touch.

Fast flowing water can also act as a barrier, preventing the recently raised dead from passing across it. Medieval castles were equipped with moats and waterwheels to ensure moving water surrounded the inhabitants, providing an effective protection against many monsters.

Once my packmate had invited me onboard, we quickly headed up to the first floor.

In a switch from the 'normal' rules, Jacob had copied my layout style and provided guest accommodation on the 'ground' floor, whilst his own bedroom and second lounge was upstairs. I dumped the jacket I'd worn against the seasonal chill over the back of a chair, and my packmate disappeared into the kitchen. He came back with two chilled, frosted bottles of beer. Offering me one, we chinked them together before Jacob took a long pull from his.

"This is probably a complete waste of our time." I admitted as I collapsed into the nearest chair, taking a sip of the beer. Though I prefer wine, a good, chilled bottle of quality beer can be just as enjoyable as a glass of aged Merlot, and I savoured the sharp tang as I looked at the bottle. Something Nordic, imported. *Kostritzer Black Lager*, the bottle told me. *Toasted bitter flavour with bittersweet herbs. A gentle tingle balanced with an elegant and intensely aromatic freshness. Finished with delicate bitter notes and a malty sweetness on the palate.*

This from a beer? Right.

I certainly got the bitter and sweet notes, though wasn't sure what herbs they'd used. These days, anything green seemed to be classified as a herb by mortals, whether it actually did anything or just grew where it shouldn't. Calling them weeds was probably insulting, a label deemed a slur by the herbalists and vegetarians of the world. Possibly just ground leaves?

"Why?" Jacob asked as he settled down on the larger sofa. Any anger at me babysitting him to check his alibi was buried deep, since all I was getting from him was a world-heavy weariness and that faint stab of emotional pain. The loss he still carried around from Lucille's death.

I gave him the crib-notes from my meeting with the Morrigan, seeing his brow furrow at my casual chit-chat with a major fae immortal. Both he and Jessica had made it clear they were uncomfortable with my level of involvement with the Courts, especially now that I supposedly held allegiance to all three for different reasons. Ivory and Shadow by my appointments as Knight and Errant, Wyld by my blood.

Jessica at least accepted the situation as 'complicated' and trusted me to handle the various entities that thought they had their hooks in me with equal levels of *fuck-all chance*.

My packmate, however, was in a word '*distrustful*' of anyone and anything linked to the Courts, given the long history of lycans having to deal with their condescension and blatant fucking around that usually ended up causing us all manner of headaches. Despite being the ones who had contributed to and bound themselves to the Accords, the fae often thought themselves above the law and ignored them as they saw fit. Me meeting with one, even one who as it turns out is family by blood, just gave Jacob another reason to worry.

"So as much as I know you like to play the big, scary wolf," I wrapped up, taking another swig from my beer. "Looks like the thing that killed the mortals in the park, and has been snacking on pets and wildlife across town, is a bigger, badder arsehole come answering ol' Moggie's summons. Letting you off the hook. Sorry."

Jacob mulled over my little revelation, swigging from his beer, but then shook his head.

"Still. Jessica wanted you to watch me. So, you might as well get comfortable." He told me, showing his allegiance to our alpha's wishes, no matter his personal feelings on the matter. Too bloody well trained as a soldier. "Unless you have more important places to be …?"

I sighed theatrically and gave him my wry smile.

"Quit fishing. You're crap at it." I told him, seeing him crack a small grin too. "She's sleeping at my place, and knows not to expect me back until tomorrow. See, I can make the adult choice too. At times."

"Hnh." He snorted, but then pushed himself up of the seat. He rubbed his hand, where I saw a small plaster had been administered to his palm. The idiot had probably cut himself to get the Wolfbane into his system quicker, knowing he'd heal anything once the effects wore off. "Whilst we're talking about doing the right thing …"

The lycan disappeared into his bedroom, closing the door behind him and I caught the sound of draws sliding out. When he returned, he dumped a small, sealed packet in my lap, tossing the contents over to me as he picked his beer back up and drank the remains of the bottle down.

Sipping from my own bottle, I looked down at the present Jacob had deposited so carefully on the seat between my legs. Familiar vials of glass stared back at me, like the ones I'd last seen packaged in boxes used to transport vital organs for surgical transplant. Greenish ooze filled each one, and there had to be over twenty full vials in the bag. I didn't need to open any of them to know what they were.

"This all of them?" I asked, knowing it was vaguely insulting to doubt Jacob but then again, he'd started dosing himself on fucking Wolfsbane. Forget alcohol being a mild poison, this stuff was death to us lycan in high enough doses, and I'd suffered from its effects far too many times to give him a free pass on this. Getting hooked on this shit made most of my fuck ups look like charming little anecdotes.

Jacob gave me his flat eyed look as reply, not bothering to answer. He was obviously tired, probably cranky and definitely not in the most forgiving of moods. But then, I wasn't one potentially hooked on a lethal Accord-forbidden substance. So I really gave zero fucks.

Jacob got back up again, heading to the kitchen. Suitable clattering and banging noises were made as I sat back and looked out the windows, enjoying the view across the water whilst darkness fully descended. The Quay lit up with the cosy warmth from numerous mortals' homes and the streetlamps. The liquid beneath us moved as something travelled up or down the Thames, the ripples eventually reaching us to gentle rock the floating fortress from side to side.

I could understand the sense of peace Jacob found here. The strong hearth he had made for himself that suited both his need for a place to set down his roots but also his warring desire to not be chained to a mortal dwelling of uncompromising stone. He'd found a balance with his inner beast, and whatever demons he'd brought back from his excursions abroad, fighting unknown and faceless enemies in different lands.

Beer makes me get a little poetical, if it wasn't obvious. Possibly a little melancholy too. It's why I tend to stick to wine.

Jacob re-appeared, fresh bottles and an assortment of small snacks divided on two platters. With the deft skill of someone who had waited tables at some time in his life, he deposited two armloads of food and drink down onto the table in the middle of the room.

We sat. We ate. We drank.

Jacob seemed to withdraw into himself moment by moment, and to be honest I had enough going on in my head to keep an inner dialogue going as I tried to work out my next steps.

Wrap things up and prove Jacob wasn't the brutal murderer to the Sisters. Once that was in the bag, I needed information about whatever the hell it *was* the Morrigan warned me was hunting us. Hunting me. *Something like me, but not.* That was about as fucking helpful as the fae ever got, always bound by their own convoluted rules when it came to revealing the truth.

But at least it gave me some leads. 'Like me' was either a pointer to us lycans or to my link to the Wyld Court. After I'd managed to clear Jacob's name of any involvement, I guess I was due another chat with dear ol' Pops. Via his sarcastic furball of a Herald, most likely.

Don't get me wrong. Herne still gave me the absolute creeps, him and his habit of forcing us lycan to be his Hounds of the Hunt, bound beyond any ability to resist his every whim. But the fact he was my father made things a little easier for me to be sarcastic about the scary as fuck bastard. That and his sworn oath to not take any of my kin until the year and a day was done.

Then there was the ongoing problem of how the hell I was going to get into the mists, to find and retrieve Ellie and her beau. Months in the Mortal Realm translated to far too long in Twilight, but if it was anything like the Real, it had probably felt like years had passed for her. And I *really* didn't want to think what that must have been like for the witch.

The fact Morgana had not come hunting for my head made me hope that Ellie was being a calming influence on the revenge-crazed immortal. That or my little trick with the Harrowing had crippled the fae enough to stop her from enacting any payback. It was a long shot, I knew, but a wolf has to hope at times.

Then I had this missing colleague of Sarah's to find, though I had an inkling I'd already done so. Or at least I'd found his pieces. I needed to talk to the survivor of that gory little mess, see if my suspicion was right and there had been *four* people killed that night and their body parts mutilated and savaged to hide the actual number. But that then brought me back to this mysterious killer, and why it would want to hide the man's murder?

"Don't think I ever told you the story how I met Lucille. How she joined the pack." Jacob suddenly spoke up, breaking my thoughts. Looking across, I saw he had finished his beer and was staring at the bottle in his hands, dark eyes hooded and far away.

"Nope. Only that Jessica and Mark kinda collected us from all over the place. Different countries, backgrounds, that sort of thing." I shrugged. Where each lycan came from before they joined the pack was often something personal, something they either chose to share themselves or kept under wraps. "I figured from her accent, Lucille came from France maybe?"

"Yeah. Dijon. Burgundy." Jacob nodded, and I gave myself a little mental pat on the head. "It was 1944. About a year and half before the end of the Second World War. I was serving with the Special Air Service at the time, stationed back here after doing my tours in Libya. The rest of the troop knew there was something different about me, and my CO actually knew what I was, but they didn't care. I was good at tracking, hunting down targets and walking out of a firefight fit for duty, so they turned a blind eye whenever I needed them to."

I listened silently, knowing this was a side my packmate had not, to date, shared with me. Jacob was a private person, the walls he locked his personal life behind fucking impossible to break through or climb. I knew he had military experience, and that he was a *lot* older than the thirty or forty years he looked like. The fact he'd been involved in the Second World War wasn't much of a surprise, as I knew a bunch of lycans had served the Allies, used to counter the German's own *Werwolf* guerrilla soldiers. Skinwalkers pretending to be mortals, encouraged to be as savage and brutal as they could be, bestial in their treatment of any enemy they encountered or civilians they could terrorise.

"Word came down from Command. We were running two operations into German occupied France. *Bulbasket* in Poiters, but the second one I straightways signed up for. Like it had my name on it. *Houndsworth*." He continued, smiling wryly at the memory. "We were going into Dijon. Disrupting any chance of German reinforcements to Normandy, the planned landings there. A hundred and forty odd of us, dumped arse-deep in enemy territory then broken up into troops to cause as much chaos and fucking mess as we could. Blow up train tracks, destroy fuel dumps, that sort of thing."

"Kill as many of the enemy as we could, so they didn't kill us."

"My job was to hunt for any *Werwolf* soldiers. The crazy fuckers the Nazis allied with to put the fear of Hitler into the locals wherever they occupied." Jacob set down his bottle, looking across at me. "Those bastards, they tortured and butchered men, women and children just to make a point. Did some really fucking awful things to any young women or men they got hold of. Raping them then nailing them up to walls for target practice. Or stripping them naked and hunting them, tearing them apart when they caught the poor fuckers. They might have been shapechangers from the

Real, but inside, they were just fucked up animals. Sick and twisted, just what Hitler needed."

"Problem was, when I started hunting, I found someone else was ahead of me. Doing the killing I was supposed to." Jacob shook his head, lip curling at the memories he was sharing. "The locals who talked to us, the resistance fighters, they told us the Germans had slaughtered a bunch of nuns, set fire to the abbey they were living in after *desecrating* the women. From that point on, they were cursed. Their own beast hunting and dragging them off to hell one at a time."

"Lucille?" I guessed, and Jacob nodded.

"She was just a youngster at the time, a foster kid they'd taken in when she'd come stumbling in one night. Naked, feral. Covered in blood. She never did say what happened to her family, her parents but I know she had nightmares. The Nazis hunted wolves and lycan, thinking they could gain supernatural powers by skinning our kind alive and wearing the hides. Be like their *Werwolf* allies. And of course, those bastard shapechangers had it in for any of our kind they found. They treated lycan worse than the mortals."

"So, I reckoned she'd escaped something like that." He shrugged, and I let him talk, knowing that our kind had faced that sort of barbaric practice throughout the long years we'd lived beside mortals. The Germans had only been one of many cultures who vilified and reviled our kind. "The nuns raised her, taught how to speak and to control herself. She was only seventeen when the soldiers came, but the sisters hid her away. They died keeping her safe."

"The Germans got wise to her eventually. Set traps. Cornered her." He continued, coming to the crux of his story. "I was tracking the *Werwolves* and her, and found them together. Lucille in a cage, the bastards working out what they were going to do with her. She'd been staying at the ruins of the Abbey, after she buried the nuns and she was spotted there. The Germans and their shapechanger buddies had Wolfsbane, and had drugged her. I think they were going to rape her then cut her up. Feast on her, maybe."

"I did what my superiors had asked me to do. I killed them all. Then I freed Lucille, and took her back to our camp. Got her cleaned up, treated the Wolfsbane and offered her a choice. She could walk away, go find a new home far away from soldiers and death." Jacob pushed himself up off the sofa, eyes still on me. "Or she could join me. Stick with the troop and fuck up a whole load more of the bastards. Stop them from doing what they'd done to the sisters she knew. I didn't even have to ask her twice."

"And she joined the pack when you came back over?" I guessed, and he nodded. "So, you've known each other, what, seventy years or so?"

"Feels a lot longer." He answered, expression set, the pain he felt tempered at the memories of her. "But you needed to know, so you'd understand. I *saw* what letting the beast loose was like, what those *Werwolves* did to helpless mortals. To people like the women who cared and brought up Lucille. And there is *no* fucking way I'd go do the same thing to a bunch of innocent mortals, and fuck with her memory like that."

"No. Fucking. Way."

I didn't bother replying, knowing Jacob had told me not to talk things over, not to share the pain. Just to make his point very loud, very clear.

"Now, let's get this over with." He nodded to the package of vials I still had the couch beside me. "I'll take one and you can see I'm not sleep-walking or creeping out to munch on the nearest fat-sack."

I gingerly opened the package, not wanting to handle the stuff even though I knew it was perfectly safe as long as it stayed inside the glass containers. Picking out one vial, I set it onto the table in front of me.

Jacob nodded once, stepping over to collect the poison. He motioned to the kitchen.

"There's more beers in the fridge. Take anything you want. You know where the shower and toilet are, and there's towels out for you." He instructed me, then pointed to the cupboards set alongside one wall. "There's bedding, sheets and pillow in those, and you're sitting on your bed. I'll let you figure that out."

"Too kind." I looked over at the clock on the wall, and saw we'd somehow passed several hours just sitting and drinking. It was past eleven now, with the night having settled across London so that outside the boat's glass panes there was just darkness split by the odd lamp or the silvery sheen of the almost full moon. "I'll try not to be too noisy, but if you're out cold on Wolfsbane, reckon you won't care much."

"I won't." He agreed, but then shot me a hard smile. "But my search history on Sky is locked, so if you order any kinky shit, I'll know. Just saying."

With no better response, I flipped him the finger, and he snorted a laugh.

Clasping the vial of poison, Jacob turned and headed off to find whatever sleep he could. Haunted by the dreams of the woman he loved, and had lost.

Chapter 20

Now, given it had been a long day, involving some pleasant physical activity for a change, and considering I was supposed to be sitting watch on Jacob, I *should* have just switched on the TV, put my feet up and found something trivial to wind down with before I crashed out too.

If my packmate so much as twitched, there was no way I wouldn't hear him, so it wasn't like he'd be sneaking out of his room and past me whether I was awake, or had chosen to rest my eyes. I was sure in the knowledge this was a monumental waste of both our time.

Yeah, that's what I *should* have done.

Instead, I waited until I heard Jacob's groans and snarls from the poison's effects start to quieten, and his breathing deepen, that I was certain he was unconscious.

Then I went snooping.

It is the height of ill manners to go poking around a packmate's home without his or her strict permission. But thankfully, we lycans are renowned for being nosy bastards, and it wasn't like I was trying to find anything embarrassing to use against Jacob the next time he pissed me off.

Well, that wasn't my *main* reason for being up and about when I should have been sitting on guard.

No, I was just trying to look out for my packmate, and maybe help stop him fucking things up for himself. More so than he had already done.

He'd said the package of vials was the only stock of Wolfsbane he had, and with that passed to me, he was out of any supply of the toxic shit. But Jacob had proven to not be thinking straight when he started dosing himself with the stuff in the first place, and I was versed enough with narcotics and the hold on their victims to know that usually, there's a stash hidden somewhere. A *final* little bit left just for emergencies.

Or whatever lie they tell themselves.

If I found anything, I could dispose of it with the rest of the Wolfsbane, and Jessica could be sure Jacob was clean and without any supplies to further fuck himself up with. Then he could heal, get his head back in the game and we could all put this sorry mess behind us.

I figured if Jacob had anything stashed, it would be fairly well hidden. Nowhere near his own bedroom or living space. No, the clever thing for him to do would be to put it under the noses of any visitors, to use them as cover to hide whatever he wanted kept secret. Let the idiots search high and low, and waste their time and energy on a fruitless hunt. Oh, Jacob would *definitely* enjoy doing just that.

Sure in my hunch, I stealthed quietly down the stairs to the lower deck. This was all in darkness, but I didn't bother turning on the main lights, just in case they somehow alerted Jacob to what I was up to.

Instead, I started at the front of the boat, where the guest bedrooms were. The bow, I think it's called. Closing the doors behind me meant I could risk turning on the overhead lights here, as I quickly checked the usual hiding places … inside the toilet's flush cavity, under the beds, behind the drawers. I checked the walls for any subtle marks or odd angles that might betray a hiding place. The bulbs in the ceiling were deeply recessed and thus not usable to store anything within their sockets, so I checked instead that he hadn't fitted any trapdoors alongside these, to use the space between floors for storage.

I *did* turn up a fairly decent arsenal of hidden weapons, carefully stored to be out of sight but easy to reach if needed. Jacob was a lycan, after all, and we expected trouble pretty much eating, sleeping or at any other time.

But I found no stashes of Wolfsbane. No evidence he'd held any of the shit back.

Switching the lights off and carefully closing the doors behind me, I went through the living room and kitchen, the bathroom and showroom with as little luck. Or the same good luck, given I actually *didn't* want to find more of the bloody stuff.

The other end of the boat, the aft or rear or boot depending on who you ask, was set up as Jacob's gym and utility space, for doing all the laundry a busy lycan needs to do if he wants nice clean clothes to face each new day and adversary in. As I approached this section, I picked up the scents I'd expect. The tang of sweat from Jacob's regular exercise regimes, the chemical fragrance of detergent and the moist undertone of clothes freshly washed and drying naturally.

There was another scent, however, that I wasn't expecting. A trace, a sliver in the air that was almost but not completely masked by the other smells.

Blood.

Now, we lycans enjoy a little rough house, and play hardball when we get the chance. The Blooding is a perfect example, where we happily maul each other and do the sort of damage that would leave most mortals crippled and on life support. None of us are shy about spilling a little claret here and there, knowing sometimes you just have to bleed to get the job done.

I've exercised before and overdone it, breaking equipment built for mortal limits, and suffered minor injuries from a shattered bench-press bar or collapsed weightlifting machine. Finding Jacob had bled in his own home gym wasn't that surprising.

The problem? This wasn't my packmate's blood.

When mortals speak of smelling or tasting blood, they talk of a coppery tang, a metallic flavour that is unmistakable. To a lycan, that's like saying red is a pure colour without nuances. Compare the shades of crimson, cardinal, maroon, cherry, rose, ruby … and try telling me they are all the same colour?

And yeah, Sarah had taken me make-up shopping a few times, and I'd been overwhelmed with the seemingly endless variances of shades on offer to wear. Let alone the price tag associated with each little piece of lipstick or eyeshadow. Talk about criminal!

What I smelt was a *lot* more than anything a mortal could naturally detect. Lycan blood was heavier, thicker with a tang of our vitality to it that I couldn't mistake. Mortal blood, well, it's flatter, mixed with a chemical burn that normally comes from all the crazy emotions that flood through their hearts, and a sort of earthy, peaty undertone that I think is a by-product of their short lifespans. You can almost taste the decay in the blood, stronger in those who are older or suffering from sickness.

And this was no lycan blood.

The trace grew stronger as I moved through the gym, nothing of it staining the equipment or towels placed around the room. I followed it into the laundry room. Definitely mortal blood, and from the flavours, a mixture of more than one. There were notes of sickness, of rot that came from abuse like alcoholism or drug use, and bitter after-tones of age. Whomever the stuff came from had not been young, and had not been in the best of health.

"What shit have you been up to, mate?" I asked softly to myself, as I started hunting round the large room. Nothing in the clothes basket, except for some gym gear that definitely needed a clean. The washing machine was equally free of incriminating evidence. No trace of the blood inside or on it.

Maybe I was jumping at shadows. There were any number of reasons why I was smelling blood down here. Jacob worked protection on the mists, as well as the tougher hunts our pack handled. Any of these could have involved interactions with mortals, possibly victims that had bled over him as he dealt with whatever horror was attacking them. Or there was always the chance some complete idiot, off their face on alcohol or drugs, had tried to mug him and he'd dealt them a bloody nose to teach them a lesson. It happened sometimes in London.

On the other hand, he hadn't mentioned any such thing recently, and the blood taint was not old. Jacob was private, but surely he would have said if mortals had gotten hurt on a hunt, or someone had been stupid enough to try to fight him.

Surely?

Several cupboards sat at floor level, filled with cleaning supplies for the boat. House. Jacob's floating home, whatever. I pushed aside bottles of bleach, scrubbing brushes and clothes, as the smell of blood grew stronger.

Pushed right to the back of the last cupboard, I yanked out an old cardboard box. Someone, probably Jacob, had scrawled *Private* on the outside but that just made me more curious.

"What're you hiding, Jacob? And why so stupidly?" I pondered, as I put everything except the box back and closed the cupboard door. This I picked up off the floor and moved over to the nearest free tabletop.

The box was light, and nothing rattled when I shook it. I was guessing it wasn't any more vials of Wolfsbane, which was a good thing. Not so good, the smell of blood was stronger now and definitely coming from inside.

I carefully pulled back the flaps, opening it away from me in case it was, oh I don't know, boobytrapped or anything came flying out of it at my face. You just never know when opening a strange box that had been hidden away and which smelt highly suspicious. I've seen the movies.

When nothing attacked me or blew up, I reached inside and carefully lifted out the contents.

It was a t-shirt and set of leggings, the sort you might wear out to go running or possibly to sleep in. Both of a size to fit Jacob, and both smelling of him enough for me to know they were clothes he'd worn more than a few times.

And both were liberally splashed with dried blood.

The t-shirt had splodges of it flaking away, and several marks that might have been made by someone's hand, drenched in blood, swiping down the material. The leggings were stained thickly on the calf sections and around the ankles, again with marks like someone had pressed against them whilst bleeding heavily.

The blood was definitely mortal, and stank enough of illness, rough living and poor diet that I couldn't ignore the obvious conclusion. No matter the fact I'd disproved my worries with what the Morrigan had told me.

This put Jacob at Greenwich Park, at the scene where the homeless people had been butchered. He had been there, and had been involved. Most likely actually done the fucking killing.

Jacob was the killer.

And that's when I caught the unmistakable stink of Wolfsbane, and heard the rasp of breath behind me.

Turns out, Jacob *could* sneak up on me.

I slowly set the clothes down on the side and turned to face my packmate. The sense of him was tainted with the rank toxicity of the poison he'd taken, but there was something mixed with it, a scent that was nothing to do with Jacob or the Wolfsbane. It was familiar, I just couldn't place it.

He was standing in the doorway to the laundry area, the light painting shadows over his broad, solid features. His eyes were closed, his breathing ragged and his stance was sending warning signals to my hindbrain without bothering to check in with what made sense in my head.

"Jacob." I greeted him quietly, nodding back to the clothes I'd laid out in full view. "Mind telling me just what the fuck those are? And why you hid them?"

He gave a throaty chuckle in reply, rasping and definitely not the sort of laugh he normally made. I always thought Jacob saw laughter as a waste of breath, to be gotten over with as soon as possible. This rasping laugh sounded more like the cackle of a hyena, as he slowly raised his head and looked at me.

This was not Jacob.

My packmate had strong Nordic features, with his blonde curling hair and sharp blue eyes. There was definitely Viking in his DNA, probably from the days of the Wolf Brothers and their voyages across the oceans, when no sheep was safe.

Now, he stared at me with glowing, amber eyes, lit with feral intelligence. Definitely not his own. His lips were curled up in a savage smile, and his features somehow seemed … heavier. More brutal. Shadows pooled unnaturally around him, and the air was filled with that weird smell, getting stronger with each breath.

"Who the fuck are you, and what have you done to my mate?"

He simply shook his head, barking that strange laugh. Then he came at me.

I'm no slouch when it comes to instinct, and knowing when someone's going to swing a punch at me. I was already reaching for my Wyld-born strength, Ivory flames shimmering around my right hand as I sought the armour it bestowed on me.

None of that helped.

Jacob, or the Jacob-lookalike I faced, simply barrelled into me. Before I could knock his hands aside, he had grabbed hold of me, pulling me close so we were pressed almost nose to nose.

"You will know me soon enough, Morgan Black." Whatever the fuck it was possessing Jacob rasped, the stink of its nature in every breath. *"For I am your God!"*

Then the fucker hurled me through the wall. Into the night amongst the crash of broken timber and shattered metal, to slam into the freezing water outside the boat.

Chapter 21

Fire

Fire is an effective weapon against the supernatural, as it will prevent many creatures from healing from mortal wounds inflicted on them. The hydra will regrow any body part hewn from it unless fire is used to cauterise the wound. Burning the bodies of the newly risen dead will often effectively prevent them from returning back to un-life, unless they are particularly powerful or possessed of a truly dark intent. Most usually this is the desire to punish their killers.

However, fire is useless against creatures of no corporeal form, and will not ward against ghosts, wraiths or any of their ilk. Nor will it be effective against creatures of undeath that have fed on the living, so vampires, ghouls and the like are not stopped by flame. Many a mortal has gone to their grave, thinking themselves safe with a simple burning torch, and learned the error of their ways before their lives are lost.

I was still fuming when I pulled myself out of the freezing water. Sodden, humiliated and confused as fuck.

No matter their great advancements in technology, the mortals still hadn't created a mobile phone that handled being dunked in Thames water that well. If at all. With my phone waterlogged, I had no way to alert Jessica and the rest of the pack to either Jacob having a psychotic reaction to Wolfsbane, or that *something* was wearing him like a meat-suit. Either way, he was out and about, and I reckoned intent on causing more carnage and bloodshed.

The scent I'd gotten from him made me think this was something using him. Possessing him somehow. Which shouldn't be possible, given our natural resistance and general ability to say *fuck you* to anything supernatural trying that shit on us. Unless you're stupid enough to invite them in or weaken yourself against them. Like, say, signing a document in your own blood to allow a hex to take hold, or in this case, dosing oneself on the only poison that royally fucks us up.

Had to be the Wolfsbane. It made sense that if Jacob had been weakening himself in a desperate attempt to get enough rest to allow himself to still operate, then this spirit or thing from the Real or whatever it was had found him pliable and easier to manipulate.

I am your God.

The four words echoed in my head as I squelched my way around the quay, headed back to Jacob's boat. I was pretty sure he wasn't at home, instead out and about butchering whatever poor bastard he came across, so I wasn't worried about another dunking. What I did want was to find towels to dry off with, fresh clothes I could nick and hopefully an unlocked phone I could call Jessica on to give her the good news.

I'd be too late to stop whatever was going to happen tonight, but I could at least warn my pack.

Part of me, the reckless and less sensible side that I let rule me a lot more than I should, wanted to do the stupid thing. Hunt for his scent and go track him on my own. See if I could be the hero and save a life. But tackling Jacob on my own in normal times would have been a feat in itself, and not one I'd have put money on winning unless I cheated and used my Court talents. Him in the grip of some supernatural crazy that thought it was a God? Well, the fact it had tossed me around like a rag doll told me it was monstrously strong, way stronger than its host. That was Alpha level strength, so I wanted serious back up before I went head-to-head with it again.

What if he hurts someone you care about? Like Felix? Your packmates? Sarah? The treacherous voice in my head whispered, and I cursed, adding speed to my steps.

Towels and clothes were easily sourced, given I didn't fancy walking around Jacob's home butt naked just in case he did reappear suddenly. That would be hard to explain, no matter if he was possessed or his normal self.

The phone situation proved trickier to solve, as I should have expected. He *did* have at least two work phones that I found without having to look too hard. Both however were locked with facial recognition, so I couldn't even use the old trick of Sellotape and an old thumb print to fool the thing's logic. My own phone, and the one OPS had given me, were out of action until I got them completely dry, so unless I sent up bloody smoke signals or something, my only option was to hightail it over to the office and hope one of the pack were still on site and working.

Smoke signals. Huh. There was always another option if you thought about it long enough. Usually a crazy one, but then, what the hell …

Mobile phones have this neat function where you can still make a call even if you can't unlock the bloody thing. It's limited to making an emergency call to 999 in the UK, which for most people is pretty useless since the last thing they want to do is call the police or fire service.

But for me, right now, it was perfect.

Five minutes after I'd spoken to a very nice young woman, both phones lit up with an incoming call. And I didn't need Face ID to pick it up.

"Jacob?" Jessica's voice came through, not clouded by sleep and as clear as if it were not some ungodly hour of the night when every sensible mortal or lycan should be fast asleep.

"Nope, Morgan. We've got a problem." I replied, and when Jessica remained silent, took the hint and filled her in on what had just happened.

My Alpha was quiet for a little longer, then when she spoke, her tone was one that brooked no argument.

"Ah will alert Emma and the rest of the pack. They will start the hunt fer Jacob, and ah will speak tae the rest of the Alphas in case any other lycan runs into him whilst he is … not hisself." She told me, no emotion betrayed in her voice that she was opening a hunt on one of her own pack. "Ah assume the report of a fire at Jacob's home was yer doing?"

"I needed to get hold of you, and I know you keep tabs on all your pack and their homes." I replied. It was thoroughly illegal, the tap that Jessica had in place to alert her if any emergencies were recorded by the mortal services at one of her own pack's homes. But since she was using her Oracle system to do it, it wasn't as if she was *really* breaking the mortal rules by using any software to run the hack. Supernatural forces weren't covered in their regulations and fine print, we'd checked. "But I can set fire to the place to make it look authentic? I owe the bastard for dumping me in the water."

"That was nae Jacob." Jessica reprimanded me lightly, as ever the soul of logic. "Burning down his home when he is obviously not hisself, and under the influence of something malign, will nae do anyone any good."

"Yeah, fine." I groused, knowing she was right. "You want me to head over and join the hunt?"

"No, I dinnae think that will help much." She replied after a moment's thought. "Better you stay at his home. If he shows up, call it in and ah will have the team there tae support you. Dinnae think of tackling him alone, Morgan."

"Oh no fear. I've already tangled with him once and you know how that ended." I growled, with the sure knowledge it would probably take way more than me to subdue him, if Jacob were possessed by some bat-shit crazy Real fuckwit. "Jessica, tell the team not to mess around. He's seriously strong, way more than normal. They need to pile on him as soon as they can, and not fuck around."

"Dinnae worry. Ah intend tae *personally* deal with Jacob as soon as we find him." She reassured me. I just had to hope an Alpha would be enough to stop him. Him and whatever the fuck was messing with him.

"Ok, cool. Just call me if he shows up."

"Ah will. Ah'll also cancel the emergency call fer the fire services, so you dinnae forget and have some explaining tae do when they show up." She helpfully offered, knowing me all too well.

"Thanks, boss." I replied before she hung up.

Two hours passed, whilst I took advantage of Jacob's facilities, washing and drying my clothes so that I could strip out of his borrowed gear and back into my laundered and only slightly damp garments. I kept an ear out for any sign of him showing up, knowing I'd recognise the strange scent that must belong to whatever creature was inside him. He'd gotten the spring on me once, but never again.

Checking the time and finding that it was gone one a.m., I brewed up some coffee and devoured the remains of the snacks left by Jacob when he was himself. I was finishing up a second mug of quality java when the phone I'd borrowed rang.

"We've got him." Jessica told me as soon as I connected.

"Where?" I asked, setting aside the mug. "Is he himself? No glowing eyes and a serious fucking God complex?"

"He showed up at the office. Emma and Georgia were just heading out when he came in through the front door." My Alpha told me. "He was himself, but covered in blood and obviously still affected by Wolfsbane. He knew something was wrong, and told them tae put him in the cells immediately. He's there now."

"I'll head straight in." I felt a cold certainty in my gut, realising he had killed again. I needed to speak to him find out who his victim had been. If it was anyone I knew.

"Ah will see you when you get here. There's a taxi headed tae your location already." Jessica had evidently known I'd want to be there when we talked to Jacob, conscious of my worries before I'd even really thought them through. "And Morgan? Ah understand yer concerns. But remember, this *is* Jacob. And he needs our help, first and foremost."

The taxi showed up within five minutes, giving me just enough time to dump my mug and plate into the dishwasher and grab up his keys from where he'd left them on the counter. I had no way of knowing if the wards would activate if I simply locked his front door or if they needed something more. But the least I could do was make sure his home was shut when I left it.

Of course, there was nothing I could do about the gaping hole in the laundry room wall I'd made when I was thrown through it. If someone were *that* interested in getting inside the boat, I'd leave it to Jacob to deal with them if and when he got back home.

That being a big fucking *if*, right now.

Forty minutes later, I walked into our offices. Daniel was manning the front desk, which at close to two in the morning was not normally a thing we bothered with. But I figured there was every chance the shit that Jacob had pulled earlier could well have people knocking on the door. Serious people, looking for the perpetrator of more bloody murder.

He gave me a nod, the easy smile he normally wore absent on his face. He was twanging like a taught wire to my senses, confusion and more than a little fear bubbling up through his normally calm demeanour.

"Jessica is with him," My packmate told me, nodding to the floor at our feet. "Emma, too. The rest of the pack are out, looking for his ... for whoever got hurt."

I nodded, knowing my packmates would be looking to clean up any evidence if it wasn't too late, and get enough details to handle the situation if it was.

Good Deeds, as I've mentioned, was laid out with a client reception on the ground floor, and our main office on the first. Jessica and Mark had claimed the top floor of the building for their living space. This is being central London, there was no attic space above us.

However, there *was* a sublevel. When it had been an embassy, the basement had been mostly used as storage, with some secure rooms set aside for *discreet conversations* that needed to take place away from public eyes or anyone listening. To protect those speaking from legal repercussions or to muffle the screams, depending on the type of 'talking' being done.

We'd made use of the additional floorspace, opening it up and blocking off all access except for a single route down from the first-floor offices and a direct entrance out back leading from the parking bays. Always handy to have an easy route to offload anything we'd picked up on a hunt without having to walk them past potential clients, or leave messy blood-trails all over the carpet.

Now the basement held cells, holding pens built from scratch with cold iron and silver. Elspeth and a few other specialists had been employed to further improve the containment capabilities, so that we had a full twenty units available for our use. Strong enough to contain most Real creatures, warded to keep those incarcerated from making any efforts to escape or to damage the building in a fit of pique before we handed them over to the Furies for due punishment.

They were certainly strong enough to hold a lycan, which is why I figured Jacob had volunteered to be shut up in one.

Part of me wanted to take a moment, grab one of the nearby phones and call Sarah and Felix. Make sure they were ok, that nothing like a crazed lycan on PCP with glowing eyes had gate-crashed their lives with intent to do harm. But since Jacob was right there, waiting, I figured I might as well get the bad news from the horse's mouth. It's not like I could do much at the end of a phone, to be honest.

So, growling with the urge to punch my packmate *very* hard, I sprinted through the office and took the stairs at the back of the meeting rooms down.

Recently, a trio of trolls had set up home in one of the holding cells, after they had narrowly escaped being turned into rubble by a particularly nasty Wyld goblin by the name of Red Cap. I'd saved their skin, and Jessica had offered them sanctuary in exchange for sworn testimonies on their involvement in the kidnapping of young men and women for both the Nighters pack and Robert Knox. Neither of whom were kicking around anymore, but she liked to know *all* the details, and the evidence the little fuckers had given us had helped identify some of the victims, which Jess had duly handed over anonymously to the relevant authorities. Some grieving parents or kin had at least been told the worst news, but given a chance to stop hoping and move on with their lives however they could.

We weren't called *Good Deeds* for nothing.

Jessica, wily coyote that she was, had also bound the trolls into becoming our version of snitches. Informants. Not stopping them from going about their illegal and immoral ways, as that would have been a useless task given this particular trio did *nothing* but break the rules. However, she had turned them, and now we had another set of ears on the ground for anything major happening in the supernatural community. It never hurt to add to our pool of resources, and I'd lost a major one when I'd first had a certain weapons-dealer gnome bound over and handed to the Furies for punishment, and then let the fucker slip through my fingers and run off to the Real.

The Furies *still* held that over me, and when things were settled here, I fully intended to jump Real-side and hunt the little runt down and kick his arse all the way back to the Furies' loving embrace.

It seemed the brothers Bung – Tol, Dol and Mull – had caught wind of the trouble that night, as they were conspicuously absent from their nest of blankets, cushions and rugs that they'd purloined to make the cell a cosy, stinking and highly unsanitary troll-hole. Probably out fleecing some unfortunates of their worldly goods, or chasing down errant pigeons and seagulls for a morning snack.

I took a breath, having run across the office space, to calm myself … instantly regretting it when I got a mouthful of troll musk. Coughing, I collected myself before I carried on into the room where I could see Jessica and Emma waiting.

And in the furthest cell, a hulking dark shape that I knew was both my packmate … but now also a brutal murderer of innocents.

Time to find out just what the *fuck* was going on.

Chapter 22

"Morgan." Jessica greeted me. Emma nodded in my direction, the hard line of her chin and the scents she was giving off telling me how confused she was, and just how pissed.

"Jessica. Emma." I looked across to where Jacob sat in the middle of the cell. Each one was furnished in true jail fashion. No benches or chairs to handily break and give the inmates primitive weapons to use on us or their fellow occupants. Or themselves. "He said anything yet?"

Emma shrugged.

"Not much. Think he was waiting for you to show up." She answered. That fact did *nothing* to reassure me.

They'd stripped him of the bloodstained clothes he'd worn, putting him in simple leggings and a t-shirt, one of the many bundles of clothes we kept around the office to deal with the problems of us Changing and ruining perfectly good gear. Normally we were clever enough to wear stuff that had enough give in it to handle the difference in body mass and shape, but there were always the odd times when we were caught unprepared. And having butt naked lycan wandering around the office floor was distracting to potential clients, to say the least.

I walked over to the bundle of stained clothes. The blood was already drying, splashes of gore soaking his pants and top, like the set I'd found in the laundry room. Bracing myself, I lifted up the top and took a long sniff.

As I've said, blood to lycans is a multi-layered substance, far from the simple red fluid mortals see when it gets spilled. It tells a story, of the owners health, their history, their state of mind when the stuff had been shed.

I was dreading scenting anything that told me this was from people I cared about. Felix, Sarah, Danny. It was a small number of mortals outside of the pack, but they were close-knit to me and perfect targets for anyone wanting to make me hurt.

The blood was … none of them. I got age, so not from anyone young, and hints to tell me that the person it had belonged to smoked heavily, drank and had several infirmities to make me think they were elderly and not in the best of health. But no one I recognised, which was a relief.

Of course, the person was probably dead, and had died scared out of their mind from the other scents in the blood, so I didn't do a dance of joy or any shit like that. Wouldn't have been appropriate.

"Now, Jacob. Morgan is here. Are you willing tae tell us what transpired tae lead you here, in this cell?" Jessica asked, her tone calm and cool. No sign of the anger she must be feeling, the stress of one of her own pack involved in such a fucked-up situation.

Jacob looked up from where he had been staring at his hands, clenched together. There was still blood staining his skin, but it looked like he'd tried to scrape some of it off as flakes littered the cell floor. Whether because, like an idiot, he was trying to get rid of evidence or just wanted the stuff off his hands, I didn't know. But Jacob wasn't an idiot.

Well, not normally.

"Not much to tell." He replied, his voice leaden. Defeated. There wasn't even any anger in his tone, just pain that ran from deep inside. Linked to the knowledge he'd been used to do something horrific. "Last thing I remember, I was heading to bed, leaving Morgan on the couch. I took the dose of Wolfsbane, then crashed out. The usual sickness kicked in straight away, but I normally ride that out pretty quick, and I fell asleep as I intended. No dreams, just unconsciousness."

He shook his head.

"But this time, it was different. I thought I was dreaming. Felt like I was moving, talking. Maybe even fighting. You were there, Morgan … then you weren't." He looked across at me, eyes hooded and dark. "Next thing, I was elsewhere. I think I was trying to get inside somewhere but couldn't. Something stopped me, and I was angry. Filled with rage. Then I remember a voice, a woman's. Older. Think she challenged me to start with. Then … screams."

He looked down at his hands, spreading them out, splaying his fingers.

"Next thing I know, I was awake, standing over a dead body. Bits of one. It had been ripped to shreds. Blood all over me. I *knew* I had murdered the mortal but I couldn't remember doing it." Jacob shook his head again, clenching his hands so that blood flaked off and fell to the cell floor. "I figured I needed to get somewhere safe, someplace I could shut myself away so I didn't hurt anyone else. The cells seemed an obvious choice."

"Do you remember where you were? And how the hell did you get here without causing a shitstorm, given you're like painted in gore?" I asked without waiting, seeing Jessica shoot me a look. I know she wanted to get the truth as much as I did, but she would want to handle things delicately. I, on the other hand, preferred the *'bull in a china shop'* approach. Gets me results.

It seemed Jacob also preferred cutting through the niceties and getting the truth told, as he looked across at me, nodding.

"It was Greenwich. I saw a street sign. *Hyde Vale Road.*" He confirmed, and I felt that *suspicious bastard* bell go off in my head again. "As for how I got here without raising the alarm? I simply mugged the first mortal I could find who was on a phone. Left them unconscious and safe, without letting them see me. Dialled up a cab from the firm and headed on in. The mortal will be ok apart from a sore head, and I wiped the phone of prints and replaced it, so he won't know it was ever used."

Jessica looked across at Emma, who nodded and pulled out her mobile. She was calling in the location of the dead mortal, to see if we could get packmates over there urgently. Given Jacob remembered hearing her screaming, it was doubtful the murder had gone unnoticed for this long, but sometimes we got lucky.

My packmate would also call the taxi company we used, to let them know to burn the number Jacob had called them on. Remove all traces of it, something they had done before and offered as part of the *professional services* for select clients. I didn't know how they managed it, but within an hour of Emma's call, no trace of that number would exist, just a discontinued service that would lead nowhere even if the police followed up the mugging and chanced a look at the phone's call records.

We had a handful of numbers to use to book their services, so it would just mean switching to one of the others. No biggie, if it meant this shit didn't lead back to our doorstep.

"Jess," Jacob switched his attention back to our Alpha, expression pained. "It wasn't the Wolfsbane. I *felt* like something else was controlling me. Something with a will of its own, and a definite goal. It wanted into wherever it was I got taken to, and it'll try again. It doesn't care about killing anything that gets in its way, whether that's mortals or … others. Don't know why it chose me, but I'm not safe to be outside these bars until you find out what it is and deal with it."

"Ah understand, and ah also know it wasn't you that did this thing." She replied, stepping up and facing him, well within grabbing distance. It was a sign that she trusted him, knew him to be himself right now. "Morgan had already informed me you were not yerself when you threw him through a wall in your home. This creature that possessed you, it claims tae be the God of us. That gives us somewhere tae start looking, but ah agree, you cannae be let loose until we know more."

"A God? Hnh." Jacob grunted, then looked back across at me. "I threw you through a wall?"

"Yeah. Laundry room. Right into the water." I shrugged, my animosity towards my packmate melting away after seeing just what a shit state he was in, how badly it had cut him to be used this way. "You've got a fucking big hole in your boat, but I don't think she'll sink. Shouldn't be too difficult to patch up, whenever you're, um, yourself again."

"Cheers." He grunted, and I caught the sense of relief he felt at finding his home was still in one piece. I'd felt the same after finding Robert Knox's retaliation against my apartment block had been blunted by my fae grandmother.

I was still getting complaints fielded through my managing agent company, about electrical short-circuits and loss of power, but I had bitten my lip to date and not asked the tenants if they would have preferred being barbecued by a supernatural fire storm. I'm good like that.

Emma interrupted any further dialogue, accepting an incoming call on the second ring. She spoke quietly for a moment, then hung up and turned to Jessica.

"Kris and Pippa are on site. The police are there too and taping off the area." She confirmed, the mortal authorities showing a surprising punctuality to calls of someone being brutally murdered in the street. That sort of thing happened too much in London these days. "No one is stepping forward as a witness, and there's no mention of a description of the suspect. Just that someone tried to break into number 67 Hyde Vale Road, then assaulted and brutally murdered the neighbour from 69 when she came out to investigate."

That pretty much nailed it for me. Whatever had been controlling Jacob, driving him like its own demolition machine, had been after the home of Sarah's missing colleague. Even I had to admit the clues were painting a big fat arrow down on this one, and I would be an idiot to ignore the link.

"Well, that's something." Jessica replied, expression set. "If nae description was given, and ah believe Jacob covered his presence and exit from the scene effectively, we should focus on identifying the entity at the core of this event. Fer all our sakes."

She placed a hand on the bars of the cell, Jacob already reading her expression and guessing what came next.

"Until we know more of this thing, ah agree you cannae be let loose. Fer yer own safety, and the safety of the pack and the mortals." She told him, and he nodded, accepting the simple truth. "Ah will arrange fer more comfortable fittings tae be brought down here, now ah believe you are in control of yerself. But in there you'll stay until we unmask this creature who thinks it can use one of mah pack as a weapon. And make it regret its ill-choice."

Jessica looked across as I coughed, raising a hand.

"This is nae school, Morgan. If you have something tae say, spit it out."

"Yes boss." I answered, and dove on in. "The address Jacob ... the thing controlling Jacob ... was trying to get inside? It's the home of the missing professor, the one Sarah asked me to locate. We've got several butchered homeless transients, killed in a similar brutal way, and the fact this mortal used to spend time with them at night as well. Everything's pointing to this thing and him being connected somehow, so I guess I'm up for finding whatever the fuck is going on here?"

Our Alpha thought for a moment, then nodded, stepping away from the cell.

"You'd best go check out this mortal's home, since this thing was so keen tae gain entrance." She instructed me. "In the meantime, ah'll reach out tae mah contacts fer any reference to a creature thinking itself God of our kin. You may want tae ask Felicity, see if anything in Elspeth's library may be of use too."

I nodded, not wanting to tell my Alpha I'd already been thinking along those lines.

"Fer now, ah think …" Jessica began.

Then she collapsed.

Our Alpha went down like something had swept her feet from under her, slumping to the floor in a dead faint. Emma was at her side in the next breath, me a moment later whilst Jacob was up on his feet and jerking his head around, searching for an assailant or where an attack was coming from.

Jessica stirred, even as Emma began checking her for wounds or sign of whatever had happened. Our Alpha coughed, beads of sweat glistening on her forehead, and she looked at the pair of us with momentary confusion.

"What happened?" She asked, voice rasping slightly as Emma helped her to her feet. Jessica swayed for a moment, before she seemed to gather herself. Taking slow breaths, she wiped at her face, staring at the faint perspiration in surprise.

"You fell over. Mid-sentence." I told her, and she shook her head, coughing once more to clear her throat. "Have you been overdoing things lately, boss? Not getting enough sleep? Not taking your vitamins?"

She shot me a hard look, and I shut up.

"It's the same thing that's happening to the rest of the packs, Jessica." Jacob spoke up, having found nothing in the basement to explain a sudden attack, anything that could be blamed for what had just happened. "Lycan feeling weak, faint. Nauseous and unsettled. But no Alpha spoke of feeling its effects."

"Until now." She agreed, breathing shallowly. "Ah can attest, ah feel a weakness that is nae natural, but was nae there a moment before. Whatever this thing is, it is spreading."

She looked at the three of us, and I caught sight of something I had never seen in her eyes before.

Fear.

"And none of us are safe, it would seem."

Chapter 23

Wind chimes

Bells, wind chimes and other musical devices harnessing the power of wind are known to ward off malevolent spirits, but also attract the attention of benevolent creatures dependent on the quality of music produced. Originally church bells were used as a means to ward off the Devil, and any demonic servants, but over time they have become a means to attract creatures of Grace as well with their melodious playing.

Bells are used at weddings to ward off mischievous or malevolent spirits, often the ghosts of former partners, seeking to cause harm to the newly weds or disrupt the service before it can be completed. Here the need is less to be melodic, and more to scare the spirits away with discordant and loud clanging.

The trick to breaking into someone else's home without getting caught is to make it look like you aren't in fact breaking in at all. Like, you belong there. It encourages any witnesses to forget your features when you become just part of the scenery.

I left the office with a new phone, the sim cloned so I had everyone's number to hand, and a few choice tools I'd need to help break into the professor's house. And maybe deal with anything nasty that might be waiting for me inside.

Jacob was talking to Emma when I exited the basement, giving orders to pass to those lycan of the pack still on patrol. Jessica had retired to the second floor, intending to reach out to every Alpha and update them on whatever it was spreading through the packs. No matter the time of morning, how early it was and whether they were sleeping or not. If we were under attack, being afflicted by something that weakened and debilitated us, everyone needed to plan for the worst.

Our Alpha hadn't looked great, to be honest, when I'd left. Her skin had a grey cast to it, and there was a redness to her eyes that for any mortal would have had them bound back to bed with medicine and the day off work. For Jessica, she just set her shoulders and focused on dealing with the trouble in hand. Whilst probably pouring herself a medicinal large glass of whiskey.

I'd arranged for a cab to drop me off near my destination, since I'd had enough of the London transport system getting to Jacob's home, and didn't feel the need to immerse myself any more in the fug of mortals that hung around the tunnels and carriages. Plus, it not being Friday or Saturday, services had ended over two hours ago. Mortals needed their sleep too.

Walking up Hyde Vale Road, with the moon bright in the sky and highlighting everything in iridescent silver, I quickly spotted the flashing blue lights that indicated police were still present and going about their business. They had taped off the road, plastic barriers set round a white tent erected in the road, with a portable generator chugging away for the lights strung inside the structure. The material was of a type to obscure any detail, but my nose picked up the strong scents of blood and spilled organs, flesh ripped and torn unnaturally. Death. A sharp stench, a stain on the street and neighbourhood that would linger far longer than the woman's mortal remains when they were transported elsewhere.

A few of the neighbours were out on the street, standing at the barricades, talking with the officers on duty. I approached, keeping in plain view and walking without hurrying. Just another mortal on his way home, letting surprise show on my face as I took in the scene before me.

"Excuse me, sir. This is an active crime scene, and we're not letting anyone through." I was told by a polite policeman as I approached the barrier.

"Oh god, what happened? Did someone get hurt?" I asked with as much sincerity in my voice as I could feign, only slurred slightly but enough to give the impression I wasn't completely sober.

"There was an incident earlier tonight, sir and I'm sorry to say, yes, someone was involved in a physical altercation. Do you live here?" The man asked, looking me up and down, taking in my details and noting them down mentally. To check against any witness statements or bring in for questioning if I happened to meet any description of the perpetrator. Of which there was none, according to my packmates.

"Yeah, but I'm only crashing. I'm sleeping on Dr Eduardo's sofa. Number 67." I nodded to the house sitting just outside the barriers, beyond the tape. By some luck, Jacob had brutally murdered the neighbour far enough away from her home that *both* houses sat outside the small ringfenced area, leaving my path there unobstructed. But it would have looked weird if I'd walked past the barriers and not asked what had happened. Mortals are serial gawpers.

"Right, well then you wouldn't mind giving me your name, sir? Just for the records?" The policeman politely enquired, and I shrugged, playing the part of someone with nothing to hide.

"Not a problem. Tomas Jeffers, no *h*." I replied, and reached into a pocket. "I guess you'd like to see some ID?"

"If you don't mind, that's very helpful Mr Jeffers." He answered, as I showed him the utterly fake driving licence I had in my totally fake wallet filled with totally fake cards and crap that any mortal man carries around with him. "And you know this Dr Eduardo how?"

"Oh, I met him when he lectured at the university a while back. We've kept in touch, and he lets me crash on his couch when I'm in the country. I do a lot of travelling, you see." I glibly lied, having concocted Tomas Jeffer's back story on the way over. He was one of several false IDs I kept and used as and when needed, just so my name didn't keep showing up on crime scene reports and start attracting too much attention.

Sadly, that wasn't a *completely* full proof plan.

"Tomas? Ah, Tomas, I thought it was you." A voice spoke up behind us, and I slowly turned, knowing who I would find walking towards me. However unlikely.

Cormac bloody Smith.

"Uh hi." I replied, extending a smile and a hand, which he duly shook.

"You know this gentleman, Mr Smith?" The policeman enquired, and Cormac smiled a genuinely warm grin.

"Oh, I do indeed. Though at times I do wonder if anyone *really* knows Tomas Jeffers, with no *h*." He replied, then dismissed the policeman and turned back to me. "It's a stroke of luck me seeing you here. I was just heading over to speak to Dr Eduardo. I guess he isn't in?"

"Uh, no. I don't think so. I was just going to crash, it being so late…?" I replied, trying to work out why an agent of OPS was here, and had been waiting it seemed for either the missing professor or someone showing up looking for him. Neither of my packmates had noticed him, so he'd either arrived later or managed to avoid their attention.

Knowing just how slippery Mr Government Spook was, it was probably the latter.

"Oh, its been so long since I've seen you. Mind if I come inside and we can chat over a coffee? It's not that late, after all?" He steered me away from the barricade and the policeman, the latter no longer interested in me now that I had been identified by someone in authority.

"How did you know I was going by *Tomas Jeffers*?" I asked quietly, under my breath.

Cormac smiled and tapped the side of his head.

"I have excellent hearing, Morgan." He replied somewhat smugly. "Maybe not as good as yours, but enough to make out whatever false name you might be using from across the street. It also helps that I can read lips, too. Now, shall we proceed?"

We walked casually to the front door, set above the street level and reached by a short flight of stairs protected by a small porch. Cormac let me go first, and followed behind, carefully blocking any view of what I did from anyone who might look our way.

"I take it you *can* open the door without breaking anything?" He enquired under his breath, and I gave him the answer he deserved. A grunt, nothing more.

Now, normally, Cormac would have been right to ask. *Normally* I would have just forced the door, and worried about locks and bolts later when it came to putting the thing back in its frame. However, I didn't want any of the onsite police hearing the unmistakeable sound of breaking wood, and come to investigate why I might have caused property damage getting into a house I supposedly had access to.

Instead, I palmed one of the many useful tools I had at my disposal thanks to Jessica's resourcefulness, her contacts in various industries and her willingness to ignore certain legalities if it helped her pack overcome any of the multitude of obstacles presented whilst working in the Mortal Realm. Like locked doors.

It was called a bump key, and owning one ... let alone using one broke several key laws with the uniformed people I had at my back. It pretty much fitted most standard front or back doors manufactured for residential housing or commercial buildings. For accessing someone's home in London, it did the trick after a few wiggles. The lock made a satisfying click, and it was only then that I thought to check there wasn't a second deadlock on the door.

Thankfully, there wasn't.

Through our Alpha's contacts, we'd also picked up some handy little tricks for accessing buildings when we didn't even have bump keys on us. Like being able to slip locks using only a Coca-Cola can at a push. It works, but is fiddly and not best done when the police happen to be standing so close behind me.

As I stepped through the open door, I felt *something*, a presence pressing against me. Like an invisible bubble, inflated to fill the entire house. A warding, definitely one set to protect and deny entry to something specific. For me, it held a moment then let me through. As if I triggered a degree of the protection but not enough to fully engage the crafting. Cormac seemed to have no problem following, not even sensing anything out of the ordinary.

I stopped in the dark hallway, looking around me. Even though the light was off, enough illumination filtered in from outside through the door and windows for me to make out details of where I stood. And a few things that definitely didn't belong.

"I *really* hope the good professor owns this place." I commented dryly, as I looked at the wall nearest me. "Otherwise he has well and truly fucked up his chances of getting his deposit back."

Someone, and I had to guess it had been Professor Julius Eduardo, had removed what looked like fairly non-descript and bland wallpaper from the walls, dumping it in tattered piles on the carpet. Then they had meticulously and with great effort, carved a staggering series of pictograms into the exposed brick, painting the harsh lines with black paint to make them stand out. These ran around the doorway, up the inner surface of the exterior walls and around every window that I could see.

There was a light switch on the wall, and I flicked it on, revealing the place in more detail. I wasn't worried about surprising anything, or revealing our presence, since I could tell the place was empty. It had that feel to it. But I really wanted to get an idea of what had gone on here, and why whatever the fuck had been possessing Jacob had wanted in so badly.

Whilst Cormac closed the door behind us, I stepped over to the wall and looked closely at the artwork enscribed there. I'm no expert on these things so I had no idea if these were Egyptian, Mayan or whatever from their look, but Sarah had said this professor had been passionate about the old South American culture and peoples, so I had to guess it was from their language. And there was one other thing … I leant in and took a good sniff of the paint lining the pictograms.

"Blood. Human." I told Cormac, easily identifying the faint trace I'd sensed from the black liquid. "I'm guessing he mixed a little of his into the paint before he used it. Either that or he's been a very naughty boy and borrowed someone else's."

The OPS agent grunted, taking out his phone and flicking to the camera app. He started taking photos, focusing on the details around us.

"You know, you never said what you're doing here." I commented as I let my senses paint me a picture of the house. It was a three-story building from the outside, with a staircase leading up from the hallway. A small corridor ran past this and ended with two doors, with a third set to my immediate right. A living room, I guessed, from the smells of paper and old furniture. It still had a working fireplace since I caught faint traces of ash and smoke coming from its direction. At the back, most likely the kitchen and dining room, given the scents of food, coffee and an acidic tang from a rubbish bin. Probably a downstairs toilet too if the bleach was any indicator.

"Didn't I? How remiss of me." Cormac replied glibly, as he finished taking photos and went to open the living room door. He shot me a look, obviously asking me if it was safe for him to enter. I shrugged then nodded.

If anything *did* go boom, he was the one stepping into the room first. Not me.

When nothing jumped out or blew the OPS agent up, I followed him in.

The living room was a mess of old plates of half-eaten food, spilled stacks of newspapers and cuttings scattered over a large coffee table and spilled onto the tattered and broken looking sofa. The fireplace had been used not so long ago, with ashes still littering its cast iron cradle. But whomever had done the burning had been paranoid as hell, having not only ignited whatever they wanted destroyed but also then ground the pieces that were left to fine ash. Leaving no handy clues captured on half-burned paper.

The room smelt of old sweat and the chemical tang of cigarette smoke, but there was one overriding flavour that even Cormac seemed to sense despite his limited mortal nose.

Fear.

Wallpaper had been stripped from every surface in here too, and the script painstakingly etched into the plaster and brickwork. I had no idea how long such efforts would have taken the professor, but given the wreckage he had left behind, it had not been done that long ago. Something had changed recently, forcing him to take such drastic actions in his own home. To keep him safe. But from what?

"So?" I prompted, figuring there wasn't much to be gained in this room and heading toward the door. Cormac went to follow, but I blocked the doorway, crossing my arms and looking at him with one eyebrow cocked. "Why are you here?"

The agent sighed, and nodded to the room's disreputable state.

"The same reason you are, I would suggest. To try and find out what happened to Professor Julius Marino Eduardo. Now, we can chat later but for now, I believe there are several more rooms to search. Might we do so before I catch you up on current events, and you tell me what you know about the slaughter outside?"

I shrugged, and stepped out of the way.

"Be my guest." I gestured for him to pass through, and he nodded in thanks.

One thing I was sure. There was *no* fucking way I was going to drop Jacob into the shit with OPS, just so they could cart him off to the depths of Tower Hill or some other secret hideaway and dissect him to see what, if anything, remained of the creature that had possessed him.

I'd find out what OPS knew, what their involvement was in this mess. And then happily lie through my back teeth if it kept my packmate out of their hands.

It's what he would have done for me. It's what made us what we were.

Pack.

Chapter 24

We hit paydirt on the top floor.

I'd been right in my guess as to the layout of the ground floor, with a dirty kitchen piled with more unwashed plates and cutlery, half-drunk mugs of coffee crowding the countertops. There was a small toilet off the back of this, and it was in here that I found pots of black paint, a bread knife marked with old blood and a stirring stick stained with crusted paint. It didn't take Sherlock Holmes to work out this was where Julius Eduardo had shed and mixed his own blood into the stuff he'd used on the walls.

The dining room was another mess of paper clippings and discarded food, scattered atop a wooden table. Three chairs were sat around, making me wonder where number four had gotten to. But there was nothing left to tell us anything. No hint about the professor, or whatever the hell had gotten him so scared as to stain the very air inside the house.

The first floor was equally unhelpful. Two bedrooms, one front and one back, sat on either side of a bathroom. Both beds looked like they hadn't been slept in for a while. Wardrobes were open, and clothes were strewn over the floor, in the haphazard manner that usually is associated with a woman frantically trying to choose an outfit for a night out somewhere glamorous. Or a man trying to find the one shirt he wants to wear amongst all the others that just won't do, to be fair. Or the general state of a child's bedroom just before their parents discover the mess and order them to clean up or all privileges would be revoked.

Just normal, everyday mess. Apart from the ever-present torn wallpaper and scratched and painted markings on every wall. Those were far from normal or everyday. Even for me.

The bathroom told me one little detail. The professor had been planning to leave his home, possibly flee somewhere else that he thought would be a better sanctuary. All his toiletries were packed away in an old bag, the sort used for travelling. I poked around, finding the usual Toothbrush, toothpaste, shaving kit. And several plastic containers marked as *Caffeine tablets, 250 mg, 100 tablets*. One was empty, the second half full, which made me think the mortal had been popping them by the dozen.

Everything I was finding told me the man's mental state had been fragile, to say the least, and he'd obviously been terrified of something. So much so that his life had fallen apart around him, and he'd taken some, frankly, desperate steps to protect himself. But from what? And why?

A single staircase led to the third floor, which was a landing with a single door at its centre. I guess it had been a converted loft, intended to be another bedroom, but Julius had obviously repurposed it with his personal fixation in mind.

It was an office, the walls marked like all the others below, but half hidden behind white boards that had been hung wherever possible, or large swathes of paper where not. A large desk, that had to have been put together inside the room since it wouldn't have fitted through the door, let alone up the stairs, was heaped with books and scattered papers, accompanied by various artefacts and odd-looking objects that must have come from some of his explorations. That, or he'd been stealing stuff from the Museum.

"What do you think we're looking for?" I asked helpfully, staring at the mess in the office. It smelt of the man, he'd definitely spent a lot of time up here, without the windows open to bring in any fresh air. "A nicely written note explaining all the shit downstairs and where the professor has buggered off to, maybe?"

Without concrete proof, which I hoped to get just as soon as the Sisters replied with a time and place to meet the survivor of the Greenwich Park slaughter, I still only had suspicions that Julius Eduardo was dead, and not hiding someplace. But Cormac didn't need to know that, so I might as well play the dumb lycan for a while and see what he knew.

Cormac, however, wasn't playing along.

"Have you been in contact with Dr Sarah Conner recently?" He asked instead, the left-field question catching me so that for a moment I had to re-align my thoughts. Hop from possibly dead man to very much alive woman.

"Uh, I'm sure you know the answer to that. Coz I doubt she's been wandering around London without you keeping tabs on her." I shot back at him, feeling my anger at how she had been treated ignite. "But ok, yep, I would say I have been *in contact* with Sarah. And on that subject, just what the fuck? You said you were taking her somewhere far away to come to terms with what she had witnessed. That she'd get help, that you lot were *experienced* in handling situations like hers. Instead, how the fuck did she end up at a digsite in the arse end of nowhere, attacked by bloody drug runners? Whose *brilliant* idea was that?!"

Cormac looked across at me, from where he was examining some of the writing on the nearest whiteboard.

"I will take that as a *yes* then." He replied dryly, before shaking his head. "Dr Conner's rehabilitation was scheduled to take place at the digsite just outside Sao Paulo, as I had arranged. A place she could devote to her calling, whilst carefully selected specialists who we arranged to work alongside her would have provided support and clarity as and when she needed it. That had been my plan, but as we all know, such things have an unfortunate habit of being screwed up by larger events. Ripples caused, you might say."

"You're talking about Moggie setting up shop in South London, aren't you?" I surmised with a scowl, knowing where this was headed. "You seriously cannot be pinning Sarah being kicked off to some Gods-forsaken site on us, just coz we couldn't stop one bloody immortal? Not everything is our fucking fault, just so you know."

"Ripples, Morgan." He replied, before taking a breath. I stepped to the desk and set my arse on its edge, knowing I was either going to get a very boring explanation as to why everything was my fault, or a dressing down. Neither of which I was particularly in the mood for.

"I am sure your Alpha is aware, but most likely you are not. London is not the only city to have seen mists arise. In the past six months, OPS has coordinated with our counterparts and been informed of incidents occurring at locations in both North and South America, Europe and Asia. New York, San Francisco, New Orleans. Frankfurt, Paris, Naples. Saint Petersburg, Odesa. Singapore, Fukuoka. Melbourne. Sites across the globe, all far smaller than what we have seen in London. Some of the mists have simply swallowed a block, a building or warehouse. But they are the same. Nothing can get in, and whatever was there before has vanished."

Fuck. I let that truth sink in, its meaning all too clear. The mists were linked to Twilight, raised by Morgana to protect her Court from her kin, from Ivory and Shadow, even the Wyld. If they had started showing up in other countries, it meant Twilight was linked to these places too. For what purpose, I had no clue but if it involved the sister of Madb, then it could be nothing good.

"Still doesn't explain why Sarah … Dr Conner was shunted off to this new digsite?" I groused. "She needed help, not more stress."

Cormac shook his head, expression closed.

"It was not my idea. Unfortunately, the instruction came from my superiors who I have little or no influence over in terms of their decisions." He admitted, shrugging his shoulders. "The discovery needed a specialist to attend, someone who might be able to verify some oddities which the initial investigation had thrown up around bones found at the site. And here was a specialist of all things zoological, only a short distance away, already practically prepared for the work. Just different bones. My superiors thought the risk to her mental stability and well-being was worth the chance that something from *our* side of things had been uncovered. Just in case it turned out to be something which needed burying again."

"Hold on a sec." I held up a hand, my hindbrain having worked through all the new information and had come up with a fairly big question mark. In blinking red. Bright neon, in fact. "If these mists have shown up all over the world, why the fuck haven't I heard about it? Seen it in the news, splashed all over the papers or all over the internet? The mists of London are all over the headlines and conspiracy chat blogs, so why not the other sites?"

Cormac actually laughed at that, a bark of joviality that broke his normally distant and controlled persona.

"Oh, Morgan, surely you know the answer to that. We had no control over the information leak when the mists initially appeared, but it has suited our purpose to keep everyone's attention locked on the event *here*, and not worrying about what is happening in their own backyard." He shook his head, the smile so out of place on his face. "I won't bore you with the details, but rest assured. OPS, and our counterparts on the other continents, are working hand in hand with government officials and many of the clandestine organisations which exist to protect us mortals from our biggest enemy. Ourselves. And we have *any* potential leaks or sources of information around the mists being a globally phenomenon sewn up tight."

"Hnh." I grunted. Mortals had shown themselves thoroughly incapable of handling the reality of the Real, of what lived amongst them, what lay before them after they died. They'd invented pantheons of Gods and Goddesses, helped along by mischievous or bored immortals who fancied a little bit of worship and adoration to pass the centuries. Whole mythologies created to salve their fears about what happened when they died, and whether the good would be rewarded and the bad punished.

The funny thing really was the number of similarities between religions, where it was so obvious mortals had stolen ideas from someone else's fantasy. Changed the names a bit, swapped a couple of sexes, and voila, a whole new religion and bunch of deities to bow to. The number of great floods that had occurred in the Mortal Realm, the place should be underwater by now. And don't get me started on the incongruity of skin colour for certain biblical characters, when a little bit of research about the natives of a region would paint a very big WTF over the artist's choice of pigment and bone structure.

But I digressed.

"Fine. So you've got a handle on the shit hitting the fan. For now." I scowled, coming back to the one point I knew he hadn't properly answered, and one I felt needed dealing with. "I still haven't heard a proper answer why Dr Conner was dumped in the middle of a bloody war zone, with drug runners and guerrillas and whatever else threatening her life, and those of her colleagues? Why was this even allowed, if the site was so dangerous? And don't give me the *site of importance* and *risks were balanced* crap. If there was a chance people were going to get hurt, someone up the bloody ladder should have blocked the expedition until it was made safe."

Cormac looked at me, his grey eyes searching mine for a long moment, looking for something. Then he shook his head.

"You seem to be labouring under a misunderstanding, Morgan, and I believe Dr Conner is as well. Which is understandable given her recent traumatic experiences, whilst you have less of an excuse." He answered finally. "The fact is, there were *no* drug related criminals working in the area of the dig site. Nor guerrillas, except possibly the hairy variety that try to steer clear of humans as much as they can where possible. No volatility at all, except from potential thieves and the local tribes people. Those who might have ventured into the site to obtain artefacts to sell onwards to rich Europeans wanting to have a nice paper weight on their desk."

He nodded to Professor Eduardo's collection of objects he had piled on his tabletop, as supporting evidence to his statement.

"That doesn't make any sense." I countered, remembering what Sarah had told me. "She said they were working on the dig site, exploring the buildings they'd discovered but then the camp was attacked. That she and two colleagues, this Eduardo guy one of them, were split from the rest of the team and extracted by the soldiers they had as guards. She remembered explosions, gunfire. Hell, she said the leader of the expedition, a Professor Stands I think, stayed back with some of the soldiers to see if they could secure the site. It's him they're hoping this professor has spoken to, to tell them about the rest of their expedition. Who got out ok."

"That would be problematic, without the services of someone with very specialist skills." The agent answered with a wry smile. "Dr George Stands is most definitely deceased, as are the majority of the United States reserve marines who were enlisted to serve as escort to the expedition. But, contrary to Dr Conner's insistence, they did not die at the hand of drug runners, bandits, mercenaries or anything as run of the mill as that. Anything as mundane, anything *mortal*. We have, in fact, been trying to contact Dr Conner to debrief her and understand what *exactly* happened at the dig site, however she has proven reticent to our requests to talk. I advocated that we do not stress her too much, given the recent events she was exposed to. Plus, as I mentioned, I did not agree with the decision to send her to this site in the first place. However, we *do* need to talk to her, and her constant dismissal of our requests might require a firmer approach to securing her co-operation, I'm afraid."

"You're saying Sarah lied to me?" I growled, my anger finding a new fuel to burn bright on. "Told me the expedition was attacked by locals or whatever the fuck they were, when that was just a bunch of BS? Why?"

It just didn't make sense. Just like whatever the hell had happened with Jacob, until I found out the truth. But this wasn't like that. It had nothing to do with my world.

Did it?

"I am simply telling you there is some confusion over what happened at the site. The place which they seem to have named *ba'alche' le máako* for some reason. I do not speak Mayan, but it's written on most of these white boards." Cormac pointed out the words, a lot of them ringed in red marker pen, with frenzied writing scrawled underneath. "Dr Conner, as well as Dr Cooper and Dr Eduardo, are key witnesses to an event that left multiple mortal casualties. Their remains left in such a way that the team tasked to investigate, after those three were transported to safety, have reported it looked like wild animals attacked the expedition site. Bodies mauled, dismembered and savaged beyond anything they had seen before. Three members surviving from a team of over twenty experienced expedition staff, and that many armed and professional soldiers."

"And now, a woman has been brutally murdered outside the home of Dr Eduardo." He rounded off, ticking items off his hand. Finger by finger. "From what the forensic team have told me, she was dismembered as if attacked by a large predator. A lion or tiger possible. Claw marks ripping her joints apart. And Dr Eduardo is missing, and has not been seen since he returned from the failed expedition. Dr Miles Cooper is claiming to be suffering from some illness he picked up in the jungle, stating he is fevered and too weak to give any sort of statement. Whilst Dr Conner simply ignores our approaches to come in and tell us what she knows."

He held up his hand, wiggling his fingers.

"You asked why I am here, tonight? Your phone went silent, and you were unreachable when I decide to try a different tact. To ask if you could convince Dr Conner to speak to me. That I felt was … *concerning*." He told me, smiling pleasantly but I read his mood and demeanour as anything but. Cormac Smith was stressed, and wound tight. "When I contacted your Alpha to enquire after you, she said you were looking into a matter of a missing colleague for Dr Conner, and then I was made aware of the brutal murder outside said missing colleague's home. Where else would you suggest

I be, when all these things seem to be pointing me in the direction of your …ah *friend*, Sarah Conner and her two colleagues?"

It looked bad. Very bad, listening to the OPS agent list out the events and circumstance that had led him here. I had no clue as to why Sarah might be dodging OPS if all she needed to do was explain what the fuck had happened over there. What she might or might not have seen.

But it put me in an awkward position, now covering the arses of *two* people I cared about. Jacob for the killing of an innocent bystander outside. Sarah for lying to the people I was supposed to be working with, and her possible involvement in this shit show.

Something had seriously gone wrong at this *maako* site, and people had died because of it. It wouldn't be fair to those mortals for me to mess with Cormac's investigation, and Jessica would forbid me from directly obstructing the mortal authorities, given that only could lead to a shitstorm of trouble for the pack.

However, it didn't mean that I couldn't do my own legwork on the side, and see if I could get some answers before OPS got wind of Jacob's involvement. Or as Cormac put it, took a firmer approach to getting their answers from Sarah.

Thankfully, the OPS agent gave me the opening I needed. Sometimes I do get *that* lucky.

"This room will need to be processed, and whatever Dr Eduardo was working on thoroughly reviewed to see if he mentions the expedition and what happened. Or what he obviously was afraid of, to so decorate his own home." Cormac looked around the study, at the disorganised mess left by the professor. Then he shot me a hopefully smile. "I don't suppose anything stands out to your finely tuned senses?"

I pretended to cast around, making a show of closing my eyes and hunting. I'd already spotted the one thing I wanted to get my hands on, but of course that meant getting Cormac to look elsewhere. Finally, I set my hands on the desk and picked up a sheaf of papers that had been scattered across it. They carried the professor's scent, saturated with a sense of fear and dread, scrawled over with his tight handwriting.

"Try these." I passed them over to Cormac, whilst carefully palming the thing I wanted to keep from him. "They smell of him, and it looks like he was working on them just before he left, whenever the hell that was."

Cormac accepted the papers, and I slipped my hands back, all the while keeping the small leather-bound book I had noted on the desk hidden. Whilst the OPS agent was looking over the notes I'd given him, I slipped the book into a pocket as stealthily as I could.

It wasn't that I was trying to hide stuff from him. Not really. I just needed to see what the professor had written in his journal, as the thing had carried not just the scent of his fear, but also blood. Like the paint, he must have written something in the thing with his own viscera, or spilt some on it when he was last inscribing in the book. Whichever, I needed to see his last entry, since in my experience that normally held pertinent details. Like what he had been thinking, or wanting to record just before he disappeared.

Like what the fuck he was terrified of, and what was hunting him.

"Thank you." Cormac told me after scanning the documents for a moment longer. "I'll get the team to check these, and see what they might tell us. They'll be along shortly, as I believe the police will be wrapping up their investigation any moment."

A sharp note pinged, and he took out his mobile and checked the message.

"Yes, they are done. Ms Wilma Ellison's remains have been removed from the vicinity, and all the statements the police think are relevant have been taken. Pity all of the CCTV in the street seems to have suffered a disastrous malfunction. Odd, that." He commented dryly, but I just shrugged. "I think we both know what that indicates."

There was nothing linking the pack to any malfunction in security camera footage, and I actually doubted Kris and Pippa had had the chance to mess with every single one before the police noticed them. More like the supernatural entity inside Jacob had blown them all. Something fairly common with the more powerful immortals. So that told us both we were dealing with something that tipped the needle on the Godzilla-meter to pretty fucking strong.

"Well, reckon it looks like you've got your hands full here." I nodded to the room, to the walls of scribbles, randomly drawn pictographs and images. "I guess I should get out of your hair and let you crack on?"

I took out my new phone and snapped a couple of pictures of the wall wardings, and the whiteboard notes because, well, you never know what might be useful. I figured the journal stashed in my pocket was the key here, but Jessica would have my hide if I made a rookie mistake and forgot to record evidence that was slapping me in the face.

And even if she was feeling under the weather, I knew as an Alpha she could make her displeasure known in ways I really didn't want to think about.

I was moving towards the door, and the stairs down, when Cormac called out behind me.

"Morgan. One moment." He stopped me, and I turned back to look at him. The journal felt like a lump in my pocket, and I couldn't help but wonder if the sharp-eyed agent had seen me palm the bloody thing.

"Here." Cormac tossed something at me, and I caught it awkwardly. A new phone.

"Your Alpha mentioned you had managed to get the last one wet, which was why you weren't answering." He told me, and smiled coolly. "Do try to remember to take this one out of your pockets before you put them in the washing machine, ok? It took me long enough to convince certain people you should have one, and they don't look kindly on anyone treating our devices frivolously."

"Washing machine. Yeah, right." I pocketed the phone, trying not to sigh with relief. "That it?"

"One last thing." He focused on me, and I winced. Here it came.

"Do please try to convince Dr Connel ... Sarah ... that it is in her best interest to come speak to us. To me." Cormac instead told me, doing his best to look apologetic. "You should know, when my superiors decide something needs handling, they can be less than subtle and not exactly the soul of sympathy. The incident at your home is a prime example. Please make her understand ... I only want to help."

I took a breath, wanting to nod and just get the hell out of the house. But I just couldn't. It needed saying.

"I'll ask her." I agreed, but then let my voice carry the edge of my next comment. "But tell your superiors. If anyone comes after her. Tries to make her go anywhere against her will. As much as harms a hair on her head … well, take what happened at my home as a prime example, but a shitload worse as *I'll* be the one doing the damage. Make *that* clear."

With that, I turned on my heel and left him alone in the study, surrounded by the scrawled ravings of a man in fear of his life, and terrified of something monstrous.

Something evil.

Chapter 25

Fireworks

Fireworks are known and used throughout Asia to scare away evil spirits. The belief is that the combination of bright lights and loud noises frightens the creatures, and deters them from doing harm to any mortal in the area they are released. Fireworks will not harm the spirits, but are considered effective as a non-lethal deterrent that does not anger the creatures, and incite them to greater acts of violence and ill will.

Fireworks are used throughout the rest of the world, but mostly for entertainment value rather than to protect lives. The fact they have been enhanced and changed to explode higher and higher in the sky might in fact detract from their use in scaring off monsters, as it is the closeness of the explosions that causes them to flee.

All I wanted to do was head home, greet my dog and curl up with the very attractive woman I knew was sleeping in my bed.

Nice, simple things.

None of which I got to do, of course.

Given the either very late hour of the night, or the incredibly early hour of the morning, I figured since I was awake I might as well crack on with finding out just what sort of shitshow we were in for. And who the ringmaster this time around was.

For the first time in my memory, Jessica didn't pick up when I phoned, so I figured she must be asleep. Or unconscious. Dealing with whatever the hell was infecting the packs. I left her a voicemail with all the pertinent details, and told her I'd check in as soon as I found something solid enough we could hunt … or hit.

An hour and a half later, I was standing outside Ellie's cottage again, knocking on the front door. I had a bag of fresh bagels, half with pastrami and pickles for me whilst the rest were traditional cream cheese and salmon, and a couple of bottles of wine, to pay my way in through the door and to ask for more help from my friend.

A bleary eyed and yawning Felix answered after the fifth time knock, looking up at me with suspicion.

"If you've been kicked out of your own home and are looking for a place to crash, try a hotel. You earn enough." She groused at me, but stepped back and let me step inside in the next breath. "Do you *know* what time of the morning it is? It's so early, it's still bloody night."

"What happened to the carefree, partygoing young woman who used to go clubbing till gone three, then sit up eating pizza with her mates before knocking back a coffee and attending lectures straight after?" I joked, but there was a truth to my question. More than one time, I'd been asked to go find Felix by Danny at an ungodly hour of the morning, only to find her still out partying with her friends, having lost track of time.

"She got zapped by some weird fucking mystical crap, and found out eight hours of sleep a day is, like, mandatory when you're dealing with the energies of the Universe." Felix snarked back at me, then looked at the brown paper bag. "That had better be something edible, coz I haven't been to the shops in days. That pizza was breakfast, lunch and dinner last time."

"Food, and drink." I untucked the bottles from under my arm, and nodded to the kitchen. "Plates, glasses and your brain cells in that order. We have some research to do."

"You know, *some* people just come to see me to chat, catch me up on things and find out if I'm doing ok." She snarked over her shoulder as she turned, the fluffy dressing gown she'd thrown over t-shirt and leggings flaring as she went in search of what I'd asked for. I'd obviously dragged her from bed, and she had dressed in whatever was nearest before she surfaced to find out what I wanted. "*Some* people don't use me like slave labour whenever they need something looked up. I'm not a bloody research assistant, you know."

"Slave labour wouldn't get paid in good food and wine." I pointed out, knowing she was only joking. If I'd even tried to keep Felix out of my world, now that she was a part of it, she'd have chewed my ear off about treating her like a defenceless mortal. And probably shown me just how undefenceless she was ... which by the scorch marks and dents on the training dummies, I'd take as given. "Plus, this should be an easy one."

I kicked the door shut behind me, feeling her wards connect and once again seal the place against intrusion. That's a weird thing with wards. You can have the most powerful seals protecting your home from any and all intrusion, crafted by the mightiest dwarrow of the Shadow Court or warlocks of Ivory. But if you left a door or window open, most of them would turn off or short circuit or whatever it was they did when they don't work. Breaking the door down or shattering the window wouldn't count. The opening had to have happened by will of the owner.

In this case, Felix had opened the door for me, temporarily circumventing the protection the cottage offered. With the sort of shit that was happening outside her front door, I figured it was probably wise not to expose her to danger *just* yet.

"So, what're we looking up this time? More random beasties that could be this, could be that and might be something else?" She quipped, returning with clean plates and glasses.

I shook my head as I divided up the bagels and unscrewed the first bottle of wine. Yeah, normally I'm a traditionalist and think a bottle should be sealed with a cork, and not one of those fake plastic versions either. But it was gone two in the morning, and I'd had a full night. My taste buds could forgive me this one time.

"Managed to narrow things down a fair bit." I told her, as I pulled out the purloined journal, and my phone for the photos I'd taken. "The book will hopefully help, but if you can look up the pantheon of the Mayans, paying attention to anything that was called *ba'alche' le máako* ... don't ask me to spell that, it's in the photos. Oh, and cross reference with any gods that were linked specifically to lycanthropes, werewolves, shape changers. That should give you enough to start with."

"Mayan, as in South American temples? Blood sacrifices, jaguars, and the whole *El Dorado* thing?" She asked, snagging a bagel and chewing on a mouthful as she spoke. "Isn't that a little bit out of scope, even for you?"

I just shrugged.

"Trust me, I'd much prefer this to be some local little shit causing trouble. But unfortunately, it looks like we've got a heavy hitter from out of town, so I kinda need to know how to handle it."

Felix nodded, and with bagel in hand, walked off to the bookshelves to do her thing with the cottage and its helpful book-finding service.

As for me, I settled down into the nearest chair with a large glass of wine, the pastrami bagel within reach, and started flicking through Professor Eduardo's journal.

Now, the temptation was to turn to the last page and see if he had been ultra-nice to me. Maybe written a short but descriptive message to tell me what we were facing, why we were facing it and how to kick its arse back to wherever it had come from. It'd make my life a whole lot easier if people were that considerate on us hunters and solvers of problems.

Unfortunately, what you normally get if you turn to the last page of a book or journal is information that makes absolutely no sense because you didn't read the previous chapters or entries. Thus, you have no idea who *Mr B* is, or why *Miss S* was so upset she shot the butler or what the hell a *bonapo* is.

Just for clarity it's the word for nephew in Bengalese.

Professor Eduardo's journal was typical of a man living and breathing his obsession. Filled with cryptic notes, references to dig sites and expeditions he had attended, finds he had catalogued and snide comments about his colleagues. If anyone ever says that men aren't bitchy, then they are woefully ignorant of the savagery that has been carried down from Neanderthals when they first went hunting together and mocked each other's hunting skills on walls with finger paints.

Flicking through it, I found the good professor never included the full year of his entries, just the day and month. I had no idea why he struggled to include the exact date, but guessed it was just one of his quirks, and he would have known the details if he ever needed to reference them. Made it a little difficult to work out a timeline for me, however.

May 24th. El Zotz. ... Pr. Londus should be commended for his idiocy in requiring us to use heavy trucks to reach the site, over 23km from the nearest town. We *have been bogged down in mud and jungle refuse more times than I can count, but for Pr. Londus, that most likely means simply more than 1 ...*

Feb 13th. Holmul. ... What honestly possessed Pr. Shen and Pr. Matlin to think this was a site dedicated to Itzamna?! Any idiot can see from the pictograms and friezes, this is a funerary site dedicated to Yum Cimil?! I do not know where these two got their doctorates, but it must have been by mail order ...

June 15th. Tikal. ... I am surrounded by idiots and morons! Who are these childish newcomers to my calling? They cannot tell a Mayan from an Incan, a sacrificial blood bowl from a shit collector! Why can't they take their new-fangled imaging devices and go bother someone else, leaving those of us with two brain cells to knock together well enough alone? ...

That was the theme of much of the journal. Rants about other professionals, about the conditions he was forced to work in, about pretty much everything a mortal could complain about. Interspersed with actual tidbits of information about his work and findings.

Reading it was seriously taxing, and I felt that the wine had been the best call I had made in a while, taking the edge off the acid tone and judgemental nature of the mortal writing in the book. Then I remembered he was probably dead, butchered, and felt a little bad about judging him.

But only a little.

Skipping forward, I thumbed past more whinging diatribe and complaints, before finally getting to the interesting bit.

July 13th. Somewhere in the arse end of nowhere. Site unnamed. God, another jungle, more bloody mosquitos and more insufferable idiots getting underfoot and in my way. But they can go to hell. A new site? Untouched, and in what I'm told is almost pristine condition. This could be the one. I can feel it in my bones, the one to put my name where it belongs, over all those other buffoons and charlatans, those college dropouts and ingrates who think one published paper means they know everything! I will see if Pr. Stands or the rest of my so called colleagues are any better than the usual chaff I have to work with. I have my doubts ...

September 3rd. Ba'alche' le máako. Finally we arrived. God, the flatfoot soldiers have been pissing me off, making us follow strict regimes as if we belong to the bloody military! Pr. Stands has made it clear we are to listen to them, however I intend to have as little to do with them or him as possible. But the site? It is simply breath-taking. We need to clear away the jungle to allow access to the buildings, to the temples, but I have already managed to decipher enough glyphs to know that is its name. Ba'alche' le máako. K'alab najo' le máako' ba'alche' to be precise. Though the use of prison or cage, I do not understand. This is not dedicated to any of the run of the mill Mayan deities, there is something new. Something old, I can feel it in the air. Like a presence. Probably spent too much time around the superstitious flat-foots ....

September 24th. Ba'alche' le máako. It has been three weeks, but we have already discovered so much new data, new details that challenge what most people thought as fundamental to the Mayan culture. But not me. I have had my own theses confirmed time and again, at every step we take in this place. Pr. Stands at least seems to grasp the individuality of what we have found. Dr. Cooper won't stop prattling on about matters of context and divergence. The man cannot see past the books he read as a child! At least his companion, Dr Conner seems able to keep quiet and focus on the amazing finds we uncover daily here. These are not simple temples to Yum Cimil, Kukulcán or Itzamna. This is a site linked to Xibalba, a prison as well as a place of worship. Showing the duality of the Mayans, and how advanced they were in their mythology compared to the other civilisations of their time. And I still sense that presence, like a hand on my shoulder as I am drawn further into the site's wonders. The moon shines down, large in the night, and I cannot help but shiver as it transports me back to ancient times.

Times of blood ...

I took a break, setting the journal aside for a moment and taking a mouthful of wine. Savouring the slight burn of the alcohol, I let my grey cells clunk and whir towards some initial conclusions.

I already had a pretty good impression of Professor Julius Eduardo, and to be honest, I was surprised someone hadn't bludgeoned him to death with an ancient stone tablet or stabbed him with a sacrificial dagger long before now. The man was seriously shitty about pretty much everyone around him. But he still didn't deserve to be dismembered, brutally torn apart like I suspected had happened.

The Mayan site sounded like the find of the century, even with my limited knowledge about the topic. Almost perfectly persevered, unique and providing new information on a culture that was known across the world for their calendar predicting the end of the world, and their supposed city of gold. Oh, and their strange mass extinction or crisis that had basically wiped them out long before the Spanish Conquistadors got involved.

Several things were making my alarm bells rings though. Firstly, Julius writing that he sensed a presence at the site. With mortals, that sort of thing normally means something powerful was in residence since it takes a *lot* to get through to their stunted and malformed senses. Forget vengeful ghosts and dodgy women in need of a serious hair cut or manicure, we are talking major league immortals. The sort that are a *real* pain to deal with.

And then there was that reference to '*Times of blood*'. Again, that sort of visualisation normally meant something or somethings *very* bad had happened at the location. Which given the Mayan's penchant for human sacrifice was not all that far-fetched.

"Felix?" I queried over to my companion, as she shuffled along the bookshelves and munched on her bagel, pulling books at random it seemed from the wooden units. Some she studied, then put back in their place with a shake of her head whilst a small but increasing number were set aside. "Can you translate these two things. Please?"

I grabbed a pen and a pad of paper that she always seemed to have to hand, probably a carry-over from when she was a university student and had to remember to always take notes. Scribbling from the journal, I noted the two phrases I needed translating then tossed the piece of paper at her.

Without even turning, she plucked the scrunched-up ball from the air with negligent ease. However, she then spoilt the whole thing by sticking her tongue out at me.

"Well, since you ask so *nicely* ..." She slipped the paper over to the pile of books she was carrying, then reached to the bookshelf and picked up a small metal container like a lip balm holder. This she popped open one-handed, dipped two fingers inside and then touched whatever the substance was to her closed eyes whilst she mumbled something quickly.

Opening them again, Felix shut the little container and popped it back onto the shelf before taking back the piece of paper I'd thrown at her and checking the contents.

"Ok. First one. *Xibalba*. 'Place of fright'. Basically, the Mayan underworld. Ruled over by a bunch of death gods and lesser spirits, like Santa and his elves but waaaaay scarier. The other one? *K'alab najo' le máako' ba'alche'*. Prison of the man beast. Though prison, maybe cage? Definitely all about the confinement of this 'man beast'."

I got that heavy sensation again as my stomach dropped a few feet.

Man beast. That was just another primitive reference to our kind, the lycan. The beast that walked as a man, or man with a beast inside. And if the Mayans had called this site a prison or cage, then that really meant one thing.

They'd captured something supernatural from what they called their underworld. A place to inspire absolute fear in their people, enough to name the place accordingly. Pretty much like the *Real*, maybe?

And this 'something' was so powerful that centuries after their civilisation had vanished from the Realm, when all that was left were ruins and etched messages in stone, this thing was strong enough to affect mortals who visited the site where it was bound. It was ancient, made those near it think of blood, and was named as a thing that changed shape. It wore both the shape of a man, and a beast.

Now something was loose in London, strong enough to possess a lycan … which to my knowledge was fundamentally impossible. And it had spoken to me. Said I would know it.

That it was my *God*.

Fuck.

Chapter 26

"Well, there's some good news." Felix told me as I settled in my chair, rubbing my forehead and taking a long, deep swig of wine. "And some not so."

It was one of those moments.

"Hit me." I replied without thinking, then held up a hand as she grinned mischievously. "As in, *tell* me. Save the punching for the dummies."

"You're getting to be *no* fun at all." The young witch replied, before setting down half a dozen books on the coffee table and sinking into the chair opposite. She took a bite out of a fresh bagel, waving it in the air as she reached for the wine.

Knowing I wouldn't get much sense out of her until her mouth was at least empty, I motioned for her to finish before she did the big reveal, and she nodded in thanks.

"Ok," Felix carried on after swallowing, setting out the books neatly. "I'm pretty sure whatever this thing is, it isn't a God. At least not of the Mayans. I've checked every reference to the official pantheon of Gods and Goddesses they ascribed to, and it's a shitload, I can tell you. But nothing that fits your perp."

"Perp?" I queried, knowing I was likely going to regret asking.

"Perpetrator. As in the thing who did all the bad things, that you're now hunting. *Perp*." She replied with a grin. I shook my head and sighed. "You need to watch more US crime dramas."

"Yeah, like I need to rot what little brains I have left *that* much quicker." I snarked back, but held up a hand to forestall her instinctive response. "Leaving that argument for another day. Give me the not so good news."

"When Elspeth gets back, I am *so* telling her how badly you treated me, and used me for all this menial labour." Felix threatened, before tapping one of the hard backed books. "But look, there *are* a few things in the Mayan mythology that could be whatever the hell this thing is. There's the *Nagual*, a human who can shape change into a jaguar, but supposedly they were just magicians. Tricksters. Not murderous bloodthirsty monsters. Then you've got the *Brujo*, wizards with the ability to take the form of an animal, their totem. Again, they didn't exactly rampage and tear other people apart, according to the books."

"They're also both mortals. Not supernatural entities, ones that might think they are a God." I commented, shaking my head. "This thing is definitely more than just a mortal with some skills with magic. Something way worse."

I tapped the leatherbound book under my hand.

"This is a journal, written by someone I think this thing killed recently. He was on an expedition to South America, investigating a new Mayan temple." I told Felix. "In here, he says he could *feel* something there with them, watching. And it was affecting him, filling his head with bloodshed and fear. That takes something powerful, something inhuman, to affect a mortal that badly."

Felix looked hopefully at the journal, and I chuckled, shaking my head.

"Sorry to disappoint but he didn't write down its name, or any helpful hint so far. Just complaints at having to work alongside pretty much any living person. No matter if they deserved it or not." I admitted, knowing I could be kinder about the deceased, but not bothering. It's not like he could get upset now. "The guy's the sort to find fault with everyone, and thinks … *thought* they were all idiots compared to him."

Felix snorted, rolling her eyes.

"Yeah, I've known a few guys like that. Full of themselves, up their own arses and thinking they're God's gift." She smirked a little. "Funny how it's always *men* acting like that. You don't catch women …"

I held up a hand, stopping her.

"When this is all over, if she is still kicking around the Mortal Realm and not hiding under a rock in the Real, remind me to introduce you to a woman called Cerce." I told her, knowing my friend was baiting me a little but not able to resist. "I can absolutely guarantee you'll change your mind after spending five minutes with her."

"Can't wait." She replied, but I knew she didn't really believe me. Felix still had a few years to go before she realised the simple truth that gender, colour of skin, politics, religion or any one of the many differences mortals fixated on to feel better about themselves compared to others played *absolutely* no part in whether one was a complete tosser or not.

Sometimes it just came down to which side of bed they fell out of that morning.

"You were suggesting it might not be Mayan at all?" I prompted, steering us back on track. "Even though this mortal carved Mayan-style pictograms into his own home's walls to ward off something thoroughly nasty, and South America just happened to be the last place he had visited before going off the rails. Where things supposedly went to utter shit. People butchered, torn apart. That sort of thing. Kinda points a very big finger, don't you think?"

"Meh." The young witch replied, rolling her eyes. "Just coz it's obvious, doesn't mean it's true."

I shrugged, accepting the point. I motioned for her to continue as I started on another bagel and took another long pull from my glass.

"So, this thing said it was *your* God. That's pretty specific so I figured I'd check what deities are linked to your kind. Lycanthropes, werewolves, that sort of thing." She flicked open one book, filled with tight script, and ran her finger down until she reached the section she wanted. "I started with a reference to the *Epic of Gilgamesh*, around 2,100 BC, where the hero dumps a woman because she turned a previous lover into a wolf. But she wasn't a Goddess or anything, and the wolf-guy died so I don't think that's relevant. Next up, I looked at Greek mythology, coz that's chock-full of people changing shapes and Gods becoming animals. There was this witch, stranded on an island in the *Iliad* …"

I stopped her, swallowing my mouthful of food.

"Cerce. Yeah, I mentioned her before." I waved a hand in negation. "You can scratch her off the list. She's moved on to genetic manipulation and making designer babies for the rich and morally corrupt. But as I said, last time I saw her, she was making ready to hightail out of here and go hide for a few millennia. Possession just isn't her game."

Felix eyed me, trying to see if I was joking with my casual reference to dealing with a centuries-old Goddess. When I shrugged, she shook her head and continued.

"OK, whatever. Moving on. This is where it gets interesting. There's this place. Arcadia, in Greece. Around 380 BC, Plato wrote about the locals worshipping '*Lycaean Zeus*', a cult based on the mortal king Lycaon. According to the stories, he tested whether Zeus was all-knowing by killing his own son and serving the bits of him to the God to see if he realised what he was eating. Pretty sick, and I don't mean that in a good way. Anyhow, Zeus was so pissed that he cursed Lycaon, turning him into a '*wolf of monstrous form*', making him immortal and forever '*hungering for the flesh of man and child*'. As this all occurred under the full moon, Lycaon was said to *have the shape of a man until moon rise, then be cursed to be as of a beast until the moon rested once more.* I'm quoting."

Elspeth had already dismissed this myth as being the root of where us lycans came from, since there was no mention of the curse being transferred or the beast-King ever fathering children to carry the blood-line on. Just one of those weird foot notes in history, a warning about fucking with the Gods.

"What's more interesting though, is the cult that worshipped this sick sod were able to change into wolf beasts themselves." Felix carried on, and my ears perked up. This wasn't something Ellie had mentioned. "Seems if a mortal worshipper asked for *Lycaean Zeus's* aid, it was known to possess them, its spirit entering them and allowing them to take the form of a monstrous beast. Usually to punish their enemies, defeat some powerful foe or open a pickle jar if they were struggling. That sort of thing."

"They had this festival called *Lykaia*, on the slopes of Mount Lykaion where Zeus was supposed to have cursed King Lycaon. The high priest served human flesh as a sort of divine sacrifice, and those that ate this '*special meat*' would be touched by their God and turned into wolf-beasts to serve their God too."

I swallowed a chunk of pastrami and pickle, mulling this over.

The fact the worshippers had practised cannibalism was hardly a surprise to me, given the long and quite nasty list of things mortals had done to themselves over the years they'd been kicking around this Realm. In the name of religion, politics or just because they could. In that way, they were akin to the immortals they worshipped, though a mortal character flaw was to blame someone or something else for their heinous actions. *'God made me'*. *'I was ordered to do that'*. *'The voices in my head told me it was the right thing to do'*. That sort of *shift the blame* shit went on a lot.

Immortals were more likely to use the *'Because I could'* or *'Who was going to stop me?'* argument to explain their various fuck ups.

"Ok, so we've got a demi-God in Greece who kind of fits the description. Possessing people, turning them into monsters. Using wolf-men as its servants." I replied slowly, not wanting to be too critical but seeing an obvious plot hole. "Those bodies in Greenwich *did* look like something had snacked on them, so that maybe fits with the cannibalism angle. But that was *Greece* mythology. Unless I'm really bad at geography, there's maybe ten thousand miles between there and South America and the Mayans, and our man Professor Eduardo and his journal. There's nothing to connect the two cultures."

"Oh, ye of little faith!" Felix rolled her eyes at me, in a manner that was so Elspeth I almost got goose-bumps. It was like my other friend was sat there, lecturing me just like she had done countless times, and I felt my gut clench at the weirdness. Then I shook my head and wolfed down the remains of the bagel, letting Felix continue as I pushed the awkward feelings back into their box.

Thankfully, she didn't seem to have noticed my little blip, instead jumping into her theory.

"We all know the Greeks and Romans banged heads for a long while, until I think it's safe to say the Romans won and kicked their Grecian butts. Took their entire pantheon of Gods and Goddesses, and made them their own." She explained as I settled back to listen. "Zeus became Jupiter, Poseidon to Neptune, Ares to Mars and so on. Bit like adopting the orphans of your enemy after you've beaten them."

"As *anyone* knows, the Roman Empire spread across much of Europe, conquering pretty much every country they invaded and making them either citizens or slaves." She continued, tapping the book she was reading from. "It's common knowledge the Romans were really close to their Gods, and practiced all manner of weird shit to connect with them. It's not a big stretch to think a demi-God that could possess its followers and imbue them with inhuman strength and savagery would be popular with the common soldiers of the Roman legions. Army-grunts always want to be bigger and badder than their enemies. Leastways in the books and movies."

"Rome eventually pulled out of Europe and its entire empire collapsed pretty much in the late 400 AD. But it left behind a shitload of stuff, including the myths and religions it had practised whilst occupying most of the continent. Some of the Gods of old Germanic lore and Scandinavian Viking myth were based on those worshipped by soldiers they had once faced as enemies. That they had then taken, and made their own in new stories and mythology. From Zeus to Jupiter, to Woden, then Odin, like."

"The Vikings. Now they were all about shape-shifting Gods. Wolves that turned into men, and men imbued with the spirit of animals. Like the *berkserker*, a warrior possessed with the spirit of the Gods to become something bestial, terrible in battle, insatiable and unstoppable. Sound familiar?" Felix pointed out and I heaved a sigh, nodding as the links, no matter how tenuous, connected. "And guess what? A little-known fact is the Vikings actually sailed to Mexico, after they tried to hit Ireland and missed by like bloody miles. They got involved with the local tribes of South America way before the Spanish invaded and royally fucked them over."

"And you know that how?" I queried, my brain working through the connections Felix had made, the jumps that might be guesswork and pure conjecture, or might actually be actual fact.

"Ha. You think I spent so much time studying without picking up all manner of random facts and shit?" She laughed, then managed to look a little abashed. "Actually, there was a guy I kinda hung out with for a bit. He was majoring in ancient European folklore, and he had a certain Chris Hemsworth-*Thor* about him. He had the deepest blue eyes …"

I held up a hand, screwing my face as if nauseous.

"Ok, enough detail! I'm eating here!" I protested, and she snorted but thankfully stopped describing the object of her affections, albeit for whatever brief period that had been for.

I finished my food and set the plate aside, working it through. It actually made a fair bit of sense, given how mortals liked to 'borrow' myth and superstition from each other, usually those they had brutally conquered and then claimed as their own. How many 'holy' days like Christmas or Easter in the Christian religion were based on *pagan* rituals celebrated for hundreds of years before their God started messing about with stone tablets and wooden crosses?

"Just so we're clear. You think this thing is some sort of old demi-God from Greek mythology? One the Romans borrowed, and took with them on their campaigns across Europe?" I walked my fingers along the sofa arm, imagining the passage from one set of worshippers to another. "This thing then stuck around when the Romans were booted out, working its way through the old tribes of Europe and their shamans and priest until it got to the Vikings. Who then took it on their voyages across the sea, landing in South America and into the laps of the indigenous tribes there. Our warm and friendly Mayans?"

Felix nodded as she munched on her last bagel, then nodded to the journal.

"What's the betting there's some story your professor translates, about this *God* of theirs being transported over dark oceans by pale warriors, maybe travelling through their Underworld or something and the Vikings are the dead guardians. *Druagr*, like in the horror movies?" She hazarded a guess, obviously having read or seen as many myths and legends turned into popular fiction as I had, and knew how they tended to go. "They might even say it came to them seeking help, that they were doing the right thing by freeing it from the Vikings. Sacrificing its old followers and making it their own God, and just keeping the chain going of bunny hops from one culture to the next."

"*Still* doesn't explain why this thing thinks it's the God of Lycans. Except that bloody name." I grumbled but Felix was having none of it.

"Hello?! Doesn't explain, my arse!" She snapped good naturedly. "Zeus *Lycaean* or *Lykaois*? A cursed King turned into an immortal who could change its followers into beasts? A festival in its honour called *Lykaia*? Just how many references to *Lycan* do you need?"

"Ok, ok! I get the point!" I held up my hands in mock surrender. "It's some solid research, and it all *sounds* like it makes sense. In the sort of weird and twisted way I'm getting used to these days."

Felix nodded, looking mollified. To be fair, for someone who up until six months ago had only dabbled in the supernatural as a bit of fun and with the firm belief that it was all nonsense, the young woman had adjusted her thinking dramatically in a very short period of time. With Elspeth missing in action, Felix was proving invaluable with her ability to source information and make connections which we'd relied heavily on the witch for previously.

Still didn't mean I wouldn't occasionally throw some sort of sarky comment at Felix. Just to keep things normal between us.

"Let's go with your theory. That this is some old Greek god of werewolves, and its been bouncing from one bunch of idiots to another until the Mayans got their hands on it." I scooted forward so I could reach the coffee table, snagging up a pad and pen, and scribbling *Greek God Lycan* down on the paper. I then added in *Greeks – Romans – Germanic – Vikings – Mayans* one after the other and linked them like a flow chart. Then I wrote two question marks under the last one. "You said the translated name of the place was '*Prison of the man beast*'. That doesn't sound like they were worshipping this thing, but keeping it locked up instead. Right?"

"Well, prison normally *does* mean that, yeah." She drawled, but then shook her head. "Just don't get too literal on my translation. I don't *read* ancient languages, the magic sort of uses what I know in my head and fills in the blanks. There's been a couple of times when something just won't translate coz I don't know any word that it would be like."

"Let's stick with it being a prison." I suggested, tapping the two question marks. "According to the professor's journal, he said this place was linked to their version of hell, *a place of fright*. That makes me think they were more afraid of this thing, rather than outright worshippers of it. So why take it or whatever they did in the first place? And how did they capture it if it was something from their version of an underworld?"

"Not forgetting, if it was imprisoned, how the hell did it get loose?" Felix reached over and scribbled another question mark with her comment underneath.

I just grunted, making a leap of logic from my long experience with mortals.

"That's an easy one." I replied with a world-weary sigh. "Someone probably broke the important seal which had warnings all over it to say *don't break*, or removed an item from a specific room where warnings said *don't take anything*. That sort of thing happens *all* the time with mortals. No offence."

"None taken. People are idiots." Felix agreed, crossing through her own question.

It was at that point both my phones kicked off. The one from OPS buzzing, my work one playing the tune I'd set as a ringtone.

"*'Paint It Black'*?" Felix shot me a smug smile as I drew it out of my pocket to shut off the music. "And you mock my taste in music? Hypocrite."

"You're just tone deaf." I quipped back at her, but then held up a hand to forestall any further abuse as I took the call. The number was hidden, so I had a certain idea who might be calling at such an ungodly hour of the day, and worse, why. Given they'd rung both my numbers at the same time to make sure they got hold of me.

"Who's dead?" I cut to the meat of things.

"Five security guards and seven research assistants, at the last count. There may be more." Cormac Smith told me with absolutely no emotion in his voice. Just stating the facts. "There's been an incident at the Natural History Museum, and I want you down here. Now."

Shit. Twelve mortals dead, and the way Cormac spoke, there could be more. The museum was where Sarah worked, where Professor Eduardo had too. Far too close to home for me not to think this was all connected.

"I'll be there as soon as I can." I told him, thinking I'd just dial up a cab on the company. This time I could add it to the expenses OPS were covering for our unofficial / official partnership since Twilight had intruded.

Hey, us mutts have to pay the bills too.

"Don't worry about calling a taxi. There's a car sitting outside Miss MacElvy's cottage, waiting for you." He replied, with that faint trace of smugness that showed just how much he enjoyed letting me know he or his organisation were still keeping tabs on me.

"Aww, you shouldn't have." I snarked, but the line was already dead.

Felix was looking inquisitively at me, and I knew she was about to ask where *we* were headed. I cut that line of enquiry off straight away.

"*I've* got to go check out something. Maybe nothing, maybe something like Greenwich." I told her, and slid the journal across the table to her. "See if you can find out anything from that. Proof that your theory is right, maybe. How to find and stop this thing, also good. I'll check in with you later, with food."

I could see Felix wanted to argue, but common sense told her she would do more good hunting out the things I'd asked. So, with a begrudging nod, she picked up the journal and stifled a yawn from behind her free hand.

"Give me some time to dig out anything, and catch a few more z's." My friend told me. "And if I have nightmares from eating stodge so early, you'll be taking your punch-bag's place for the next session."

"Yeah, yeah. You hit like a girl anyhow." I snarked as I pushed myself up and headed toward the door.

It closed behind me with a more solid thump than normal, telling me Felix had *helped* it close – probably hoping to catch me and send me on my way with a sore arse for my joke.

The car was idling just down from the cottage, which was why I hadn't sensed it pull up. Another typical governmental type, with dark windows, non-descript vehicle make and dull paint job. Enough effort to make it blend in and look like every other one on the street, so much so that it shouted out loud its real identity. Sometimes mortals just can't help but get things wrong no matter how hard they try.

I slid into the back seat after identifying myself, and with no further word between the driver and I, we slipped off the curb and back into central London.

Chapter 27

Effigies

Mortals have learned to create horrifying effigies to ward off evil creatures, creating them to ward their homes, their land or in fact anywhere they wished to be free from fear themselves. The meaning of the Scarecrow, used now to deter avian pests in the fields, has been lost to a time when the mannequins guarded the fields from tricksome fae seeking to steal crops and ruin the food of the farmer. Carven creatures, gargoyles, have long been crafted and fitted to dwellings and places of worship where mortals know evil creatures are drawn to, and used to ward the buildings and make them a formidable sanctuary.

Mortals don grotesque masks in festivals throughout the year, most especially on the darker nights when it is believed spirits and monsters are emboldened and come seeking their prey. They have used effigies of these creatures, set upon pyres and burned in full view, to strike fear into the creatures as a warning of what they will face should they seek to cause harm.

The good news? No way in hell was this anything to do with Jacob.

The bad news … well, it was definitely our supernatural wannabe-God of bloodshed and violence. Both of which it had committed with gusto and savagery that went beyond anything a simple mortal could have achieved.

No way this could be mistaken for anything but unnatural.

The Natural History Museum was lit brightly by the ever-present search-lights set at ground level, spearing up through the gloom of the night to illuminate the grandiose structure in all its glory. Banners advertising the latest exhibits and attractions fluttered in the late October breeze, but this morning any eyes would have been drawn to the flashing blue lights and police tape strung up to barricade off the main entrance. Its steps were guarded by armed police holding their stubby rifles close to their chests, eyes alert for any sign of trouble.

Cormac Smith met me as the car he'd sent pulled up by the wrought iron gates, clad in his ever-neutral grey suit. Against the cold autumnal weather, he'd thrown on a long coat of, no surprises, grey material and had added a hat. A fedora or trilby or something that definitely wasn't a flat cap, to ward his head from the cold.

The OPS agent eyed my somewhat less warm attire, seeing how I had dressed to be inside that night babysitting Jacob and hadn't expected to be bouncing around London, and simply shook his head. Then he motioned for me to follow him.

"What happened? And why am I here?" I asked quietly as we walked down some stone steps. I'd expected us to head to the rear entrance, keeping out of public sight, but it looked like Cormac intended us to head in through the main door in full view of anyone interested.

Uniformed officers moved to meet us as we neared the barricades and tape, but Cormac simply flashed a badge and they melted back except for one who held the tape up for us to duck under. He eyed me for a moment, and I winced slightly as I recognised his scent.

The last time I'd met this particular officer of the law, he had been standing on one side of another barrier, this time blocking the little mews where Danny and Felix lived. Before Felix moved out to explore her career as a witch, part timing as a demolitions expert. I had been fresh from our little tussle at this very establishment, when I'd gotten the news Felix had been kidnapped and someone had assaulted Danny in his home. I hadn't been in the right frame of mind to play nice, and had let my mood get the better of me.

Hurling the man into a gathering of trashcans *might* not have set the pair of us off on the right footing, I realised belatedly, so I kept my hands down at my side and simply nodded as Cormac and I passed him by. The policeman gave me a cool, blank look in response, and whispered something into his shoulder mike. Something about *two incoming, one of DI Allen's contacts* if my wolfy ears heard him right.

No mention of rubbish bins, which I took as a good sign. But he'd tagged me alright.

We mounted the steps, passing the armed police officers, who remained vigilant and untroubled as we passed despite me sensing their attention on us. Quite the feat, to be standing guard facing forward, eyes scanning ahead, and still able to look us over. Without moving a single muscle.

Inside the massive building, the sense of something bad having happened rolled over me like an invisible wave. Bloodshed, fear, pain … the air was saturated with suffering and the sourness that always accompanied death. I drew a sharp breath, bracing myself. Whatever *had* happened, it had been nasty.

The grand hall of the museum used to have a fully articulated skeleton of a Diplodocus on show, fondly known as Dippy. That poor beast had taken a very severe pounding the last time the pack and I had been here, suffering quite a bit of structural damage after I clambered over the thing and an enraged shape-changer bashed through it several times. The damage done had been blamed on a gas explosion on the premises, which also explained a few gaping holes in the floor and some damage to the other exhibitions. Though no-one yet could offer a reason as to a missing chunk of fossilized flesh that had been removed from the Giant Sloth exhibit. And we weren't going to tell them said shape-changer has snacked on the relic to takes its form. It just wasn't worth the conversation and questions to explain that little mystery.

Whilst Dippy was being lovingly restored, a Blue Whale had taken pride of place to welcome visitors. Hanging above the floor on multiple secure chains, spanning the entire length of the hall and grinning slightly at some unknown joke. Probably something to do with mermaids and starfish, but I was only guessing.

Gazing up at the enormous beast, even knowing it was only a model and not a fossilized creature, I still couldn't help but feel a little awed that something so big existed and would probably have had the most pleasant and enjoyable life if mortals hadn't found a use for pretty much of all its body parts. Even eating its blubber, which made me a little nauseous thinking about that fact.

Cormac cleared his throat quietly, and I dragged my attention back to the case in hand. More police filled the open space, forensic teams in white checking over a section that had been cordoned off whilst armed officers stood to attention and watched everyone.

"Down here." The OPS agent directed me, and we ducked down a side passage opposite the entrance to the massive gift shop. Not that I was thinking of browsing, but the place always had something for pretty much everybody. Soft cuddly toys for the children, dinosaur shot glasses for the adults. That sort of nice balance.

We headed through a set of doors marked Private, meeting another pair of armed police officers stationed behind them. The scent of blood got a lot stronger as we descended a level, then one more, and I realised where we were headed.

The last time my pack and I had been here, we'd tracked our way down to the sub-basement level, a massive section below the main building dedicated to storage and artefact inspections. Large glass-walled units were set up with all the latest gadgets to allow specialists to inspect ancient scrolls without tearing them, open sealed caskets without releasing deadly spores into the air and generally make sure the finds taken from all around the world were handled carefully and respectfully in a place that had an air of almost reverence about it.

This was distinctly lacking this morning.

Two more officers opened the next set of doors for us, and the stench of death hit me hard as we moved into what looked like the epicentre of a small explosion. Glass littered the floor, fragments as small as coins joined by massive, jagged shards. Small yellow triangles, numbered with black digits, had been set amongst the destruction, highlighting footprints amongst the broken glass. A bloodied handprint. Something that looked like someone's shoe, with the jagged stump of an ankle sticking out of the opening. Evidence, carefully tagged by the crime scene team.

Blood was splashed over the nearest walls, coating the remains of several glass offices and splattering the floor and walls in arcs and puddles. Other, more viscous fluids were pooled together along with lumps of raw meat, that most likely had once resided inside someone. Someones' in fact, given the number of bits littered around the large area.

"I'm informed there were twenty or so staff working tonight on various projects. Labelling recent discoveries or finalising items for new displays." Cormac informed me as we walked carefully through the destruction. More specialists in white body suits knelt on the floor or stood, inspecting particular sections or taking photos with expensive looking cameras. All turned to look at us as we stepped around the evidence, no-one stopping us to ask if we belonged there or warning us to watch our step. Just silent, grim appraisals before they turned back to their tasks.

"At around two thirteen am. Dr Miles Cooper, a professor and lecturer of Plant Sciences, specialising in Forest Mycology and Pathology, accessed the building with his credentials." The OPS agent continued as my ears perked up. Dr Cooper was Sarah's colleague, the third member of the team to survive whatever the fuck had happened in the jungle. "Despite him stating he was unwell, not fit to meet us and give his statement of what occurred on the recent expedition, it seems he was hale enough to want to work on some samples he brought back from that ill-fated journey. Properly catalogue them, as some were thought to be unique to the area in which they were found and needed testing for possible toxins."

"I'm pretty sure no poison did this." I noted grimly, waving a hand around the blood-bath. It looked like full scale slaughter had occurred, with a side order of demolition. "What happened?"

"Dr Cooper *happened*." Cormac answered quietly. "Those of his colleagues who survived have given statements to say he appeared unwell. Sweating profusely and pale, as if sickened with something. They thought he might have picked up some virus in the jungle, for he started shouting whilst working on the plants he had come to check, knocking items off the desk at which he was working. Acting violent."

"Two colleagues, concerned for both the samples and Dr Cooper's own health, went to check on the professor. That was when things went dramatically wrong." He gestured to the most badly damaged room, where spikes of glass coated in blood were all that remained of the walls. "Statements are a trifle confused, and something affected the security cameras so that there is no footage to substantiate what the men and women describe. But the common thread is that Dr Cooper *changed*. Became something from a horror movie. Bestial, savage. With glowing amber coloured eyes, an animalistic visage and enhanced muscularity. Talons, which he used to rip the two helpless men apart before they could defend themselves or escape."

Amber eyes. That did it. I'd stared into those very same eyes on Jacob's boat, and knew all too well that nothing mortal had eyes like that. It had been the creature again.

"Dr Cooper, or whatever he had become, commenced to slaughter those colleagues within easy reach. He dismembered and tore them apart, and evidence suggests he fed on parts of the bodies." Cormac continued, his attention on the room but I could feel the weight of his eyes on me even though he wasn't looking in my direction. He must've learnt the trick off the armed officers upstairs. "Several brave, or foolhardy, men tried to restrain him, but he proved too strong and dispatched them. However, this did allow Dr Alice Kenwick to unlock the security doors and summon the on-site guards. Sadly, she was killed before they could assist."

"The guards sought initially to take Dr Cooper down with non-lethal force, utilizing tasers and batons, but after several of them were killed, I believe they reassessed the threat level they faced." The OPS agent pointed out several holes in the remaining glass, fracture patterns from high velocity shots. "The museum has recently upgraded its security since that unfortunate *gas leak*, and then the events at the Southbank centre where priceless items of Arthurian legend were destroyed. Of the guards who still live, I have a report saying they shot Dr Cooper well over a dozen times, but he remained active. Believing him high on drugs or wearing concealed armour under some sort of costume, the guards retreated back upstairs, drawing him away from the unarmed men and women who were hiding in the room. It was there, as the guards attempted to summon additional support, that the professor was seen to return to himself. At which point he succumbed to his wounds, and expired."

I looked round the room, seeing things happen in my mind as Cormac had told them. The creature, spirit or whatever the fuck it was …I was *so* not calling it God… had rampaged through the place like a bulldozer, spreading gore and body parts in a frenzy. This hadn't been methodical, but a riot of savagery and slaughter. Nothing about its actions indicated intelligence, a sense of purpose and intent. This just seemed like the workings of a rabid beast that had gotten loose and was biting and clawing at anything that got in its way. But that didn't gel with the presence I had felt looking at me from Jacob's eyes, the cold intellect I'd faced. That had spoken to me.

We couldn't be dealing with two creatures, could we? Fuck, that just wouldn't be fair.

"You asked why I called you here?" Cormac finally replied to my earlier question. "If you would step over here? I think you'll find this … interesting."

I followed the OPS agent as he moved nearer the far end of the room, where the forensics had set up some sort of small tent. It was far too small to be covering a body, but I still got a sense of foreboding, a *'what the fuck now?'* feeling as Cormac reached down and pulled back the covering.

Entrails. Definitely human from their scent, and from more than one person if the discolorations were anything to go by. A mortal has something like twenty-one feet of intestines inside them, all nicely coiled up and packed into the meat sack with the skill of someone who really knew how to squeeze things into a tight space. These ones had been torn free, ripped apart and chewed on from the bite marks I could distinctly see in several lengths.

And then they'd been arranged, forming words. Two of them.

Morgan. Bla.

Chapter 28

Oh, *balls*.

"I can only assume Dr Cooper was disturbed by the entrance of the security guards," Cormac commented dryly, as I eyed the attempt to spell my name with mortals' intestines. "Otherwise, I am sure he would have finished naming you, and possibly written whatever it was he wanted you to know. But it does beg the question … *why* is most of your name to be found here, at this crime scene? This not being the first time it has appeared at the scene of slaughter."

The time he was talking about had been by the hand of my half-brother, Jack the Ripper. After he butchered a Sister of the Arch and used her blood to write me a little poem, threatening people I cared about before coming for me. I hadn't seen OPS at the scene, but I wasn't surprised to find they were aware of the threat left for me.

I *really* needed the monsters to stop leaving me messages. It was starting to get a little embarrassing.

"I believe the police have a number of options as to what name was being spelled here, so for now I think you are safe from enquiry." He told me, but I recalled the policeman on the barrier who remembered me from before. I couldn't be sure that Gregory hadn't said my full name in hearing distance when I visited Danny, but thanks to Jack's waxing poetical, I knew there was at least one police report with my name splashed all over it. In blood. So definitely on the shortlist.

Conscious that Cormac was watching me, I quickly gathered my thoughts and worked out what I could and couldn't tell the OPS agent. Whilst wondering just what sort of trouble I was in right now.

"Firstly, we don't know what this thing is." I put that out there straight off, clearing one point of issue that I know would be a major problem between OPS and the pack, if Cormac thought we were hiding things from him. "The Sisters of the Arch alerted me to an ... well, an incident in Greenwich Park two nights back involving some of their flock. They requested we keep all details from going any further until we knew what had happened, and so far all I've managed to find out is a *possible* link to Dr Julius Eduardo. Hence me showing up at his flat last night, and finding you there. None of us even suspected that this thing might target his co-worker, or cause this sort of carnage. That's the truth."

Cormac eyed me coolly, his expression closed, eyes narrowed as he mulled over what I had told him. The Sisters being involved complicated things for him, since they sat outside his jurisdiction given their religious affiliation. It was quite possible that they *would* have asked to keep all the details of the attack locked down, and probably thought I would do so anyway, so I wasn't exactly lying through my back-teeth. Just paraphrasing what *could* have been their intent.

"If it helps, I'm due to meet with a survivor from the attack in Greenwich Park whenever the Sisters tell me it's ok, and let me know a meeting place and time." I offered up, trying to appear helpful when I knew I was withholding key evidence from a man I was supposed to be partnering with. Even if he didn't officially exist, and the organisation he worked for didn't either. "I'm hoping to get some more information from them, at least a better idea of what the fuck this thing is."

Cormac nodded, not bothering to look at me but his attention still on the scrawled, bloody name.

"You think this ... *creature* was not killed when Dr Cooper died?" He finally asked, and I shook my head. "What evidence do you have to substantiate this?"

"Evidence? None. We're not *sure* of anything right now." I countered, but then gestured around at the carnage, the mayhem caused. "But honestly, unless the museum has started issuing '*special*' ammunition to its guards, and by that I mean cold forged iron fused with silver and bathed in pure salt tipped bullets, then the only thing that was killed tonight was a mortal. This thing gets inside its host, uses them like a puppet, then fucks off again. I don't know why, maybe it can only possess a host for so long before it gets tired or bored. But I'm ... *we're* pretty sure it has possessed at least one other person than the professor here, and that means it can move around and get out of Dodge before anything threatens its actual life."

Cormac grunted, and I braced myself for the inevitable question that was coming next. Who else did we know it had possessed? Which of course I couldn't answer.

Instead, he sighed, rolling his shoulders as if shifting a very heavy weight.

"Fine, Morgan. This is how we are going to play this." He told me, with a definite edge to his voice that brooked no argument. "This will be an unfortunate accident in the laboratory, toxic substances released with hallucinogenic properties, whilst inducing a psychotic episode in a museum employee. Resulting in multiple fatalities. Including the affected employee. The survivors will sign non-disclosure agreements to protect the institute they work for, and will be given leave of absence to recover from their ordeal. With strict instructions not to share details with anyone, the penalty of which would mean legal action and possibly affecting their permanent records."

"Meanwhile, I will ask of you two things." He continued, the tone in his voice telling me he was *not* asking. "Firstly, that you *strongly* recommend to Dr Conner that she contacts us and allow us to debrief her on matters concerning the Amazonian site. Especially around the events concerning the deaths of her colleagues and the marine soldiers sent to guard the expedition, in relation to bandit or drug-related activities versus what we believe to be the truth."

I bristled at the unsubtle accusation thrown in there, Cormac stating Sarah was lying. But he held up a hand, and I bit my lip. See, I can play nice when absolutely necessary.

"We can discuss the rights and wrongs of my wording later." He told me, then carried on with his instructions. "Secondly, that when the Sisters of the Arch contact you with a meeting time and place for this survivor, that I join you."

I shook my head, knowing that second request was out of my control.

"They said only me. And if I brought anyone else, that would breach our agreement, and trust." I answered him honestly this time. "And 'trust' me, the last thing either of us want is the Sisters pissed off over a broken promise."

Cormac simply shrugged.

"I will accept *full* responsibility, and any penance that they wish to ascribe is mine to bear, and mine alone." He told me with firm finality. "I too wish to see this survivor, and hear what manner of creature we face. I will expect to hear from you shortly, both on the matter of Dr Conner and this meeting. Unless there is anything else, I think we are done? Good night Mr Black."

The dismissal was unarguable, a verbal *thanks now fuck off* from the OPS agent. And there wasn't really anything I could do here apart from get in peoples' way and possibly draw attention to myself.

With a nod, I left Cormac standing in the middle of a scene of absolute carnage and bloodshed, the scents of pain and death surrounding him like a thick fog. The mortal man looked shrunken for the first time since I had met him, buckling under the heavy burden he carried, his strength at its limit to bear what was an impossible burden. To keep the rest of his people, his race, safe and unaware of the horrors that really existed, the terrors that stalked the shadows and hungered for blood and flesh. Cormac had lost colleagues facing off against the creatures of *my* world, yet he still got up each morning, put on his grey suit and faced the world to keep it from falling into utter oblivion. For just one more day.

Knowing all that, I did feel a little bad hiding the truth from him, keeping him in the dark. But I owed Jacob more, as a friend and packmate. The last thing I wanted was for their worlds to collide and to see a fellow lycan dragged off to Gods knew what sort of interrogation and torture the OPS used to get answers. That just wasn't happening.

I'd find this thing, this insane fucker who thought it was a God of Lycans, and I'd kick its arse from here to the Real before I let it hurt anymore people. Anyone I cared about, or even loved.

I'd made it outside, past the cordon of armed police and almost to the gates of the institute and freedom, when I realised someone was coming up on me, fast. I turned, taking a calming breath and forcing myself not to react instinctively … as I'd already found out that tossing an annoying police office into the trash has consequence.

Of course, it *had* to be that police officer, unarmed except for his baton and spray, all safely checked at his belt. His handcuffs, the new carbon-fibre restraints that were harder to break free from than ice on a lamp-post once you'd frozen your tongue to the bloody thing, were also safely checked and not in his gloved hands … a good sign that made me think the officer wasn't looking for payback.

Just yet.

"Ah, Mr … *Black*?" He stopped his quickened pace as I faced him, and settled on his two feet. He had gloves on against the chill of the October air, and he clasped his hands together to keep them warm as he addressed me. "It is Mr Morgan Black? From the incident involving Mr and Miss Price?"

That's the price you pay when you don't use a fake ID, a fake persona because you are actually friends with the people in trouble. Certain individuals, like police officers, tended to remember who you are and what your face looks like. At the most inconvenient of times.

Knowing there was no use lying, and in fact that would make things far worse, I nodded once.

"Yeah. Look, if this is about me tossing you in the trash …" I began, formulating the best apology I could manage without actually meaning a word of it. But the officer just shook his head.

"No, that's … look, I understand. Mr Price is a friend of yours, and I was standing in your way when you wanted to get to him, after he and his niece had suffered a traumatic event." He explained with surprising clarity. It's not often mortals show that level of insight, especially when employed to enforce the laws and rules of the Realm. "Thing is, I wanted to … look, it's Detective Inspector Allen. What happened to him. Or didn't."

I kept a poker face, not even a tick betraying my recognition of Elspeth's love. The man I'd firstly put in harm's way and been a major factor in his death, and then helped bring back to life by way of a Goddess's favour. Everything this mortal police officer was *not* prepared to know about in any shape or form.

"Look, this isn't the time or place but, well, you showing up, I just thought …" He carried on, as I quickly scanned over his shoulder to see if anyone was paying attention to us. Anyone coming to investigate why I'd been stopped leaving the scene of a bloodbath. Possibly putting two and two together to make one suspicious suspect. But we seemed to be alone, just me and him.

"DI Allen. Greg. We all heard what happened. Him calling in a suspected bomb threat, then ignoring protocol and going in without back up, thinking to save the bloody day." The police officer shook his head, but I didn't get the scents I was expecting from him. Not the mockery, the judgemental or similar emotions most mortals give out when they talk about someone doing something monumentally stupid. No, what I was getting was a sense of honour, yet sadness that spoke of a core faith in the DI, belief that he had done the right thing no matter what anyone said. A brotherly bond, that normally came strongly from pack. "We heard he was … that he died at the scene. That he saved lives. But then MI6 or some division of the spook squad came in and took over everything. And then somehow lost his bloody body. He vanished, from a secure forensic institute, with all the cameras fritzing and no-one remembering a thing of what happened in the time he was delivered there."

Mortals gossip. This is the one fundamental truth that has remained unshaken throughout long centuries, and has frustrated all the secret institutions and hallowed bodies who safeguard information too dangerous to be known by the common man, too upsetting or challenging to ever be released into common knowledge. There is *always* someone who talks about something they shouldn't. Let slip a secret after one too many drinks or when relaxed with a member of the opposite sex, or sometimes the same. Secrets burn a hole through most mortals' moral compass and reservations. Proving too much to keep quiet, keep a lid on. To not share.

As had happened here. OPS took over the clean-up of the shitshow that had led to the DI's death. A cover story had been released, '*brave police officer saves lives but at the price of his own* …' No other names had been mentioned, the rest of us kept from public scrutiny, and those officers who had been called to man the perimeter of the site bound to silence over anything they *might* have seen or heard. Simple, clean and a nicely wrapped up ending to the man's life.

That should have been it, end of story.

But Elspeth had meddled, proving that love truly *does* trump common sense and any vows a person might have made in their former life. She had defied her Goddess, involved herself with an escaped Real prisoner and enacted a scene that would fit any one of the *Oceans'* heist movies like a glove.

End result? DI Allen had effectively vanished.

The police officer looked at me, exuding a cocktail of emotions that were carefully hidden from his face. Confusion, pain of the loss of a friend and colleague, anger at the cock-up made by OPS even though he didn't know they existed. And one last thing.

Hope.

"Thing is? Look, your name pops up in his case files. Mixed up with some stuff that doesn't make a lot of sense." He told me, settling the matter for me whether the police knew about me or not. "But when you are involved, things *happen*. Missing people turn up. Bad things stop happening. That sort of thing. With no explanation, but nothing concrete that he thought meant actionable steps needed taking. Like if we were dealing with a vigilante or wannabe superhero. Those idiots in the US who dress up like the movie characters and go patrol the streets until someone shoots them."

I just shrugged, not wanting to confirm anything, nothing that could be used against me in a Court of Law. Given I was speaking to a police officer right here and now. But he just shook his head.

"I'm just a police constable, not a detective or anything. I'm not sniffing for a lead here." He told me, and I read the honesty of his words in the air around him. "But, if you are something *different*? If DI Allen got caught up in something and the fact there's no body means *anything*? Just, I don't know, tell him things are getting crazy. There's stuff getting reported … just, tell him he's needed. If he can, we need him back. No questions asked. That's all."

I read the hope in his voice, the need this police officer had for DI Allen to be ok, to be alive and able to come back when they needed him. The trust this man had in someone to make things right, to handle the crazy and make it all ok.

But I also knew *exactly* where Gregory Allen was, and just how impossible it would be for him to help. To be the saviour this man, and maybe anyone who worked with him, wanted him to be. And what I had to do, no matter the pain it would cause.

I took a breath, and schooled my expression into what I hoped was a fitting look.

"I'm sorry." I told the officer, seeing him wince, not able to hold back the pain my words caused him. "DI Allen, to my knowledge, died when he attended a suspected bomb alert at a restaurant just outside the Tower of London. There's no way I can pass word to him because … Look, he's dead."

The police officer, who had not yet given me his name, squared his shoulders and exhaled slowly. Calming himself. His eyes met mine, and I read the denial in them. The simple fact he wasn't going to accept my story, just like he and others had not accepted the company line given them already. But he wasn't looking to cause me trouble either.

"Then all I can say is thank you for stopping to talk, Mr Black." He told me, holding out a gloved hand. Which I took, and shook carefully, as I always did around mortals. "I hope you have a good rest of the day, and if anything changes, anything at all? Just ask for PC Daniel Chambers."

"Of course." I replied, honestly this time. Then I turned on my heel, and crossed the barriers, slipping through the gates of the museum and away from the blood, the slaughter. The pain I left behind me.

Strangely enough, it wasn't the agony of the dead that followed me as I left. Just the sharp stab from a single mortal soul, whose hope I had crushed, and stomped all over. It was the eternal struggle, and I'd chosen my path as I always did. Knowing I was serving the greater good by thoroughly shitting over doing the right thing.

Don't ever tell me my job is easy.

Just don't.

Chapter 29

Pets

It is a known fact that mortals rely on animal companions to ward them against supernatural monsters. Cats are able to see through glamour, veils and most of the ways creatures attempt to disguise themselves to prey on their victims. Dogs will bark at malevolent spirits, the loud noise often frightening the creatures away.

Owls are often mistaken as conduits for the spirits of the dead, but instead ward homes in which they roost from wandering spirits who might seek to enter and make the dwelling their new home. A cockerel's cry at first light is deadly to a basilisk, and will turn the creature to stone if it hears the raucous cry.

A quick phone call to Jessica found her awake and able to confirm Jacob was still safely locked in his cell. He could not in any way have been to blame for the mess at the Natural History Museum. Even though everyone said it had been Dr Miles Cooper.

The way this thing was shaping up, I was beginning to doubt even the simplest assumption. That a packmate I had known for years couldn't commit bloody murder on some helpless mortals, or that a bunch of mortals had completely mistaken a colleague for some other stranger before he wreaked bloody mayhem.

The saving grace being some utter bastard had been to blame for that act of barbarism, controlling the mortal professor just as it had my packmate.

Jessica also told me the Sisters had been in touch. A particularly rank and smelly gnoll had stopped by the office, a shuffling mass of rubbish and discarded materials that the mortals tossed onto their streets with no regard or care. To the gnoll, a creature used to burying itself in the foulest shit and filth, it was like Christmas every day it shambled the London pavements.

It had passed on a message for me. *All Saints, Margaret Street. 9pm. Come alone.* Then it had shuffled off, taking with it a bottle of good whiskey from our Alpha's stock, and a promise that I would abide by their wishes.

Jessica had been *less* pleased when I admitted I wouldn't in fact be keeping to what the Sisters asked. That in fact I needed to show up with Cormac Smith in tow. But after I explained the corner I was in, and that I'd managed to keep Jacob's name from being linked to the killings in Greenwich, she unwound a little. I still reckoned I was due to be assigned some *real* shitty cases when all this settled down, just to teach me a lesson. But I could deal with that later.

Life was an eternal learning opportunity, according to Jessica Walker. And not the sort you could bunk off from to go smoke behind the bike sheds, or hook up with your partner of whatever sexual persuasion to explore all those fun things you just learnt about in Biology.

After the call, I checked my phone and found it was closing on four in the morning. High time I headed back home, to reassure my mutt that things were ok after my previous night's frolics, and check in with Sarah. Who I hoped was still fast asleep in my bed, who I now owed some very bad news to. Not only was one of her colleagues missing presumed dead, at least to us, but now the other survivor of her escape from South America was deceased, after killing a bunch of people at her workplace.

This sort of bad luck normally meant those involved had done something monumentally stupid. Way beyond stepping underneath a ladder, or breaking a mirror. Crossing the path of a load of black cats. This level of bad luck usually involved a serious curse or bad juju, and *had* to be linked to the Mayan site they all visited. And interacted with something there, to awaken the sort of malevolent spirit that horror writers *love* to create, to inspire terror in their readers or watchers, and try to retell the centuries-old lessons that mortals simply cannot learn.

Don't touch shit.

Don't go into the dark, scary room and whatever you do …

Don't mess with the big bad scary thing that has warning signs written all over its room, prison, dwelling or abode.

Breaking any of the three basic rules invariably leads to pain and the sort of scene that requires a clean-up crew with industrial strength solvents for the stains. Sort of like what I'd just seen in the sub-basement of the Natural History Museum.

Bear was snoring thunderously as I slipped open my front door, having grabbed another taxi on the work account and then spent fifteen minutes patrolling the area around my home for any sign that Jack had paid a visit. Thankfully, it seemed my half-brother had learnt his lesson from the last time, and there wasn't a scent of him to be found anywhere close by.

I *still* needed to let Cormac know the bastard was back in town, though not in a fit state to pick up his old habits. Gutting and feeding off women of negotiable favours, that sort of thing. Whether he was still sickened by the wound given him by Gregory, or just broken from having his arse well and truly kicked by two mortals, I wasn't sure, but the Ripper was definitely not the terrifying murderer of yesteryear, or even six months back when I'd faced him. Before, he wouldn't have cut and run after encountering my wards. At least without hunting down and brutally murdering someone on my doorstep to leave as a calling card. He'd fled, and that told me a lot about where his head was at, and what he was currently capable of.

Fear does strange things. Even to the strongest creatures. Soldiers having survived the most brutal and horrific of encounters will suffer PTSD, and whilst they might still face down an armed assailant threatening someone they love, they'll cower and run for cover if they hear a car back-fire, or a child run up behind them and shout "Bang, you're dead!". Firefighters, having rescued lives from a burning tower block, will be unable to light the fire on their gas hob, fixated by the flame. Seeing it devour everything in their mind. It paralyses, disrupts every natural instinct and at times makes the afeared almost act like a completely different person.

In this case, Jack the Ripper should have already started brutally murdering and devouring young defenceless mortals by now. Unbound and at large, a killer from the shadows, a stalker and twisted genius in all things murderous and agonising. Yet instead, having crawled from the deep waters of the Thames, dragged himself from the muck, he lurked and hid, making only one rash attempt on my home and then running when he was repelled. Not once had he left me any messages in the blood of his victims. Not once since he had returned had he attacked anyone I cared about to cause me pain.

Of course, the pack knew of his existence and were alert for his return. And Felix was safe as long as she stayed in Elspeth's home, locked behind wards far older and more powerful than mine. The sort to turn him to cinder and dust if he was stupid enough to try to attack her.

That just left Sarah, Bear and Goldspur, plus her father, in my home. And my half-brother's rash and idiotic attack had ended before it even begun. It made me suspect Jack was a shadow of himself, broken and fear ridden. Possibly dying. That didn't mean he wasn't dangerous, and I'd keep an eye out for him in case he had one last trick to play, but I had far bigger and scarier fish to fry right now.

My trollhound stirred as I stepped onto the floor of my living room, cracking open one eye and giving me a welcoming huff before settling back amongst the roots of the apple tree. That at least told me nothing had happened whilst I was out, otherwise Bear would definitely have made it clear I'd missed out on the action and probably owed him extra sausages for his heroic defence of our home.

As I've said, he and I are very much linked and have a bond closer than anything even a lycan might expect with a packmate. And I could read his mood from simply his sighs and grunts, the roll of his eye and sometimes even just the snores he made. I treasured him, and he tolerated me. It worked.

Goldspur did not stir, another sign nothing bad had happened in my absence, so I simply grabbed a glass of water to wash the taste of death from my lips, and a hot shower to rinse off the rest of me. Crime scenes leave far too much trace on anyone visiting them, like the less than pleasant aroma those individuals employed to dispose of the waste mortals produce throughout their lives have ingrained into their very skin.

Showered, slightly boiled from the heat of the water, I dumped my clothes in the nearest wash basket and then slid into leggings. Call it pessimism, but I prefer these days to have even the barest clothes on in case something happens whilst I'm asleep and I can avoid the embarrassment of fighting butt naked until I Change. Call me weird but I think that way at times.

Then I slid into bed, curling up beside Sarah as she slept soundly. I got a muffled sigh as I enfolded her in my arms, and then I told the world to sod off for a while and slept.

Morning brought with it the painful task of telling Sarah what had happened.

"*Dios mio.*" Sarah shook her head, eyes wide as she gripped the mug of strong coffee I'd made her, sat up on the bed amongst the twisted sheets. "*Dios mio*, that's ... terrible."

"Yeah, that's one way of describing it." I agreed, knowing I sounded a little less than the sympathetic other half that I could be, delivering such bad news. But the whole situation was a mess, and I was still trying to work out how the three of them ... Sarah, Miles and Julius ... were mixed up in it. "Look, my contact at OPS said Miles told them he was too sick to meet up and talk, but then he headed into the museum to work. Does that sound right?"

"You're telling me my colleague turned into some kind of crazed monster and butchered a dozen people? Some of them people I work with, I *know*. How is that meant to sound *right* in any way?" She replied after a moment, anger sparking in her response before she slumped and shook her head again. "No, I don't know why he would have gone back into work. I thought he had some sort of fever, I *knew* he wasn't well. That's why we agreed to wait, to talk to your OPS when we'd found Julius, and Miles was well enough. It just didn't seem right to do so before ..."

"Before you could get your stories straight over what happened?" I queried quietly, seeing her flinch a little but knowing I had to ask. I had to know what was going on with the three of them. "My guy also said there were no drug runners. No bandits. That *something* killed most of your expedition, and a load of soldiers who were there to guard you. But it wasn't something with guns or conventional weapons. Nothing *human*. And now this thing with Dr Cooper? Is this what you didn't want to tell OPS? Was it him all along?'"

Sarah shivered, taking a long pull of her coffee before looking up at me. Her eyes were wide, deep pools that normally I'd love to just lose myself in. But now I saw the pain filling them, the loss.

The fear.

"Miles was human. Like me, like Julius." She finally replied, taking a breath to calm herself. "He'd just lost his wife to cancer, and two years before that they lost their only child to a drunk driver. Drove into them at a crossroads, smashed up their car and their boy who was on the back seat. He threw himself into his work, he told me. It was the only thing keeping him alive, stopping him from simply walking out in front of another car and ending it. He wasn't a *monster*, Morgan. Just a man, hurting and wanting to forget what happened."

"Julius … Julius was obsessed with his own importance, his excellence in his field of study. A *burro desagradable*, my mother would call him. Half the time I wanted to slap the man for being so obnoxious, but he was brilliant too. He was single-handedly responsible for some of the most amazing finds and studies of a culture and people who seemed so far ahead of their time, they were thought of as Gods themselves. The only things monstrous about him were his manners and complete lack of tact!"

Sarah set her mug aside, and reached over, enfolding her hands over mine. I felt her emotions through the touch, the feelings she was struggling with. And the honesty in her words.

"There's gaps. Things aren't really clear even now about what happened at the digsite. Maybe I hit my head, maybe this *non-human* thing your OPS contact is certain killed my colleagues did something to us." She told me, and I nodded, knowing just how easy it was for most creatures of the Real to fuck with mortals' minds. They'd been doing it since time began, for shits and giggles, and they'd gotten bloody good at it. "Whatever, Miles and I agreed we would only speak of what we knew after we found Julius. When the three of us could talk, and understand what happened to us. That's why I asked you to find him, why we … shit, *I* need to speak to him. This is what he lived and breathed, and if anyone might know something about what was done to us, it is Julius."

I sighed, bracing myself but knowing Sarah deserved the truth.

"Thing is, I've been over to his place. Last night, well, this morning." I admitted, and I caught the widening of her eyes, the spark of hope that quickly faded to trepidation. "I didn't find his ... I didn't find *him*. Nothing to say he's ... you know ..."

"Dead." She replied, her tone laced with fear and pain. "What did you find?"

"A shitload of weird stuff. Protection runes carved into every wall he could get to. Drawings of what I can only guess are Mayan symbols and rituals, and the sort of mess that tells me your Julius Eduardo was also scared shitless and living in fear of something." I answered her truthfully, seeing her head drop and her shoulders shake with barely repressed emotion.

"But I found his journal." I told her, seeing Sarah jerk her head up again, eyes widening. "I've got a friend looking it over right now, to see if it has anything in it that can help. And look, I'm only telling you this so you know I'm still trying to find him, I'm not giving up. But I'm meeting someone later, someone who might know something about him. Where he was, where he might be. It's a lead, and apart from his book, it's the only one I've got."

"No, Morgan, that's brilliant!" Sarah replied, reaching over and giving me a quick hug. "I *know* you're trying your best, and if this thing works out, if Julius is alive, he can help us figure what's going on. And maybe how to fix it."

Before I could comment on the tenuousness of *maybes* in my experience, she pushed herself off the bed and started gathering up her clothes.

"And you're going *where*, just out of interest?" I enquired, seeing her shoot me a guilty look for having been read so easily.

"I can't stay here, *chulo*, not after what you just told me." She replied, slipping into her clothes with the ease of someone used to dressing in minimal space and without the leisure of time. "I need to go over to the museum, speak to people. I can maybe find out what Miles was doing there last night, but I need to check in on who ... who got hurt. Then I might swing by my apartment and pick up a few things, if I'm camping out here for a while."

She held up a hand as I went to remind her just what sort of mess was going on, with her in the middle of it.

"I *know*, but I need to do this. I'll be safe, I'll be around people I trust, and I won't take any unnecessary risks. Like walking into a dark corridor when the lights won't turn on, or investigate a suspicious sound on my lonesome." She told me, smiling with enough bravado to try to mask her own pain and fear. "And then I'll come back here and you can protect me, *mi amor* like we agreed."

"At least let Goldspur come with you. Like we agreed." I countered, but Sarah shook her head.

"Even if she can … how did you say … *glamour* herself to look more normal? I won't be able to explain why she is with me at work. Most of the places I'll need to go are restricted to museum staff only, let alone if I want to check on what Miles was working on. The labs are kept secure and only senior staff are allowed access." She told me, pointing out the obvious hole in my plan, one I hadn't even bothered thinking about. "No, I know you are worried. I am too, but this way, I'll be able to get in, do what I need to do and be back here safe all the sooner."

I could think up a hundred arguments as to why what Sarah was thinking was *exactly* the wrong thing to do. But she had that look about her, the fear and pain in her eyes pushed down and locked away, and a set to her jaw that she had told me was inherited from her mother and grandmother. And it was one all her family knew well, and never bothered arguing when it came out to play.

"Fine. Just be careful." I told her, as she disappeared into the en-suite to do any one of the mysterious functions women do in private, to make themselves *presentable*. "I still don't know much about this bloody thing, and what it wants. Apart from publicity."

"You have Julius's journal. I'll bet there's something in there that solves this whole thing." She called out, the bubbling of water and spitting sound marking Sarah cleaning her teeth. "Then we can wrap this whole mess up, and get back to what we started last night."

When Sarah stepped back into the room, her hair was combed and tied back, and her makeup had been carefully done to highlight those rich Spanish features of hers. With her tanned skin, she glowed with health, and I felt a little lump settle inside me on seeing her standing there so naturally, in my home again.

"Keep looking like that, *mi amor*," She told me, as I stood. She leant in, rising up on tiptoes to kiss me on the lips before whispering in my ear. "And I promise I'll show you what a *good catholic girl* knows about being very, very wicked."

My grin was answer enough.

I called her a cab on the company account, knowing Sarah would otherwise hit the early morning commute for most mortals coming into London or leaving it. Nature programmes following herds of wildebeests across the Savannah have nothing on the zombie-esq horde that engulfs the Underground stations and bus stops of the capital city first thing in the morning. The least I could do was make sure she didn't have to spend an hour or so squashed into the armpit of a fellow traveller. Or worse.

With her safely on her way, I set about the tasks sat squarely in front of me.

Get washed, dressed and fed.

Walk and feed Bear before he started eating the furniture.

And finally …

Find out what the fuck this thing is. Stop it killing any more people, and put it back in its box.

Permanently.

Chapter 30

"You are *not* going to believe what I found."

Felix told me, sitting on the edge of my desk and devouring a raspberry jam filled doughnut with surprising grace. Not a single speck of dusted sugar smeared her lips or face, and her clothes were pristine.

Her size six and a half feet were parked on the arms of an empty chair, clad in purple boots laced halfway up. These were accompanied by a double layer of striped torn tights, a gypsy style wrapped skirt that reached to her thigh and a loose multi-coloured blouse decorated with knotwork and corded detail. All in all, she looked like something that had been birthed from an explosion at a colour factory crossed with a knitting group on drugs, but the desired effect definitely took the eye off her snow-white dreadlocks and slim features that were, day by day, looking more and more fae-like.

That last detail was definitely a matter I found a little disturbing, seeing the young woman I had known for quite a few years change in so obvious a way, linked to her exposure to and now frequent use of fae-magic. Formed from the Veil, that barrier between the Realms that, turns out, was the ruins of the Twilight Court and its lands. Destroyed in a fit of pique by Oberon many centuries ago when he betrayed his fae-kin and stole their magic for his own.

Yeah, that nice and sweet-talking Oberon you hear about in Shakespeare, the one mouthing lines such as '*Sound, music! Come, my queen, take hands with me,*
And rock the ground whereon these sleepers be....' and '*Fare thee well, nymph: ere he do leave this grove, thou shalt fly him and he shall seek thy love....*' is a complete work of fiction. In truth, the Lord of the Ivory Court is an arrogant, self-centred and vastly obnoxious arse-hole with the might and power to make sure no-one ever threatens his rule of the prime Court, nor takes him to task for his many acts of pettiness and selfishness.

In a word, he was fae through-and-through.

And I was a little worried Felix was slowly losing her mortalness, and being transformed into one of them through her connection to Twilight. Not a good thought.

But that was a worry for another day.

"I give up. Pretend I tried a few times to show how dumb I am, and we can move onto the big reveal." I replied, sipping a large mug of hazelnut-creamed coffee and trying not to wince as I watched my friend devour what had to be a small mountain of sugar and unhealthiness carefully hidden as a harmless treat. "I'm guessing you got something from the journal?"

"Well, *obviously*." Felix sighed theatrically, shuffling as if she was going to get up and leave. "Frankly, if you're not going to make any effort, I'm not sure why I bother spending all night reading instead of sleeping, wasting my time doing *your* work for you …"

"You want to know about this thing as much as me, probably more so." I replied with a dry tone. "And I never asked you to stay up all night doing research, given you *told* me you needed eight hours solid sleep these days. Is that why you're snaffling all the doughnuts like they're going out of stock, because you got overtired and need the energy boost?"

"Ha!" Felix snarked, finishing off the crumbs on her fingers before, with a sigh, pushing the box out of her immediate reach. "Be like that. You want to hear what I found or not?"

I rolled my eyes at the witch, but nodded, knowing I wanted answers more than our usual verbal banter this moment.

"This Professor Eduardo, he certainly had a thing for the Mayan culture. All its mythology and legends, all the Gods and Goddesses and mystical stuff." The young witch settled on the desk, placing the worn journal I'd left with her on her lap and flipping it open. "If you get past all the self-importance bullshit and crapping all over anyone else who was *intruding on his field of expertise*, this guy practically lived, breathed and slept this stuff. I mean, this is next-level. Nothing else was important to him, apart from this."

"Good to know. Can we skip to the great reveal?" I quipped, earning a hard stare from Felix.

"Typical man. I bet you skip-read books and jump to the end to know how it all wraps up before you're even halfway through." She accused, but when I just shook my head, she took the hint and continued.

"Ok, so he spends a lot of the journal trashing all the existing Mayan discoveries, saying they were like the dross, the easy-finds. He was convinced there was something greater hidden away, something that explained why they mysteriously vanished. Something they discovered that at once explained some of their amazing breakthroughs but also their weird disappearing act." Felix explained. "Like, a culture that managed to chart the solar system with an insanely specific calendar of the heavens, invent zero in mathematics as a constant, understand gravity and water pressure to build underwater aqueducts that supplied water at pressure to the buildings on the surface, could *suddenly* over less than a hundred years practically vanish from all their cities and homes. Leaving behind practically everything, no bodies, no trace of where they were going or what caused them to pack up and bugger off."

"He found clues, references in texts at some of the smaller Mayan sites. Hints that led him to believe there was a 'special place'. A place of worship but also a prison, where something had been contained. The secret to their knowledge and accomplishments, a powerful weapon they could use against their foes if need be." She explained, flipping through pages and pointing out hastily scribbled notes, diagrams etched on the thin paper. "Some place no-one had found so far, but also somewhere that only the 'worthy' could ever find. A place you had to be drawn to, summoned if you were deemed special enough to locate it."

"Sounds a lot like the stories of the Isle of Mist, and Avalon." I commented dryly, knowing the Arthurian legends *far* too well after my recent interactions with key players from those times. "*Only the worthy, the just, the true of heart might find its location* … yada yada."

"Yeah, pretty much that." She looked across at me, and I read from her expression that I was about to learn one of the key facts she'd found. "Except, this place was like a door to their *Xibalba*. Their 'place of fright'. Think Hell, just about a thousand times worse. And it wasn't the *true of heart* or the *just* that it summoned. Not even close."

"This place, it's linked to those who endured great loss. People who suffered something truly traumatic, enough to really fuck them up. Leave them scarred." Felix pointed out an underlined short phrase in the journal. "This is your *K'alab najo' le máako' ba'alche*. 'Prison of the Beast that walks as a Man', with a few alternative translations like 'Lord Beast', 'Animal in Man'. But you get the idea."

"Yeah, I think I get the picture." I replied. "Sounds like Dr Eduardo's site was more like something from Clive Barker's *Hellraiser* than the next Wonder of the World. Figures."

The Real was not a fairyland, a Disney-esq wonderland of bubbles and sparkles. It held just as much terror as joy, as much fear as delight. Madb's icy Forest that sat outside her inner Court was an icy hell-hole filled with the still living bodies of her enemies, spiked through with ice and made into trees for her enjoyment. And that was a positively warm and cuddly place compared to other locations I knew existed beyond the Veil.

"I get the reference, but it dates you, old man." Felix snarked, but nodded at my analogy. "Whatever the Mayans had imprisoned there, it was linked to their version of Hell. I figured it had to be the creature, spirit or whatever being the root of all the suffering, so I did some backtracking. Turns out the Vikings had their *Niflheim*, where Hel the Goddess basically ruled and was particularly shit-scary. Almost as good as Cate Blanchett."

"There was one of the Vættir, one of the spirit creatures linked to Hel and Niflheim. *Niŏ-Garmr.*" Felix rolled off the pronunciation of Scandinavian lore effortlessly, which told me she'd been practising so she didn't sound foolish. "The first part of its name denotes some shameful act, some stain against honour, whilst the second part denotes its links to the great *Garmr* who guards Niflheim's gates. A monstrous wolf-like beast that always hungered for blood and flesh. Sound familiar?"

I grunted, seeing where this was headed but wanting to let Felix show how much effort she'd put into investigating this thing, the hard work she'd done. It was solid research, the sort of valued help I'd always looked to get from Ellie. Her pupil, ward or whatever she was, was doing the witch proud.

"Oh, and I found a few references to certain Viking rituals, where *Niŏ-Garmr* is named. Mostly for strength before battle, swearing the blood of their enemies to this thing if it gives them the power to overcome them. That sort of thing." She noted, before continuing.

"In old Germanic, they use *nīþ* to denote the same sort of thing, a stain of honour or social stigma. There are stories of the *Nīþ-Gyflin*, a creature that haunted the darkest of places, a spirit which could grant its followers bestial form and strength in exchange for blood sacrifices, ritual slaughter. Again, kind of like *Lykaois* and the Greeks."

"I couldn't find a specific reference to anything in Roman mythology, but that kind of makes sense." She rounded up, looking over at me. "The Romans were two-faced bastards when it came to their pantheon and worship. Everything had to be Jupiter this, Mars that. All official-like. But unofficially, soldiers used to pray to all manner of smaller spirits. Offering up all manner of things to keep them safe, grant victory in battle. That sort of bull. This thing may just have hidden, laid low after it was 'adopted' from the Greeks. Kept off the radar."

It made a helluva lot of sense, but there were a few holes that needed filling before I felt we had this spirit, immortal or whatever the fuck it was named.

"Before you start poking holes in my research," Felix told me, somehow reading my expression and intent. "I haven't finished. I cross-referenced Mount Lycaeon with any records of Roman battles or stories. And guess what? A centurion called *Gaius Marius* left a written record of him and his legionnaires being sent to that area, to deal with rebellious dissidents against Rome and some barbaric cults judged by Jupiter to be wiped out. He wrote of men who became wolves, of seeing them feast on the flesh of the fallen in both forms, and of the High Priest calling on their God to gift them victory as he sacrificed young children on a stone altar."

"The Romans somehow won, and they killed all the cultists, but they kept the High Priest alive. He was taken back to Rome, and died horribly." Felix wrinkled her forehead in distaste, and I figured I didn't need to know the details of what had been done to the mortal. "Gaius mentions they also took the knife and bowl that the Priest was using, having been instructed to bring back any artefacts of these false gods as spoils of war."

"Annnnnnd …" She grinned, holding up her hand and counting off her fingers. "The stories of *Nĭŏ-Garmr* mention an old knife and bowl used to draw blood, spilled in honour of the spirit and dedicated to its endless thirst. And *Nĭp-Gyflin* was known to use a knife to cut those that sought it out, taking their blood in an ancient bowl and drinking from it before it granted any powers."

"What's the betting, if you go ask your friendly girlfriend who works at the museum, that they found a bowl and knife at this Mayan temple? Possibly Greek-looking and very old?" She grinned, and I sighed, knowing someone must have let slip the details of Sarah and me, my pack being worse gossip than a load of teenage schoolgirls. "And so … tada! I give you, *Lykaois* of the Greeks who became fuck-knows who for the Romans, *Nĭp-Gyflin* to the Germanic tribes, *Nĭŏ-Garmr* to the Vikings and *Ba'alche' ku xúmbal bey juntúul máak* to the Mayans. You can tell me how great I am now."

Something went click in my head, and I slapped my forehead as realisation hit.

"That's what Miles was doing at the museum. And why this thing was trying to get into Eduardo's house." I realised, it being painted in bloody big letters now in front of my eyes. "It's after the bowl and knife. One of the three must have packaged them up before they fled, and this thing needs them for something. But it couldn't get into the house so it killed the neighbour because it was so pissed off, and then when it was in Miles, it couldn't find them either in the museum so it went on another killing spree."

"It has got major anger issues, is what it is." Felix told me, but held up a hand as I pushed myself up as if to leave. "Hey, where are you going? I ain't finished with my marvellousness yet. And you *still* haven't said how great I am."

"Can you tell me in twenty words or less?" I explained as I pulled out my phone and dialled Sarah's number. "Coz I need to run to the museum and see if they have those items listed, and what happened to them. And then I've got to find someone and get them to safety, because this thing has definitely killed one of the three people who survived that expedition, maybe two, and that just leaves one who might know where the things it wants are."

Felix bit back whatever sarky comment she was going to make, setting our normal banter aside. She was clever enough to read when she could push things, and when it was time to *adult*.

Sarah's phone went to voicemail, so I typed her a quick text. Just to say hi and I wasn't checking in on her, but seeing how she was. Nothing to be worried about, whatsoever.

"Look, Morgan. This thing, it's *bad*." She told me, tapping the journal. "There's things in here, stuff this Professor learned. This thing they captured, the Mayans wrote that they took it from fearsome warriors that beset them from the underworld. They obviously hadn't seen Vikings before, so they called them *terrible white giants*. But they managed to kill them, and must have claimed all their belongings. And that's how this spirit got to them, maybe. I don't know."

"But it *knew* things. It was like an oracle, showing them stuff it knew that was far ahead of their knowledge, their skills. It's the reason they did so much stuff, managed to become so great." Felix acknowledged, but her expression told me there was a price to be paid for its gifts. "But it demanded sacrifice. Human sacrifice. Blood and flesh. But that's not the worst of it."

"This temple seemed to call to those who had suffered. Like this spirit fed on it somehow, needed their pain. But it wasn't enough, so the high priests started selecting *chosen* from their own people. Men or women, always people who had families. Partners. *Children*." She told me, and her voice caught a little at the sheer horror of what she had learned. "Morgan, they *forced* the chosen to sacrifice anyone they were close to, cut out their hearts on an altar and bleed them. Their wife or husband, brothers, sisters. Kids. All for this God of theirs, this *Ba'alche' ku xíimbal bey juntúul máak*. Then when the chosen had killed everyone they loved, they were given to it. Like a host, or a body for it to use. But it kept them alive, knowing what they had done, feeding off their pain, their horror."

She looked at me, the pain raw in her eyes from what she had learned.

"This happened over and over, every full moon it demanded a new chosen. A new sacrifice. Until the tribes rebelled. They supposedly spoke to their old Gods, and were ordered to cast the priests of this creature down into its own prison. Alive. Then they were offered a chance to redeem themselves, to make good for the wrongs done in this thing's name." Felix shivered, as she recalled the details she had read. "The Gods opened a portal, a door to *Xibalba*. The remaining priests forced everyone, including the children, to pass through. They scoured through their entire civilisation, removing any trace of this creature and its link to them. Its name. The things they had done. All the while forcing each tribe to pass into their *place of fear* to be punished."

It certainly explained why the Mayans had seemingly disappeared without trace, over such a relatively short space of time. And why nothing had pointed to so traumatic an event in their past … if the priests had been tasked with eradicating any proof, any possibly link back to this creature and what it had forced them to do.

"Eventually, the priests were the last left of the peoples they could reach, of those who had been exposed to the foreign God and all it had taught them. They left behind a few tribes who were too far away to have been contaminated, too isolated to know anything about it. Then they closed off the prison where the creature was still contained, and followed their people into *Xibalba*."

"To suffer the horrors of their underworld, and pay for their sins. Hoping some would prove worthy, and join their true Gods in the afterlife."

"Morgan, it was *horrible*."

Chapter 31

I hadn't figured on returning to the museum so soon after the events of last night. But life likes to play little jokes like that on me. I was getting used to showing back up at places I'd prefer to avoid for a while. Leastways so I could put any unpleasantness aside and actually enjoy the visit.

Oh well.

The building was still cordoned off, with barriers firmly in place and the gates closed. A message on the imposing barriers read that *due to unfortunate events, the museum would not be open to the general public for a short while. All tickets pre-booked would either be refunded or honoured for a later date*, which I thought was a nice touch by whomever was overseeing the debacle of an employee turning into a monstrous beast and killing numerous colleagues.

A harried looking museum guard uniform started to give me the standard *sod off nicely* spiel, but I dropped Sarah's name straight away and flashed my fake wallet badge, saying I needed to speak to her urgently, or one of her colleagues and that I had been on-site last night.

After a quick chat into the guard's hand radio, I was escorted through the gates and met by another guard who escorted me along the path and up the steps. Silent, professional and obviously distracted by the events of last night, the man didn't ask me for my reason for wanting to speak to Sarah, or what my business was. I guess someone somewhere had recognised me, given the number of guards and staff on-site when Cormac and I were present.

I made it up the steps without incident, the guard stopping just shy of the front door but nodding for me to head on in.

Inside, the area that had been sectioned off was now clear, the floor pristine and any indication that a man had died there wiped clean. Staff were hurrying around, checking exhibits and generally making themselves busy whilst they obviously tried to not to think of what had happened in their place of work.

I felt the woman's attention on me as soon I slipped through the door, her shoes clicking on the stone underfoot as she approached. Tall and slim, her blonde hair worn in a professional bob. Pulled back from slim, pinched features that showed the stress she was obviously trying to hide. The woman was dressed in a business suit, and carried an air of authority about her which told me straightaways I was looking at Sarah's boss.

That, and the fact I'd met her a couple of times before, when things were more settled between the pair of us. Her name was … June … May … something to do with the month of the year.

"Morgan Black? This is a surprise." She greeted me, holding out a hand which I shook. "I hear you were with us last night, and part of the investigation? Have you joined the police since we last spoke?"

"Uh, no. Look I'm really sorry, but it's been a long day and I've missed too many coffees." I lied, trying to look as apologetic as possible. "I just can't …"

"Oh, sorry. It's Jan. Jan Beccaloni. Head Curator for Sarah … ah Dr Conner's division here at the museum." Jan smiled warmly, letting me off the hook this time for forgetting her name. "So, you're here on official business?"

"Sort of." I nodded towards the door off to my left, knowing it led down to the vaults and where things had gone horribly wrong not so long ago. "I'm attached to things a bit tenuously, but still officially. It's about Dr Miles Cooper, him and Sarah and Dr Eduardo. And that expedition they just returned from."

"Oh gods, yes. That frightful mess." Jan indicated we should move away from the staff milling around, and guided me through the main hall and off down one of the corridors. She swiped a card through a reader beside a door marked "Museum Staff only" and I followed her down another short corridor before she pushed open a door and motioning for me to head inside.

It was a small office, with a table, chairs, coffee machine and various ancillary items to indicate someone worked here. A computer was pushed as far into the corner as possible, whilst manilla folders were stacked haphazardly in various trays. A few choice pieces of either art or fossilized animals were parked on the desk and along a small section of shelves, keeping company with various ring binders almost bursting with paper.

"Coffee? Water?" She offered, as she closed the door behind me.

"I'm good, thanks." I knew the museum didn't exactly splash out on expensive caffeine providers, working on the principal that quantity was better than quality for its late working staff. Call me a coffee snob, but I like something that doesn't taste like it could also be used to strip wallpaper at a pinch.

"Yeah, it is pretty appalling stuff. I keep meaning to sneak in a decent machine …" Jan told me as she took a seat. I joined her, settling into the sort of chair that was designed to numb your backside after a few moments seated in it. "So, how can I help you today, Morgan? Or if this is *official* then should it be Mr Black? I believe the police have taken every statement and witness report from last night, and their forensics team have completed their analysis of … well, the scenes. Was there something more they needed?"

"Morgan is fine, thanks." I tried to be as easy going as possible, not wanting Jan to dwell of how tenuous my reason for being here was, and the fact if asked I doubted the police would have authorised my return visit. "It's just a couple of things really. I know Sarah was coming in this morning, to speak to her colleagues about what happened. Check in on everyone, that sort of thing. I thought I'd catch her if you haven't got her doing anything important?"

Jan looked at me for a long moment, before shaking her head and making an apologetic sound. Her expression was one of confusion.

"I'm sorry, Morgan but there must be some mistake." Jan told me, as little alarm bells went off in my head. "Sarah … Dr Conner is on official leave of absence, mandated by the Department given the frightful events she and her colleagues went through on the expedition you mentioned, pending a psychological ruling that she is fit once more for work. She isn't working on anything that I am aware of, and definitely has not been in today. I haven't seen her in weeks, to be honest and I was hoping she was taking the time to, well, take her mind off what happened."

"She hasn't been in today. Not just to pop in to check on her workmates?" I queried. "No chance you might have missed her? Dealing with all this thing, or anything else?"

Jan shook her head, but shifted her chair in an ear-screeching move across to the computer.

"I haven't seen her, and I've talked to all the staff in our department who are in this morning. I'm sure any one of them would have mentioned if Dr Conner had come in today, as we are all aware of the … *circumstances* of that expedition." Jan shook her head, and I read the truth from her scent. "Quite shocking, in this day and age, that drug pedlars and mercenaries can put at risk defenceless scientific research expeditions with such impunity."

She tapped a quick set of codes into the computer, and scrolled through several options before tagging one and bringing up a new screen. Running a finger down the monitor's glass surface, she tsked under her breath before looking back at me, shaking her head again.

"Our IDs are all monitored when we access the museum, and which areas we enter and exit. It's a security measure, in case of fires and the like." She told me, tapping the screen with one finger. "And Dr Conner's ID has not been used, as I said, for over three weeks to log in anywhere, from the front door or elsewhere. She *could* have come in and not used it, I admit, but then all she would be able to access would be the main lobby and public exhibitions, and that wouldn't enable her to talk to any of my department since we work further in. And no-one would have let her through without swiping her card. We know the rules."

Ok, no real cause for concern, I told myself, schooling my expression to hide the stab of worry that Jan's words caused. Sarah wasn't answering her mobile, and had decided *not* to do the one thing she'd promised me she would. To stay safe and not put herself at risk given the shitstorm that might be following her, given she was possibly the last survivor of the expedition.

The fact she hadn't been at work for weeks did make me wonder what the hell she'd been up to before she came to find me. But I reasoned, her time was her own and if it had taken Sarah that long to decide she wanted to speak to me, I didn't think that too weird. Hell, after what she'd witnessed, I was still a little stunned she had pretty much leapt back into bed with me.

I wasn't complaining, mind. Just stating a fact.

"Ah, ok. My bad. Must have got the wrong day of the week or I just wasn't listening properly." I re-ordered my brain, not wanting to worry Sarah's boss and start some awkward questions. Just going for the standard excuse used by most men. "Not a problem. There was just one other thing I wondered if you could check? I'm not keeping you from something?"

"Mr Black. Morgan. A member of our staff, whilst afflicted by some virus or disease he picked on that tragic expedition, assaulted and killed a number of his colleagues and our in-house security team." Jan replied with a deep sigh, the sadness and pain riven through every word. "Anything that means I don't have to dwell on the details of the … incident, well, it's a welcome relief. I've spoken to all my staff, excepting Dr Conner. So for now, how can I help?"

Ah, so that was the cover story they were using. The old *driven mad by mysterious illness* and *temporary insanity* scapegoat. To be fair, from what both Cormac and Sarah had said, Dr Miles Cooper *had* seemed unwell. Feverish and not himself, but that could have been due to a mosquito bite, fatigue or the stress of having most of his colleagues butchered by something inhuman and evil in the jungle. That would do it, too.

But at least it gave me the excuse I needed, to ask without having to try bribing anyone or strongarm them for the truth. Someone *volunteering* to help me was kind of novel, in fact.

"Good, just glad I'm not adding to things." I smiled, then got on with my request. "The thing is, it's a bit of a weird one to ask."

"You wouldn't believe the weird questions I have to field in my day-to-day job, Morgan." She smiled back at me and leant back in her chair. "So go on. Surprise me."

"Ok, but I warned you." I replied with a small grin. "It's actually about that expedition, so I'm sorry to remind you of it. Were there any utensils brought back by them? Possibly, and I know how weird this will sound but … a *Greek* style bowl and a knife, maybe?"

Jan looked at me with a cocked eyebrow, and I read that I had scored a hit from her expression and scent. Sometimes things do line up for me. Not often, but sometimes.

"I am definitely *intrigued* as to your source of information, Morgan." She answered finally with a wry smile. "As those details were kept to the senior department heads only, and the persons involved instructed *not* to speak of the matter until a proper analysis had confirmed or disproved the initial findings. Care to tell me who snitched?"

I held up my hands, shaking my head sadly.

"Sorry. Part of the investigation, and on a need-to-know basis. Plus, I promised I'd keep them from getting into too much trouble." I lied, knowing that my real source, a young witch with far too much sass, wasn't going to fly here. "So, was there?"

Jan nodded once. She typed another query into the computer and checked the inventory that was displayed.

"From the initial reports and satellite uploads, plus the details Professor Eduardo, Dr Cooper and Dr Conner provided on their return, there was an absolute wealth of materials to be salvaged from the site." Jan told me as she read through the listed items. "Most of which seemed in unbelievable condition, like they had been preserved despite the passage of time and harsh environment of the jungle. From the simplest of tools and utensils, children's' toys and items of clothing, to extravagant pieces of artwork on the two temples' walls. Statues of the Mayan Gods and Goddesses. Offerings to the deity for which the site had been raised. Weapons and armour from the soldiers guarding the place against rival tribes or other enemies. All left to be trampled underfoot by ignorant drug runners and disgraced soldiers on the run from their own criminal past. Destroyed by gun fire and grenades. Such a damned waste!"

I grunted a mumbled agreement, remembering the damage we'd caused in the museum when we'd confronted the Mistress and her minions. We hadn't even tried to protect the exhibits and ancient pieces of cultures long past, remains of creatures long dead whilst we were fighting for our lives against a shape changer and an insane immortal. Best not to dwell on that.

"But they were able to retrieve a small number of items, a few cases already packed and readied for shipment. Mostly trinkets and small curiosities. The sort of thing we can put on display almost immediately, to start getting a return on the expenses of the expedition." Jan told me with a roll of her eyes. "Everything these days is costed in terms of what income it will generate the museum, what return will be seen on the monies we spend sending our staff out to God knows where, to face all manner of challenges. All in the name of discovery. And profit."

"Here we are." She focused on the screen. "At first we thought there had been a mistake, someone had accidently slipped these in from another case. But they are listed in the notes, and named by Dr Cooper and Professor Eduardo in both their statements. *Item thirteen. One glass bowl, circa 1st century B.C. Translucent deep golden brown, vertical rim with rounded edges, convex curving side tapering down to flat bottom with integral outsplayed. Slightly oval base ring with thick edges. Two smoothed handles set on either edge, of the same material as the bowl. Intact, some pinprick bubbles, a few larger bubbles and striations; dulling, pitting, and faint iridescence. Traces of dark material staining the inside of the bowl, substance to be identified but initial thoughts to be biological in origin.* And *item fourteen. One obsidian sacrificial knife, of a design akin to the Greek kopis but smaller. Possibly 1st century B.C. but maybe earlier. Hilt of forged bronze, blade of worked obsidian. A single stone piece, expertly fluted along each blade edge. Sharpness tested and confirmed to be as if newly forged. Stained with similar biological matter.*"

Jan turned away from the computer, looking across at me with a questioning expression.

"Are you allowed to tell me *why* these items are so important that you had to come back here this morning, to check their existence?" She asked, then stopped at a thought. "You don't think … there was nothing *illegal* about them? We are not handling smuggled goods stolen from another institute, and this whole drama with Dr Cooper is somehow because of that, is it?"

I shook my head, heading off the usual random direction that mortal thoughts tend to race to if left to their own devices.

"No, no. Nothing like that. It's just a detail, is all." I reassured her, seeing her shoulders slump with relief. "You mind if I ask, when you read that bit about the knife? *Sharpness tested and confirmed*. What does that mean? Did they cut something with it?"

"Someone, more like." Jan sighed, shaking her head. "Professor Eduardo. He was convinced someone was playing a trick on him, that they'd planted a fake knife and bowl at the site to disprove or throw off his findings at the site. *Immature young boys and girls playing stupid games* I believe his accusation was to the rest of his team. So he picked up the knife and made a show of cutting his hand with the thing. Of course, it was sharp obsidian so you can imagine the mess. The cut needed stitches, plus a thorough cleansing given what we believe was on the blade. He was lucky to keep the use of his hand, the unprofessional fool."

That clinched it for me. They'd not only taken sacred relics from wherever they had been stored, probably breaking whatever protective warding the Mayans had used to contain the creature linked to the objects, but then Professor Eduardo had spilled blood with one of the tools. Enacting whatever rite the creature, this *Lykaois* of ancient Greece, had used with its worshippers to grant it power, enact its will.

Letting the bloody thing loose. Bloody, stupid mortals.

"I can tell that's not good news to you. I know we're just talking about an old bowl and knife that didn't belong at the site where they were found in, and someone foolishly cutting themselves whilst not thinking straight. I can't see any significance or link." Jan told me, her mind obviously working through all the reasons I could be asking about these things in relation to what had happened with Miles Cooper and coming up blank. "But I guess that is why you do the job you do, and I'm just a Head Curator at the museum. Right?"

I shrugged, knowing I didn't have any answers to give the woman. Nothing she'd firstly believe, and secondly anything she needed to know. Better she slept well at night, and didn't know just what was loose on the streets, killing people and causing me such a bloody headache. Blissful ignorance, as the Accords dictated.

"Last question, if that's ok?" I asked instead, and she sighed but nodded. "Are the bowl and knife still here? Locked up somewhere, ready to be displayed and get the monies rolling back in?"

Jan shot me another one of those looks, and I knew I was pushing my luck. But she screeched her chair back to face the computer, and tapped in a few details. She scanned the information, tsking under her breath, before closing the screen down for the last time.

"I've got good news and bad news, I'm afraid." She told me, and I took a breath, mentally crossing my fingers and hoping my luck held out a little here. I was on a streak, I just needed it to last that little bit longer.

"Bad news then." I asked, and she nodded.

"Good choice." Jan smiled then pointed toward the door through which we'd come. "The bowl is ... *was* still here. It and a few other boxes were in one of the viewing rooms downstairs. Where Dr Cooper had his ... ah episode. We're still compiling a list of the items he damaged or destroyed, but the bowl is definitely deceased. Irreparable. I'm sorry."

I took a breath, cursing silently but guessing that had been only one of the items *Lykaois* had used Miles Cooper to get into the museum to find. And if it had destroyed the thing, then either it was of lesser importance to it, or one of the things needed to lock it back down again. I was going to have to gamble on the former.

"And the good news?" I asked hopefully.

"The knife? That has been tagged as having been removed from the museum's location. It's not something we do regularly, preferring to keep items on site for study, but ..." She held up her hands, shrugging. "What with his personal interest and credentials, when he asked it was deemed a low risk to the item, and better for him to continue to study something whilst he was on medical leave."

"He being?" I had to ask, even though I had put two and two together, and made a full fat bullseye.

"Professor Julius Eduardo. The finder of the knife and bowl, and the idiot who cut himself with the darn thing." She filled in the blank, and I tried not to punch the air.

The knife was still kicking around, and the professor had taken it offsite. Probably realised the truth about it eventually, and that had been what had driven him to go off radar and build an '*anti-Mayan god*' nuclear bunker out of his home. So it hadn't been around when the wannabe God walked Miles into the museum, which probably explained the hissy-fit and bloodbath when it found its favourite carving implement missing.

But that then led to more questions. How had Professor Eduardo realised he'd cut himself with a cursed knife? Why didn't the thing just inhabit him if it needed its knife so badly? And where the hell was the knife now?

Supernatural creatures linked to objects tend to be able to sense them, unless you block the artefact somehow. Think lead shielding to negate Superman's X-ray sight. Cloaking technology to hide war planes. But if you didn't have the means to make a ward to hide the thing behind, you can always use a living one. Other supernatural creatures of the Real can negate or blind curses, their own nature acting like a smoke screen.

So either the professor had built a warded box to keep the thing inside, or he had used some other supernatural entity to cloak its presence.

And I had a sudden sneaky suspicion I knew just what he had done. Who might have told him the truth of what he had, and why he'd been hanging around with the transients in Greenwich Park, leading to his rather gruesome death. But I wouldn't know for certain if my guess was right until I met up with the Sisters of the Arch and this Grubbins tonight.

Until then, I had a missing woman to locate, and make sure nothing nasty had caught up with her. Plus check in with my Alpha and see just what shit state the rest of the packs were in. And catch up with Felix and let her know her guess had been right, as well as finding out what else she'd learned from her study of the journal. Whilst stopping her eating the office out of anything edible.

Oh, and let Cormac Smith know about the meeting tonight, unless I wanted a seriously pissed off OPS agent on my hands.

And there I'd been, not so long ago. In bed with the woman I loved and letting the world deal with its own issues. A period of relative calm and happiness, just for a short while.

I should have known it couldn't last. Something always goes *boing*, normally right in my face.

It's like a law, or something.

Chapter 32

Incense

Though often used to aid enlightenment and a more spiritual state of mind, incense is also used to drive away evil and malevolent spirits which find the smell abhorrent. Much like burning sage, incense can be used to cleanse a dwelling if a supernatural entity has settled in and made it their home.

The blessed smoke can also reveal what has been hidden from mortals, breaking any glamour that has been fixed to a structure to alter its appearance. Many a tricksome spirit has had its plan to cause a mortal sleep in a pigsty or sewer disguised as a fancy bed or home ruined by the burning of incense. In a pinch, the incense burner can often be heavy enough to use as a weapon if the supernatural creature takes offence at its tricks being revealed.

After extracting myself from the museum as speedily as possible, thanking Jan for all her help and hinting she shouldn't mention my visit to anyone, I hit the street and went about ticking off the first item on my list.

Find Sarah.

I tried her mobile again, but it still went to voicemail. Now there were handful of reasons she might not be answering, and all but one of them were normal and no cause for alarm.

Of course, when one of them *could be* that she was lying dead someplace, gutted and fed on by a monster trying to hunt the mortals who had taken its sacred objects and thus freed it from captivity, that sort of sticks in one's head.

Deciding that me continuing to call her and magically make her pick up the phone was a non-starter, I made a best-guess as to where she might be, and headed off to Holland Park, and her home.

I figured Sarah might have headed there to go through any of her stuff she brought back from the expedition but hadn't yet handed over to the museum. Like, maybe, a sacrificial dagger of obsidian. It was a wild stab in the dark and probably not true, given it had been Professor Eduardo who had checked it out, and she and Dr Cooper had been trying to reach him for a while now. But there was always a chance.

If she *was* home, and going through her stuff, then it was one reason why she wasn't picking up her phone. Sarah got lost in work all too easily, and it wasn't uncommon for her to disappear for hours at a time when she had promised to only be "five minutes". When there was a possible discovery to be made, or a strange new species to be explained, Sarah quite happily left the world to itself with the sure knowledge she'd catch up on anything urgent when she resurfaced.

What with morning traffic already choking the London roads, I decided to walk to Holland Park from the museum, keeping a fast pace but making sure I was aware of my surroundings. Just in case I walked past Sarah without realising, or something unpleasant jumped out at me whilst I was distracted. Like my half-brother.

My brain, of course, was working overtime on all the things Felix had managed to learn from her two sources, the cottage's full library and the professor's journal. As well as the additional information I'd received from Jan at the museum, and what I'd seen at the house in Greenwich.

On one hand, it seemed fairly obvious that the immortal spirit we faced was Lykaois, this Greek king cursed by Zeus for his pretty poorly thought through test. But that still left a few things to clarify. Like what, in fact, was Lykaois? Had it in fact ever been a mortal, or was the story just some bullshit dreamt up like the myths around the Lords and Ladies of the Courts, and most of the fae themselves? If so, then it was likely this thing was Wyld Court from the little I'd learnt about it, and the way it behaved. About as bat-shit crazy, but even more bloodthirsty than my half-brother or the Red Cap, or any number of creatures I'd faced from that party-bunch.

Setting aside its real nature, what did it want? The message it had growled to me whilst inhabiting Jacob sprang back to mind. *"You will know me soon enough, Morgan Black. For I am your God!"* Not too helpful in terms of explaining its reasons for messing with my packmate, apart from making me think it had grown weary from its hundreds of years of captivity, and was after a new cult, a new set of followers. And it seemed to think the lycans fit the bill this time.

Oh, and how the hell was it picking its 'hosts'? So far, it had gotten inside Jacob and Miles Cooper, and one of those two should have been pretty resistant to being possessed by anything. I recalled the discovery Felix had made, about how this thing or its priests had nominated *chosen ones* from amongst their people, and what they had been forced to do. To sacrifice those they loved, killing them brutally as an offering to the God before they themselves became its glove puppet. And the simple fact Sarah had let slip about Miles Cooper. About his loss, his recent state of mind.

I added that to the facts about Jacob. Him taking Wolfsbane to help him cope with the loss of Lucille. Weakening himself to get to sleep. For him to do something so fucking stupid was a fairly big sign of how much pain he was in, how fucked up he was.

So maybe, just maybe, this thing could only take over would-be hosts that were emotionally tormented, suffering and weak. Letting it feed off their pain, whilst it drove them around like a rental car, wreaking havoc until … what, the host rejected it? It ran out of energy, and had to return to its natural form? And what was that?

And how did the knife and bowl fit into the mix? The knife had been used to draw blood, I was positive on that guess, and from what little I knew about such ceremonies, the bowl was probably for drinking the fluids gathered from the sacrificed. If they were so necessary, why had Lykaois destroyed one in a fit of pique?

Maybe the fact it *wasn't* using the artefacts, reliquaries or whatever they were, maybe that was why it kept bouncing from host to host? It couldn't settle, couldn't seal the deal without at least one of them. Which would explain why it wanted to find the knife.

Oh, and let's not forget the really big question. Where the *fuck* was it now? Where did it go when it wasn't taking control of people and racking up the body count?

The questions dogged me as I walked briskly through the streets, dodging the pedestrians milling in front of me, avoiding the sluggish traffic that choked the London roads like congealing fat running through sewer pipes. The air was alive with the buzz of the city, awash with the smells of the people living, working, *being* there. A smog that if you could see it, would probably look like some psychedelic haze from a 1960's music festival, bright and savage and choking.

Oh, and I am sure that in other stories, the brave and plucky lycan would have simply been able to track the errant mortal by her scent. Tracking through the busy streets and dirty alleyways, following her path like an illuminated trail leading eventually to her location with pinpoint accuracy.

This lycan, however, was faced with trying to catch Sarah's scent amidst a barrage of fumes, aromas, stinks, smells and aromatic assaults that the mortals produced everywhere they existed. Forget needle in a haystack. Distinguishing my love's aroma from the thousands of smells that existed in the London air on a standard day was like trying to find one specific snow-crystal amongst an artic blizzard. Blindfolded, and by taste alone.

No, I was down to betting on blind luck letting me find her, and the fervent faith that she was safe and well. Just because I didn't want to consider the alternative.

Turning into her road, I slowed my pace as one smell spiked through the morass I was surrounded by. Sharp, metallic and tinged by the chemicals of fear and pain. Aged, but not infirm.

Blood.

A small crowd had gathered on the roadside beside the park's metal fence, near the gates where I'd stopped before to find them closed and locked. As I walked slowly toward the gathering, I saw police tape had been set in place around the entrance to the green space, and a couple of harassed looking police officers stood within the confined space whilst various men and women shouted out questions at them.

"What's going on here?" "Has something happened in the park?" "What's that dog doing, is that…?" "Why won't you tell us what's happened?"

I stopped at the barrier, recognising one of the police officers immediately.

PC Daniel Chambers caught my eye, expression showing a short stab of surprise before he beckoned me to step inside the cordon. Ignoring the various complaints thrown my way by the nearest people pressing up against the flimsy barrier, I ducked under the tape and moved to the gates and the pair of officers.

I immediately noted a couple of things. The gates to the park were open, the chain broken and the notice of closure lying in shreds on the concrete path. Also, the scent of blood was coming from just inside the park, strong enough now for me to know whoever had shed the stuff must be lying just inside, out of sight of the pavement.

Oh, and I caught the sound of muted growling, a lingering rumbling snarl that told me there was a dog present and it wasn't in the best of moods.

"Mr Black? What a surprise." PC Chambers told me, but I just shrugged. "What are you doing here?"

"Looking for a friend. She lives just down the road from here, and I was hoping to catch her at home." I answered truthfully since there was no reason to lie. Yet. "What's happened, and who's dead?"

The police officers both eyed me suspiciously, but I just pointed to dark splashes on the park's concrete path. Thick and sticky, they were unmistakeable in the October's daylight.

"I know what that is, and there's enough of it to make me think someone is seriously hurt, or worse." I explained my logic, keeping it simple. "But there's no ambulance, and you are both guarding the scene so I can only assume there's a body close by. Am I right?"

PC Chambers exchanged a look with his colleague, then nodded, once.

"What happened?"

"We were notified of a potential incident about an hour ago, from an anonymous caller to 999 reporting a possible fatality at this site." He explained, as the other officer stiffened, his expression confused. "We got here about forty minutes ago but …"

"Dan ... PC Chambers. This isn't procedure." The other officer stated, eyeing me suspiciously. "This ... *civilian* hasn't even identified himself yet. What is he, 'plain clothes' or something?"

"He's *special*, Davie." Dan replied, nodding to me. "He was at the Natural History Museum with the other *special* last night, and he used to work with DI Allen on the weird cases. Him and his mates. It's ok, I'll take the heat if anyone asks but this is exactly the sort of thing he handles. Right, Mr Black?"

I nodded, leaving my fake ID in my pocket. Sometimes having a person vouchsafe for you was worth pure gold, for explaining why you were poking your nose in business that you had no right to be involved in, or why you were asking the awkward questions.

"If you've been here for forty minutes, why's there no forensics? No ambulance and crowd control?" I queried, knowing if there *was* a body lying in the park, the police should have had people crawling all over it by now. Especially if they linked it to the animal killings at the place. "And why's it open? It was closed last time I was here, a day or so back."

The other PC shot me a suspicious look, obviously picking up on the pertinent detail of me being at the scene of another possible murder, alongside the museum killings, but PC Chambers just shook his head.

"It's the dog, Mr Black. He won't let anyone inside or near the body. Attacked PC Moss here when we tried to take a look at what's happened." He admitted, and his colleague grimaced, pointing to some shredded material at about ankle level. Given the mortal police used fairly robust uniforms, the dog in question had definitely been aggressive to have ripped it. "We've called in the Canine unit to come handle it, but they're backlogged and won't be available for another hour or so. Until then, all we can do is keep the general public out and wait."

"And yes, the park was locked previously. A call's been put into the local council to see if that was revoked for any reason, but to our knowledge it was closed until we showed up." He continued, nodding to the broken chain. "Looks like someone broke into the park, though the chain and lock haven't been cut. More like wrenched apart but God knows how. Then the man and his dog must have gone in for some reason, and he got attacked. Until we can get past the dog, we can't tell much else."

I breathed a small sigh of relief, pushing aside the stab of guilt. Whomever it was lying dead in the park *wasn't* Sarah. It wasn't good that someone had been killed, but it wasn't her. I reckoned I could spare a moment and see what had happened here, given it *was* just down from her home.

"Look, maybe I can help out?" I offered, seeing PC 'Davie' Moss stiffen as I guessed I overstepped his line of acceptable behaviour. "I'm good with animals. Maybe I can get the dog to calm down. Let you guys go check things out? I'll stay out of your way, and I won't disturb anything."

"That won't be necessary, Mr Black. As my colleague said, our own Animal Control unit will be along …" The police officer started, but stopped as PC Chambers shook his hand at him.

"They'll be ages, Davie. And Mr Black is here now." He told him, ignoring the other's scowl as he looked back at me. "If you're offering to help, then I'll happily take it."

"I'll have to call it in." Davie admitted sourly, already reaching for his shoulder mike as he stepped away from the pair of us.

"Tell them I'm letting him through." Dan replied, as he nodded for me to head through the gates. "Go on, Mr Black. See what you can do, but watch out for your ankles!"

I slipped through the gates, taking a closer look quickly at the chain and lock that had secured them shut. The police officer had been right, the metal was twisted and wrenched, with links bent open and the lock almost shattered. Whatever had happened here, it hadn't been a tool that cut the metal. Instead, brute force had been used to rip the barrier open. And no mortal, at least the normal ones not dosed on anything illegal, could do such a thing.

The blood trail was short, beginning at the gate and ending a few paces into the park, off to the left and on the grass. I immediately saw the slumped body of a man, twisted in death, his clothes ripped and shredded to reveal the flesh beneath. That looked to have been savaged, white bones gleaming amongst crimson gore with chunks of innards hanging out of the gaping wounds.

But what caught my attention was the dog planted in front of the body, glaring up at me with its muzzle pulled back and teeth bared.

"Ah shit." I whispered, recognising it immediately. "Albert, I'm so sorry."

The bulldog glared at me for a moment longer, his eyes filled with anger and pain. Blood stained his fur, most likely most of it from his owner lying dead behind him, but I could see at least three slashes on his upper body that looked nasty. Blood had clotted, darkening and matting the fur, and he favoured his opposite side from whatever injury had been done to him.

I crouched down, carefully avoiding the splattered blood, and held out my hand for the dog to sniff.

"Remember me? It's Morgan. I met you and … Frank? Met you here before. It's ok, I'm not going to hurt you." I spoke quietly and calmly to the dog, letting it feel the truth in my voice, knowing the words wouldn't mean much to it. "You don't need to be afraid."

I'm sorry to dispel another common fallacy about lycans and animals but we can't 'speak their tongue'. It's not like our words are translated to canine, and their barks and growls become English or whatever we speak. That would be really cool, but might be somewhat disheartening when we heard exactly what our companions thought of us, swear words and all.

Instead, animals can understand our intent, what we are trying to make them understand in more basic terms. That they are safe, we mean them no harm, that we'll protect them, feed them and the like. Or the reverse, to back off and not attack when the situation required it. Especially when we accidently barrelled into their backyard whilst on a Hunt, to avoid any confusion with the dog just protecting its home and family.

It's different between Bear and I, but that bond was strong from all our time spent together, let alone the trollhound's somewhat different nature to most common canines. Let alone my weird nature … I had yet to really understand what being a child of Herne *actually* meant apart from being abandoned for my *own good*. Supposedly.

With Albert, I just let the bulldog know he was safe, that I was here to help, and my sorrow at his packmate's death. For that was what dog owners are to their dogs. Pack. Not owner and pet, not even best friend, it was closer than that. A bond of faith and trust, that both will protect and love the other, and do their utmost to keep them safe. It's a simple truth a lot of mortals should understand, but somehow never do.

The bulldog gave one last growl then, with a pitiful whine, he limped over and leant into my hand. I gave him a gentle head rub, as I quickly checked his wounds. Three slashes, left by claws of some kind. Not deep, thank Gods, but they would need tending. Thankfully, our office had all the necessary equipment to patch up lycans in any of our shapes, and we kept supplies onsite just in case we came across hurt animals that needed tending. It's a pack thing, a lycan thing. Sets us apart from all the real monsters out there, and besides, mortals are far too lax around keeping their pets safe and well. The least we could do was help things a little if we came across any creature that needed our aid.

Knowing I was on the clock, with the officers waiting to hear that all was ok, I quickly eased myself up and left Albert slumped on the concrete path. I crouched down by Frank Appleby's side, giving him a quick once over.

The poor bastard had been gutted, his inside torn out and his chest savaged by deep claw marks. His face, frozen in death, was twisted in extreme pain and his eyes were wide, horror filled. He had definitely seen the thing that killed him, and by the reddened marks around his throat, he had been grabbed and pulled into the park before being eviscerated. I couldn't be sure, but none of the torn intestines looked to have been bitten or chewed, unlike the bodies in Greenwich, and there were no obvious tracks in the grass and dirt to show the host changing from beast back to mortal shape. This looked rushed, hurried, as if Lykaois had not had long. Maybe just enough time to take control of whomever it used as a host, break into the park and wait for the first mortal to pass by.

But then either it had been interrupted or its control over its host had slipped, since it had not been able to feed like before.

Either way, this was definitely the same monster. And it was just down the road from Sarah's home. Past time I got out of here, and found her.

And I hope to Gods she was still safe, otherwise this Lykaois was going to find out just how *cursed* it really was.

Chapter 33

"All ok now." I told the two police officers as I stepped back out of the gates. Reckoning on Albert not being up for much walking given his injuries, I had him held carefully in my left arm, cradled to keep his wounds from tearing.

For his part, Albert seemed to have used the last of his strength guarding the body of his former owner. Now his eyes were closed, his breathing rasping from his mouth, and he was a limp weight for me to carry.

Then again, compared to Bear, the bulldog was practically a featherweight, so I didn't find him much of a burden.

"You definitely have a thing with animals." PC Chambers told me, as PC Moss shook his head and ducked through the gate to being the preliminary examination of the scene. He was already talking into his shoulder mike, and I caught the words *checking if Mr Black has in any way affected the crime scene*, telling me I was still not winning things with the police officer. Oh well, I'd cry into my pillow later.

"Albert's tired and hurt." I nodded to the dog, turning him slightly to show the wounds he bore. "You said your Canine Unit won't be along for a while. In that case, I'm happy to take him back to our offices. I can give you the address, but we have some stuff we can use to patch him up. Unless you know of any next of kin who're here to take him?"

"Ol' Frank ain't got no next of kin." A voice intruded, and I turned to find an older woman standing at the barrier, looking at Albert with a sad expression. "Albert there was the only thing he had in his life he loved, and the pair were inseparable. Ain't no-one now for that dog to call friend, or place to call home. Fact you've got him means …"

"Ah, Miss Withers, please. There has not been any formal identification made, so we cannot say anything more than we have already."

The police officer interjected smoothly, stopping her before she could suggest what me holding the bulldog meant for their neighbour.

"Huh. Do what you need to, but we all know what it means for that fella to be holding Albert, all bloodied and hurt." She replied, a tear in her eye. "I'll tell you this for nothing. Ol' Frank was a fool, saying it were just kids messing around in there that did the killing of them animals. Ain't no kids done that, nor done him in. Mark me, we ain't safe to walk our own streets. But you get on with your *formal identification* as you please, mister policeman."

With that, she wiped at her eyes and then turned, walking off. It seemed she was the spokesperson for the gathered residents, as pretty much everyone else followed her. Not a single one stopped to check on Albert, or to offer any help. They simply left, to go grieve on their own.

I turned back to face PC Chambers, who wore a sad expression.

"First the museum. Now this. Since those mists appeared on the South Bank, things have just been getting worse, and we're no better off knowing why." He spoke softly, showing his frustration.

Then he gathered himself, seeming to remember his position of responsibility, his office. Not just some mortal to admit how fucked up this was, but someone to remain detached. In control. A figure of authority others could rely on. Even if all they did was turn their back and walk away.

He seemed to remember my offer after a moment, and nodded, expression turning grateful.

"That is incredibly kind of you to offer, Mr Black." He told me, nodding back to the gates and what lay beyond them. "We've got our hands full until the forensic examiners show up, and they won't be able to take, ah, Albert in anyway. If you can look after him, and just leave your office address so we know where to reach you in case anyone *does* in fact come forward for him, that would be a big help."

"No problem," I replied, carefully juggling the dog and slipping free one of the many official business cards I kept on my person just for such situations. I wasn't expecting the Met Police to sign up as a client of ours, but you never knew when it was handy to just leave a card where someone might see it and find us a useful option they hadn't known existed.

"*Good Deeds?*" PC Chambers noted, as he took the card with one gloved hand and read its details. I guessed he was one of those unfortunates who suffered from bad circulation and was forced to wear gloves and such as soon as summer was over. He probably had a woolly cap under his helmet. "Well, you certainly live up to the name. I'll call this in, and if we have any questions, I'll make sure they know where to find you."

I took that as my cue to exit, and slipped under the tape with Albert held close.

I wasn't too worried leaving the two police officers at the scene since I figured Lykaois was well and truly gone. So far, the bastard had struck at night except for this one time, doing its killing under the cover of darkness … oh and then another little lightbulb went on in my head.

The moon. We had been nearing a full moon for the past couple of days, when this thing seemed to have shifted up from killing small animals to satisfy its hunger to starting on bigger prey. Mortals. Now, the whole full moon and werewolf thing is a complete myth in terms of us lycan, but maybe, just maybe, this thing was bound by older laws. Felix had mentioned something about the cult linking the full moon to their rituals, their worship of this thing so there was the chance it was affected by the moon.

I needed to check, but I was pretty sure the full moon was due either tonight or tomorrow. And that might mean Lykaois was going to get more powerful. I figured whether it found its knife or not, this thing wouldn't be shy about celebrating being free and with suitable hosts to let loose wholesale bloodshed and slaughter.

I *really* needed to find Sarah, then go speak to Jessica and possibly Cormac. We needed to plan for the shit seriously hitting the fan.

Carrying Albert, ignoring the few odd looks I was shot by the last few people who loitered on the street outside the park, I walked as fast as I could down the road and ducked into the side street on which Sarah's house sat. Then, with as much restraint as I could manage, I banged on her side door.

Hard.

It took five minutes, but eventually I heard the sound of someone moving inside. Quitting battering the door, I did a quick check around the house as I waited, making sure I couldn't see any sign of forced entry, or sense any trace of anything like Lykaois hanging around. Since meeting it whilst it possessed Jacob, I was getting familiar with its scent, that spicy-burned mustard tang that might be its favourite aftershave or even the smell of its sweat. Whatever, it was definitely a tang that hung around where it had been, since the air in the museum had had trace elements of it, as had the area where Frank Appleby had died.

Nothing seemed amiss, so I stepped back in front of the door, cradling a still slumbering Albert.

I caught the fresh scent of citrus shower gel, the aroma of wet hair and Sarah's own scent as the door opened to show her standing just inside, wrapped in two towels.

"Morgan! What're you doing here?" She queried, looking first at me and then at what I carried. "And what are you doing with Mr Appleby's dog? And is that *blood*?"

"Can we speak inside?" I asked quietly, and she immediately stepped aside to let me in.

Sarah's home was a study in minimalism whilst at the same time decorated with many unconventional items. Her entrance hall wasn't filled with a clutter of shoes, coats and the general pile-up that mortals accumulate at the entrance to their home and never manage to shift despite their best efforts. However, she *did* have the arching skeleton of a spear-fish mounted on a wooden plinth just above head height. It supposedly was a family heirloom, of a size not seen in the oceans today and hand-caught by some great grandparent from way back in the day.

I carried Albert through, even as he grumbled and snorted his way to wakefulness. The kitchen lay down the end of a long corridor, with a washroom set on the right and a sitting room laid out on the left. Both I knew were decorated in Spanish tones of ochre and wood, with the furniture of the lounge designed for houses filled with sunlight and the heat of the Mediterranean sun. No massive loungers, corner sofas or such for Dr Sarah Conner, instead she kept to comfy long wicker sofas with fading woven throws covering their seats and cushions. All gifts from family and friends, accumulated over the years despite her black-sheep status for turning her back on the family business.

Passing these, I headed to the kitchen. This had been re-modelled when she first bought the house, fitting a central island in the floor space and then shoe-horning in a large old-style hob and oven that must have been assembled in the room itself, given the simple fact it would never had made it through the door let alone the narrow corridor. The walls were tiled, again with bright warm colours, and Sarah had managed to assemble a variety of hanging baskets from various nooks and positions, all filled with fragrant herbs spilling over their pots.

I set Albert down on the island top, and he cracked open his eyes to check his new surroundings. Sarah stepped close to the dog, concern writ all over her features as she leant in to check his wounds.

And Albert immediately backpedalled on the countertop, a snarl rumbling from his throat as his back fur bristled.

"Ok, you *really* need to change that perfume you picked up in South America." I chided her gently, as I motioned for her to back away.

Sarah looked hurt, but nodded and moved off to the sink to pour some clean cold water into a pot. This she passed to me, as well as a fresh cloth, before she stepped back to the kitchen door.

"Mr Appleby. Frank. He's dead." I told her, not sparing her the reality of what had happened. I was more than a little pissed to find her here, at home, when I had asked her to stay safe and not put herself in harm's way. Especially now that someone had been murdered by Lykaois practically on her doorstep. "The thing that was inside Miles? It must have tracked you here, and killed Frank when he took Albert out for his walk. I reckon it was waiting for you to step outside, but got bored and decided it needed some entertainment to pass the time. Hence Albert's wounds, and the blood. Which is not all of his own."

Reassuring the bulldog I meant no harm, that all I wanted to do was help, I gently scrubbed at the blood staining his fur, matting in his wounds. Albert grumbled, shivering under my ministrations, but he seemed to settle down after a moment. Allowing me to check the severity of his wounds.

Thankfully, I'd been right with my first guess. The claw marks weren't deep, so I had to assume Albert had simply gotten in the way of Lykaois's attack on Frank, and suffered from trying to stop his death. For whatever reason, the creature hadn't finished the dog off, instead leaving it alive when it fled the kill. Before it could feast on its bounty. Again, I had no idea *what* could have caused it to leave before it started eating the mortal, except I was fairly sure the police arriving had not been a factor. If it had been present when they showed up, I'd have expected the body count to be higher.

"Frank's dead? But how ... what would that thing want with me? I ... oh *mi madre*. That's horrible!" Sarah replied, eyes fixed on Albert. "Is that why you're here?"

"You didn't answer your phone." I told her, keeping my voice calm, my emotions in check. Now that I knew she was safe and well, I was fighting just a little to not be pissed as fuck with her. "I went to the museum to find you, just to make sure everything was ok after last night's shitshow. But Jan told me you hadn't been in. When you said you were going there to make sure everyone was ok. That's what you *told* me."

I left the statement there, without asking the question. Leaving it up to her how she wanted to respond.

Sarah switched her gaze from the bulldog to me, her dark eyes wide and pained.

"Oh, Morgan. I'm sorry. I really am." She went to step into the kitchen again, but Albert bristled, and I waved for her to stay put. "I ... I really meant to go in, but after the taxi dropped me off at the museum, I just didn't know what I was going to say. What I could do to help. Miles got sick ... this thing got into him ... because of *us*. Because what we found out there, what we brought back with us. I just know it. So we're to blame for the people who lost their lives. People I know, that I've worked with, shared time with. Friends, not just colleagues. It's *my* fault they died."

Tears coursed down her face, as she leant against the doorframe. All I wanted to do was walk over to her, enfold her in my arms and tell her how wrong she was. Except, of course, the truth was she was right. It *had* been because they broached the sacred temple or prison or whatever the fuck the Mayans had built to house Lykaois. They'd taken the tools of his ritual, and bloody stupid Professor Eduardo had even spilled his own blood with the knife. Everything the spirit most likely needed to break free and start causing mayhem and slaughter all over again.

"What did you do?" I asked quietly instead, settling one hand on Albert as the bulldog heaved a heavy sigh. His wounds were clean now, but I still needed to get him to *Good Deeds*, so I could patch them up. And update Jessica on things.

"I … I walked for a bit. Just trying to make sense of it all." Sarah told me, brushing the tears from her face, then nodding back behind her. "Then it struck me. If we released this thing, if it was because of what we did at the temple, then maybe we can put things right? Put this thing back in its box, and seal it back up. I came back here, to check through anything I hadn't given over to the museum yet. To see if anything might help. I … I just want to make this right."

It sounded logical, plausible and wholly believable. The scents I was getting off Sarah did not in any way make me doubt her, or think she was trying to trick me. She was upset, deeply upset. There wasn't any faking that. But I also sensed her frustration and guilt, and that burning passion of hers to set the record straight.

"Ok, I get it." I told her gently, letting my anger fizzle and die, seeing the woman I loved struggling to deal with a situation she was in no way experienced to handle. "Just, next time, call me when you decide to change the plan. I almost had a heart attack when Jan said you hadn't been in. Oh, and there's about a million missed calls on your phone. The one you're supposed to answer, remember?"

Sarah managed to look embarrassed, that emotion a spike of heat amongst her sadness.

"I'm really sorry, Morgan." She told me, gesturing down at the towels. "Things got a bit jumbled in my head. I must have put it down when I got in, but I can't remember where. I think all the stress is getting to me, as I sort of woke up in the shower, but I don't remember getting dirty enough to want one. Crazy, huh?"

A chill burned down deep inside me, a flicker of fear that I bit down hard on before it escaped and showed on my face.

"Yeah, funny. You forgetting things. That's more my job, isn't it?" I joked, then asked offhandedly. "What *do* you remember? The last thing, before I was breaking down your door?"

Sarah cocked her head, motioning to the towels again.

"Well, obviously me being in the shower, *mi chulo*," She told me after a moment, smiling a little. "But before that, I know I stood outside the museum for a while trying to get the courage up to go inside. Then I just walked for a bit. Not sure where, just around. Eventually I must have headed back here to start searching. So, maybe that. I think. Why?"

"Oh, I'm just checking if you're going senile, starting to forget important stuff. Like the fact you promised to take me out for a proper date and dinner, and made me promise not to try to pay for it!" I joked, the lie slipping free to hide my worry. The last thing I wanted Sarah to do was to start dwelling on any missing time, any forgotten portions of her life. Especially recently.

"Yeah, that sounds *just* like the thing I would say, *mi amor*. Of course, it means I get to pick the restaurant." She grinned back at me, the lie accepted. I breathed a little easier. "So now what? Is Albert going to be ok?"

"I need to get him back to the office, so I can patch him up. Then I'll ask Jessica if anyone can look after him until we can find him a permanent new home." I replied, and then, as an offhand thought added. "Look, grab whatever you think you found that might help, and come in with us. It'll help to get all the information we have in one place, and this way I won't keep calling your phone every five minutes until I know you are safely back at my home."

Sarah nodded, and shot me a warm, loving smile.

"Give me ten minutes to change and grab some of my things, if I'm going to be staying at yours until this all is over." She told me, already unwrapping the towel from her hair to check how damp it still was. "I'll throw in what I have from the expedition too, and we can see if anything helps. Wouldn't it be great if I had the answer to this mess and we can stop anything more horrible happening?"

"Yeah, that would be simply awesome." I told her, then tried my luck as an afterthought. "One thing, did Professor Eduardo leave anything with you? Anything from the site? Like, oh I don't know, anything he found there?"

Sarah thought for a moment then shook her dark locks.

"Sorry." She replied, and I shrugged, knowing it had been a long shot anyhow. "Anything Julius had would probably still be at his home. He wasn't much of a sharer, you might say."

"Yeah, I got that." I shrugged. "Ok, you pack, I'll call us a ride."

Albert, sat on the kitchen island top, chose that moment to show his thoughts on my plan. Fragrantly.

"*After* I open a window. And maybe light a candle!" I shot a look at the bulldog whilst trying not to choke.

For his part, the old dog simply gave a snort and closed his eyes. Totally at peace with his attempt to gas me for my efforts.

Chapter 34

True to her word, Sarah took very little time to stuff a bag full of everything she might need. Showing her obvious experience and well-seasoned practice of travelling light, but also making sure she only took what she herself could carry.

I personally knew she detested those wheeled luggage bags, her complaint being their owners should take a mandatory test like you did to drive a vehicle. Since most of them were lethally inept at navigating anywhere with a fully loaded suitcase without running over your toes, banging into you from the side or trailing them far behind to cause the person behind them more stress.

Instead, Sarah had a battered carry-all that she could fit an astonishing amount inside and still sling it over her back to hike up a mountain or into the depths of a jungle ... and at the end of the day *still* have a dress uncrumpled or free of creases to wear at a suitable event. A woman of many talents.

Whilst she was busy gathering her clothes and toiletries, I had done a very quick and light scan of the house. Those chunks of missing memories had the warning bells ringing in my head, and whilst I had gotten no scent of Lykaois from Sarah or around the home, the death of Frank Appleby just down from her home was a fact I couldn't ignore.

Thankfully, unlike when I searched Jacob's home, I found no scent of blood. No bloodstained clothes. No evidence that Sarah had been involved in the butchering of an old man, or had been hunting and killing animals where she lived. All I *did* find was a freshly cleaned house, the sharp smell of bleach filling the air and her washing machine running on a high temperature wash.

Nothing to worry about, at all. I told myself.

I'd booked us a cab on account, and called into work to tell them I was headed in with Sarah and an injured animal. Marcus had taken the call, and I immediately caught his worried tones, stress and maybe a little fear laced in his response to me.

"Morgan, thank fuck! Glad you're heading in. It's Jessica. She's ... oh, just get in, ok?"

With that cryptic and worrying instruction, I bundled Sarah into the front of the cab, whilst Albert and I took the rear seats. I'd specifically asked for a vehicle that would suit our needs, since the bulldog *still* wasn't settling around Sarah despite her having washed all trace of that perfume and body scent off her, and chosen a neutral deodorant instead.

Between the way Bear and now Albert had reacted, I was wondering just *what* was in that perfume she had brought back with her. *Eau de la latrine,* maybe. It certainly didn't set my nose off in any bad way, but that didn't exactly mean it wasn't upsetting to actual canines.

Traffic was still bad, so we crawled our way from Holland Park to *Good Deeds,* taking roughly the same time as if we'd decided to walk the distance. But even though Albert wasn't exactly a heavy load to me, he was still in pain, and I reckoned he could do with the break from either being lugged about by me or waddling along under his own steam. And of course, I reckoned I'd save Sarah hoiking her travel bag along as well, since I couldn't carry that and the injured dog.

Mr Considerate, me. At times.

When we pulled up at the office, I carefully manhandled the hurt dog out whilst Sarah hung back. Albert, for his part, was half asleep, snorting the odd snore but thankfully holding off on releasing any more noxious gases.

Getting in the door, I found Marcus waiting for me. And I immediately guessed what the problem was.

"You look like shit." I told him, and he managed a smile despite his pale complexion and sweat soaking whatever skin I could see. Normally, Markus looked like a gym instructor, the sort who handles the heavyweights of Hollywood or professional wrestlers. He's *solid,* just the sort to laugh off anything but the worst possible injury.

Not so much now.

"Yeah, well. Least I know I only look like this coz I'm sick." He snarked back at me, getting up from behind the reception desk with only the barest of groans. "You look like that *all* the time."

"Point." I gave it to him, then nodded to the stairs. "I'm guessing the boss is just as bad?"

"Worse." He confirmed, and I shook my head before motioning for Sarah to join us as we headed up. Markus deftly slid her bag off her shoulder before she could object, but I heard the faint hiss he let slip before he half staggered ahead of us.

"What's wrong with him?" She asked, but I just shook my head again, not knowing what the fuck was going on.

Lycan just don't get sick. We get hurt, sure, and need downtime to heal up broken bones, wrenched joints, that sort of thing. But colds, flu, diseases … pretty much most things that threaten mortals just take one look at us and fuck off elsewhere for easier victims. Wolfsbane screws us over royally, and definitely weakens us but unless *everyone* had suddenly got as stupid as Jacob, that couldn't be the reason.

No, this was something else, and I was at a loss as to what it could be.

Coming up to the first floor, I stopped, as the reality hit me like a sucker punch.

The rest of the pack were slumped at their desks or over the couches dotted around the office, but it wasn't just them. Other lycan, from the packs of London, were filling up what arse-space they could or even just stretched out on the floor looking thoroughly miserable.

Emma saw me and raised a hand, her fiery red hair lank and looking like she hadn't bothered combing it for a while. And I'd seen her not so long ago, looking as spry and vital as normal. Kristoff didn't even manage that, just raising his head from the desk for a moment before letting it thud back down again with a muted groan.

There was no air of sickness around the pack, nothing that made me think this was anything like a virus or plague. Whatever it was, it looked like it was sapping them of their strength, leaving them weak, enfeebled.

Normal.

"Shit, is this everybody?" I asked Markus, who had taken the chance to park himself on the corner of a desk. He drew a breath, rallying himself before he shook his head.

"Jess is down, as is Sean and Patrick." He answered finally, waving a hand at the rest of the floor. "East London Hunt's been hit hard, like us, so Rian and Josh are basically covering everything with whom they have that can still stand up. We've had to tell the mortals, so they've taken over manning No Man's Land, but it won't be long before word gets out we're in no shape to keep the peace. Then the shit'll really hit the fan."

I grunted, acknowledging the simple truth. As much as OPS and the regular mortal authorities might be able to stop the small problems like idiots trying to get into the mists, they were in no way ready to pick up the slack if those Real denizens of the Mortal Realm realised the Red Cloaks were out of action.

Let alone if Morgana decided six months mortal-time had been enough to hatch some elaborate revenge on us all, and come crashing out of Twilight like the psychotic deranged but all powerful fae I knew her to be.

Shit, what *if* this was her, somehow? In normal times I'd have turned to Ellie to ask her to identify whatever the hell was going on, but she was beyond reach. Leaving me two choices.

"Is Felix still around?" I asked Markus, seeing him nod, jerking his head upward.

"She's with Jessica. Been trying to see if there's anything she can do to help." He replied, his expression telling me not to get hopeful. "So far, I think she's managed to stop her falling over, but that's about it."

"Ok." I gripped his shoulder, feeling the shivers wracking his body that he was fighting to control, and gently pushed him down into the chair by the desk. "Sit your arse down and rest a bit. I'll go check things out and be back to see what I can do to help."

Markus shot me a grateful look, leaning back in the chair and uttering a soft groan.

First thing, I set Albert down on the soft carpet, far enough away from Sarah not to start him off again, and headed back downstairs. There were just two things I needed to do, and neither took long. Fitting the "Sorry We're Closed" sign on the door, then switching the automatic answerphone into the office number to pick up any calls coming in. That way, no-one would be disturbed from feeling like utter shit, and have to come staggering and falling on their arse down the stairs.

I re-joined Sarah, and motioned for her to follow me. Picking up Albert again, ignoring his grumbled complaints, I headed through the office, nodding to those lycan who were conscious enough to greet me with a weary wave or pathetic nod of their heads. It was scary, seeing them all laid low so quickly, so fragile. So mortal.

Taking the stairs up, I stepped into Jessica's private sanctum.

Felix looked up from where she sat on a sofa, pouring over a thick, ancient tome, bound in leather and with yellowed pages.

"Oh Morgan!" She tossed the book aside and hit me like a small battering ram, wrapping her arms around me as I frantically tried to juggle the bulldog and not be carried over by her momentum. "I ... shit, I don't know what to *do*!"

Well, that answered my first question, as I gently prised Felix off me and set her back on her feet. Following behind me, Sarah remained quiet and forbore to comment on what a young woman of, I had to admit, very attractive appearance was doing wrapping herself around the man she loved ... showing the good sense and judgement that I loved *her* for.

"Hey, calm down. It's ok." I told her, looking into her eyes and letting her panic still, quietening her with my own measured breathing and solid presence. "First thing, are you feeling ill in any way?"

"What?" She shook her head, focusing her thoughts from wherever they had run off to. "Uh, no. Not even a sneeze. It's just all you lot, your pack and the other lycan. And Jessica. They're all getting sick and ..."

"Yeah, I saw. Let's park that for the moment." I told her, as I nodded to the bedroom door which was currently closed. "Jessica in there?"

Felix nodded, as her eyes settled on Albert, flicking from noting Sarah hanging back quietly behind me. "I've been keeping her drinking fluids, and watching her temperature, but that's about all that works. Nothing I try seems to stick."

She waggled her fingers, indicating she'd tried using her magic. I shrugged, not surprised that whatever was attacked us was impervious to anything the young witch might try. Felix was strong, no doubt about that, but this thing had to be complex *and* powerful to override our natural resistance, and curing an illness meant understanding it first and foremost. Leastways that was what Ellie had told me on more than one occasion.

Healers are often demeaned these days as second rate who simply wave their hand and knit wounds, salve pain and make things better with barely any effort. But their chosen profession was one steeped in personal sacrifice and learning, understanding each and every ailment by the simple practice of suffering it themselves. It wasn't masochism, just the simple truth that to fix something properly, you had to know what was wrong, and what needed leaving alone. It was all too easy to *heal* someone and accidently cause them to grow an extra limb, or suffer weird-ass side effects that were of no help whatsoever.

In comparison, Felix was like a child attending school for the first time, and being asked to construct a fully functional and working rocket that would not only carry passengers into orbit but also keep them safe and return them in one piece. She would have to understand engineering, mechanics, the laws of psychics, biology and a host of other stuff, when all she was really ready for was finger-painting.

"Look, I've got to go check in with her." I told her, thinking through what I needed that she could help with. The first was easy. "This is Albert. He got into a fight and his wounds need tending. Can you help him?"

Felix leaned in and ruffled the fur under Albert's chin, eliciting a rumbling deep in his chest as his eyes closed in pleasure. She beamed up at me, holding out her hands.

"Totally! He's adorable! I'll get those cuts sorted out, no problem." She accepted him off me, her muscles bunching under his solid mass but she straightened and rubbed his deeply furrowed forehead with obvious delight. "What about his owner? Is he or she …?"

"Out of the picture. I'll fill you in on the details later." I answered her truthfully. She had seen the carnage in Greenwich Park without losing her breakfast, lunch or dinner. She could handle the truth. "But for now, if you can fix him up, that would be great."

Having handed over my burden, I turned back to Sarah. She had watched the interplay between Felix and I silently, but simply smiled at me warmly when I returned to her.

"I've got to check in with my boss. If it's ok, do you mind just waiting here until we're done? Then we can go over what you know, and hopefully make a little more sense of all this." I asked her, and she nodded, having picked her bag back off Markus when he collapsed into the chair. This she now set down on the floor, and nodded down to the floor below.

"I have a little experience of dealing with victims of malaria and jungle fever." She told me, reaching up to bind back her hair and roll up the sleeves of her blouse. "I can lend a hand if you like, until you're done. Just fetching drinks and checking on your … friends?"

"Friends is a good word. And yeah, that would be great." I smiled at her generous offer, knowing she could have very well asked to sit this out and leave matters that had nothing to do with her alone. But not Sarah Maria Conner. That wasn't the woman she was, or ever had been. "The kitchen should be fully stocked downstairs. Unless Felix has eaten us out of everything already."

"Oi!" Felix shot at me, but then turned back to making coo-ing noises and fussing over Albert. The dog, for his part, was rumbling and snorting with pleasure from the affection being shown him. I reckoned he was going to be alright in her hands.

"No problem, *chulo*." Sarah replied, stepping towards the stairs then looking back at me. "I'll see what I can do to help, then come find you again."

I waited until she was definitely out of earshot, the scent of her fading enough for me to know she was out of range, before I waved to Felix.

"Hey, one other thing?" I asked quietly, as she broke off inspecting Albert's claw wounds.

"What?" The young witch asked, obviously picking up on my hushed tones. "And why are we whispering suddenly?"

"Because I want this to stay between us, obviously." I nodded my head back to where Sarah had gone. "Is there any way you can do something like, I don't know, check if she is … herself? Uh, like if there's anything that has messed with her head maybe? Or is still inside her somehow?"

Felix's eyes widened as she guessed what I was making such a piss poor job of asking.

"You think *Lykaois* has gotten to her?" She asked in hushed tones, and I winced, remembering how many times we'd been using this bloody thing's name now that we knew more about it. And how names attract attention. But that was the least of my worries right now. "And you brought her *here*? Are you mad?!"

"Probably. Completely." I agreed, then shook my head. "Look, I don't think this bastard is still around, but I need to know if its gotten to her. If she was still possessed, the wards would have reacted to its presence and since things haven't exploded, I'm pretty sure we're safe."

Felix nodded, looking a little sheepish at having forgotten our office was warded and a safe zone. To be fair, that had been a test I'd thought to run on Sarah back at her home, realising if this bloodthirsty arsehole was just puppeteering her, then the new and improved protections around the office would go off like the fourth of July crossed with the fifth of November.

"But something's not right, and I need to know if it's just me being paranoid or something worse." I added, nodding to Albert as he snorted in displeasure at the cessation of fussing. "Bear and he both reacted badly to her, and my mutt was … *is* besotted with her normally. Plus she pulled a vanishing act, and turned up just down the street from that bastard's most recent kill. And she's the last one of the three people who survived whatever actually happened in the jungle and even she admits she's got blank spots in her memory. All I need to know is, is it *her*, or it looking back at me."

Felix took a breath, thinking before shaking her head, expression apologetic.

"I'm sorry, Morgan but I really wouldn't know where to start." She explained, confirming my fear. "It's bad enough trying to guess what's wrong with the rest of you lot and try to help. But trying to sense if she is possessed or whatever you want to call it? That's like trying to ask me to design a space rocket or something equally crazy."

I snorted a laugh, struck again how Felix and my minds' sometimes tended to be attuned the same way. She shot me an odd look, not expecting me to laugh at her apparent lack of skill to help me, and I just shrugged.

"It's ok. It was a long shot." I told her, and nodded to Albert. "Best you get on with fixing the old boy there, and I'll go check on the boss. She's due an update on all things weird and shitty."

"When you're finished, I did some more reading of that journal. There's stuff you need to know." She told me, and I tried not to wince. I wasn't sure how many more revelations I could take today, and had to wonder at the sort of mind Professor Eduardo had had, to uncover so many Gods-awful things about the object of his fascination ... and still bloody well mess with it.

Mortals. The only species I knew that should have a warning label printed on them at birth.

Chapter 35

Stake to the heart

A common misconception is that vampires alone can be killed by piercing their heart with wood. Many supernatural monsters are weak to this strategy, however the issue is that they often have hearts in different places or multiple organs so that a mortal need to find the right place to strike to slay the monster.

Often wood is not required, but it is the commonest weapon to find at hand. A broken chair leg, a pole, even logs taken from the fire and broken into handy stabbing tools will serve. The trick when attempting this is to get in close enough to shove the weapon into the right place, and then get out of reach fast enough to avoid injury. There is usually no second chance offered.

I slipped into Jessica's bedroom quietly, not wanting to disturb her if she was asleep. If she was, I planned on leaving her a scribbled update of what we'd found, what I suspected and my immediate plans, and then get the hell out of the office before she woke and realised the depths of my idiocy.

"Ah, Morgan. Ah'm glad tae see you." She spoke up as I stepped in through the door.

No such luck.

Jessica was curled in her bed, sheets and duvet bundled around her like an old woman trying to stay warm in winter. She looked haggard and weary, bags under her eyes and her skin a grey colour in the light of the lamps she had on so she could work on her ever-present electronic notepad.

The smile she shot me, though, was as warm as ever, and I felt a measure of strength through the bond with my Alpha. Something certain I could rely on, in all the craziness that had been going on around me.

"You're looking … uh …" I offered, and her smile grew sharper, as she chuckled weakly.

"Exactly. Ah look just as bad as that, and feel ten times worse." Jessica told me, but then set aside her pad and motioned towards one of the free chairs that sat in the room. "But ah am sure you did nae come tae see me, simply tae tell me how ah look. Felix has apprised me of yer investigations, but ah think you have more tae tell me."

"I really wish I didn't." I answered her truthfully, as I settled down into the chair. "But yeah, things have been happening. It's all getting a bit crazy, even for me."

Jessica chuckled, then coughed a rattling wheeze that sounded decidedly unhealthy. When she caught my look of concern, she waved a hand at me, brushing her ailment off.

"Dinnae worry. Ah'm not ready tae join Mark in the Hunt just yet." She told me, referring back to the lycan's view on death. Joining those we'd loved and lost in the Wild beyond the Veil, hunting free forever. "Now, list out our problems fer me."

It didn't take long for me to run through everything that had happened since I left the office this morning, and the few guesses I'd made about this *Lykaois* and what it might be after. And finally, my recently discovered worry that Morgana was behind this somehow.

Jessica listened intently, coughing occasionally but letting me finish before she spoke.

"Ah am well aware of that particular fae's potential tae cause us problems," She commented dryly. "But fer now, until ah see more evidence tae suggest her hand in this, let us focus on the creature who is obvious and the cause of so much pain and sorrow."

"The fact this creature has been able tae take control of Jacob does in some way affirm its supposition tae being linked tae our kin." Jessica continued, but stopped me before I could voice what I thought of its alleged Godhood. "I dinnae say it *is* our God, or the root of where we came from, what we are. Just that there is a link betwixt us. Obviously, it sees this tae be one of deity and subject, and is seeking tae find a new set of followers. As those that last did so have been dead these many hundred years."

"As tae yer thoughts on it being a thing of the Wyld Court, ah expect you may be right. It certainly fits the brief of the fae and other creatures ah have experienced bound tae that province." She eyed me, knowing my history, where I came from. My link to the Wyld. "It may also be why this thing seems tae be inordinately focused on you, Morgan. It has revealed itself tae you, spoken tae you, and spent time studying you. Your life, your links tae threaten. It wants something of *you*, of that ah am sure."

"It can go screw itself, if it thinks it's getting me to call it God or any shit like that." I growled, and Jessica nodded, smiling.

"Ah would expect nae else." She replied, but then tapped her pad as she thought. "Ah think you had best expect this thing has you followed, and is keeping tabs on you somehow. Yer suspicion about the Sisters, and this Professor Eduardo may indeed be true, but if so you could be leading it tae the one thing it seems tae desire if you attend this meeting tonight. It might be better if someone goes in yer place …"

"Uh, like who?" I shot back, gesturing to her. "Pretty much most of the pack are flat on their back, or will be if this virus or illness or whatever the fuck it is keeps spreading. And the Sisters are expecting me. It's bad enough I've promised to take Cormac with me, but if someone else shows up instead of me, I'm pretty sure they'll see that as a complete breach of our agreement. And I really don't want them pissed at me. It's bad enough the Furies still want my hide, let alone a bunch of mystical nuns who to be frank are just plain scary at the best of times."

Jessica shrugged, accepting the point even if she did not agree with my decision.

"Look, I know you're not going to like this, but I don't think I've got much choice in the matter." I told Jessica, seeing her eyes narrow as she braced herself for what I was about to suggest. "Felix isn't Elspeth, and the rest of the Witches-R-Us seem to want to treat us like dogshit they'd rather not step in until she agrees to join their coven. I think I've got to ask *family* about whatever is affecting all the lycan, and maybe if they know about this *beast that walks as a man* arsehole."

Jessica sighed after a long moment, then pointed to the door of her bedroom.

"If you are going tae summon *family*, then ah'd appreciate you do so in the next room." She told me with finality. "The last thing ah want is the stink of the fae filling where ah'm trying tae get some sleep."

Then she nodded, her eyes tired.

"You are right. We'd be foolish to nae seek help when we are so afflicted." She admitted, and that was like a punch to the gut, hearing Jessica admit we were weakened, that *she* was too. We relied on our Alphas to be the solid core of the pack, and drew on that to stand against whatever we faced. Losing that strength meant we were vulnerable, weak against anything looking to take us down. "Ah grant you the right tae summon who you choose tae the office this once, so at least you won't set off the alarms and cause your packmates downstairs more trouble."

I nodded gratefully, pushing myself up and walking to the door. I had it open, and was about to walk through, when Jessica stopped me.

"Morgan?" She called after me, and I looked back, seeing her almost lost amongst the rumpled duvet. Somehow *smaller*, which tore at my heart.

"If you're right, and the Sisters are keeping this artefact, then the moment you take it from them, you'll be alerting this thing tae its location." She told me, expression grave. "You'd best prepare tae run *very* fast, if you dinnae want to simply hand the thing over, and maybe let this thing go trouble someone else?"

I shook my head, knowing it had crossed my mind to simply find the knife and somehow bargain with *Lykaois*. If it wanted the bloody thing that much, maybe I could force it to deal, to promise. But I'd faced that idea and realised just how idiotic it was.

Lykaois wasn't going anywhere, with or without its favourite chopping tool. The thing wanted to shed blood, to feed its hunger, and to form a new cult in its honour. If it even did agree to fuck off and leave us be, I'd only be passing the buck over to someone else, setting them up to be its victims and playthings. And that wasn't in me to do.

"Ah thought so too. But ah had tae check yer thinking." She told me with a small smile. "Oh, and one last thought. You said whatever is affecting all the lycan. This illness or attack, whatever it is."

"Yeah? So?" I asked, and she looked pointedly at me.

"Not *all* the lycan. You are fit and hale, from what ah can tell. Think on that. And now, if you dinnae mind, ah'm going to try tae sleep. Try tae keep the noise down."

With that dismissal, I closed the door quietly behind me, and went about calling on the help I'd hoped not to have to ask for, but now was my only real option.

Chapter 36

"Morrigan, do you mind if we skip the *thrice ye shall call* thing this time? I'm a little pressed and could do with your help. Please?"

I figured it was worth a shot, given how I knew my fae grandmother on my father's side kept tabs on me. She'd made far too many snarky comments about my failed attempts with Sarah, and other things in my life, for her not to be sneaking peeks on me.

After I'd finished with Jessica, I checked in on Felix and Albert. After her inability to help the lycan, the young witch had thrown herself into aiding the injured hound. His wounds had been thoroughly and professionally cleaned, and then either she had managed to do the neatest and smallest job of sewing them up or she had cheated and called on her magic to fix them. Albert wasn't a lycan, so had no resistance to get in the way of her craft. I was just a little surprised at the skill she'd used wielding it.

With that done, Felix had procured a bundle of blankets and pillows from our stores, and put together a lavish and very comfortable bed for the bulldog to recover in. She'd finished things off with some treats taken from the kitchen, cold sausages factoring largely in the meal she'd prepared.

As Albert snored blissfully with a half-eaten sausages tucked beneath his jowls, I'd motioned for the young woman to come help me for a moment. With nothing more to do, she agreed, and I sent her down to keep Sarah occupied whilst I grabbed as quick a catch up with my immortal contact as I could. The last thing I wanted was Sarah walking in on us, and me giving the Morrigan the perfect chance to grill her. Or scare the life out of her, more like, knowing my relative's sense of humour.

With all that done, I'd settled down on the couch in Jessica's living area, and readied myself for dealing with the as ever frustrating but oft times helpful fae.

"I'll even offer …" I started to promise, reckoning owing the Morrigan a no-strings favour was a tempting enough offer for her to ignore protocol just this once.

The next moment, the room around me blurred and I had that familiar sense of travelling without actually making a single move.

My arse plunked down on fresh grass, and I breathed in a lungful of air totally free of the smog and pollution that filled London. Looking around, I found myself sat on thick rolling verdance, curving off down on every side. A large stone building, ancient in design with a massive, carved archway for a door and small ornate windows set three by three in its upper stories. The roof looked like it had been taken from a castle, with the sort of blocks perfect for archers to hide behind and pepper any unruly element with arrows if they dared assault the building.

It was unmistakeable, and a long, long way from where I'd just been talking to my pack Alpha. Where I'd left my witch friend and my on-again partner.

"What the hell am I doing on Glastonbury Tor of all fucking places?" I asked the empty air, figuring the answer would not be slow in coming.

"Once more you are dressed wholly inappropriate for times of war, Sir Pup." The Morrigan's icy tones replied, managing to convey subtle humour and a slight reprimand with the ease of a being who had been alive for millennia. "I would think, given that which stalks your city, feasts upon the innocents and not so innocents whom you say you protect, even those you love … you would be garbed more appropriately. But then, knowing you, maybe not."

I turned, to find the fae standing by the arch leading inside the Tor's building. She wore her customary leather armour, scarred from many battles, wrapped with rags taken from the shrouds of the fallen warriors she had ushered into the afterlife. Usually by way of a particularly brutal death, surrounded by the broken bodies of their foes. It still disturbed me to think that after fighting whatever war, battle or skirmish they found themselves in, either winning or losing the day for their cause, lord or just the settlement of a long-standing grudge, these poor sods had succumbed to their wounds only to have the last thing they saw being … her. Pools of dark fire for eyes, fox-thin features of shadow-grey, tattooed with runic script. And a smile so sharp you could cut steel with it.

She leant on a different weapon this time, her normal staff exchanged for a lance of dark metal. The spearhead was ornate but more than anything else, lethally tapered to a point, curving slightly along the back edge to give her both stopping power from a thrust and a very nasty slicing edge to use against any who came against her.

"You're looking particularly warlike today, granny." I greeted her as I pushed myself up to stand, even as my nose twitched. I'd been distracted by the pureness of the air out here, so far from London and its atmosphere so dense you could almost feel it clinging to you as you travelled about the city. But now, I caught another scent. Bright and sharp in the air, all too familiar, all too alien for where I found myself sitting.

Blood. Not fresh, but definitely in enough quantities to be something more than a paper cut or scratch from a thorn.

"My attire is suitable for the present state of all Realms," She replied gravelly, then sniffed as she looked at my casual clothes I'd thrown on for the office. "Something you should consider, 'ere much more time passes."

"Yeah, I'll throw on some armour and clank about the place, looking like a right pillock." I promised her, smiling sweetly before nodding to the building on top of the Tor. "I'm guessing you brought me here coz of what's in there?"

"Firstly, you do not need armour to attain such a description." The fae answered with a sickle-slim smile, then pointed at me. "Secondly, *you* called on me. In such an uncouth and ignorant manner, I might add. You are lucky I answered at all, if not with the pointed end of my lance."

Shrugging, I let the threat slide by as I knew there was little chance of the Morrigan actually skewering me here and now. Skipping the Court protocols to call on her was *far* down the list of the thing I'd said and done that deserved her kicking my arse from here back to London. I reckoned I was fairly safe from being turned into a lycan-kebab, heavy on the red wine sauce.

"And I am thankful you did." I graciously told her, seeing her smile grow wider at the obvious attempt to ingratiate myself. "I need help."

"That much needs no announcement." She quipped before I could continue, and I bit back the sigh and rolling of eyes that I felt was due. I sought her aid, and her sarcasm came hand in hand with that.

"Ok, I earned that one." I held up a hand to forestall any more dressing down or abuse, at least until I had gotten my questions out of the way. "Thing is, we think we've worked out what that thing you warned me about is. The bastard stalking me, and leaving corpses all over the bloody joint."

"I warned you, pup." She answered with more than a little ghoulish delight. "This thing, it is savage and bloodthirsty, and will not stop unless it is dealt with like any mad animal. And put down."

"I'm getting that impression." I agreed, thinking back to the damage the creature had done in the museum simply because it couldn't find the thing it wanted. The mortal neighbour butchered in the street when it couldn't get into the professor's home. How Frank Appleby had been torn apart and tossed in the bushes. The thing had serious rage issues. "Thing is, you said before you didn't think this thing was of the Wyld. But some of the stuff we've found contradicts that. The scent I've gotten from where its been, just a feeling about it. I was wondering. Could you be mistaken? Could this be just some arsewipe from the Wyld looking to settle an old score against, oh let me think, the son of the current Lord?"

The Morrigan eyed me for a long moment, then simply shrugged.

"The Seers could not say what this thing's nature was, nor any affiliation to a Court." She replied, her dark eyes unreadable. "Only that it is fixated on *you*, and your kin. And that it shares some sort of bond with you. That should be enough for you to hunt it, and kill it before it hurts any more that you care for."

I went to rebuff her casual sentence, knowing I was bound by the rules of the pack to try to capture and detain this thing just like any other Accord breaker or rogue Real denizen. But the Morrigan cut me off, her expression hardening.

"Do not be foolish, pup." She told me harshly. "This thing is not some simple goblin caught tricking foolish mortals, or a troll peddling in stolen mortal children. This thing is a *killer*, and as such, needs to be treated as such. Find it, end it. Before it ends you."

"Now, what else did you wish to speak to me about, so that we can move onto matters of actual *import*." She crossed her arms, leaning her spear against one shoulder, arching one slim eyebrow.

Knowing I wasn't going to get any more information out of the fae on that subject, I shoved my frustration aside and moved on.

"Ok, fine. Something's making all the lycans sick. Weakening them, like a virus. It's almost as if they've all caught something like influenza or something." I admitted, bracing myself for the obvious rebuke. "We're out of ideas what the fuck it could be, and how to treat it."

"Lycan do not get sick." The Morrigan did not disappoint me, shaking her head so that the bone braids clacked together. "You seem fit and hale, so it cannot be that bad."

I shrugged.

"It doesn't seem to be affecting me. But everyone else is pretty much fucked over. Even the Alphas." I replied honestly. I could trust my grandmother with this fact, knowing she wouldn't exactly run off and announce to the world that it was open season on the packs. "I was hoping you might know a thing or two about what could mess with lycans. Other than Wolfsbane, and I can promise it isn't that. But it's definitely something."

The Shadow fae looked at me for a moment before stepping up close and laying a cold hand on my forehead.

"I told you I'm not affected." I went to move her hand away, but snake-quick, she slapped my own with the haft of her spear. "Ow!"

"Foolish pup. Leave me be." She told me, closing her eyes. I felt a coldness spread from her touch, sinking into me, moving as if searching. It was definitely up there on the weirder feelings I'd felt. "Your connection to your pack is strong enough, for me to gain a sense of what might be troubling them."

I stood there, on the grassy hillock, feeling more than a little exposed as the fae mumbled to herself, too low even for me to hear what she was saying. Then, finally, she let her hand fall as she stepped back. Her dark eyes were thoughtful, and even more worrying, I sensed a troubled air to her that I had never felt before.

"So, what is it?" I asked, but the Morrigan shook her head.

"You know as well as I, that I am bound by the laws of the Realm and cannot simply *give* you a straight and simple answer." She told me, and I cursed that little clause in the rulebook of dealing with all things Real. Whoever had written the laws on how mortals and immortals interacted had decided that they needed to make things as complicated as possible. It was the same sort of logic that also ruled on what a mortal could and could not wish for, if offered by a supernatural entity. Enough subclauses to make sure the Realms could never be truly threatened, and that whatever the wisher asked for usually came back to bite them in the arse.

In this case, the Morrigan was actually speaking the simple truth. Whilst standing in the Mortal Realm, she was unable to give me a straight answer to any question I asked. She could hint, indicate a direction I should look in and signpost however she might like to get me to the answer I wanted, but she couldn't just come out and tell me.

"That is *so* bloody annoying. Just saying." I growled, but the Morrigan shrugged, smiling like a shark.

"Would you prefer that we were unbound in our answers, when mortals might ask all manner of troubling things? Like the *launch codes to all the nuclear weapons in the world* or *the secret of eternal life, to cheat death* or even *how do I murder someone and make sure I am never accused*? Such trifling matters, with such weighty outcomes." She replied with a knowing smile. "Is it not safer that we are bound, and so keep the mortals from waking to a world in ruin because of one man or woman's simple greed or stupidity?"

"Yeah, yeah." I groused, but I knew she was right. "Ok, lay the hints on me. What *can* you tell me?"

"Your packmates are indeed afflicted, but I cannot say by what and how." She replied after a moment, obviously carefully choosing her words.

"The source of this thing, I have already told you to be wary of. Seek what you already hunt, and you will find your answers. Of that I am sure."

I sighed, knowing on the one hand she was doing everything she could to help me, but still feeling so bloody frustrated. *Seek what you already hunt?*

"It's that bastard, isn't it?" I growled, realisation hitting me. "Somehow it's fucking around with the lycans, making them weak. Easier to prey on, or subjugate or whatever. Fuck, *is* it the God of us?"

The Morrigan's laugh was cruel and harsh, like the sudden cawing of a hundred crows, a full murder of them. She eyed me with dark fire in her eyes, shaking her head at my words.

"Gift it not a title unless you truly believe it deserves it." She warned me. "Gods and Goddesses are simply those that the foolish are naive enough to put unquestionable faith in. The desperate, who they turn to when they do not believe in themselves. The guilty, wanting to seek some solace, some higher power to blame for their actions or seek absolution from. This creature may be linked to the lycans but its nature is far from Godly."

"Besides, *you* are no simple lycan." She reminded me, like Jessica had done. Almost echoing her words. "Whether this thing has a bond with those of your pack, you are not of the same ilk. So quit thinking like them, and put this matter to rest. I have something more … *disquieting* to share with you."

Well, that was me well and truly told. I knew I wasn't going to get anything more from the Morrigan on either subject, so with a small sigh I waved her on. Time to find out what she, of all creatures, would find *disquieting*.

Thinking on that, I braced myself from something particularly nasty.

I was not disappointed.

The Morrigan led me up to the tall stone building that sat atop the Tor, and I tried to recall anything I knew about the place. The ruins of a church, if I remembered correctly, dedicated to St Michael. Lots of stories and legends about the place, including one grim truth … the Tower, all that remained of the church that had once stood there looking out across the green lands of England, was the site of execution for the last Abbot and two of his monks. I didn't remember what happened to the other two, but I recalled the Abbot had been hung, drawn and quartered for supposed treason by Thomas Cromwell. In fact, according to various records of the time, he was killed for 'robbing church property', which was the excuse dreamt up by parliamentary officials when they didn't find the considerable treasures of the Abbey they'd expected to when they turned up unannounced to 'officially' rob the place.

You have to love mortal politics. Just so … twisted.

Anyhow, the only thing left was the Tower, and that was a hollow shell. Tourists came up to the top of the hill on sunny days to stand beside the majestic tower of stone, or step inside the cool confines and look at the sky overhead.

The Tor itself had been linked, like many sacred sites, to the Goddess for a long time now. Ellie had celebrated with her sisters, and joined in several processions of the Wiccan community on the significant days of the year. I'd joked about a bunch of witches dancing around naked atop the Tor giving the locals with binoculars heart attacks, and earned a clip round the back of my head for my humour. But it was a fact, this site, like Stonehenge, Arbor Low and a handful of other places across the breadth of England, was linked to the many-named but single immortal bound to the land. Whose lifeblood witches, warlocks and all those creatures who manipulated magic drank from.

The scent of blood grew stronger as I stepped through the tall, wide archway that split the tower in two. This was joined by the reek of death, that bittersweet tang of decay and finality which was unmistakable.

I stopped, looking at the tableau in front of me. Momentary shocked.

It was a ritual, obviously. A circle had been drawn on the worn stone, swirling symbols running smoothly from one to another, entwining like vines. And around the inner boundary of the working, at each cardinal point and then mid-point in between, knelt a single figure. They all wore ceremonial cloaks, stitched with the leaf and vine motif to denote Nature, but the hoods had been pulled back to reveal eight women of varying ages and descriptions. All of Elspeth's age or older, and at least three were instantly recognisable to me.

"Theresa Shaw. Mary Wilson. Sinead O'Keefe." I spoke their names quietly, taking in the rest of the details. "Shit, and there I'd thinking they were just giving us the cold shoulder coz of Felix. Not … *this*."

"Your surmise is correct." The fae commented dryly from where she stood, watching me intently. "Their shoulders are indeed cold. Cold as death."

The eight witches, for that was whom I guessed knelt in the inner circle, were not alone. Around the outer edge, an equal number of men also knelt in mirroring positions. All eight of these were of middle years, but fit and healthy from their muscular bodies which were naked except for loose leggings. They were barefoot, and almost every inch of their skin was tattooed with more vine and leaf motifs, but with carefully formed script flowing around and entwined with the blessings of Nature. The stories of their lives, those that had come before, the history of their order.

Each had a sickle, small enough to be handled with one hand, at their side and sprigs of dark mistletoe woven into their braided hair.

"Now what the hell are a bunch of druids doing here?" I asked the thin air, knowing the order still existed, and still jealousy warded the worship of the Goddess, Tera as I knew her. On this patch of ground and most other continents around the world.

"Druids and witches." I commented as I slowly walked around the scene, carefully placing my feet so as not to disturb anything. "That's like putting cats and dogs in the same box, or adding fire to petrol. What the fuck are they doing together?"

The one thing they both had in common was the fact they were dead. Very dead.

"Note the details of their wounds, pup. Take a moment and tell me what you sense." The Morrigan told me as she waited in the arch. As a sacred site to an immortal not of her Court, I guessed the fae wasn't going to be stepping any closer unless she wanted to risk triggering any lingering ward or protection.

I carefully squatted, avoiding the blood staining the stone underfoot, and checked the nearest druid. He had died as he knelt, no obvious defence wounds to show he in any way resisted the killing stroke. Which was surprising, given that whoever had attacked him had slit his throat from ear to ear, opening a wide ribbon for blood to gush down and cover his bared chest.

I leaned in, inspecting the wound as I felt my insides clench and anger kindle inside me. Fading, almost gone now, but still lingering were two unmistakeable scents. One, I'd been smelling far too much of recently, that burned mustard that I now linked to Lykaois, but the second was all the more familiar. A stench of madness, fear and anger, carrying notes of pain that had not been there before. Underscored by the touch of the Wyld. The odour of someone who had recently come back into my life, intent on causing trouble and pain to me and those I cared for.

And the wound. Precisely angled with no ragged edges. A surgeon's slice, with inhuman strength behind it. Knowing exactly where to cut for maximum damage, with a weapon that followed the bastard's hand like a glove. Or finger.

"Jack. Fucking Jack is working with Lyk…" I went to snarl, but the Morrigan stopped me with a hissed warning.

"Name it *not*. You know the law, so draw not its attention unless you wish to face it here. Far from your pack, from any who might aid you. Alone." She told me sharply, and I bit my lip, forcing myself to think through the anger.

"Ok. So *Jack* and *the arsehole* are working together. None of that makes sense, but fine. Leaving that one aside, what were these witches and druids doing here?" I looked around, not recognising any of the symbols arrayed on the floor, not that I knew that much about magic rituals and what did what. I normally left that to Ellie. "It can't be a warding, otherwise how the hell did Jack get inside the circle to kill the women? And why didn't anyone fry my fuckwit of a half-brother's arse before he came anywhere close? They must have sensed him, hell, smelt the bastard the way he stinks."

"Mayhap they were occupied. Their minds turned elsewhere, their guards lowered whilst they desperately attempted to … well, do whatever they were here to do." The fae commented without actually giving an answer, which was quite a novel trick. "What is certain is, the shedding of their blood *here*, in this manner? It can only hurt She whose heart is bound to this site."

"Tera." I shook my head, pushing myself up and stepping away from the ring of death. "It's an attack on the Goddess, killing her followers and despoiling her sacred site. But how the hell does that help the right royal *arsehole* if all he wants is a new cult, a new set of followers? Going up against Tera is like throwing stones at a mountain to make it fall over. Fucking *stupid*."

"You would be right, pup." The Morrigan commented dryly as she stared at the murdered men and women. "If this were the only site like this. But as the sun passed overhead, I have witnessed similar sites. A full half dozen of them. And at each site, Her followers remain as if in communion with Her, seeking to perform an act such as you witness here. All slain, viciously and cruelly, by one hand but guided by another."

"Fuck." I loosed a breath, shaking my head. "Seven sacred sites, with murdered witches and druids at every one? You'd only want to do something that fucked up if you were trying to despoil all the sites, wound the Goddess badly. Leave her weak. But the *bastard* doesn't need to! Why the fuck is he attacking *her*? And why hasn't she just wiped the floor with him? This is *Tera* we're talking about, as in Terra Firma. Literally the *ground on which we all walk*."

I spun at a new sound, and watched as the stone floor of the Tower cracked and broke apart. I stepped clear, as tendrils writhed up out of the broken earth, surging up and over the bodies of the slain. Within the space of one moment to the next, any trace of the butchery was wiped clean as a carpet of moss and grass took its place. A single, solitary white flower rose up, opening its petals under the cold sky above. A solemn, sad note to those who had died there.

"The Goddess does what She can." The Morrigan answered as a response to my angry questions, turning and stepping back out of the arch. "As must we. You have a hunt ahead of you, pup, and an enemy to find and deal with. For yourself, for those you love … and now the Goddess of the Realm you protect. No pressure."

I followed her out into the sunlight, feeling the chill of October settle into my bones just a little deeper. I thought we had enough to handle with a psychotic and possibly insane supernatural creature freed from its prison and wanting to set up shop in London as our God and master. Now I had my half-brother back on the scene, killing witches and druids with impunity, and threatening the Goddess that wished me to find Elspeth. She who protected this Realm even more surely than the Veil.

Some days, I truly wonder if I shouldn't just take Bear and go Troll-hunting in the Real for a break. A few decades, maybe. And not have to carry this sort of shit all the time.

I wish.

"Ok, so you've somehow made my day *that* much worse. Thanks." I told the Morrigan, seeing her smile viciously in response. "Mind popping me back home or to the office so I can get on with unravelling this mess?"

She looked at me with those dark eyes of hers, and her smile widened with wicked intent.

"Oh, don't you dare …" I growled, but the fae simply shrugged.

"There is a price to be paid for not following the correct protocol when performing a summons, pup. The proper words bind each one to aid the other, to reach an accord together. Without those words … well. You understand." She told me, as an icy wind spun up around the Tor, pressing against me with the sharp scent of winter. "Consider this a learning exercise, on *not* cutting corners. Or next time I shall cut something in return."

With that, she faded away and vanished. Leaving me standing like an idiot on top of Glastonbury Tor, over a hundred miles from where I needed to be.

I swore, loudly and profusely, as I dragged my phone out of my pocket. It wasn't like I had much option. It was too far to walk, even for me to run, and my wallet was sat on my desk in the office with every possible way of paying for a train fare helpfully out of reach.

When Jessica got the next taxi bill on my account, she was going to *kill* me.

Chapter 37

Total Body Trauma

Whilst most monsters are immune to modern weapons, given the impurity of the base metals used and the lack of imbued intent imparted to the weapon by machine rather than the hand of a smith, it is also true that disrupting a monster's body in the most violent of ways can still be an effective deterrent.

Whilst beheading or dismembering a monster often only inconveniences it and enrages it further, blowing its entire body to shreds, burning it to a complete crisp or shattering it after freezing it in sub zero temperatures can cause the monster extreme pain and often force it to flee. Once it has gathered itself together.

Three and a half hours later, I stomped back into *Good Deeds*.

We'd hit traffic on the way, otherwise we might have made it a little sooner. But until someone invented the flying car, we had to stick to the roads and queues that tended to fill them most of the time.

I'd fielded calls from both Felix and Sarah, both checking where the hell I'd vanished to. It was easier telling Felix since she was familiar with my world, and the simple fact I could be in one place one moment, then almost at the other side of the country the next thanks to immortal meddling. Sarah, however, was left more than a little confused at my apparent vanishing act. I think she had got the impression I was still pissed at her for not sticking to the plan we'd agreed, and had walked out without even speaking to her instead of being whisked all the way to Glastonbury by the nightmarish version of Mary Poppins.

The sign that the office was closed was still up, as I slipped inside. Checking my phone, I saw I'd managed to lose pretty much the afternoon what with all the running around and crazy revelations, and it was nearing five now. Four hours before I was due to meet Grubbins and the Sisters, and see if my bet was right.

And four hours to make sure Sarah was safely ensconced back in my home, behind solid wards, and for me to make one last stop to see if I could fix the bastard that was on the hunt for its favourite butchery tool.

Felix greeted me as I made it up the stairs, looking up from handing over a cold compress to Emma as she sat slumped at her desk. Seeing me, the lycan pushed herself up from the seat, ignoring the young witch's squawk of complaint, and staggered over to face me.

"Tell me you've got something." She part asked, part demanded. I could feel the waves of frustration rolling off her, the fact she looked ready to collapse if I blew on her too hard adding to her stress. "Tell me you know what the fuck this is, and how we beat it."

I nodded, having most of the picture even if I wasn't sure how everything was connected. Gently, I settled Emma down in her chair, feeling her try to resist but then give up and slump back. Exhausted from that small effort.

"I've got to talk to Jessica." I told my packmate, then nodded downwards. "Have our smelly little bastards shown back up again?"

She nodded, grimacing as a thought struck her.

"Please don't tell me you're getting a cure from *trolls*." Emma shook her head at the very idea. "Fuck, I'm not sure I'd take the medicine for this fucking illness if they're involved."

"No, nothing like that. Just a couple of other things I need." I reassured her before nodding to the mug of steaming lemon and honey I saw sitting beside her. "Now, drink up and get some rest. I'll need you back in fighting shape real soon."

"Any time, Morgan. Just tell me who I need to hit." She answered, barely hiding the wince as she picked up the mug in shaking hands. "Or cough over. Or fall on, right now."

Turning away, I found Felix and Sarah both waiting for me. Sarah, it seemed, had focused on ministering to the sick lycans, fetching hot drinks and making them as comfortable as she could. And woe betide the foolish mutt who tried to argue with her, as I'd received the tail-end of a few

Spanish-spoken dressing downs when I'd been the one with the odd injury that I tried to shrug off in her presence.

"Glad you're back." Felix told me, nodding to the room. "I don't think anyone's getting any worse but whatever this thing is, it's not letting up no matter what we try. Magic bounces off you lot like rubber balls, and regular medicine is plainly useless."

"Yeah, I figured." I replied, then indicated my next stop. "Just going to go check in on the boss, then you can catch me up on what you've both been up to whilst I was dragged hallway across England."

"Be quick. Sarah and I have news." The witch told me, and I shot my love a look. She shrugged, nodding her agreement.

"We've been talking, *chulo*, and I've been helping Felix here with the journal." She explained briefly. "It's not my field of study, but I know Julius, so was able to help work out some details that we think you need to know."

"That's great." I told them both, only having winced *slightly* on hearing the fact the pair had been talking. Last time one of my acquaintance did that with Felix, I'd been slapped with a tenancy agreement about a mile long, with enough clauses to make my teeth ache.

I obviously wasn't subtle enough, as both Felix and Sarah rolled their eyes like they'd been practising.

"Typical man. With all this going on, he's worried about us girls talking about *him*." Felix snarked, and Sarah laughed gently. It was good to hear the sound in the office, given how the rest of my pack were giving off serious *woe-is-me* vibes. However, there was a trace scent to her, of fear, sadness. A sliver underlying the humour. I'd need to ask about that soon, and find out what had upset her.

"Play nice, Felix." She replied, her eyes dancing with mirth. "Most men would have been running a mile by now, at the thought of two beautiful women such as us talking about their faults and failings. Morgan is at least still standing here."

"Just shows he's an idiot." Felix replied, making them both laugh harder.

"That's my cue to be anywhere else but here." I told them both. "If you ladies will excuse me, I'll leave you to your entertainment."

Then before either could answer, I quickly headed on up to see Jessica, and give her the good news.

She took it well, all things considered.

"Ah would ask if you were kidding me, if ah thought you the sort tae think this a joking matter." My Alpha told me as she drew a breath, having listened to my update on all things fucked up. "As it is, ah think we can agree matters are far worse than they seemed."

"That's putting it mildly." I acknowledged with a sigh.

Jessica was sat up in bed, her skin still clammy and off-colour, and the room smelt of sweat and fatigue. I could tell Felix or Sarah had been in, since there was a collection of cups that smelt strongly of lemon and honey, and surprisingly a half-eaten bowl of chicken soup from its lingering aroma. Someone obviously bought into the idea that boiled poultry and various vegetables was a cure-all, or was getting desperate enough to try anything.

"Then there is nae other choice." She set down her pad, and with effort dragged the covers off the bed, swinging herself so she was seated on the edge of the mattress.

"Uh, Jessica, what are you doing?" I asked, seeing her take a moment to gather her strength. She was dressed in a loose t-shirt and jogging bottoms, possibly the most casual I had ever seen her. Not that I knew what she wore to bed … I hadn't even wondered. You just don't. But seeing her wearing a Warner Bros cartoon t-shirt with the Tasmanian Devil emblazoned on it somehow still made me respect her all the more.

"Ah'm getting out of bed. Ah intend tae shower, change in tae something more suitable and then, Morgan, ah intend fer you and ah tae work out how we kick this particularly being's backside so hard, it'll nae even *think* of causing trouble fer a century or two. Maybe more." She growled, and her eyes flickered with the strength of her anger and general pissed-offness. "Do you have anything tae say on the matter?"

"Just that if you fall on your backside trying to do all that, I'm letting *you* take all the blame when Felix starts fussing over you like a mother hen." I joked, seeing her smile in reply. It did me good, seeing her up and out of bed, even if she was still afflicted by whatever curse or hex Lykaois had managed to fuck the pack over with. However, it was possible.

"Morgan, ah would appreciate it if you would step outside, and wait fer me out there." She told me sharply, as she gripped the bottom of her t-shirt, obviously about to strip.

"Oh, right. Sorry!" I beat a hasty retreat, closing the door firmly behind me.

It took Jessica about half the time I'd expected to get herself into some semblance of herself, but she was still far too pale and hesitant when she joined me in the living room of her quarters. I'd rustled up strong coffee with extra sugar, and several double chocolate brownies that I knew were her favourite little treat, for when she felt she deserved a pick me up. I think it was something Mark Walker had introduced her to, when they were first courting, since she always seemed to linger over a single bite, and there was an air of sadness about her when she had one. Chocolate is one of those things you *really* have to work at to feel sad whilst eating.

Crucially, both Felix and Sarah had joined us, seated on the sofas. Felix was sipping a thick milkshake she had procured from somewhere, whilst Sarah had a cup of hazelnut coffee cupped in her hands, enjoying the aroma almost as much as the drink itself.

I'd had to convince Jessica to include Sarah in our discussion, given she was simply a mortal and not really part of our world, part of our business. My argument was simple; she had been helping Felix translate Professor Eduardo's journal, and was now involved given she'd witnessed the truth about the pack, about me. Oh, and she had first-hand knowledge of where the root of all our problems had been imprisoned, and might help find some way of putting the bastard back in its box.

Given that, and the sure knowledge that if this were a mistake, I'd bear the price, she had ceded to my request. Grudgingly.

"Felix, how about you start?" I offered, as Sarah and Jessica faced each other across the coffee table in that way which mortals have perfected through countless encounters. The way they *weren't* looking at each other, whilst their attentions were most definitely on each other. Like two cats, each nonchalantly circling the other and pretending they were focused on anything else.

"Ok, but you need to answer a question first." She told me, tapping the journal that she had not let out of her sight since I had given it to her. "Was there a knife at the museum, like in the book?"

I nodded, and then sighed.

"There *was*, both a knife and a bowl. Dating back to Ancient Greece at the least. Possibly 100 BC or earlier." I explained, remembering the details Jan had told me. "The knife was some sort of obsidian sacrificial weapon, and it and the bowl were stained with what the museum labelled *organic material*. Which I'm guessing was blood."

Sarah looked up, dark eyes sparking with a memory.

"I remember it. They were in a chamber, right at the bottom of the second pyramid. The one which was inverted, and led into the ground." She spoke up, brow furrowing as she tried to focus on the details. "The room was sealed, and we had to break through a blocked-in door to get inside. But there was a central shaft leading down from the top of the pyramid, where there was the traditional altar stone and statues dedicated to the God the Mayans worshipped there."

"*Ba'alche' ku xíimbal bey juntúul máak.*" Felix rolled the name off like she had been born to speak ancient Mayan, and Sarah nodded again.

"That's what Julius said was the name of the spirit they worshipped. There was a ritual they performed. A blood sacrifice each full moon to honour it." She blanched and I guessed she was remembering the details. "*Mi dios*, it was horrible. They …"

I held up a hand, forestalling her.

"It's ok. We all know what they did, and what the poor bastard they named as the chosen had to do. So, let's skip the gruesome details." I told her and she smiled gratefully. "So yeah, there was a knife and bowl taken from the site. But when Dr Cooper … Miles … when he was possessed by this thing, he destroyed the bowl. I *think* he was looking for the knife, but Professor Eduardo had already checked it out himself. Taken for personal research, according to the records in the museum computer."

Felix smiled grimly, obviously happy to hear what she'd been expecting.

"The bowl wasn't important. Just a receptacle for the blood that was spilled. They could have used anything to hold it. A mug, chamber pot, anything." She replied, showing she had definitely been doing her research. "It's the knife that's important. It's the link between this spirit and its host, part of the contract that allows it to enter whoever is chosen after they are properly conditioned. Weakened, made to feel the ultimate fear and pain. This creature not only feeds on the negative emotions, but it needs them as a sort of conduit, to allow it to function and control whoever it targets."

"It wants the knife because without it, it's not able to complete the ritual?" I asked, seeing the obvious issue here. "But that can't be right. This thing already possessed Jacob whilst he was under the influence of Wolfsbane, and Miles Cooper too. Neither time involved the knife unless I missed something pretty obvious."

Felix nodded, her smile a mirror to how Ellie always looked when she was about to reveal just how brilliant she was. It made my stomach clench.

"You did, Morgan, but that's ok. You're only human …" She quipped, and I rolled my eyes at her before spreading my hands to indicate she should get on with the reveal. "It's the fact the knife *wasn't* involved that explains why this creature is still popping in and out of hosts. It's not able to properly bind itself to another, probably not even able to control whoever it gets inside completely. And depending on the strength and nature of the host, it's on a ticking clock before it's kicked out."

"But Sarah helped me figure how it might have found a way round that. A shortcut." The young witch opened the journal near the end, flicking pages until she got to a specific one. Holding it up, she showed us a section of tight script, along with hand-drawn sketches of Mayan pictograms. A figure bending another over a stone altar, knife raised. And then another, similar figure standing along, cutting their hand whilst a particularly demonic image hovered nearby, tongue extended.

I had to admit, the creature depicted certainly had *wolf-like* details about it. Enough to make my skin crawl.

"It's the blood." She told us, tapping the second image. "This creature might not have its knife to complete the ritual, but if it can take over the host and then get it to cut itself, and *feed* itself blood then that allows it more control, a stronger hold on the other."

She looked across at me, expression suddenly showing regret.

"Given what happened to Dr Cooper, I can't check to see if he cut himself. To confirm my theory." She admitted, but I realised there was another person she *did* have access to. A very close friend, a packmate. "But Jacob, well, I guessed it was worth a shot."

"He had a plaster on his hand." I remembered suddenly, zeroing in on the detail from when I'd sat opposite on his boat. Before things went Due South at high velocity and I took a dunk in the water. "Shit, I just thought he was cutting himself to get Wolfsbane into his system quicker."

Felix shook her head.

"Jessica allowed me to go speak to him." She admitted, and I cocked an eyebrow at our Alpha. That sounded all too much like we were treating him like a prisoner, not a victim. Probably a poor choice of words on Felix's part, but Jessica's expression was set and closed. Her scent however told me just how upset she was that someone so close to her had been used so badly. "He has no memory of hurting himself, of getting cut. But it hasn't healed properly, so he thought it was something he did whilst dosed. I think this creature possessed him, then made him shed blood that it then tasted, strengthening its hold on him so his normal resistance wouldn't stop it using him for longer."

"Hence the Greenwich Park bloodbath and it being able to use him to try to break into Professor Eduardo's home. With another murder to add to its tally." I grimly deduced, seeing her nod.

"Ok, so we can safely assume Miles did the same thing. Cut himself under its influence." I continued, seeing Sarah flinch at the name of her dead colleague. The scents rolling from her made me want to move to her side, fold her in my arms and tell her it was ok. But now wasn't the time. "At least now we can keep an eye out for anyone with a cut they don't remember making, as a potential host for the bastard."

Silence greeted me, and those emotions roiled out of Sarah even more strongly.

"Uh, Morgan." Felix began, but stopped as Sarah shook her head, shuffling forward on the couch. She looked across at me, her rich brown eyes wide and full of fear. And shame.

"Ah, shit. No." I growled. I'd made sure. She hadn't triggered the wards when I brought her into the office. But the reaction of Bear, of Albert. The odd cleanliness of her home ... the warning signs had been there.

"I'm so sorry, Morgan." She told me softly, as she carefully rolled up her right sleeve. I remembered she'd taken to wearing what I thought was some sort of large South American bracelet of worked leather and beads, the sort of thing you see modelled in the more high-end fashion boutiques as *ethnic chique*. She'd had it on when I faced her just out of the shower, and even kept it on in bed, but I hadn't thought it worth questioning. Being otherwise distracted, idiot that I am.

She unclasped this, revealing a folded square of bandage, padded to hide any leakage from what lay underneath. I even caught the scent of antiseptic spray, that masked any smell from the wound. As I cursed, she carefully pulled this free, and my nose immediately caught the scent she'd been hiding from me.

The cut was still angry and red, puckered from where she had broken the skin and shed her blood.

I'd been right. Sarah was a host for the bastard.

Fuck.

Chapter 38

"When?" I growled, clamping down on the riot of emotions threatening to overwhelm me. "When did you do that?"

"I don't know." Sarah replied honestly. Felix and Jessica remained silent, and I guessed my friend had told my Alpha as soon as they both realised what the significance of the cut was. Whilst I was dragging my arse back from Glastonbury Tor. "I told you, things are confused, blurry. There're moments from the expedition I don't remember properly, especially at the end. I was told how we were extracted, how we got back to London but I *don't* remember it or who told me. Like it happened to someone else. And since then, it's like sometimes I wake up and don't remember where I am, how I got where I was. Like I sleepwalked. I found the cut a while ago, but keep forgetting about it, like I'm not meant to focus on it."

"Probably this creature, tampering with you every time its taken control." Felix commented quietly, and I shot her an angry look. "Hey, I'm sorry but it's just the truth. She's been its puppet all along."

I swore again, but bit down hard on the anger seeing Sarah flinch, and Felix looked more than a little upset too.

"Shit, sorry. Felix, it's not your fault." I told her, shaking my head and gripping my hands together hard. "And Sarah, sorry too. I'm being stupid, just a bloody idiot. I should have checked, should had realised something wasn't right when Bear reacted to you. It's ok, we'll fix this."

"Dinnae worry too much, Morgan." Jessica spoke up, having kept quiet whilst this little revelation was made. "Ah too felt more than a touch aggrieved tae find this creature's effect on those closest tae us. But you are right, we *will* fix this. And tae that end, we need tae agree our next steps."

Pushing herself up with only a small grunt of effort, she stepped to a whiteboard Felix had carried up from downstairs. One of the ones we'd used previously to track Robert Knox and try to identify the mystery immortal he had been working with. Once things had gone so badly wrong that Twilight was reborn with Morgana as Lady of the Court, we'd figured that matter closed and cleaned off the boards for re-use.

"Ah think it is safe tae say, our first priority is tae secure this knife." She elegantly updated the board, as ever putting to shame my scrawl. To be fair, when Jessica had learnt to write, ink and quills were still in style, and she had never lost the flair from writing with such tools. "Once we have control of this reliquary, the creature in question should nae have any chance of permanently acquiring a host. And most likely, it will focus its attention on us rather than any other defenceless victim, and so limit the damage it can do. So, we need tae find it."

"Morgan, you are meeting with the Sisters tonight." She looked at me, and I nodded. "If yer suspicion is correct, you will need a way tae lock this thing away so you dinnae draw the creature's attention tae you. *If* you can convince them tae hand it over. *If* they have it."

I shrugged, knowing just how many 'if's' I was basing my hypothesis on.

"Uh, should we really be sharing our plans with … well … her?" Felix spoke up, looking across at Sarah. "No offence, but you *are* a host for this thing. And we don't know what it can or cannot do if it pops back inside you. Read your memories, for one thing?"

Jessica exchanged a look with me, and I shook my head vehemently.

"We are *not* sticking Sarah downstairs with Jacob." I refused the suggestion before it was even voiced. "And before you think I'm not thinking straight, hear me out. Sarah is not like us, she's not as strong even if this thing can make her change form like it did Miles Cooper. There's no need for her to be caged like Jacob."

Sarah jerked, her expression showing she hadn't realised just what we were talking about doing to her. I held up my hand to reassure her.

"It isn't happening." I told her, before looking back at my Alpha. "There's a good chance this thing is working with Jack, and using him as a ride-along if what I found at the Tor is anything to go by. That bastard tried to get into my home recently, and was sent packing. Sarah will be safe there, behind my wards and with Goldspur to keep her company. That's non-negotiable."

I know I sounded belligerent and angry, but I'd just found out the woman I was in love was serving as a host for the immortal bastard trying to fuck all of us up. Me in particular. One of my packmates was already locked up in a cell below us, because he too had been used by this creature. And now Sarah too? I definitely was not reacting well to the news.

"As you say." Jessica replied, letting me read in her eyes the trust she was placing in me. "But fer now, ah think it best we do not share the location of your meeting. Just in case."

Sarah actually nodded, making the call for me so I shut up.

"Ok. So that is one line of investigation tae follow." My Alpha then also added an additional line to the first point. "In case yer suspicion is nae true, then ah think Professor Eduardo's home is the next likely location. Given this creature's attempt to gain entrance. Whilst you and Agent Smith are meeting with the Sisters, ah will check if they recovered any such item from the house, and if not, negotiate fer some of the pack tae be allowed in tae look fer it."

"If anyone's fit to stand, let alone go rummaging around a house." I countered but Jessica shook her head.

"This thing, this affliction? Ah will nae let it lay us low." She vowed, her anger at being so weakened granting her a measure of strength. "If needs be, if none other of the pack are strong enough, ah will do the searching myself. Ah will speak tae the other Alphas and see if they are fit fer the task."

"Fine. What else?" I queried, as Jessica updated the board.

"Felicity. Morgan and ah have grave news fer you." She turned her attention to my friend, who looked surprised and more than a little apprehensive at the lycan's words.

"Shit, it's not my dad is it?" She asked with a tremble in her voice, but Jessica smiled and quickly reassured her.

"Nae, yer father is fit and hale. This is about the witches ah know who have approached you tae join their coven." She explained, and Felix looked confused.

"I've told them I need time. I'm not ready to take any vows or make promises to a Goddess." She replied, looking between Jessica and me. "They aren't causing trouble because I won't join their club, are they? Coz that's just shit, and I can't believe their Goddess …"

"Nae, not that." Jessica stopped her. "Morgan has been made aware of a grave ill done, most likely at the hand of this creature, and the creature you know as Jack the Ripper. The witches, ah am sorry tae say, have been killed. Seeking to help their Goddess in some manner we dinnae understand."

"Oh, shit, they're dead? What, all of them?" Felix asked, shocked, eyes widening at the terrible news. "What happened?"

At the same time, Sarah looked between the three of us, even more confused.

"*The* Jack the Ripper? You can't be serious?" She asked, but I simply nodded. "Is that who tried to get into your apartment before? It's *Jack the Ripper* who's angry with you, who you thought I needed to be careful about bumping into?"

I shrugged, knowing all this must be coming as shock after shock to Sarah. Lycanthropes being real, witches existing. Supernatural creatures possessing people, including her. And now a killer back from the grave over a hundred years since he should have been dead, and well and truly buried.

"Welcome to my world." I softly told her, and she sat back on the sofa, obviously trying to come to terms with this new information.

Turning back, giving Sarah some space to think, I focused on Felix.

"It looks like they were involved in some sort of ritual. Them and a bunch of druids, which means this was serious, since normally those two don't mix." I explained, the memory of the sixteen dead people fresh in my mind. "I *think* this creature is trying to weaken Tera, make her vulnerable by killing Her worshippers. I was told its happened at another six sites across England in the past twenty-four hours, which means whatever it wants to do, it needs to do it now, or soon. And for some reason the Goddess is either in the way or a possible factor in fucking up its plan. Hence, lots of dead bodies."

Felix looked stunned, and more than a little afraid, before a thought struck her.

"Hold on." She gestured at herself. "I haven't joined their coven, or taken any vows. According to them, I'm not even sourcing the same font of magic as them, since I got all this stuff from whatever Gary did to me. He was using power from the Veil, which is what Twilight was turned into. I'm linked to that, not the Goddess."

"Exactly." Jessica confirmed, adding a second item to our *to do list*. "Ah dinnae fear you are a target in this thing's plan tae attack the Goddess of the Mortal Realm, but ah do think we need tae know what has happened tae Her. What Her worshippers were trying tae stop happening. Ah need you tae set aside yer research into this creature, and see if you can learn more of this matter."

Felix nodded, putting the journal down on the sofa beside her.

"I can start by finding out who is still alive, who might know what their sisters in the coven were involved in. I've got a list of contacts from all the times they've been round to check on me and see if I'd made up my mind." She admitted. "It's back at the cottage, but hopefully at least some of them are still safe, and might talk to me rather than either of you."

"Ah thought so too. If they are afraid, feared fer their lives, they will nae likely desire contact with Redcloaks, nae matter that all we wish tae do is help." Jessica agreed, assigning Felix to the second task.

"And what about me?" Sarah now spoke up, looking firstly at Jessica, then at me. "What can I do? Because if you think I'm just going to sit on my backside whilst you risk your lives, dealing with this *bastardo* who has hurt and killed my friends, and used me, then you should know that is not going to happen. *Si diablos no.*"

My Alpha looked at me, but I just shook my head, nodding to Sarah. No way was I going to try and say what she could or couldn't do. I wanted to keep her as far away from this fucked up mess as I could, but it was far too late for that. She was involved, right at the heart of it.

"Ah would prefer tae have you kept from any further involvement, given yer … *situation*." Jessica admitted, and I saw Sarah's jaw clench as she started to form a suitable rebuke. "*But* ah can see that is not mah call tae make."

"No. It isn't." Sarah replied simply, obviously changing her words at hearing Jessica's reply.

"Then, if Felicity is otherwise occupied on matters concerning the attacks on the witches, ah would ask fer you tae continue looking through your colleague's journal." My Alpha added a third task to the board. "Whilst we know what this creature wants, at least what it needs, we are nae further in finding out how tae deal with it. Tae trap it and return it tae its prison. You must try tae remember what you saw at the temple, and what your colleague wrote about the room where you found the bowl and knife. Something there will speak of their efforts tae contain this thing, tae undo the damage done by removing the items."

Sarah nodded, and Felix handed the journal carefully over to her.

"Now, ah think ah need tae speak tae yer packmates, Morgan." Jessica set the whiteboard marker down, taking a breath to stead herself. "It's past time they got over feeling ill-done by, and got on with what we all need tae do. Keep the peace, and safeguard those who cannae protect themselves. Nae matter what state we are in."

I nodded, knowing what I had to do. And bracing myself for the unpleasant task ahead of me.

"Sarah, if you don't mind staying here for a little bit, we can head back home and get you settled and safe once I've done one last thing?" I asked her, not wanting to expose her to any more of the weirdness that comprised my life. Especially this particular sort of *smelly* weird.

"You're not going to disappear on me again?" She asked, only half joking, but I shook my head.

"No. Nothing like that." I reassured her, before nodding down at our feet. "I've just got to go talk to three brothers about a couple of things I need, and for all the love I have for you, I *really* want to keep these particular smelly bastards and you from ever meeting. You'll thank me, I promise you."

"Especially your nose."

Chapter 39

The Brothers Bung were just as I remembered them.

Filthy, smelly and somehow a mix between totally craven and aggressively pugnacious.

"What does wolf want? Want another leg maybe?" Tol, the oldest of the three, growled at me as I rapped on the bars of the cell they'd taken over for their nest.

Bol, the middle troll, smiled nervously at me where he sat, busy plucking feathers from a dead gull. No matter that we'd offered up a selection of foodstuff from our kitchens for them to eat whilst they were our 'guests' the three trolls seemed to always revert back to their penchant for eating gull-surprise. The surprise being just how smelly the concoction was, and whatever else went into their cookpot.

Sol, the youngest of the three, gave a squeak of fear and immediately flung a ragged blanket over the trinkets he had been sorting. The three brothers were clan-less, friend-less and so low on the food chain that with us permanently dealing with the Nighters pack and Robert Knox, even enemy-less. Which in the Real underworld was almost impossible. Someone was always out to get someone else, for a vendetta nursed and kept alive far longer than mortals might ever consider holding a grudge.

When Jessica had first indicated to the trio of scruffy trolls that their dealings with Talen and Sal Orben, corrupt lycan Alphas, let alone their connection to Robert Knox had marked them as undesirables and a target even amongst their own kin, they had readily agreed to relocate to the offices of *Good Deeds* and provide their connections and knowledge in repayment for protection. However, in the months since then, it seemed everyone was simply happy to just forget they existed, no-one wanting to waste the effort messing with our pack simply to gain a little vengeance on the miserable brothers.

It looked like the Real community thought we'd done them a favour by taking the Bung brothers off their hands, and were in no way interested in their return.

So, for lodgings and the offer of foodstuffs they didn't need to steal, we got three smelly little informants who knew the darker, and smellier underside of the Real community. With furry ears to the ground, and a wealth of knowledge that them being troll-kin, they were party to.

"I need two things." I told the three of them, keeping my distance. When I'd found them lodging at a particularly seedy troll strip-club, they had been at the mercy of a particularly nasty and sadistic Wyld goblin called Red Cap, who had been slowly subjecting them to ultraviolet light. All three still bore scars from his efforts, and Tol had lost one leg to the deadly light. Something he seemed to think was my fault somehow, and brought up at every opportunity.

"No limbs today, thanks." I answered Tol's accusation, ignoring the troll's snarl. "One piece of requisition and a bit of knowledge, with a side order of *give me no shit coz its been a bad day already*. Deal?"

I let a little growl of my own add a timbre to my words, and I saw the trolls stiffen. Tol tapped his fake leg … which looked like he'd taken it from a grand piano … against the floor angrily, but Sol and Bol both grabbed hold of their kin and whispered furtively in his matted and filthy ears. Probably reminding him that if they caused any of us lycan trouble, they'd be out on the streets in the very next breath.

Threatening trolls, by the way, isn't really something I enjoy, especially when they are the lesser kin, small and relatively harmless. No threat to me, except maybe from fleas and any other small critters they'd picked up. But it had been a long couple of days, I'd just found out the woman I loved was a carrier for a possibly insane and definitely psychotic supernatural entity with delusions of grandeur, and I had a nagging feeling the shit we faced this time was going to be the straw that broke us.

We'd lost pack, Jacob deeply wounded from losing the woman he cared for, whilst Alphas from the other packs had been slain. The running of the Hunts was at risk, with far fewer lycan left to cover London than we needed. And now all this was kicking off, with something weakening all the lycans and a crazed psycho declaring itself our God. Whilst it revelled in murder, butchering witches and mortals at every step.

This time, after the smoke settled, we might not get back up again.

"What you need then?" Sol enquired, the youngest of the three being the *quartermaster* and *forager* of the three. If this had been wartime, he would have found his perfect role as the dodgy soldier to go to, to find anything. The sort of military personnel who skirted legalities and rules, but could lay his hands or claws on pretty much any item, if the price were agreeable.

"Something I can stick a knife in, to keep the creature it's bonded with from knowing I have it." I explained. "A pouch, bag or even a box but something I can carry around without it being obvious. I need it to be fae proof, scrying proof and just about whatever proof from anything sniffing traces of blood, magical links and that sort of thing. Especially curses and hexes linked to it."

I figured Lykaois was linked to his knife, through whatever curse or ritual had bound it to the creature. Cursed items such as a knife that, when used to cut a person, weakened them and allowed another to possess them, tended to have a tether to its owner. And the last thing I wanted was *that bastard* to know its location as soon as I found it. If my hunch was right.

The trolls huddled together, whispering and growling. There was a lot of ear pulling, skulls knocking together and tugging of each other's chins as much as words spoken, given that trolls are very physical in their communications. More than one person had mistakenly thought a pair of trolls were fighting when in fact they were just greeting each other and asking how the other was doing.

If you need a point of reference, just listen to how South Africans speak to each other, or any of the Slavic cultures ... Russians, Ukrainians, Polish ... catch up with friends and family. You'd think someone was declaring war.

Finally, Sol bit down hard on Tol's ear, causing the other troll to snarl but back down, and turned to face me.

"Got maybe what you want." He told me, wrinkling his muzzle and showing his teeth in that troll way that said *now we bargain, and I find out what I can scam off you.* "Genuine 'bag of holding'. Fing goes innit, no-one knows it's there. Only you. Stick whatever you want innit. Just fink of the thing you want, and out it comes."

"Sounds useful." I replied, bracing myself. "So, what's it gonna cost?"

Sol looked back at Bol and Tol, the last brother scowling and opening his muzzle to speak.

"And before you even think it, nope, you ain't getting my leg. Or getting to lop it off. Or any leg, for that matter." I shut the troll down, seeing his eyes flash red with anger. "Legs are off the table, so move on."

Then I had a thought, and stopped them from speaking.

"For that matter, my first-born child, or in fact *children* mine or otherwise are also vetoed. As are any items *legitimately* belonging to someone else that you just 'want', and also any service you ask, for me to go beat up, threaten or in any way involve contact with someone or something that has in the past upset you." I counted items off my list. "Nor will I offer services to clean your abode, obtain to cook seagulls or any animal, vegetable or mineral you name, or break any of the mortal, Court or Accord laws for you. All off the table, as well as legs."

Sol's ears flopped, and he turned back to have another whispered conversation with his brothers. I caught the edges ... *wolf said 'seagull. Maybe we could try pigeon? ... don't know what wolf has against legs ... what he mean, clean?* ... before the smallest troll turned back to me.

"This thing. Knife you want to hide. Cursed, is it?" He asked, and I thought about it for a moment before nodding.

"I'd say most likely. Something like a *hexen-wolfen* belt but far worse. Anything it cuts binds that person to another. Really bad juju." I explained, keeping it simple.

"And this thing, that you hiding knife from. You're gonna deal with it. Permanent-like?"

I could see where this was going, and actually it wasn't so bad a solution to the problem of what to do with the knife when we'd dealt with Lykaois. If possible, I'd want the creature and the knife separated, so it could never possess anyone ever again. Then it would just be a knife with a *really* bad history.

So I nodded again.

"Ok. Knife for bag." The troll offered. "Deal with knife-thing, then when done, give us knife. Promise."

Sol held out one grubby paw and I hesitantly shook it, feeing its little claws close around my fingers, and all manner of unknown substances smear against my skin. But then again, I'd dealt with grimalkins, so the trolls were just disgusting rather than truly stomach-turning.

"What info you wanted?" This was from Bol, the middle troll. Whilst Sol ambled off to rummage in their stash of goodies, his middle brother questioned me. Still plucking feathers from the dead gull, obviously not wanting to miss lunch. Dinner. Or whatever snack he was aiming to prepare.

"How do I negate a cursed weapon? Break it from its owner, that sort of thing?" I asked, and saw Sol perk up. He had a small bag in one hand, obviously the thing I'd bargained for. It looked like a knackered old belt pouch, the sort that was popular in the 1980s and earned the dubious name of *bum bag*. Definitely the sort of thing I'd expect the trolls to peddle in, and if it was what I was after, I was checking its authenticity before accepting it.

It's not common knowledge but trolls are about as good smiths and forgers as the Dwarrow. Whilst fairy tale stories all tell of dwarven blacksmiths, dwarf cobblers and magical armour and weapons created by the clever and gifted dwarrow-kin, there is rarely a mention about trolls and what they make.

There's a good reason for that. Trolls are incredibly gifted, especially the greater troll-kin. But it's an incredibly niche talent, since they don't make magical swords which can cut through metal and stone. Nor armour that is impervious to projectile weapons, or cups that heal those who drink from them.

Nope, trolls can make absolutely amazing magical items, but only if they are *cursed*. You want a hexed ring that will drain the life from its wearer and turn them into a shade, go talk to a troll, not an elf. Tolkien had that one wrong. A sword that will defeat any opponent but after the tenth one, will slay its wielder instead? Go find a bridge and talk to your local troll.

Even lesser troll-kin like the Bung brothers had the knowledge inherited through their genes to know about cursed objects, hexed items. Nasty jinxes and cruel jokes, bound and inlaid into normal object to normally thoroughly fuck up the foolish mortal they were gifted to, or bestowed upon.

"You want break thing? When we bargained?" Sol accused, shaking the bum-bag of holding in one small fist. "Wolf thief, liar!"

"No. I'm not." I argued back, having expected something like this and planned how best to explain. "I just need to know if there's a way I can break the link between the knife and the creature it's linked to. Break the curse, make it harmless. So the bastard cannot feed through it ever again, or use it to take control of another. Then you can have the bloody thing."

"Comes with blood? Not tell me that." Sol countered, eyes narrowing. "Who's blood? Old blood? Mortal blood? Blood from people who come want it back?"

I shook my head, remembering who I was dealing with here.

"That's just a phrase. Ah, forget it. Give me the bag, and you'll get the knife as soon as I know how to stop it being bad juju. That's our deal."

Bol had another whispered conversation with his brothers, before grabbing the bag off Sol and shuffling forward. The troll offered the bag to me, which I quickly took just in case the brothers changed their minds, then cocked his head.

"One who cursed knife around?" He asked, but I shook my head again. I doubted very much whoever had been involved in creating the knife and its link to Lykaois was around to ask them politely to remove it, and then kick hard in the backside for being such a fuckwit. "Bad. Wolf know who cursed knife?"

I shook my head again, and the troll shrugged, out of ideas.

"No fee, no know then." He told me, helpfully. "Need know who cursed knife to know how undo. Not know, could be million ways was made, and each has different way of stopping curse. Could *break* it, suppose but if knife powerful, need sort of power wolf don't have. Maybe Courts, maybe not."

Sol made a strangled snarl at Bol's suggestion that I break the knife, and grabbed his brother's ear, dragging him back. Guessing I was about done with any answers from the smelly three, I slipped the bag into a pocket and carefully backed out of the doorway to the cell, as all three trolls started snarling, biting and shaking fists at each other.

"Morgan."

Jacob's voice stopped me, and I turned to find him watching me from the confines of his own cell. Far enough away from the Bung brothers so he wasn't disturbed by them, though there wasn't enough air freshener in the world to hide their stink.

Walking over to his cell, I faced him as he sat on a chair, obviously having been catching up on his reading given the pile of books he had in there with him. There was a simple bed, a washbag and bowl of fresh water, and a plate with what looked like the remains of a meal stashed neatly to one side. I wouldn't call his accommodation particularly welcoming, but compared to the rest of the sparse chambers we kept our hunts' prisoners in, his was relatively homely.

Jacob himself looked in far better condition than the rest of the pack. His eyes, though darkened and still a little bloodshot from his use of Wolfsbane, were clear and alert and he wasn't shaking, or pale like the rest of the lycans. There was no acidic stink of sweat, the sort from fever and illness, and he watched me with a focus that told me he was all there.

"You aren't sick." I commented, and he nodded, expression stony.

"You noticed." He replied, then sighed. "Whatever the fuck's wrong with Jessica, the pack, fuck, all the lycan, it's this thing's fault. I can *feel* it."

"Yeah, I'd reached the same conclusion." There was no harm talking to Jacob, and he had personal insight into what we faced, what sort of creature we were dealing with. That sort of intel, you don't pass on. "When it was inside you, did you feel anything? Get, oh I don't know, an idea of what it was thinking? Anything that could help?"

Jacob thought for a long moment, then shook his head, expression pained as his brow knitted together.

"I don't *remember* a thing. Not really." He admitted, and I could read the frustration in his voice, in the scent he gave off. He *wanted* to help, but was benched. Like I'd been when it came to guarding the mists. I couldn't help but feel a *small* sense of justice there. "It happened after I took the Wolfsbane, and I was going under. Maybe … *anger. Hunger.* I didn't see anything or share its thoughts, just sensed some of the things it was feeling. But that could just be my imagination?"

"You got one of those? Wonders never cease." I snarked, and Jacob grunted a short laugh.

Then he pushed himself up and stepped up to the cell's bars. Gripping them, he leaned into them, pushing his face against the cold iron.

"You're going after it's reliquary, aren't you?" He said, showing he'd been listening to the conversation I'd had with the Bung brothers, and possibly had spoken with Felix on this when she'd asked to check him for cuts. "The thing it was after when it possessed me. When I killed …"

"*It. It* killed." I corrected him. No matter the fact it was Jacob's hands that had done the deed, he had not been in control. That put all the blame at Lykaois's feet. "You've done a stupid thing, but not that."

"That time I spoke with you about. When I met Lucille." He went on, shrugging off my attempt to make him feel a little better about himself. "When I hunted the *Werwolves*. Those bastards, they killed for pleasure, to horrify and terrify the locals so that they'd do whatever the soldiers told them to do. Betray their own, give up everything they owned and had earned, sacrifice *anything*. I saw the damage done, and I swore I'd never let that happen. By my hand or another's."

He fixed me with his bright blue eyes, the weight of the emotion like a tsunami behind them.

"You get that knife." Jacob growled, and I nodded, once. "Get it, and then you bury it in this bastard's heart. Whatever it takes, no matter the cost. This thing needs to die, Morgan. That's the only way we'll be free."

With those cheery words, he turned away from me, stepping back and grabbing the chair so that it swivelled on its base. Then he sat down, his back to me, slumped with head bowed.

Grieving. Hurt.

I left before I tasted any more of his pain, closing the door behind me so that I didn't hear the muted sounds of his tears.

Chapter 40

Sacrifice

Not something that most mortals will wish to try, but certain supernatural creatures become vulnerable only when they are about to feed on their victims. Certain hags, invulnerable to any weapon or device, will suddenly become weak against even simple mortal weapons when they attach themselves to their prey to devour them. Usually this means the victim is incapacitated and unable to fight back, having been drawn away from allies and secured in the creature's lair so as to ensure its own safety. However, if one is willing to take the risk and to somehow have trusted companions nearby, the victim can allow the creature to begin feeding and so become vulnerable to attack.

The timing of this gambit has to be perfect, to not attempt the attack too early and risk alerting the creature nor leaving it too late and endangering the life of the victim. This is why the tactic is not often used.

Time passed quickly after that.

I had a half formed, cock-arse plan shaping in my mind of how we were going to deal with Lykaois after I'd obtained the knife. Its sacrificial reliquary. There were more holes in it than a suit of chainmail, and one particular risky-as-fuck part of my idea that I was less than wholly confident about.

But what the hell. You only die once. Unless you know a witch with stolen life energy and have her break her oaths to a Goddess to bring you back.

Sadly, mine was on loan elsewhere. But hey ho.

So, failing that, I just did the best I could. And made sure only those people who needed to know what I needed them to do, knew. That way, there were less arguments and questions about my overall sanity.

"You sure about this?" Felix asked me, expression doubtful.

"Sure." I lied through my back teeth, shrugging. "Hey, you had my face on a punchbag just the other day. Now I'm giving you this. Don't tell me I'm not good to you."

"Ha!" She snarked, cocking her head as the obvious thought struck her. "You cleared this with Jessica, right? And you've told Sarah what you want me to do?"

"Sure. Why else do you think I'm asking?" I lied again, pushing the guilt aside.

I knew Jess would never sign off on this plan, or the jumbled ideas I had that were slowly sticking together to look vaguely plan-like. There was too much risk, and I was putting me directly in the cross-hairs if things went wrong. Which they invariably did. So I decided not to tell her, and deal with the verbal dressing down later. If I was around to get one.

As for Sarah … she just wouldn't understand. As much as she had learned about lycans, about me, in the past day or so, this was all new to her. She still believed in the fundamental laws governing the Mortal Realm, without the experience that even a newbie like Felix had under her belt to show that things weren't always as they seemed, and the word *impossible* was actually less final than mortal usually thought.

Plus, I had that niggling doubt around her, knowing she was a host to Lykaois. We were missing our expert on all things spooky and freaky, and Felix hadn't uncovered anything more on what was and wasn't possible with this creature. It might be able to listen in on its hosts. Read their minds whilst not possessing them. Know things we didn't want it to know.

I reckoned, with that suspicion, it was better not to worry her unduly, or risking screwing up my plans before I even had a chance of trying them out in the first place.

"Ok. Well, if they've said ok … guess I'll do it." The young witch shrugged, nodding her acceptance.

"Thanks. Just, you know, don't be too vindictive when picking a spot." I told her, seeing her grin evilly but shrugging again. "You need to practice or anything?"

"Nah, I'm good. Dad made sure I got some practice in whilst we were in America." She replied, shaking her white dreadlocks. "Just in case I wanted to try out being a cowboy or something, I guess."

I figured Danny's reasons had been less comical than that, and more linked to Felix's family-roots, and the very real chance that they might have sent people after the pair of them. In that case, the sort of skills he'd had her practice didn't seem *that* odd, but were of little or no use back in the good ol' United Kingdom with its stricter laws.

"And the other thing? You been practicing, right?" I queried, knowing this was just as key as the first part. "Because you won't have much time …"

Felix stuck her tongue out at me, shaking her head again and sighing.

"Stop worrying so much, grandad. We're good." She reassured me, rolling her eyes. "I'm not up on making a combined one, but I can lay down a simple containment in my sleep. Just keep any monsters off me for a minute, and you'll be fine. Well … not so much, but you know what I mean."

"A minute's about all you'll get, if the shit is going to hit the fan as I expect." I told her, but nodded. Two down, now to work on the rest of my half-baked idea.

Given I was putting a lot of trust into something I'd purloined from the Bung brothers, I ran the bum bag of holding through a couple of tests. Simply stuffing things into it, and then calling them back. The magical bag worked like a charm, not increasing in size of weight even when I stashed several swords and daggers in the thing, and I got everything I put in back out without issue. The trolls had come through with this little gem.

Of course, I had no idea if it would block Lykaois from sensing its knife was in the bag. That part I was going to have to trust, but the small bag blocked anything I could scent from whatever I stashed in there, so I just had to hope we were good.

By the time I'd finished with the trolls, grilling Felix and running my odd little tests, Jessica had made an appearance on the office floor and in no uncertain terms, made it clear that the rest of the pack needed to get over their feeling like crap and be up and about.

Emma, given Jacob's incarceration, slipped into the role of lead enforcer. She soon had Vivian, Scott, Marcus and Kristoff downing buckets of coffee and cramming food into themselves before heading back out, to re-join OPS and the mortal authorities called in to cover the mists whilst we were laid low.

Whilst the pack got organised, Jessica put in a call to the other Alphas. They'd agreed we needed a show of force on the streets, and under them, just in case word had indeed gotten out about the lycans being struck down and not up to scratch. Hunts were re-prioritised, and numbers combined so that if any Real lawbreaker were stupid enough to think of taking advantage of our weakness, they'd find themselves facing more pack members than usual. Enough to put the stupids down, handle the crazies but still not exhaust the lycan too obviously.

For their part, the Alphas had decided they needed to take to the streets too. For the first time in a *long* time, they'd be patrolling alongside their packmates, handing out slap-downs and concluding Hunts. That was another difference between Talen and Sal Orben, and every other Alpha we knew. Those two had had no honour, no sense of responsibility, and definitely had not stood with their pack when the going got tough. Talen had run away, whilst Sal turned into the very monster which had been partly to blame for the Nighter's destruction. They hadn't deserved their titles.

Whilst the packs organised their rotas, and Felix headed back to her cottage with the present I'd given her, to start her own investigations into who in her circle of contacts was still alive, I took the chance to book a cab and get Sarah back home.

"Shouldn't I stick around?" She argued, tapping the journal she'd been tasked to read and hopefully find an answer as to how we trap the bastard once more. "What happens if I find something out and need to tell you *really* quickly?"

"You'll be safer at my place." I reassured her, knowing my wards were better in this situation than those around the office. There, the protection had to be tailored to deal with the influx of clients, deliveries and all the other random people who stepped inside the building because it was, first and foremost, a place of business. There were still the laws of invite, meaning I was *mostly* sure that a creature like Lykaois couldn't simply wander in and take possession of its hosts directly, but I wasn't certain. Whilst I *did* have proof my wards had rebuffed Jack recently which meant Sarah would be safer behind them.

Plus, she would have Goldspur and Bear with her. If those two couldn't watch over one mortal, and keep her from trouble, I don't know what could.

I travelled up with her in my private elevator and dropped her off at my front door, opening it up and motioning for her to head on in. She stopped just inside, even as I heard Bear grumble awake upstairs, and felt the dryad awaken from wherever she was resting.

"Morgan, I'm … look, when this is all over …" She started but I stopped her, shaking my head and stepping over the threshold to simply kiss her. Long and lasting, drawing strength from the simple contact.

"We'll talk. When I get back tonight." I told her, seeing her nod and swallow whatever she had been about to say. "Don't open the door to anyone, and if you *do* make a breakthrough, call Jessica. Her number's on the fridge, under the big red Emergency Contact sticker. Or me, but if all works out right, I might be a little busy running like Roadrunner to stop to take a call. Ok?"

"Just as long as you run home to me, *mi amor*." She told me with a mock stern expression before kissing me back one last time. "And say *Meep Meep* when you do."

I pulled the door closed even as I heard Bear's thumping tread on the stairs. She'd be safe with those two looking after her, and I wouldn't be distracted, worrying about her. At least that's what I told myself, as I jumped back into the waiting taxi and headed back to the office, for my date with the Sisters.

It was nearing half eight when Pippa shouted up to me from the downstairs reception that we had visitors. For a lycan only measuring five foot six, and weighing in at under nine stone, she had powerful lungs and the sort of shout that any drill sergeant-major would have sold their grandmother for.

"Watch yerself, Morgan." Jessica told me, from where she stood beside Emma, reviewing the current list of Hunts we had to cover, and who was doing what.

She still looked like I could knock her over with a well-placed punch, but her eyes were alert and full of energy, and her scent was stronger, more settled. She was making the effort to give her pack strength, prove we weren't beat no matter what was done to us. And it was working, given how only Pippa and Kristoff remained in the office. Every other lycan was out, warding the mists or running Hunts, making sure they were seen and felt.

"Ah still dinnae understand this creature's plans." She admitted, a continued point of frustration for us all. "But it has gone tae great lengths tae weaken us, tae sow fear and confusion where it can. And now this attack on the Goddess. There is more going on here than some simple creature's delusion tae Godhood, and its desire tae feed its centuries old hunger. So be careful."

"Always." I promised, before stopping as a thought struck me.

"What happened to Albert?" I realised I hadn't seen the bulldog for a while, nor heard his unmistakable panting and unmelodious snores. Let alone smelt his farts. "No-one came to collect him did they?"

"Nae, they did not." My Alpha replied, smiling. "It seems Felicity and the hound formed something of a bond whilst she tended tae his wounds. Whilst you were delivering yer charge home, Albert made it clear in nae uncertain terms he was nae staying put when the young witch went tae leave. And she seemed nae unhappy about the idea either so ah saw nae harm in her taking him."

I remembered how she had fussed over him when I had first brought the wounded dog into the office. The simple joy she found in healing him. Given how much negative shit she'd had to deal with, since finding out she now was something other than normal, something more powerful, more frightening … it was a small win amongst the crap we were dealing with, to have her find some love and a bond with an animal that needed help.

Of course, she hadn't tried to sleep anywhere near the dog when he started snoring properly, and bulldogs were renowned as being up there on the decibels for nasal resonance. I'm sure she'd cope. Eventually.

That fact cleared up, I headed down to find my date for the evening.

I found out we were definitely going to piss off the nuns when I got to the reception area, and found not one but two people waiting outside the door for me.

Cormac Smith was in his business greys, the overcoat he wore against the October chill as muted as the rest of his clothes. He nodded to me as I popped the front door open, and caught my expression at not finding him alone.

"PC Chambers. You here about Albert?" I spoke before the OPS agent could, seeing the other man smile and nod as I named him.

The policeman was still in uniform, gloves and hat firmly in place, his cheeks tinged red from the chill in the air.

"Uh good evening, Mr Black." He replied, then nodded over to his companion. "Mr Smith suggested I might be of assistance tonight. That whatever you and he are involved in relates to ongoing enquiries about the events at the Natural History Museum and Greenwich. Oh, and Holland Park."

I shot a look at Cormac, who shrugged.

"We often make use of local law enforcement staff for specific tasks." He blithely replied. "In this instance, I thought it might be wise for a police presence to remain *outside* our meeting place. In case anyone else thinks to join and rudely interrupt us."

I sighed. It made actual good sense, if all we had to worry about was mortals putting in an appearance. But Cormac knew the thing we were dealing with was as far from mortal as you could get, and nothing that a single police officer could handle. More likely he'd just end up getting hurt, maybe killed.

Before I could argue, and work out how to tell Cormac how stupid he was being without actually mentioning the reality of what we faced, PC Chambers pulled out a folded piece of paper.

"There was another reason I thought it correct that I comply with Mr Smith's request." He passed me the folded paper, nodding back the way I had come. "It's actually about the dog you took into care at Holland Park. Albert, you said?"

Nodding, I unfolded the sheet to find it to be one of the standard mortal forms, full of small script, subclauses and a very large area to sign one's name with a section of almost unreadable fine print underneath indicating the potential implications of signing your name and then breaching the aforementioned unread rules.

"Well, as my colleague mentioned, it wasn't *exactly* protocol for me to release the dog into your custody." The policeman smiled with an embarrassed blush. "So it would *really* do me a favour if you or the owner of this establishment could just sign this release form, so the paperwork is all proper and correct? Otherwise, someone will check and then ask the Officer In Charge of the case, who'll then ask my sarge, who'll come down on me for skipping procedures …"

I held up a hand, biting down on the urge to roll my eyes at the levels of bureaucracy involved in simply saving a wounded animal from a crime scene.

"I'll go ask my boss if she'll cover for this." I told him, seeing his expression lift with gratitude. "Come on inside, and we'll get this signed. Then, I guess we need to be on our way? Unless you've invited anyone else along for tonight's fun, Mr Smith? A marching band, maybe? Cheerleaders?"

My sarcasm fell on stony ground, as Cormac shook his head and smiled.

"No, no-one else, Morgan. I believe the good constable and I will be enough to be of any service, should you encounter any difficulties. Long words to translate, and the like."

I grunted, opening the door and letting them both in.

Mortals. Sometimes, just sometimes, I think the monsters have the right idea … it's not like one *little* bite would do all 'that' much harm.

Chapter 41

Jessica had signed the policeman's form, rolling her eyes that I had thought we'd be able to skip their rules and regulations.

With that done, and after I stashed a couple of handy tools about my person, we skipped off along the yellow brick road to go meet the wizard. In this case, the scary-as-hell Sisters of the Arch and their ward. Cormac was probably Dorothy, PC Chambers the tin man and I was a cross between Toto and the Cowardly Lion.

The Scarecrow didn't make this cut, though I did wonder what with my hare-brained scheme I was hoping would put an end to a centuries old supernatural monster from the Real, whether I wasn't covering his brainlessness too.

All Saints Church, on St Margaret's Street, was a suitably gothic looking example of 1800's architecture, where those tasked with designing a place of worship were told *make it dark, spiky, and easy to spot with a single tower like a finger to God*. It sat on the edge of Soho, that den of depravity and sinkhole of sin, meaning all manner of odds and sods washed up at its doors. The sort of scummy tide you see off the coast of the British Isles after the great cargo ships have traversed the watery channels a few times.

Given it was late October, night was already firmly entrenched by the time we made our way to the church's front door. A single gate-house had been fixed between iron railings and more dark brick, with twin lamp posts on either side of the entrance to light the way for any near-sighted sinners. The sky overhead was heavy with cloud, but occasional glimpses through allowed me to see the almost perfectly circular moon hanging high in the sky. Tonight, probably tomorrow, was full moon. Linked again and again incorrectly to us lycanthropes, but also an important time for Lykaois and its ceremony. So maybe we'd found the true root of that particular myth.

Cormac indicated to PC Chambers that he should stay outside the church, patrolling the front, and to stop anyone wishing to enter. He was given leave to tell them there was a private event happening in the church, that it would be open for visitors and its congregation from the following day and apologies for any inconvenience caused. And then move them on.

I sniffed the air, alert for any danger. Any sign Lykaois or that bastard Jack were in the area, but all I got was a noseful of London funk. Usually worse in the summer heat, the air was still heavy with the stench of mortals, their industry, their footprint on the world around them. The sort of foot which needed a bloody good pedicure, scrub and possibly boiling to be rid of all the associated smells.

Finding nothing immediately untoward, I motioned to Cormac and we headed inward.

Inside, the church opened up on glorious splendour.

A single large chamber, fitted with pillars forming arches on both the right and left of the main room, with the altar set at the far back of the church and separated by a low wall cutting across the floor. Overhead, the ceiling rose high into a majestic peak above the place of worship, with ridges running back to where the general congregation sat and knelt to pray. Two side entrances sat inset on the far left and right, leading to the back rooms and possibly some other entrance for the priests and laypeople who worked and celebrated in the building.

It was a study in olden-day paintings of saints, and carefully maintained white marble stonework. Light from long stemmed chandeliers gleamed off every surface, giving the place a warmth you would not have thought possible having seen the exterior of the church.

Our footsteps echoed on the tiled floor underfoot as we both entered the church proper. No one was to be seen either in the rows of pews set between the arching pillars or up on the altar which gleamed with flickering candlelight. But the place had that *feel* to it. Sanctuary, solemnity, a haven against the darkness outside the doors. Incense spiced the air lightly, not the overpowering musk that sometimes was employed to daze those attending services and induce visions such as the American Indian shamans employed in their trances. No, this was simply a scent of the holy, the profound. Unseen but still there.

I was surprised when Cormac stopped by the holy water font and dipped his fingers in, crossing himself before walking between the church pews. The OPS agent didn't strike me as the religious sort, given what he knew of the Real and Mortal Realm, but then again sometimes knowing the truth just enforced one's personal beliefs in the intangible, the ineffable.

I knew for a fact I didn't believe Oberon was *The* God and Creator, with capitals, just a very powerful immortal in charge of the Ivory Court and de facto Prime power in the Real. Whether that meant there *was* a singular creator, that was to blame for the mess the Realms were in and how mortals managed to evolve from happy tree-based furry primates to the monsters they were in their most evolved state, who knew? And if someone did, they weren't telling.

Probably too scared of all the hate-mail and questions they'd be sent. That and the bad reviews about the weather in the Mortal Realm, and the bedbugs. Or cockroaches.

I cast around, checking for any sign of anyone lurking in wait or just accidently being in the wrong place at exactly the wrong time. A trait which most mortals seemed to have inherited in their basic genes. But nothing pinged my suspicious bastard radar, the place seemed deserted. Empty.

Which was bloody weird, all in itself.

We got to the last row of pews, and Cormac slipped down to sit on the one of the right. I remained standing, alert for anything, looking around us.

"I am sure the Sisters will be along momentarily." He told me with that simple assurance that everything will run to schedule, that most Governmental officials lived by. Everything in its proper time and place, and leave the chaos of unplanned events and non-scheduled actions to the foreigners.

"We are, in fact, already here." A voice spoke up, and I jerked to look behind us.

The Sister stood in the entry way, clad in her soiled and stained habit, all but her eyes hidden behind the veil all her kind wore. But those eyes of hers flashed red with restrained fury, a temper on a very short leash.

Beside her, a figure huddled. Clad in a dirty long coat and with a hood drawn over its head, the creature … Grubbins, I expected … kept its features hidden. But it was manlike in form, two arms and two legs, hands wrapped in dirty gloves and feet shoved into old worn-out boots. It hunched down, as if weighed upon by something heavy, or eager to avoid any sort of attention.

I *knew* we had been alone a moment ago, and that the church had been empty when we arrived. But the nun and her charge were most definitely there now, the stench of the unwashed countering the faint sweetness of the incense, whilst the Sister filled the air with the crackle and hiss of contained lightning.

"We were assured you would abide by our rules, and come alone, Morgan Black." The Sister focused those red-raging eyes on me and I stiffened, feeling the lash of their touch but refusing to back down. I'd dealt with the Sisters before, had almost gained what I felt was their trust, even a little friendship. At least with two of their order, before they were brutally slain by my half-brother and his equally twisted companion, Baba Yaga.

I shook my head, and nodded to where Cormac now stood, having risen at the other's appearance.

"His fault. You know I normally stick to whatever any of your order asks." I replied honestly. That had usually been something as simple as finding a bottle of the harshest whiskey one could buy, to share amongst the transient congregation of whichever Sister I needed to speak with. And in London, rotgut was not hard to come by. "I'm just here to speak to your friend, and ask one question of you."

The Sister shifted her gaze from me as the OPS agent stepped up beside me, hands open.

"My apologies, Sister." He began, nodding. "As Morgan Black says, my being here is not any of his doing. I am …"

"Cormac Wessen Smith. Regional Inspector and Divisional Advocate of London Central, OPS." She cut him off, reeling off an impressive set of job titles I did not know he had. I just thought of him as 'agent'. And sometimes 'arsehole'. "We know who you are, and who those are whom you work for. There are times we have worked towards the same goal, your organisation and my order, but there are times when we have crossed paths and found ourselves on different journeys. I *trust* this is not one of them."

Cormac shook his head, if at all disconcerted by the Sister's knowledge, not showing it.

"We just want to keep the mortals safe. Keep the Accords from being broken." He replied, simplifying his job down to almost kindergarten levels. "Something is loose in the city, something which threatens to do them harm. More harm than it has already done to those of your congregation. We would see it stopped, however that may be."

The Sister's eyes flashed, and I caught the scent of her rage threatening to slip its leash. I had dealt with the Sisters before, and knew they were powerful, but this one? She felt like a ticking bomb, ready to explode.

"Sister, before we go any further, I believe we have not been formally introduced." I interjected, knowing the protocols usually involved with meeting any of the Order. It made things easier, everyone knowing who everyone else was. "And I don't believe we've met?"

"No, Morgan Black, we have not." The Sister replied, before nodding once. "You have known my Sisters Wrath, Gluttony and Sloth. Two gone to eternal service with the One we serve. Slain most foully whilst involved in matters pertaining to *your* lineage, and one you asked us to find. A mortal, deceived and controlled by she who now sits upon Twilight's throne."

It seemed the Order was indeed plugged into all the gossip channels, since they had eyes and ears on all the streets. Well, the grubby, dirtier ones. The fact they knew Jack was my half-brother was concerning, since I was trying to keep that fact from getting out. Not only because he'd done enough damage the last time he was out and about, he'd earned the enmity of the Sisterhood as well as a few other factions in London and I wasn't willing to take the blame for my kin's actions. No, the main reason was it would mean people then knew of my connection to Herne the Hunter. Lord of the Wyld Court. My father.

I still wasn't sure what that meant *exactly*. Whether I was heir apparent, or was a lycan in actual fact instead of some bizarre melding of immortal and mortal. My mother had been the mortal; a witch and scientist, involved with

OPS and its sister agency, DOPA. And something of a force to be reckoned with, from the little I'd been told about her.

Either way, I was trying to remain just another faceless lycan, one of the pack, a Redcloak and nothing more. Until at least I knew what being Herne's son meant for me, and those that I cared about.

"I am Sister Spite," She introduced herself, and for once I found her title more than fitting. "I am charged with watching over those of our flock who face greater trials, those whose path to redemption is blocked by adversity and strife. I am their guide, their shield and their comfort when times are dark."

The guide and shield I could get, but the idea of Sister Spite being *anyone's* comfort seemed a little farfetched. But who was I to judge?

"And this is Brother Grubbins." She introduced her companion, as it huddled beside her. I took a small step forward, seeing it flinch, and held out my hand. A simple gesture, watched over by the nun's fiery glare, to try and put the other at ease.

"Hi. I'm Morgan Black." I introduced myself, seeing the other's arm twitch, as if to take my hand and shake but stopping itself. "I'm just after a few questions. About what happened in Greenwich Park …"

And that's when my nose, filtering through the storm that was Sister Spite, the noisome stench of Brother Grubbins and the subtle aroma of the church, tapped me on the proverbial shoulder and pointed out a small, but undeniable fact.

Underneath the sweat, the dirt, the filth … I knew the scent coming from Brother Grubbins. I'd stood in a house, smelt the same from clothes left tossed around the place. Smelt it from furniture, from a place of study. From a journal rigorously kept up to date with each entry, each new event the owner had participated in.

Until the very last one.

But that made no sense. The smell of the person I was sensing was dead, murdered in Greenwich Park with two other transients to hide the fact. Unless …

"Holy shit." I exclaimed, forgetting I was in house of worship, and in the presence of actual clergy. "Brother Grubbins As in ... *grubbing around?*"

I saw the other flinch, then their shoulders slump in defeat. Their secret was known. Carefully, the transient reached and slowly slid their hood down, revealing ...

"Professor Julius Eduardo."

Chapter 42

Oath-breaking

For some of the fae creatures, the oaths they swear are solemn and binding promises that if broken, inflict great pain on them and can actually kill them. Obtaining an oath in the first place is often not that difficult, as the fae are barterers and love nothing more than making deals.

However, to then engineer a situation where the fae is forced to break their side of the bargain takes great skill and cunning. If the fae is alerted to the attempt, it will most likely exact a hefty price from the mortal, above what has already been promised. And fae, given their long lives, do not forget an insult done them and will spend a mortal's remaining years ensuring they get their retribution.

I saw him flinch again as I said the name, and the Sister beside him moved a step closer, settling one arm around his shoulders.

"The one you name is no longer with us." She told me bluntly, eyes blazing. "Brother *Grubbins* has willingly joined our congregation, and left that echo of his life behind him. Where it will remain. Are we clear?"

The mortal shook his head, taking a step forward and away from his guardian.

"It's ok." He told her, then looked over at me. "You're right, of course. The others called me Grubbins for what they called *grubbing around*, the work I did investigating what had been buried and lost. Grubbing seemed to fit, so I became Grubbins when …"

"When you needed to disappear. After you let something loose in South America." I prompted gently, seeing the Sister glare at me but knowing I needed answers. And here was the very man who had actually been there. Been the one to start this horrendous chain of events.

"Oh, I did worse than let something loose." He replied hoarsely, skin paling under the dirt that caked him. He peeled off one of his gloves, showing a healed mark on his hand, the sort of off-colour skin that had been a fine cut in his flesh. "I cut myself with its knife, you see. I set it free, so it then took control of me. It *made* me do things. Horrible things. I killed my colleagues, the guards set to keep us safe … all to feed its hunger. Its need to slay, to torment, to brutalise. And it let me remember, let me see what I had done. And it fed off my own guilt, my own shame too."

"That's kind of its MO." I told him, remembering what Felix had said about how Lykaois had convinced its priests to make the chosen one kill their own family, anyone they cared for or loved, before it took control of them. "And so, you shipped it back with you, hidden away, with Sarah and Miles unaware? Just you three lucky survivors, until it got back here. But *why*? What does it want here?"

Grubbins shook his head, visibly shaking as he relived the memories of what he had been made to do, the horrors inflicted on others at his own hands.

"It was *summoned*." He told me, eyes wide, breath starting to come in shallow gasps. "I felt it somehow, in my head, when it was controlling me. A need it had to be here, to do a thing. But that wasn't enough, it wanted more than just to serve. It wanted to be strong again, to be what it was before it was locked away. Worshipped, feared. A god."

"And there was a name." He recalled, looking at me with sudden surprise. "Yes, yours! Morgan Black. Over and over. It was the reason why it was called, but I don't know why."

"Oh, for fucks sake!" I growled, again ignoring where I was standing. I hadn't yet been struck down by lightning for using bad language on holy ground, so I wasn't too worried. "Why do they keep leaving *my* bloody name? Can't the monsters be original for once, and ask for Benedict Cumberbatch or someone? Anyone!?"

Cormac sighed, the OPS agent obviously wondering the same thing but failing to voice his own thoughts on the matter.

"Putting that little fun fact aside." I growled, refocusing on what I needed to know. "This thing, it's here now. It's fucking around with my friends, people I care about. And it's killing people. So you need to tell us … how do we put it back in its box? You deciphered what the Mayans did to imprison it, so how do we replicate that?"

Grubbins shook his head, expression stricken.

"You can't!" He almost wailed, arms wrapped around himself as he shook. "When the Mayans first encountered it, they killed all its worshippers. The Vikings who had sailed across the ocean, the Gothar who travelled with them. Its priest. The Wulf-gard that were its warriors. They slew them all as blood sacrifices, blunting its hunger and weakening it as it fed on its own worshippers. Just enough to keep it appeased with more human lives whilst they built the temple and prison to contain it."

Grubbins, the professor he had been almost thoroughly transformed from the cocky, arrogant expert to now a humbled and desperate soul, scrubbed at his hand that bore the wound inflicted by the knife. As if by even talking about the thing, he felt its touch. Which was entirely possible.

"It gifted them knowledge beyond their primitive understanding, power over their rivals, wealth beyond imagination. All for the price of bloodshed and death. Every full moon, a chosen forced to sacrifice their loved ones, then themselves given to it as a host, a form for a brief time. So it could take human form and expand its influence, take over more lives. Enslave more and more." He explained, the horror of his knowledge writ on his haggard features. "The knife is the key now. The only thing it needs to fully consume someone, to bind itself to a new form. There are no chosen to feed it, no blood sacrifices to quench its thirst and quieten it. No followers to slay, to weaken it."

He looked me dead in the eye, fear roiling off him like he was sweating it from his skin.

"Only its knife. Keep that from its grasp, that's all we can do."

"Oh yeah. The knife." I turned to face Sister Spite, meeting her burning stare. "See, the thing has been hunting that particular piece of cutlery since it got here. Least so I can tell. It *was* in the museum, locked away and out of reach until it could get inside someone who had access to where it was being kept. Which *should* have been immediately, given it had

Professor Eduardo here under its thumb already. Ever since he cut himself with the bloody thing. What happened? How did he slip the leash?"

The Sister eyed me for a long moment, clad in her dirty and stained habit. The veil she wore gave her the ultimate poker face, but eventually she seemed to come to a decision, nodding to me.

"We became aware of this ... *item* and its capacity to do great ill shortly after brother Grubbins's return from his travels abroad. Before he sought to make amends for the wrongs he had done, and turn his back on the life he had led." She answered with a much softer tone than she had used before, the anger in her eyes dimming a notch. "He was known to our community, and had been kind to those we ward without ever looking for anything in return. A single flicker of goodness amongst the darkness of his own deceit, arrogance and a thorough delusion of his own self-worth. When he approached us, seeking not absolution but penance for his wrongdoings, we agreed. Not only would he put aside his past triumphs and empty trophies that had fuelled his belief in a singular importance, but he also would obtain the foul item from where it was stored and bequeath it to us. To hold and ward until someone *worthy* sought it. For the single and only reason we might relinquish it."

She looked over at her charge, who had fallen silent after his long speech.

"My Sisters removed the foul link to the item and its owner when brother Grubbins handed it over." She shook her head as I went to speak, reading my mind before I was even sure what I was going to ask. "And no, Morgan Black. We cannot remove the ties that others bear to this creature. Only that which was done by the knife, and with this single act of contrition. Those others who have been marked by this creature? They are not for us to free."

I sighed, realising I should have guessed it wouldn't be as easy as bringing Sarah and Jacob to the Sisters to break the link between them and Lykaois. Life didn't deal me such simple solutions.

"Fine. But I'm the last person to call myself *worthy*." I chose my next words carefully, knowing it was as much the intent behind them that the Sister would taste and weigh, as the words themselves. "Sister Spite. I humbly ask you to bequeath the knife handed to you by brother Grubbins to me. So that I might put an end to the violence and pain it has caused, and prevent it taking a single life more. I ask that you trust me with this cursed item, so that I can use it to bind and imprison the one linked to it, and entomb it in a place where it can do no further harm, threaten none other. I seek to free those I care for from its grasp, and stop it from hurting them or any other. That is all I desire."

Sister Spite weighed me in those burning orbs of hers, the heat of them almost scorching me as I felt the press of her mind against mine. Reading my intent, seeking to understand whether I was truthful or not.

Given I had no other intent than see the bastard Lykaois, and my half-brother if I could manage it, put down once and for all, I wasn't unduly worried about the Sister's inspection of me. Sure, if she had said she would only give the knife to someone *pure of spirit* or anything like that, I'd be a little more worried. Too many impurities kicking around me to think I'd pass the test.

But worthy? I could scrape that one. Barely.

Sister Spite held me with her burning eyes for a long moment, then gave a short sigh.

"It is a testament to how desperate times have become, when the benchmark is set so low." She told me, crushing my ego just that little bit. "However, I guess you will do."

I bit back the instinctive sarcastic reply, seeing Cormac shake his head once beside me. Seems he too could do a little mind reading when he wanted to.

The Sister reached into her robes, and carefully drew out what she had kept hidden there. As she slid the folds of cloth away, brother Grubbins shied away, obviously wanting to be nowhere near the thing as I looked on a weapon of pure evil.

Given that fact, it was a little anticlimactic. You see artists draw weapons that contain vile spirits of hunger, with hooked blades and runes inscribed spelling out the evil things done by their wielders. Glowing red with hellish flames, sometimes with an angry eye set in the weapon's pommel, stolen from the socket of a God and glaring madly back at the world. That sort of thing.

The knife in the nun's hand was curved like a Greek kopis sword, with a thick machete like blade and a wide fuller inset into the stone. Its hilt had the traditional double grip of its larger counterpart, with a hook at the end of curl back over the wielder's fingers. The obsidian of the blade gleamed, the green-black sheen polished and looking not so much ancient as well cared for. There were no runes, no markings on the weapon itself, making it a fairly ordinary looking tool of bloodshed and slaughter.

But the aura of the thing? Now that was not ordinary. There was a heaviness to it, a weight like all the souls that had been shed by its fine edge were bound to it, chained to it. I could almost hear the screams of its victims, they felt so close as I looked at the knife. And the scent of blood literally *dripped* from the weapon, so that I expected to see crimson staining the cloth that the Sister had wrapped it in.

The thing was horrific, evil and definitely nothing that I wanted to have anything to do with. Sadly, I had little choice in the matter.

I accepted the knife off the Sister, feeling my skin crawl as I held it. Then, not wanting to keep the thing out in the open any longer than I had to, I opened up my bag of holding and dropped it in, snapping the thing closed and firmly sealing it away.

That done, I took a breath and looked across at Cormac.

"Well, I'm done. Did you have anything more to add?" I asked the OPS agent, hoping he had enough to take back to his bosses as well.

"Do not tarry with that thing," Sister Spite instead told me, even as brother Grubbins huddled back beside her and moved away from me. I didn't take it personally, since I now had in my possession the cursed item that had ruined his life and led him to turn his back on everything he held dear. "Hunt this creature as you will. But know it will be coming for *you* now, if it did not already seek you."

"Given it had my name bouncing around its head, and made one of its hosts scrawl it in blood and entrails on the floor of the museum? I reckon I guessed that one already." I replied a little blithely, seeing her eyes flare with red flame. "What I *do* still want to know is …"

My question was interrupted as the door to the church creaked open.

"Morgan Black, you brought others than this mortal with you?" Sister Spite almost snarled at me, but I held up my hands, pointing to Cormac instead.

"Not me. This one's with him."

PC Chambers stepped into view, his uniform shining in the candlelight.

"Ah, Police Constable." Cormac stepped in front of me, walking past the Sister and charge, walking up to the other. "I thought we agreed you would remain outside on patrol? There is nothing here you need to be concerned about."

I noted several things in that moment.

PC Chambers had his helmet lowered, casting shadows over his face. Almost as if he were hiding it from view. And brother Grubbins had started jerking like he was having a seizure, shaking whilst his face had drained of what little colour it had had.

"Uh, Cormac! Don't get too close!" I shouted out, even as the Sister of the Arch pushed her charge behind her and raised her blood-red eyes to glare at the newcomer.

"What are you talking about?" Cormac shot a confused look over his shoulder. "It's only …"

Taking his eyes off the police officer for a moment.

Who, with lazy speed, lashed out with one hand with almost negligible effort … and slapped the OPS agent so hard that he was hurled through the air to crash amongst the wooden pews a good twelve feet away.

Then the man slowly raised his head, fixing us with a pair of glowing, slitted amber eyes raging with inhuman fury, as the stench of burnt mustard and spices filled the air.

Lykaois had arrived.

Chapter 43

"My knife. You found my knife. I *felt* it." The creature rasped, as it slowly stalked up the central aisle of the church. "Give it to me. Now."

"I think I can speak for all of us here," I replied with a snarl as I stepped away from the Sister, giving me some room to move. "When I say *fuck* that for a game of soldiers. With knobs on."

"Cretin." It snarled at me, twisting PC Chamber's face into something ancient, something bestial. "When you are mine, I shall make you rue every word you uttered that was not in glorification of my name. Rue!"

It swung its attention from me, gazing at the nun.

"My knife. You had it, I can smell its taint on you. You hid it from me, and have hidden it again!" Lykaois took another step forward, the body it was inhabiting still not entirely under its control as it lurched a little. "How dare you steal from me! Give it to me!"

"Begone from this place, foul creature." Sister Spite drew herself up, eyes flashing with righteous fury. "How dare *you* step inside this holy sanctuary?! Begone, fiend, before I cast you screaming into the night."

"Fah! Silence your tongue you wrinkled crone! Useless virgin, withered hag!" Lykaois snarled in reply, a vicious smile wrinkling its lips. "This place? Holy? Your pathetic godling was a puny, mewling child when I stalked the night. Slaking my hunger with hot blood, savouring the taste of sacrifices to the glory of my name. You and your *saviour* do not frighten me."

But then its gaze slipped to the side, noting the figure cowering at the Sister's side.

"But what is this? Who else seeks to keep me from what is mine?" It snarled, taking a long sniff. Its amber eyes widened, a growl hissing from between PC Chamber's lips. "You! The mortal who freed me, who was my first chosen after so long! You hid from me, locked yourself away behind bars like those craven sun-worshippers crafted for me. Took my knife and hid it from my sight! Come to me!"

The command shivered in the air, a lash that should have jerked brother Grubbins forward, his body unable to fight the link between immortal and slave.

But that link had been severed. Instead, he cowered back, stumbling away from Sister Spite as he jerked and shook.

"No. No! You are not my master anymore!" He cried, eyes searching for a way to escape, a place to hide. "Leave me be!"

"You broke my sacred link with this mortal." Lykaois snarled at the nun, amber eyes pulsing with renewed fury. "For that I will make you *suffer*."

The gunshot was like a cannon going off, slamming the air with thunder.

Lykaois and the body he was wearing were hurled back in a small explosion of oddly coloured smoke, crashing back through the pews on the left and disappearing from sight.

We all turned to find Agent Cormac Smith back on his feet, grey suit ripped and definitely worse for the wear. Blood stained his forehead from a nasty gash, but he stood firm on his feet, braced as he cradled an incredibly large and bulky handgun. Gods knew where the hell he'd hidden that thing, as it hadn't shown as an awkward lump under his jacket or anything.

"Whoa, Agent Smith!" I crowed, then took a suspicious sniff at the air as a familiar stink sang to me. "Did you just shoot the bastard with *Wolfsbane?!*"

"Concentration of Wolfsbane, holy water, silver nitrate and pure salt particles." He replied, voice tinged with more than a little pain. He gingerly extracted himself from the wreckage of the wooden seats, limping over to my side. "Nothing that should harm PC Chambers, but effective against most category one or two entity types. Especially those reported to change shapes, and take on a bestial form."

"I'm guessing that hand-cannon is not standard issue OPS equipment?" I nodded to the thing, which looked like it needed someone like *Hellboy* to wield it. The kickback alone must have been murder on a simple mortal. "How many shots does it make?"

"Six, but I find one is normally enough." He replied, but brought up the gun once more as a snarling roar split the church air.

"You'll … need … more." Lykaois's voice rasped out, as it re-emerged.

The shot had impacted dead centre on PC Chambers' chest, smearing his police uniform with the substances combined in the gun's round. But Lykaois seemed undiminished, its amber eyes blazing as it snarled at us, obviously furious at having been shot.

"Now … you'll …pay." It rasped angrily.

Then PC Chambers *Changed*.

I hadn't seen what Dr Miles Cooper had looked like when Lykaois had taken him over at the museum, and Jacob had still been in his mortal-friendly suit when I faced him on his boat. I had no idea what to expect.

To be fair, I now could understand why this bastard was linked to us lycan, and might think it was the original of the species.

PC Chambers was a regular sized mortal, pale skinned with the sort of musculature that came from a job requiring a certain level of fitness. He had been clean shaven, and always wore his helmet so I had no idea what colour hair he had apart from a guess of *dark* from his eyebrows.

Lykaois savagely warped its mortal shell, the tight police uniform shredding and ripping like some old Hammer Horror cheap suit. Its body bulged, coarse light grey fur mottled with darker stripes rippling over thickened muscle and bone. Sharp pops sounded as the body rippled and grew, its ribcage ballooning whilst its hips and lower legs reset to be back bent and set upon splayed feet tipped with savage talons. The beast's face broke apart with a wet tearing sound, the muzzle pushing out to open and snarl, showing rows upon rows of jagged fangs. An obscene tongue, fat and slick with mucus, slipped free and tasted the air as those amber eyes fixed on us with hungry intent.

The gloves PC Chambers had worn shredded as the creature's hands twisted and grew. As the material ripped, I caught sight of the small but open cut on the right palm. A twin to the one Sarah had. A link to Lykaois, the sign it had tasted the blood of its host.

Lykaois now stood over seven feet tall, weighing in well over eighteen or nineteen stone if I could hazard a guess from its muscled and heavily boned body. It *looked* like a werewolf, with long fingers and sharp claws, panting with the after-effects of the Change as its stunted ears twitched atop a thick skull. Only its fur was odd, the rippling white-grey offset by jagged patches of a darker hue. Almost like lightning bolts carved into its hairy hide. Hell, there was even a tail, stunted but definitely there, swinging behind the bastard.

I caught the sidelong look Cormac shot me, and shook my head, scowling.

"I don't care if it looks like a fucking duck, and its quacking!" I snarled, feeling the Change in me rise to meet the challenge. I bit back down on it, knowing I wasn't here to fight but to get the bastard's knife as far away as possible from it. "The fucker is *nothing* like me or my pack. Nothing."

"I am your *God*!" Lykaois almost screamed, spittle spraying from its maw as it snarled its fury. "Give me my knife! Serve me!"

"Fuck off, like I already told you!" I shouted back, tapping instead the Shadow and Ivory Court brands.

Armour began to form around me, ice coating my clenched fist like a jagged gauntlet. Cormac levelled his gun again, as Sister Spite started chanting under her breath, Latin rolling from her lips like a song.

Lykaois stood before us, talons gleaming ... the next moment, the bastard *shifted*, disappearing from where it stood. The next thing I knew, I was slammed like I'd been hit by a freight train, hurled from my feet in a spray of fiery sparks as claws scratched across my hastily formed armour. I sprawled back, feeling wood break under me as I destroyed another set of pews with my tumbling.

Cormac, somehow sensing the attack, dove to one side this time and fired his gun again. The cannon roared, his shot taking Lykaois in the side this time. Whatever was in the shell seemed to have little effect on the creature, but the force of the shot at least staggered it, eliciting a savage howl from its gaping maw before it vanished again.

"No!" Brother Grubbins yelled, too far away from his ward to have her shield him from the danger. The next moment, the professor turned vagrant jerked and bowed like he was about to break in two. Talons speared through his chest, as Lykaois appeared behind him and spitted him on its fist.

Blood burst from the mortal's mouth, gushing from the wounds in his chest, and he writhed in agony until Lykaois tossed him aside, letting that snake-like tongue worm over its talons and taste the blood staining its hand.

Then it glared back at us, where I was pulling myself out of the wreckage of the seating, and Cormac was covering it with his gun.

"You cannot hurt me with your petty weapons and simple Court tricks." It snarled, laughter bubbling up in its massive chest. "I am a *god*! Bow down and worship me, and I *might* let you live."

"He just doesn't get the hint, does he?" I growled, feeling the Ivory armour settle fully in place now. I hefted my icy fist, imagining slamming it hard into the other's face. Repeatedly. "I guess all that time locked up by the Mayans has made him a little slow."

"If your intent is to bait this creature into rash behaviour, or enrage it further," Cormac told me blandly, firing off another shot that Lykaois this time dodged. "Then I fail to see how that will in any way improve our position. Please enlighten me."

Before I could reply, Sister Spite stepped between us.

"This is not your fight, Morgan Black. Nor yours, Cormac Wessen Smith." She told us, red eyes fixed on Lykaois. "This … *creature* has desecrated a holy sanctuary. Slain one who was in my care. Spoken ill words against the one I serve. My sisters and I will not stand for this."

Cormac went to reply, probably mention something noble about us fighting together having a better chance, that she was but a simple nun. That sort of idiocy. I just grabbed his arm and shook his head, knowing what was about to happen.

"You think I fear you, you and your sisters of dirt and grime?" Lykaois snarled as she took a step forward. "I shall gut you as my other host did your Sister Wrath, spilling her blood just as easily I will yours."

"That one shall pay the price for his deed another time." She answered, as the air around her rippled and thickened, gaining a timbre as the smell of incense burgeoned. "But you? You shall learn the price of crossing our Order. And may God have mercy on your shrivelled soul. Daniel Alan Chambers, I summon you!"

Light, pure and brilliant like the first rays of the sun, shimmered into being around Sister Spite. Where before, she had been a figure of dirtiness and muck, her habit stained with the waste of those she tended. Their blood, their tears. Now, as I grabbed hold of Cormac and half dragged him back and off to one side, knowing I needed to find another way out of the church, she transformed into a figure of pristine wrath. Her habit shone, and behind her, twin folds of shining glory shimmered into being, wings arching out to beat the air around her. Above her now pure cowl, a crackling band of energy burgeoned into life, a halo that scorched the air as she took a step toward her foe.

"Daniel Alan Chambers, I say to you … you are judged! Your sins are known to me. Step forward!" She called, and Lykaois bellowed as light shimmered over his bestial form. It coalesced into a shining figure, small against the towering monster in which it had been encased.

The policeman's soul.

"NO! He is mine!" Lykaois howled, barrelling forward to strike at the nun. "You cannot have him! He is tainted! He has wronged others, caused suffering! He is *mine*!"

"I see your truth, Daniel Alan Chambers." Sister Spite focused on the glowing form. The light around her intensified, radiating furious sparks as Lykaois beat at her, seeking to rend the life from her body. "You have indeed done ill to others. Judged them not on their actions nor their merits, but by the colour of their skin, their origins. You have brought harm to some that did not deserve it, and this weighs upon you most heavily. You must atone, and in the Light, you shall. Step forward, and be judged."

The soul wavered, drawing back towards Lykaois as its own nature sought to fight against what it had done, what wrongs it had committed. Unwilling to accept the truth of its own errors. The Sister's aura burned brighter as Lykaois howled ever more savagely and renewed its attack on her. We, it seemed, were momentarily forgotten.

"Go. Take the knife. I shall hold the creature here as long as I may, and judge this soul." The nun's voice spoke to us even as she bent her will to the battle she fought. "Your time to face it is not now, so begone from here and prepare. Do not waste this chance, Morgan Black."

The air inside the church had begone to throb, as lightning speared out from where Sister Spite and Lykaois wrestled for the officer's soul. Cracks started to appear in the pillars supporting the vaulted roof, whilst the broken pews around us started to smoulder and burn. Smoke began to fill the air, as fires crackled to life all around.

"Come on!" I yelled at Cormac, turning away from the conflict. There wasn't anything I could do to help, and the whole reason I'd come was to obtain the knife and get it the hell away from its owner. Brother Grubbins ... Professor Eduardo ... the man's death would be for nothing if I failed now.

We raced out of the main chamber, light blazing now like the surface of the sun, as my nose led me to another door, tucked away on the right-hand side. Through this, finding ourselves in a room filled with cassocks, robes or whatever the clergy called the garments they wore, along with stacked bibles and gleaming chalices locked behind glass. Another door, another short corridor, and we burst out into the fresh night air.

Behind us, shafts of light shot through the church's roof to light the darkened sky. There was a massive, rumbling groan, then the central spire collapsed downward. Through the roof, smashing this to ruin, and breaking apart inside the church with the shattering of glass and rending of metal. Flames shot up, the inside now an inferno, and we backed away from the slowly crumbling building.

I checked my belt, relieved to find that in all the chaos, I hadn't dropped the bag of holding and its contents. That would have sucked, but also would have been my sort of luck, the way things had been going.

Sirens howled in the distance, even as shocked mortals started gathering outside the collapsing church. I kept an eye out for anything moving as we easily mingled with the crowd, alert for anything trying to break free of the blaze. But it seemed the Sister had kept Lykaois bound until his host was destroyed. Nothing moved, except for the walls as they groaned and crumbled.

Cormac was already on his phone, calling in the incident and arranging for a clean-up crew to be on site before the emergency services arrived. It wouldn't do for some luckless fireman to find the burned, horrendously disfigured body of a policeman amongst the mess, but I had to hope that PC Chambers had found some peace from whatever the fuck he'd done to earn the attention of Lykaois. Personal pain, tragedy … the creature needed something bad to have happened to be able to take over a person, bad enough to haunt them. Cause them to grieve, to suffer.

He'd seemed normal enough to me, no sense of the bastard about him. Just a world-weary mortal carrying too much weight on his shoulders, still fucked up over the loss of a friend, a colleague. Not carrying some deep dark shame, nothing to make me think he might be hiding something even darker, even nastier inside.

That aside, we had the knife. It had cost the life of a man I already thought was dead, and another who I hadn't suspected I couldn't trust. Blood stained this thing wherever it went, but now I had a small window, one slim chance, to maybe put an end to the slaughter and mayhem that followed it like its own personal soundtrack.

One gamble, and this time I wasn't betting on walking away so easily from the ending. Having met Lykaois properly now, I'd gotten a feel of the creature. It was horrendously powerful, maybe not as much as Morgana but in its own right, truly monstrous. Facing off against it, I wasn't placing bets on me winning despite all my tricks, my Court talents. My Redcloak training, or even my weird-ass nature.

There was a real chance I was going to fail. And that meant more people I loved getting hurt. Or worse. And that I couldn't let happen.

So. Time to maybe load the dice just a little. See just how far I was willing to go to keep them all safe. Toss in a plan B for when things got really fucked up, and I faced the final question …

What would I pay, to keep those I loved safe?

Chapter 44

Shadows

The shadow of certain supernatural creatures is imbued with a life of its own, often moving differently to its corporal form. Vampires especially are known to have shadows which move differently to them, and often show the creature's true nature even when they have taken mortal form.

However, certain demonic creatures can be harmed by snaring their shadows, affixing them to a surface with silver or cold forged iron. The shadow will seek to elude its fate, slipping into the smallest cracks or through the tightest of spaces, but it can be captured and used to inflict pain upon its owner.

The tale of the Pan deals with how a shadow can be torn from its owner, and that this causes great discomfort to both parties. However it is not thought to be fatal to harm a shadow, or sever it from the corporeal form.

I hung around whilst the fire services and police did their thing, keeping back the crowds and ensuring the blaze did not spread to the neighbouring buildings.

It was a little stupid of me, I know, to be lurking at the scene of destruction when I had Lykaois's knife stashed on me, and might have been recognised by any sharp-eyed witnesses as having been in the church just before it burned down. Logically, I should be hightailing it back to *Good Deeds* or my own home, to get behind wards and relative safety so I could plan out my next move.

Logic almost always fails in the face of gnawing guilt. Guilt that I'd let more people die on my watch. And the unnerving worry that this time, I was well and truly in over my head.

I lurked, and watched. And thought.

OPS had shown up in a pair of dark vans with tinted windows, the *suits* who exited the vehicles looking like they'd stepped from a production line of 'government agent 101'. The only obvious difference between them being their gender, but these days, who knew if that was even a factor.

Cormac directed their initial forays into the much-collapsed building, having stowed away his hand-cannon and now acting as the agent in charge. When the police and firemen questioned who the people were already on the scene, putting their lives at risk and monkeying with the scene, he simply flashed whatever ID worked for them and stamped on any jurisdictional arguments. *This is my scene, and I say who goes where and when.* That simple.

The OPS agents removed one body from the rubble, enough of its ragged clothing identifiable for me to know it belonged to PC Chambers. But no other body was found, no trace of either Sister Spite or brother Grubbins, so I had to hope she had made it out and taken her deceased ward with her. A niggling doubt reminded me how Sister Gluttony have done an Obi-One Kenobi on us and vanished when she died in *Good Deeds*, but I had to hope that the lack of brother Grubbins's corpse meant she'd made it out ok.

If not, that meant I was three for four Sisters of the Arch, all who had lost their lives recently having been involved with me in some shape or form. It was not a good scorecard.

Whilst I waited for things to settle, and to make sure there was no trace of Lykaois still lurking around to fuck things up even more than they were, Cormac stepped away from directing all the various emergency services, and stopped by me to request a thorough and complete debrief on the knife that the creature had been after. The knife which the Sister had in her possession, and that I'd come looking for.

The knife I hadn't told him about.

I told him as much as I wanted him to know, and definitely not everything. That we'd come upon details of the knife whilst looking into anything that could link the recent killings to the South American expedition. That I'd checked with the museum, and been told by Sarah's boss that a knife *had* been in their possession but was checked out by Professor Eduardo. Then when we'd found out the Sister's ward, the survivor of the attack in Greenwich Park, was in fact been the professor, I'd put two and two together, and guessed he'd passed the knife to them for safe keeping.

Nice and simple. Without revealing our actual source of information and where all my suspicions had sprung from.

He listened carefully, then reached into a pocket and took out a wrinkled piece of paper, which he then carefully unfolded. It looked oddly familiar, and I felt a small sinking feeling as I picked up a scent from it. One that I had smelled firstly in a chaotic, messy office at the top of a building in Greenwich, and then from a journal I'd purloined from said office.

"I believe that all sounds about right, from what I've read here." He told me, as I recognised the page as being of the same type of paper that Professor Eduardo had in his little book. The one I'd stolen from his home, under Cormac's nose. "The professor, before his rebirth as brother Grubbins, seemed particularly keen to make sure whomever read his journal should heed this warning. *Do not let it get the knife. With the knife, it can be whole again. And the killing will start once more.* An easily understood statement, given the more disturbing facts he writes about before that. ... *It fills me, speaks to me of its glory, its right to rule all. Makes me kill for it. Feed for it. The hot blood. The soft flesh. I can only hope the Sisters will accept me despite my sins. I hear those I have killed. They call to me. Oh god above, will I ever not hear their screams?* ... That sort of thing."

I went to reply but Cormac stopped me, shaking his head and pocketing the piece of paper.

"Funny how we didn't find any journal in his office, nor in fact in his home." He commented dryly, looking back at the church. The fires had been put out, but a thick pall of smoke hung over the ruin like a shroud. "No-one seemed to know of its location. Not his colleagues or anyone else we spoke to. It simply ... vanished. I can only hope that were someone to find it, they would make good use of the information it contained."

Finally turning, he looked across at me, expression grave.

"I will not ask you to surrender the knife, despite the fact I am certain it is an item of significant potential and as such, is safest in our care." He told me bluntly. "Instead, I only ask that you exhibit extreme care and caution, since the Sister did indeed consider you worthy enough to bequeath it to you. I would not have our office seen as challenging Holy decisions, whether I question their sanity or not."

"Gee, thanks." I growled, and he smiled in reply.

"You're welcome. Now, it is half past ten at night and I would suggest you have far better places to be than loitering around the scene of a recent and tragic fire at a historic church." The OPS agent carried on, effectively giving me the polite *fuck off* I'd been expecting. "Not that I would presume to direct you in any way, but you *might* want to consider checking in with your Alpha on how things went tonight, and any plans you have in place to use that item to close this little business down. Purely just a thought, of course."

"But before you go." He added, almost as an afterthought. "Your Alpha *did* call to put a request in to search Professor Eduardo's house for any small item that might have been smuggled from South America. I think we both know she meant the knife, so I have politely told her there is no need for any of your colleagues to be allowed into the late professor's home. Just in case my agents find you or your team loitering around there again."

I shrugged. There really wasn't any point in us heading there, now we had Lykaois's knife. Before he died, the professor had thoroughly crapped on any hope of us replicating what the Mayans had done to trap the bastard. I didn't reckon Jessica would sign off on sacrificing anyone to sate its hunger long enough for us to build a suitable pit. Let alone us learning the correct warding to use to contain it.

And anyhow, I'd be fucked if I spilled one drop of blood for this thing. Its blood, maybe, but no-one else's.

"Good, I'm glad we're clear." He smiled, then his expression grew troubled. "She also mentioned your recent discovery regarding key Wiccan representatives. I have despatched agents to their homes, and those we know in their community and others linked to them, to ascertain how many have been lost to this brutal act. Our own experts have attempted to contact their *spiritual leader*, but She is not answering, and they tell me all they sense is a wounding, a sickness through their connection. Which seems to be catching, as I have a handful call in sick after their aborted interactions. I do not know if the matters are linked, but I have ordered any remaining attempts cancelled until we understand more of the situation. We are working on it, if you would care to inform Ms Walker."

With that, he turned and walked back towards the vans and his OPS colleagues, leaving me to chew over what he'd revealed.

The fact Cormac knew I'd taken the journal was water under the bridge now. Them having it wouldn't have saved Professor Eduardo, or PC Chambers. Not even Miles Cooper or the museum staff Lykaois had slain whilst using him as a meat suit. Or so I told myself, not wanting to think otherwise.

The situation with Tera was more troubling. If the Goddess was somehow out of the picture, then that left the Mortal Realm at a significant disadvantage against the Real. If ever Oberon or Madb got it into their immortal heads to make a play for power, it was as much the threat of facing off against the Goddess as the Furies for breaching the Accords that made them think twice. I didn't want to think of what might happen if word got out that Tera was no longer the deterrent she once had been.

Fuck, as if I didn't have my hands full already.

But there was nothing I could do to help sort *that* problem if I even knew where to start. Instead, I had a cursed knife, infected people I cared about, and an utter bastard to deal with.

Nice, simple things.

I had three stops to make that night, and me sitting around twiddling my thumbs whilst watching mortals put out a fire wasn't getting either done.

So, calling up a taxi, I left them to it and headed off, as prompted to do so by my ever-friendly neighbourhood OPS agent.

First stop, the office.

I checked in on Jessica, finding her upright and organising the packs. With her was Jarthi Patel, the remaining Alpha of West London. The Indian lycan looked equally vulnerable, sickened and afflicted, but managed a smile as I strode up the stairs.

"Ah can tell you were successful," Jessica told me, looking me up and down and taking in the last scrapes and bruises that were already healing.

"Dare ah ask if you felt the need tae wrestle with the Sisters tae obtain what you sought?"

I shook my head, knowing she was only joking. Well, maybe half-wise.

"*It* showed up. Inside the policeman Cormac Smith brought along to keep the peace." I commented dryly, trying not to find dark humour in that little nugget of insanity. "It managed to sense the knife, which was my fault for leaving it unwarded for even just a moment. So it came hunting, and then got into a fight with the Sister over the soul of its host. I'm not sure who won, but the church is a pile of rubble now."

Jessica sighed, but I knew she wouldn't blame me for the wanton destruction of property. We tried to keep buildings standing as much as we could whenever we got into scraps, as we knew she had a fondness for the older architecture of London. Plus it's always a pain having to dig oneself out from under a ton of masonry, bricks and rubble, then lie to any mortals nearby that you hadn't been caught underneath. Otherwise, *golly, I'd surely be flat as a pancake. Squished completely flat, yes indeed. What luck I happened only to be standing near it when it fell! Now please leave me alone.*

"Anyway, we've got the bloody thing now." I carried on. "Oh, and turns out our mystery survivor from the Greenwich Park murders? That was Professor Eduardo. He'd taken up religion, thrown over his old life and was going by the name brother Grubbins after what happened in South America. Surprised the fuck out of me when I worked out who he really was."

"You said *was*." Jessica noted, one slim eyebrow cocked, and I shrugged, looking apologetic.

"Yeah, when *it* showed up, it took offence at him not being its pawn anymore. He didn't make it either." I admitted.

"More bloodshed." My Alpha clenched her jaw, not best pleased at my news. "Ah am become wearied with the trail of destruction and death this thing leaves in its wake. It needs tae stop. Now."

"Working on it." I agreed with her, motioning back the way I'd come. "Just wanted to pop in, check all was good here and give you the news. Then I'm off to go see a certain witch and check on her progress."

"Ah, Morgan. Are you nae forgetting something?" Jessica asked, nodding to the pouch at my waist. "You risk much, travelling with that upon you. Should we not store it in the safe here, until we know when it will be needed?"

I shook my head, already having thought about that long and hard.

"Nope, I reckon having this anywhere near any of its host is just asking for trouble." I countered, reminding her of who we had downstairs, and why. "I can't say for sure the bastard can't sense the knife's location through them, and we're fucked if it gets its paws on the bloody thing. So, I'm stashing it somewhere safe, where I *know* this fucker hasn't got anyone on its payroll."

"And you think this friend of yours, this witch, is strong enough to ward herself against this cursed reliquary?" Jarthi spoke up, and I guessed Jessica had updated the Alphas on what we faced. What I was chancing. "Cursed items, they call not only to their owners, but to anyone who might be weak, vulnerable. She will need to resist its whispers, which is asking a lot of her."

"Which is why I'm stashing it, then bundling her up and relocating her back at my place." I countered, again having thought this through and worked out the best possible solution I could come up with. "The cottage is heavily warded, and I reckon I won't need to store it there for long. Just enough time for the bastard to get in touch, to make its play for a deal. Then ... well, we'll see."

Jarthi looked across at Jessica, who studied me for a long moment before eventually nodding.

"Ah trust Morgan, and he is nae one tae put those he cares fer in unnecessary danger." She replied to the unspoken question, whether I'd gotten my Alpha's blessing on the plan. "This is his hunt, fer more reasons than just chance, so ah support him fully. Until we need tae do otherwise."

"Thanks, boss." I replied, then remembered Cormac's other news. "Oh, and OPS are looking into the witch killings. I didn't tell him who I think is responsible, otherwise I reckon they'd have tried to take over this whole thing. And just get in the way, or killed. But they're looking."

"Ah advised them tae alert the community of the danger they face, the need to stay safe and not risk any more rituals that put them in harm's way." Jessica admitted. "OPS will nae be long in figuring out this thing's involvement, or its partner, given their recent interactions. Best not dally too long getting this matter dealt with, or ah suspect we will be facing some hard questions tae answer."

I noted Jessica's choice to remain vague about Jack, keeping the fact he was my kin under wraps as we'd agreed. Those closest to me knew, but there was no need for the pack or other lycans to know of my *difference*. Not until it became a problem.

That done, I jumped back in the taxi I'd asked to wait, and headed over to Felix's. Second stop, the witch's cottage.

Thankfully, Felix took little convincing to throw a few things into a bag and vacate the premises along with a much revived and grumbly Albert. I stashed the knife in its bag of holding in the unused fireplace, hidden under some aged, scented logs that completely hid any trace of it from sight or smell. The young witch locked the place up with the wards as we left, with me carrying her bag full of clothing, research books and what I'd handed to her in the office as she led the waddling bulldog to the waiting car.

With the knife safely hidden behind wards, I realised it had even been preying on me. A weight I didn't realise I was carrying, a subtle headache nagging at the back of my mind. No whispers, but then the thing was stashed in a pocket dimension only narrowly linked to the Mortal Realm. Any effects it normally had would have to work extra hard to reach me whilst I was carrying it in the bag. Other than a dull ache and feeling like I needed to spit out a bad taste.

That done, Felix, Albert and I headed to my final destination. By now it was gone half past midnight, as the taxi pulled up at my apartment block. Keeping Felix close, I did a quick scout around, checking for Jack or any host that Lykaois might have keeping eyes on me. Finding nothing, we headed upstairs.

Bear greeted us as I ushered Felix and Albert in the front door, dog-lead in his mouth and the sort of expression on his massive face that told me I wasn't quite done yet. The two hounds sniffed each other, Albert obviously thoroughly confused as to the hairy mammoth he was presented with, but

Bear seemed to accept the fact we had visitors with good grace. Dumping the lead down, the trollhound licked the other dog soundly across his rumpled chops, and Albert's stubby tail started tentatively wagging.

With that matter settled, I motioned Felix to head on in, as I took my hound out to stretch his legs and relieve his full bladder.

Standing in the cool night air, I looked up as Bear thoroughly doused the nearest bush in pungent urine. The moon shone bright and if not full, was only a sliver off complete roundness. Tomorrow, that would be its high point. A time sacred to Lykaois when the bastard would be at its strongest. And I'd have to face it down, free my friend and the woman I loved, and lock it down so it would never hurt anyone again.

All whilst keeping myself and the other I'd involved in my plan alive and safe. When the bastard I was going up against had already tossed me around like one of Bear's chew toys. And that wasn't at its strongest.

With that cheery thought, I hurried the trollhound along, heading back inside and to go get whatever sleep I could manage, beside Sarah.

Before I risked everything to keep her safe.

Chapter 45

Electricity

Few supernatural creatures are affected by electricity, lightning or the like. Normally, this being a natural energy, they are immune to its effects. However certain creatures are weakened to it as they have fashioned protection or their form from a substance that would normally be harmful to them. Iron. Certain hags are known to have replaced their teeth and nails with iron spikes, whilst other creatures have replaced their scales with iron armour to protect themselves. Having done so, they are then weakened to lightning or mortal-fashioned electricity, which conducts through their body and causes them great pain.

There are days it pays not to get out of bed. No matter the innocents who needed saving, the villains to be arse-kicked back into touch. The best thing to do is just pull the cover over one's head and tell the world *Not today, sorry*.

Today was one of those days.

It dawned with no sign of Lykaois or Jack. Nothing to say the bastard was coming for its knife, or wanted to deal. No message from OPS to say there'd been more murders, any more evidence of its rage and desperation. Nothing.

"Maybe Sister Spite actually did for the bastard?" I suggested quietly, whilst Sarah showered in the en-suite and I caught up on breakfast with Felix and Bear.

Goldspur had greeted me with the morning light, knocking on the bedroom door and informing me Albert needed to relieve himself whilst Bear wanted to go chase some squirrels, and that Felix deserved sustenance. Which as hearth-owner, I was honour bound to provide.

I couldn't even argue, seeing how she was right.

With the first task seen to after a minor struggle and the realisation of how difficult it was to walk two different sized dogs at the same time, I worked on the second. Coffee, pancakes, sausages and bacon soon filled the apartment with delicious aromas as I settled back on my sofa with a thick, strong brew and let the warmth soak into my hands.

"Nnh chanff." Felix replied, her mouth full of freshly cooked pancake. Washing it down with coffee, she tried again. "No chance. This thing is old-world bad, and predates the Sisters of the Arch, the Catholic Church and their religion by a few hundred years at least. She might've knocked it on its arse in the church, but it won't be down for good. That's your job."

She slipped a sausage off her plate and let Albert snatch it from her fork, the bulldog grunting in purest joy at the tasty treat.

"*Our* job." I reminded her, knowing there were more involved in this thing than just me, more than me to do what needed to be done. My usual plan of hitting it until it stopped just wasn't going to work here.

"Yeah. Remind me, you told your friendly government agent his part yet? Or you still want to just surprise him and see his expression?" She snarked, and I grinned too. Couldn't help myself.

Sure, giving Cormac a heads up on what I planned, and what I'd need him and his lot for, was the clever thing to do, but I'd been far too sensible recently and needed to half-arse things a little just to be myself. Plus, if I *did* tell him, he'd only point out every flaw in my plan and do his best to take over. That, and talk to Jessica, and I really needed her *not* to be pissed at me right now.

So, right now, only the people involved who *needed* to know had the pertinent facts of what I'd planned. And even then, Felix was still in the dark about all the details, and hopefully might never know my thoughts on plan B if I messed up royally.

"This thing has been popping up all over the fucking place these past couple of days, but *now* it decides it needs some rest and goes quiet on me?" I growled, downing a mouthful of coffee and spearing a sausage. Beside me, Bear rumbled, and I broke it in half, tossing him one section whilst I wolfed down the other. Both dogs started making satisfied rumbling noises, synching their stomachs even though they had only just met.

"Give it a break." Felix replied with a roll of her eyes. "Its had a bad day. Its favourite host turns up but the Sisters have freed him from its grasp. Its knife goes missing meaning it loses another host trying to find the thing, then shows up again only to disappear before it can grab it. You lock up one of its last remaining hosts, and the other is sitting pretty behind your wards here. Oh, and a *nun* kicked its arse. In public. It's probably still hiding under the sofa, hoping everything just goes away and leaves it alone."

"No chance" I echoed her words, feeling the truth of it. "The bastard is licking its wounds, but if anything, it's more pissed than it was before. Hopefully. At least then it won't be thinking straight, just be nice and stupid. I don't need it being clever."

We were interrupted by Sarah joining us, having thrown on loose pyjama pants and one of my t-shirts. Which on her was more like a short dress. She slipped onto the sofa beside me, and gratefully took the mug of coffee I offered her.

"So, what's the plan today? Any dragons need slaying, *chulo*?" She quipped, sipping at her coffee and making a contented sigh.

"Only one." I replied, and saw her stiffen.

Sarah hadn't slept well last night. We had spent a fair amount of time awake, talking rather than any other activity. The fact she was Lykaois's host. That she had kept it from me, even though that had been its doing not hers. The very real fear of what she had done whilst under its control, even though she had no memory of her actions, any deed. No matter how terrible.

In the end, I had pretty much just listened, and held her as she cried. Then I'd just told her this was going to be over soon. Whatever it took, I was going to stop it from doing this to her again, to anyone again. And then, we'd just see how we were. No pressure, no demands. Just us, starting afresh.

I knew just how worried and distracted Sarah was by the fact she hadn't questioned *'whatever it took'* when I let that one slip.

"Anyway, I reckon it's best if you hang out here today." I told her, sliding some pancakes onto a plate and adding bacon, sour cream and raspberries before Felix devoured everything in sight. I put this in front of

Sarah, as she looked over at me, already about to argue. "Look, I need to check in with the office. Make sure everything is ok. And given half my pack are still sick as proverbial dogs, I'd better lend a hand patrolling the mists. It's all been quiet there recently, so it'll be a waste of my time. But still. Until something happens …"

Which, I should have known, were words I must never, ever utter.

Because things literally went to hell in a handbasket as I took another swig from my mug of coffee.

My phone buzzed to life on the table, and I had that sinking feeling as I locked eyes with Felix. She mouthed the word *jinx*, but I just shook my head and grabbed up the phone and hit accept on the call.

"Morgan?" It was Emma, sounding more than a little harassed and pissed off. "You'd better get your arse over to the office. We've got problems. Big problems."

"What's happened?" I asked as I pushed myself off the sofa, dreading whatever shit had hit the fan. "Is it Jacob?"

"No. It's Molly. From London Lower." My packmate told me, and I thought back to the minor Earth Goddess who was co-ruler of the Real habitat existing beneath the city's streets. Way beneath. We weren't exactly on the best of terms, given I'd had a hand in the almost destruction of her paramour and co-ruler, Rous, God of Rats and all things small, furry and flea-ridden. That and then also exposed him when he betrayed us to Morgana and Robert Knox, dealing under the table to protect his own skin. "She just put a call in to Jessica. Seems Rous is back, and up to his old tricks. He's declared for Twilight and has stirred up the Lows to make an attempt on the mists. Molly wants us down there to stop him."

"Oh for fuck's sake!" I snarled, gripping the phone hard enough so that it made a disturbing crunching sound. "Can't she keep a grip on that weaselly little shit herself? It's not like they've dealt fair by us anytime recently. Let them sort their own mess out."

"Jessica says no. We can't risk them getting into the mists. Maybe allowing *someone* to take over the Lows and set Herself there too." Emma told me bluntly, her own frustration clear in her voice. "We're low on numbers, so you are up. Stop drinking coffee and move your arse."

Sometimes I really did wonder if the pack had my home bugged, given their uncanny accurate guesses as to what I was doing when I picked up any call.

Emma ended the call, and I slipped the phone into my pocket, turning to look back at Felix and Sarah.

"Me and my big mouth. Something happened." I told them both, seeing Felix roll her eyes as she was proved right. "I've got to head into work, but I *still* reckon you should stick around here, both of you. Jessica's asked you both to do some research, so maybe you can help each other?"

There was little I figured Sarah could help with Felix talking to the witch community, but the younger woman might need the company if there was more bad news. And Sarah *definitely* could use the other's experience if there was any chance the journal held that last nugget of information. How to lock down Lykaois permanently.

Though, having spoken to Professor Eduardo, I wasn't holding out much hope. I hadn't told Sarah what had happened at the church, that I'd met her colleague for two simple reasons. She'd had enough bad news, and hearing the man had been alive, in hiding but now was dead would just be another sucker punch to her. And secondly, it gave her something to do, some way of helping that meant she would stay safe behind my wards and not venture out … tempting Lykaois to take control of her once more for whatever reason.

Leaving the pair to get acquainted, I jumped back into my bedroom to throw on more suitable clothes for what I was about to face, and then grabbed one of my handy carry-alls and filled it with the tools of my trade. Cold iron and silver, and a fully stocked vial of fresh garlic cloves just in case someone tried to poison me again.

I wasn't aware of any specifics about the God of Rats, but I figured at least this time, my old way of dealing with a problem might actually be the right one. Hit it, and keep hitting until it stopped being a problem. On the other hand, I *really* wasn't looking forward to facing off against a creature comprised of *hundreds* of living rodents. With sharp teeth and claws. And Gods knew what sort of diseases.

I was going to need a long shower after this was done.

Packed, I grabbed one last mouthful of coffee and the single solitary pancake that Felix had kindly left for me. Then, as the witch tactfully turned away and hummed to herself as she made a fuss of Albert, I kissed Sarah.

"Stay here. Stay safe. Call me if you need anything." I told her, and saw that mischievous sparkle in her eye as she smiled. "Hold *that* thought. I'll make good on it when I get back."

"You'd better." She whispered to me, and kissed me hard back.

"Enough already! Sheez, get a room!" Felix groused and I bit back a laugh.

"Same goes for you. Call me if you hear anything, ok?" I told her, and she nodded without turning around.

Bear lumbered to his feet, coming up to me and pushing his head into my stomach. I gave him a well-earned ear scratch, and he huffed his approval before rolling his massive body and settling back down beside Sarah as she curled up on the sofa. I didn't even need to tell the big softie, he knew he was on guard duty.

The taxi was already waiting for me downstairs, so I slung my bag onto the backseat. As I went to slide in after it, I thought I caught a faint taint to the air, a familiar nasty stink of madness and rage mixed in with Wyld Court musk. And I could feel eyes on me, that prickling at the back of my neck as I carefully scanned my surroundings.

Nothing seemed out of place, no unexplainably dark patches of shadow where there shouldn't be, no extra tree that had not been there before or random piece of trash piled up as if recently discarded. None of the usual give-aways that something was hiding under a glamour.

Just the smell, and that warning of eyes on me. But even as I looked around, these faded and disappeared. Gone like the pile of food I'd rustled up for breakfast this morning, in about the same short period of time.

"Imagining things now." I growled to myself, and ducked into the taxi. "Jumping at shadows like a complete bloody amateur. Gods, I need a break."

I figured Emma or Jessica had instructed the driver of my taxi to get me to the office as quickly as possible, since he seemed hell-bent on jumping every red light, dodging London buses and clearing the odd pedestrian out of our way with sharp blasts of his horn. Either that or he was on a Star Wars trip, believing himself to be Hans Solo doing another Kessel Run in fewer parsecs this time. Which made me Chewbacca, as I growled and bounced around the back seat.

Whatever, we slammed to a halt outside the office, only for Emma to grab open the door and wave me out impatiently.

"Stop for coffee and some sightseeing, maybe?" She growled at me, and I shook my head, only just remembering to grab my bag off the seat before the taxi took off again at only a touch below lightspeed. "C'mon, we're on the clock and the shit's hitting the fan down there."

It seemed we could only spare Emma, myself and Pippa to sort out whatever the fuck was going on in London Lower, which on any normal day would have been fine given all three of us were strong lycans in our right. Except today, Pippa looked decidedly shaky whilst Emma seemed to be using her anger to keep her on her feet. Both had dressed for dirty work, loose combats and stretchable tops which would handle them Changing if need be, and each bore similar kit-bags to mine.

So, bags only slightly clanking as we moved quickly, the three of us headed at a fast pace to our nearest route down. Pan's statue.

Only to encounter our first problem.

It was gone.

"Who the fuck *steals* a statue?!" I growled, taking in the sculpted base that formed the lower section of the monument. The animals cast into the metal all looked somewhat abashed, having stood in frozen silence whilst the boy who never grew up was roughly hewn away from the top portion of the sculpture. "I mean, they say you should lock your shit away in this city, but a fucking statue?! That's not right."

Whomever had done it had not been gentle either. Great rents in the metal showed where the thief or thieves had hacked into the surrounding section and literally carved the Pan statue out of its seating. They had been careless enough that they'd left one of his booted feet behind, torn through and looking particularly sad as the only remnant of Pan remaining.

"Someone doesn't want visitors. I wonder who." Pippa commented dryly, stepping up to the abused monument and checking the damage wrought. "This was done by something with great strength, and very fine blades. Ones which can cut metal so easily, but done with rage or in a frenzy. They wanted this portal destroyed quickly."

"I can think of one particular bastard who fits that description." I growled, but the air was long since washed clean of any scent to confirm my suspicion. "Where now? Got to be another portal to the Lows round here somewhere."

Emma pulled out a scrunched-up sheet of paper from a pocket, scanning what was written there.

"Molly thought we'd face opposition coming down, maybe from Rous or just because we said we were bringing you." She answered and I grimaced, remembering I was *persona non grata* down below. "There's the Lions at Trafalgar Square, the Crutched Friars at Aldgate, ah, and …"

"Any gates that *aren't* statues?" I interrupted, looking at the destruction wrought. "I have a suspicion we'll find something similar has happened to any of the more obvious ones."

"You think we've got a statue hater out there?" Pippa asked, and I shrugged.

"Either that or someone knows the main routes down to the Lows have bloody big stone monuments parked over them to act as gate-keepers." I quipped sarcastically. "I think we need one of the more active gates."

"Ok, how about the Hob's Knobbly End?" Emma asked, and I grinned, cracking my knuckles.

"A goblin pub. Perfect." I rolled my shoulders, looking forward to a little permissible violence. "Let's go knock on their door and politely ask to use their facilities."

Chapter 46

"Fuck off, Redcloak."

The goblin growled at me from the safety of the doorway, having cracked it open only wide enough to see who was disturbing their merriment.

The Hob's Knobbly End sat in a little cul-de-sac in Ducks' Lane, Soho. It *looked* from the outside like an old boarded up restaurant, with graffiti sprayed over the brickwork, and enough rubbish piled up to make any gnoll think it was its birthday. Windows were either boarded up or covered in grime and muck, not letting a stray glimmer of daylight through. The whole place looked like it was ready for demolition, praying to be reincarnated as a swanky coffee house or designer shoe store.

In fact, it was one of the more well-known Goblin Bars in Soho, renowned for enticing mortals for some 'harmless fun' by the resident Real denizens. Nothing ever of Accord-breaking potential of course, or risking actual harm, but running close enough for us lycans to have visited the establishment on a semi frequent basis.

The story was usually the same. Late at night, after some heavy drinking or partaking of chemical stimulants, the chosen mortals found themselves outside a transformed establishment. All trace of wear and tear removed, the bar gleaming with exoticness, the locals jolly and welcoming or glamorous and enticing depending on the intended victim. They would find themselves plied with strange drinks, offered delicious food and engaged in conversations about pretty much any subject they chose. Sometimes even the odd snuggle and kiss offered out of sight, in the darker corners.

But something would start to feel off, the friendly and welcoming drinking buddies changing out of the corner of the eye. The drinks tasting delicious one moment, foul the next before back to how they originally tasted. The food becoming stomach churning foulness before their eyes.

Rice becoming maggots, crispy friend vegetables turning rotten and stinking. That sort of thing. Then back to delicious treats.

Until, finally, one of the 'locals' would let their glamour slip fully, revealing their hideous visage. And around them, the poor mortal would find all the others equally changed, as savage and gross and terrifying as their wildest nightmares. That normally was enough to send the victim running, their wallets or purses purloined, and any valuables removed artfully as they staggered to freedom. Or, for the true hardened drinker or drug-taker, they would lose consciousness, only to wake somewhere entirely different. Usually butt-naked and adorned with paint and refuse.

Of course, if ever the victims plucked up the courage to return to the site of their torment, they would find it locked, run-down and empty. The goblins inside hiding their sniggers behind their hands, as they watched with savage glee the mortals' obvious distress through spy-holes.

Goblins are, when it comes down to it, little shits. So I didn't feel too bad about what I had in mind to do next.

"And a good day to you too," I told the goblin, as I stepped up close and pressed one hand against the door. "Official Redcloak business, so if I were you, I'd step away right smartish."

And then I shoved. Hard.

There was probably another two or three of them leaning against the portal, aiming to keep it closed. But I hadn't given them the time to properly get a grip, plus I *did* sort of cheat and tap into my Wyld-born strength. Much more than any simple lycan should have.

The door slammed open, crunching into the goblin I'd been speaking to and sending it flying backward with a strangled yell. Several others crashed unseen behind the door, confirming my suspicion, as I offered up the way to Emma and Pippa with a savage grin.

"After you, ladies." I offered, receiving a laugh from Pippa and a roll of the eyes from Emma.

Inside, the goblin bar was without glamour, and in a word, a dive. Not as bad as the troll strip club I'd found the Bung brothers hiding in, but nothing that a flamethrower and a few jerry cans of fuel wouldn't fix. The word *rat-hole* sprang to mind, and I immediately realised why … the bar, an old rickety wooden affair that looked late Victorian in style, had rodents strung from its rack. These had stiffened in death, and had been coated with some sort of glaze. Honeyed rodent. A favourite bar-snack, I remembered, even as one of the patrons casually reached up and plucked one down, biting off its head and chewing noisily whilst peering at me with angry red eyes.

There were about a score of goblins to be seen, but I smelt a lot more, lurking out of sight, up to no good. As we stepped inside, I heard the door shut firmly behind us, and the interior darkened considerably. Now the only light came from flickering candles in small lanterns set around the main drinking area, and wicked stubs that had been stuck to the bar top and set alight in what looked like skulls from various species. There was a general rustling of bodies, the odd flexing of muscles and gleam of bared teeth. And lots of angry eyes glaring back at us.

"Right, gentlemen. We won't keep you." I slapped my hands together, taking the lead. Not because Emma wasn't fit or able to, but just because I had a suspicion and wanted to let it play out. For her part, Emma had already agreed to let me go in first, happy for me to field any violence for a change. "If you can just open up your door to the Lows, we'll be through and out of your hair … well, long greasy strands of whatever you have on your head … forthwith. Chop chop!"

"I fink you broke me shoulder, you bastard." The goblin I'd hit with the door growled as it clambered back to its feet.

It was typical of its species, about five foot nothing but solidly built. Green warty skin, bowed legs and ape-like arms, with a face that looked like someone had shoved its nose back into its skull. It wore a dirty chainmail shirt of fae-iron, and had the hilt of a knife sticking out of its belt. Definitely not the sort you'd meet at a goblin tea party from the mortal fairy tale stories.

"Probably only sprained, and I *did* ask you to move." I smiled back at the Wyld fae, seeing it clench its fists, ready to swing. "I'd think twice before you start anything, so just show us the door and we'll be on our way."

Now goblins, when drunk, can be violent and ill-tempered but most of the time they aren't actually bad creatures. As I'd said, utter bastards when it came to tormenting mortals but besides that, they tended to keep their knobbled skulls down and not cause us lycan much trouble. Even a large gang of them wouldn't think of messing with a lone Redcloak, let alone three of us together, so its temper and general behaviour was more than a trifle odd. Unless you figured they'd been told something.

"I 'eard tell you ain't feeling so good." The goblin spat, wrinkling its face into a broad leer. "In fact, I 'eard someone's done a number on you'se lot. Made you weak. Vulnerable. Hur."

"You hear some weird things, mate." I replied blithely, seeing the rest of the goblins in the bar start to press forward. Various tools of their trade seemed to find their hands, gleaming dully in the candlelight. Knives, clubs, a random assortment meant to cause immediate and long-lasting pain. "Last warning. Show us the door. Or else."

"Fuck you, Redcloak." It replied, dragging out its knife. The thing was jagged, hooked and just the sort of weapon to cause maximum pain with the minimum of skill. "I fink I'm gonna make you into a nice fur-coat, and maybe some mittens. Then I'm gonna take this knife and shove it right up yer friends'..."

I didn't bother letting it finish.

The goblin described a perfect flat trajectory as I slapped the knife from its paw and punched it so hard it flew through the bar and crashed into the far wall. Wood exploded around it, as the middle section of the bar itself collapsed in and around the goblin. The wall it had crunched into must have been mouldy or rotten, as the brickwork hardly stopped its flight. Eventually it came to rest, with only two knobbly feet sticking out of the hole it had made. Bubbling moans came from the darkness hiding it, and bright silver blood coated the fractured wood it had shattered in its flight path.

"*Now* I reckon I've fucked up your shoulder. And a few other things too." I politely pointed out, then slowly looked around the rest of the room. "Anyone else been hearing how we're weak? Vulnerable?"

The bar's patrons did a wonderful magic trick, weapons slipping back from sight, everyone suddenly wishing to be anywhere else and totally not involved in any thought of violence upon the lovely Redcloaks in their establishment.

"Thought not." I growled, before reaching over and dragging the goblin lurking behind the bar out from its hiding place. It had on a ragged uniform, a white apron thrown over its armour and tied at the waist with the fading black words embroidered on its front. *'Kiss The Barman'*.

I snorted.

"The door. Show it to us." I growled menacingly, making the frightened gobbo squeak. "And whilst you're at it, who told you the Redcloaks are weak?"

"'E said … 'e said not to say nuffink!" The goblin stammered as it dragged itself from my grip. Under our watchful eyes, it dragged a heavy wooden table off a rug at the far corner of the room, pulling back the stained and moth-eaten material to reveal a large square trapdoor with a thick ring pull. "'E jus' said not to let you bloody bastards down, if you came askin'."

I grunted, my suspicions confirmed. Someone was looking to stop us from getting to the Lows, and had tried to do so by fucking with the portals topside and making sure we encountered trouble at any other way we tried. The sickness wasn't affecting me, but the rest of the packs were definitely weakened to the point that even these goblins might have been a problem if I hadn't been with Emma and Pippa.

"Who?" Emma snarled, but I waved a hand, cutting off any reply.

"I'll fill you in on which fucker I think is to blame when we've sorted things out below." I told her, nodding to the ring. "I doubt it matters now, and you *did* say we were on the clock."

"Fine." She slapped the goblin round the back of the head, staggering it. "Open the bloody thing then."

The trapdoor groaned open to reveal a set of stairs leading downward. Old, stone stairs, like the ones you see built into tombs and mausoleums. Thankfully, torches on the walls sprang to life as the trapdoor thudded against the floor, lighting the *long* way down.

"Close up behind us, if you would be so kind?" I told the sullen looking goblin. "As for the rest of you? Feel free to pass the word to any of your *friends*. Don't go trusting any bastard telling you the Redcloaks are down. Unless they want to join your mate in that hole in the wall. Free of charge."

With that, I followed my two packmates into the Way down, and let the goblin hurriedly slam the trap door shut over our heads.

Chapter 47

"Where the *Hells* have you been?" Molly demanded, her lush richness momentarily replaced by an angry scowl. "I *said* this was important! Or do you think just because this is the Lows, we are less important than your business Upside?"

We'd descended the stairs down from Upper London, passing through that strange layer of interdimensional crafting that allowed the Lows to exist beneath the city without needing to have been built *per se* and interfere with the city's physical foundations. Nothing had accosted us, no welcoming party looking to fuck with the lycans as we eventually got to the bottom and made our way into the Lows proper.

The feel of the place was far different to when I'd last been down here. Before, when I took Elspeth with me, the residents had been out and about, mingling and getting on with their business of selling pretty much anything they could lay their hands, paws, claws or tentacles on. After that, I'd found the place in a state of terror when a small bunch of us chased a rogue lycan Alpha through the maze of tunnels, finding his victims strewn in his path, bloody and torn. And finally, we'd used the Lows to gain access to where Robert Knox and Morgana had planned to enact a ritual of resurrection, thinking we were getting a jump on them both. Then it had been virtually deserted.

Finding out that Rous had betrayed us, and been playing us all along with a spy in our midst, hadn't really endeared us to the Rat God bastard. It was a perfectly acceptable theory that we'd drag our heels if the Low Rulers called on us for aid. Acceptable, but totally wrong.

"Your Ladyship," Emma interjected before I could frame a suitable response. One with few words and maybe a hand gesture or two. "We came as fast as we could. The Ways to the Lows have, as you warned us, been interfered with and we met a little resistance that needed handling. But we are here now, to handle the problem *you* requested our services for. So shall we get on with that?"

When the mists had descended on London Upper, they had also sunk down and somehow managed to reach the Lows as well. Whilst Upper and Lower London do not share the same geographical space, a small section of the farthest tunnels had been swallowed behind the roiling nothingness that was Twilight reborn. That and several families of trolls, a couple of aged harpies unable to fly and a coven of hags who had unfortunately only recently moved in.

Barricades, like those in use above, had been put in place and both Molly and Rous had organised armed patrols of their gnoll guards to make sure none ventured past the barriers and made any attempt on the mists. Or anything came out of them, seeking to prey on the Low residents.

We were standing at the largest of these barriers, a massive affair of stripped wood and bent metal hammered together and reinforced with rope. To make the blockade effective, the rulers had had as much cold iron as they could bear embedded in the structures, and strewn the entire open ground with rock crystals of pure salt as well as nasty little caltrops of iron as well. Anything of the Real trying to cross *that* would find themselves in excruciating agony after only a few steps, and be stripped of any of their strength and magical protection to help heal their wounds. Vicious, but effective.

Molly faced us with a band of her guards, forty or so gnolls, all heavily armed and glowering at us like we were the ones causing trouble. The Earth Goddess kept back from the blockade, but I could tell from her expression that it was discomforting her, cold iron and salt deadening her usual seductive nature and bountiful beauty.

Someone, and I had to assume it was Rous, had ordered some of the residents of the Low to tear a portion of the barrier down. Silver blood stained the wood and metal, and I could see several bodies collapsed in the tunnel beyond. Mortals these days at least used machines to clear mines out of the way, whereas Real creatures still seemed to think throwing lesser beings' lives at a problem worked so why change?

"How many went with Rous, and how long ago did they breach the barricade?" Emma asked, as I set my kitbag down on the floor and opened it up. Pippa did the same, and we started tooling up for the *fun* ahead. Silver-iron swords and knives, clip-on riot armour for my companions. I had my Ivory armour to call upon, so wasn't bothering with the extra protection.

"Maybe a full score of our people. Two of the ogryn clan, and the rest Wyld fae except for one Ivory Court who had recently joined us." She replied, eyeing the warily weapons as I tested edges to make sure things were still nice and sharp. Those two ogryn and the Ivory fae were going to be a problem, but hopefully working together we'd be able to put down the insurrection quickly. That meant getting to Rous first and foremost.

"You *will* seek to resolve this matter without violence." Molly told Emma, hearing me snort with dark humour and scowling. "My Lord might be … *not* entirely acting wisely, but these are citizens of the Lows. We are charged with their well-being and safety, and so I must ask you to show restraint and good judgement. *Where possible.*"

That last was shot at me, along with an angry glare but I just shrugged and nodded to my packmate. She answered for us.

"Your Ladyship. *You* called us." Emma reminded her, voice calm but with a steely undertone. "Before I answer you, I would ask you a question."

There was no way I'd have been so polite with the immortal, but Emma was a professional and between her and Jacob, had run too many hunts and tactical operations that required more than just the ability to hit something hard for me to question her methods. She had this.

Molly looked at her, expression slipping back up a gear into neutral.

"Ask on then."

"Why haven't you dealt with this yourself?" Emma immediately asked, gesturing to the glaring, glowering gnolls that surrounded her. "You obviously have the numbers, and if your partner simply has a score of followers, I would think you most capable to bringing him and the rest of them to heel. So. Why not?"

Molly bit her lip, obviously debating whether to tell the truth or simply fob the Redcloak off with some glib reply. But Emma's expression told her without words just how well that would go down. And she needed us.

Finally, she sighed, shaking her head.

"The fact is, lycan, I am … *afflicted*. We all are." She answered truthfully, the taste of it in her words and expression. "Some sort of malaise, a weakness which saps my strength and means I am less than I was. We all feel it, and I was doubtful of my chances to deal with my paramour effectively as I so suffer."

"Let me guess, Rous seems to be unaffected?" I asked quietly, not wanting to break Emma's control of the dialogue but needing to know another little detail that would confirm my suspicion. "And he had a visit from someone recently, just before his little mutiny?"

Molly glared at me, but then nodded twice, answering both my questions.

Emma looked at me, and I shook my head, not willing to go into the details here, and instead motioned for her to continue. She managed a suitably withering look, then turned back to face Molly.

"Then, since you could not resolve this matter, we will. As we see fit." She bluntly told the immortal as she set her own bag down and extracted a brutal looking cold-iron machete. She set its point against the floor with a solid crunch of breaking stone. "We'll try the tact and diplomatic approach first, of course. But if that fails, they will give us no other choice. Either accept that, or tell us to leave and we'll let you clean up the mess."

Molly gritted her teeth, her jaw set but by her own admittance had no way of dealing with Rous and his mob. Eventually she simply turned on her heel and stalked off, the gnolls falling back to protect her as she retreated.

"Tact and diplomacy huh?" I grinned at Emma, who cocked an eyebrow at me, expression deadpan serious.

"Yeah. I'll ask Rous nicely to stop being such a fuckwit, whilst I'm pounding as many of the fucking rodents he needs to stay in shape to paste." She replied, earning a chuckle from Pippa. "What's this about some mysterious visitor?"

"Not important right now." I shrugged off her question, pointing to her half full kitbag. "Why don't you finish getting dressed, so we can get this stupidity sorted and head back to the weird shit up top?"

Emma didn't push, guessing I had good reasons for not telling her everything. And me, I was just eager to get my hands on Rous and ask him some very pointed questions. Pointed as in at the end of a sword, poking sharply.

Chapter 48

Blood of the Dead

Whilst names of things often refer to their appearance, like Ladies Fingers, this is in fact in relation to a mortal's blood after they have died. Certain supernatural creatures like vampires and ghouls, which feed on living blood, will be weakened if they unknowingly imbibe fluid taken from a deceased mortal. The reaction can be minor, causing the creature to become faint, unsteady and weak, or more extreme when the victuals are taken from a much longer dead subject. Leading the supernatural creature to suffer agonising cramps, fractured blood vessels, vomiting and hallucinations.

Fully tooled up, the three of us moved into the tunnel beyond the barricade. This being the far end of the Lows, the décor was definitely *subterranean* with rough stone underfoot, walls roughly hewn and braced with timber like some old abandoned mine. Light was provided by lanterns hung in nooks, their glowing radiance pushing back the darkness for those of the dwellers in the Low who needed at least a little something to see by.

We'd only gone a short distance before we caught the sound of Rous speaking, his chittering voice unmistakable.

"…You too will feel strong once more! I have been promised, and behold, I am vigorous and powerful whilst those who would stop us are weakened and laid low." He screeched, the awful sound of a hundred and more rats echoing his voice from their own vocal cords. "The mists are not what you have been told, not death but salvation. A fresh start, a new beginning as part of the oldest and most powerful Court of them all. That of Twilight!"

That tore it. Rous was definitely being played. Letting someone else pull his strings, the idiot. And, as the three of us exchanged knowing looks, we guessed just who that person might be.

"Fear not, already those that would stand against you have been stricken down. Even my own paramour, she who spoke words of love but then turned away when I saw the truth of what we must do, she has been made a shadow of herself." Rous chittered on as we stealthily crept closer to where his voice was coming from. "Otherwise, where is she? Would she so willingly let us take this great step, if she had the strength to defy us? And those honour-less curs, those dogs the Redcloaks. They are weak, sickened and no threat to anyone. Once we have passed through the mists, I have been promised revenge against the wrongs done by them to me, personally, and each and every one of you too. They shall *pay*."

"I want him. Him and whichever bastard has been feeding him this shit." Emma growled, and I nodded. We'd reached the end of the tunnel, and carefully peered round the rough edges of the entrance to check what lay ahead.

The chamber beyond had been cut in half, shortened by the swirling mist that formed a solid barrier across the stone floor and wood-braced ceiling. In front of this, illuminated by the faintly glowing fog wall, Rous stood on a wooden box, his rat body clad in tattered robes of mouldy velvet. His body was constantly in motion, the rats which made up his corporeal form shifting and writhing in place as he preached to the small gathering in front of him. His arms were raised, rodents wriggling up and down his limbs and forming splayed fingers which he held above him. Like some weird-ass prophet.

In front of him, his followers screeched, howled and growled their response to Rous's words. The two ogres were easy to spot, small for their kind and hunched over, one missing its left arm and the other with a deformed, shrunken skull. Just the type that most ogres would shun for being weak, not strong enough to be of the clan. The single Ivory fae who stood apart from the rest of the crowd looked on with the habitual sneer of its kin, but it was a shadow of what I had seen Real side. Clad in ragged, dirty once-fine clothing, bearing a bent and broken rapier on its hip and having the deeply bruised eyes and gaunt expression of an immortal lost to some addiction or other.

The rest of the crowd were a mixture of goblins like the ones we'd found at the Hob, a few bent and withered crones and surprisingly a few gnolls that I guessed had belonged to the Lows guards before they threw their lot in with Rous. All looked like they bore wounds, silver blood staining where they had damaged themselves getting through the barricades and across the salt and iron strewn path. All looked afflicted in the flickering light of the mists, painted pale and ill of health. Here too was evidence of the malediction afflicting the Lows, with only the Rat God untouched.

"How do you want to do this?" I whispered to Emma as we ducked back into the tunnel. "I'm guessing most of that lot will give up without a fight if we get Rous."

"I agree. He's the instigator, the one making all the promises. Negate him and the rest will fold." She replied, rolling her shoulders and shaking her head to clear it. "Problem is, he's a slippery bastard. He can just dissolve into his individual rats and escape whilst we're still smacking down his cannon-fodder followers."

"How about you leave him to me?" I smiled nastily, raising my left hand and calling on the Shadow brand. Ice shimmered over my skin, forming into jagged crystals and shining shards as I froze the air around my fingers. "Reckon if I can get close, I'll do to him what I did to the gnome and Twilight fae, and freeze him where he stands. He'll just be one big rat popsicle then."

"I keep forgetting how weird you are." Emma told me, but nodded. "Fine. Pippa and I will go first, try to reason with the bastard. Keep the others distracted. You go straight for him, and do your juju thing. Don't give him a chance to get away. I want a talk with him."

Simple plans mean less complications to get in the way, less things to fuck up and go wrong on us. With the play sorted, we all three Changed into our beast-man form, making us instantly recognisable as to who we were whilst still able to speak. Just enough to put the fear of the lycan into all the bastards.

Then Emma strode out of the tunnel, Pippa a step behind and me following.

"Rous! Stand down!" Emma growled, the words snarling through the air and cutting him off mid-rant. "You've done enough damage, caused enough trouble. Now Molly's called us in and we're here to stop this fucking madness. It's over!"

"Redcloaks!" The Rat God chittered, pointing one ratty hand in our direction. "They are weak, vulnerable. Think of all the times they have threatened you, bullied you. Stopped you taking what you wanted from the mortals, forced you to be *less* than you deserved! Now they want to take this from you too! Attack them! Make them pay!"

"Stand down, everyone! No-one has to get hurt." Pippa snarled beside Emma, her red fur flickering in the torchlight like she was on fire. "Well, no-one except the fuckwit telling you to attack *Redcloaks*, that is."

"Attack them! They are weakened, afflicted!" Rous snarled, then his black eyes fell on me. "Him! That one! Take him down, and you will be richly rewarded!"

The two ogres obviously decided whatever riches were being promised were worth the risk, and lumbered forward, massive fists swinging.

"Idiots." I growled, even as the gnolls and goblins howled and charged towards us.

With Emma and Pippa looking to keep the crowd occupied, I needed to reach Rous and deal with the rat-bastard as quickly as I could. Unfortunately, that meant getting through the two ogres who blocked my path to their supposed-saviour. I did a quick calculation in my head, realising I wouldn't be able to get around the two lumbering battering rams, but would need to deal with them first.

So, letting the ogres come to me, I fed Wyld strength flow through my veins. As I gripped a cold-iron and silver sword in each fist, waiting my moment.

The one-armed ogre loped ahead of its slower kin, rearing up and hammering at me with one huge paw. Ducking, rolling under the limb, I struck at its exposed leg and swiping arm. Unencumbered by armour, I slipped easily under the fae's attack, my own swords hammering into and then through its limbs with inhuman strength. Even a lycan would have struggled to cut through the creature's gnarled hide, but fuelled by my unnatural heritage I found my blows met little resistance.

The ogre screamed, silver blood splashing out in gouts as I hewed through its massive thigh and took off its one arm at the elbow. It crumpled, collapsing on top of two goblins unlucky enough to be in its way, as its life poured out of the mortal wounds.

The second ogre, enraged and obviously not the brightest of its species, howled and trampled its dying kin to get at me. I waited as it lurched at me with both arms spread wide to encircle and wrap around me, seeking to squeeze me to pulp, then slammed both bloodied swords into its chest where I knew its twin hearts were. Again, with my Wyld strength, I met little resistance and the ogre groaned as I hammered my blades through its vital organs.

As it crumpled, silver gore bursting from its thick lips, I jerked my swords free. But a quick glance over at my companions told me we needed to change the plan. They were fending off the worst of the attacks, but the weakness was definitely hampering Pippa and Emma. Three gnolls were focused on Pippa, and she already bore one bloody gash across her muzzle where she hadn't been quick enough to dodge, whilst Emma lashed out at five goblins trying to spit her with cruelly hooked spears.

I barrelled into the gnolls, hammering my swords into the nearest one in an explosion of silver blood. It howled, staggering into the path of one of the goblins, who rammed its spear into the dying creature to get it out of its way. The second gnoll turned at my attack, trying to bring its hooked halberd round to block, but I just rolled my swords over its weapon and sank them into its chest.

The last gnoll, brave beyond sense, swung its halberd at me whilst my weapons were snared in its kin. But it had forgotten about Pippa, and her jaws closed on its throat, tearing through muscle and skin in a fountain of gore as she ripped through its neck. Its eyes bulged, then the head toppled and fell with a thud to the floor.

Wiping blood from her muzzle, Pippa snarled a thanks and leapt at the nearest goblin besetting Emma. Between the pair, they soon shattered the green skinned creatures' weapons and had three of the five bleeding their life out on the floor.

Movement in the corner of my eye had me turning from my packmates, swords raised to block the weapon lashing through the air. The fae hissed a curse, having crept up on me whilst I was distracted and thought to stab me with its flimsy rapier. I rewarded its efforts by breaking its wrist with a savage twist of my swords, eliciting a shocked and very girly scream from its lips.

Not so long ago, I would have had serious doubts about going head-to-head with a Court fae, as the bastards are ultra-strong, ultra-fast and generally as impervious as Superman to my Spot the Dog. However, things were now very different, and I snarled at the sheer audacity of the bastard, trying to stab me in the back. Not even bothering using my swords, I backhanded the slim figure so hard that I heard bones shatter and its body sailed across the room to connect with the rock wall in an explosion of silver gore and blood. The fae gave one last strangled scream, then slumped to the floor, dead.

Shocked silence descended on the cave as the rest of the crowd shrank back at the sudden violence and death. Silver blood and gore coated the stone underfoot, the bodies of nine of their kin scattered around us as Emma, Pippa and I stalked through the carnage to draw near to Rous.

"We warned you!" Emma snarled at the remaining hags, goblins and gnolls. "Back the fuck down, or you'll join your kin. We're here for the rat."

"It can't be! You ... can't be ...!" Rous chittered on top of his box, his black eyes wide with terror. "He said you were sickened, ill. Easy prey! I ... I thought ..."

"That's the problem! You didn't fucking *think*." I growled, dropping my swords to the stone floor. Rous's eyes followed them, giving me the chance to draw close to where the immortal stood. "First Knox, then Morgana. Now fucking *Jack the Ripper*? Is there no-one you won't be dumb enough to play glove puppet to? Are you *that* stupid, or don't all those rat brains you use all line up to make one decent bloody thought?"

Rous glared at me, hissing and snarling. I'd guessed right, seeing how he'd reacted when I named my half-brother. It made sense. The Wyld fae would have the strength to destroy the statues marking the Ways to London Lower, even in its poisoned and fucked up state, and certainly had been linked to Morgana before she became Queen of Twilight. Just the sort to whisper in Rous's furry, stinking ear about making a play for her Court.

But Jack was working for Lykaois now, and that bastard had no reason to be messing with Twilight or Morgana. All it wanted was its knife, a cult to serve it and a regular supply of fucked up hosts to let it satisfy its cruelty whilst possessing.

Then I remembered brother Grubbins' words.

"It was summoned." He told me, eyes wide, breath starting to come in shallow gasps. *"I felt it somehow, in my head, when it was controlling me. A need it had to be here, to do a thing."*

Fuck. There was the connection. Lykaois had been called. And the thing doing the calling, to creatures near and far, was the very thing that Jack already served. And been freed by, to keep us occupied and chasing our tails whilst She got on with her own agenda.

Rous obviously took my silence as a sign of impending doom for the immortal, for he began to dissolve, the rats making up his body tumbling over themselves in a bid for freedom.

Emma snarled at me, but I was already moving, slapping my hand against the wriggling, writhing mass that made up the immortal.

"Oh no you don't! *Freeze*, you bastard!" I felt the power flare inside me, so familiar now, bonded to me through both the brand I bore but also my connection to the Court through my family. The Morrigan, Herald of Shadow.

Rous screeched as ice flowed over it, the rats nearest to where I had slapped my hand instantly freezing. He tried to stagger back from me, but I kept my hand pressed against the now fast-frozen rodents and poured Shadow-wrought magic into him. It flowed over the immortal, fastening him where he stood as the rats forming his lower limbs solidified, and ice raised upwards, claiming them even as they squirmed and clawed to break free.

I pulled the magic back as it neared Rous's neck, leaving his head unfrozen. The rest of him was now a solid block of ice, each rat sculpted in glittering detail, his robes frozen in folded flows whilst the few that made up the immortal's head squirmed and hissed at me.

The fact I was able to stop myself from completely freezing Rous as I had both Terrigyle and the Twilight fae was both a good and a bad thing, as I stepped away from the hissing, spitting immortal. Good, that I was getting better at using the gifts given to me by the Courts. Bad, because the more I used and got used to them, the less I was like my other lycan packmates, less the simple Redcloak I pretended to be. More something complicated, with a whole load of unasked questions waiting to jump me when I stopped ignoring them.

Then immortal spat out words that dragged my head back into the game. Chilled my own blood, made my stomach knot with fear.

"Think you are so clever, wolf! Think you've won?!" Rous snarled, the rats in his face writhing with fury. "You're too late! I was just meant to keep you occupied. Keep you down here. It doesn't matter about the mists, about what you've done to me. You've *lost*."

Shit.

The Rat God hissed with laughter, screeching so hard that cracks began to show in its frozen form. I looked across at Emma, seeing the realisation blossom there too.

We'd been duped.

"Know I said I wanted him able to talk?" My packmate told me, eyeing the laughing god with bright, angry eyes. "Fuck that. Shut the bastard down, will you?"

"With pleasure." I replied, and stepped in close. Rous quietened his laughter, black eyes flaring with fear and anger, as I snarled into his face.

"If anyone is harmed, anyone I care about is hurt because of you?" I promised him, raising my hand and calling up the Shadow magic again. "I'm going to come back here and dump your frozen ass in a saltwater bath and add plenty of iron and silver. Let's see you come back from that, eh?"

I didn't let him reply, lashing him with ice cold fury until every piece of him was frozen solid.

"The rest of you? Fuck off and go find Molly. Tell her you were all idiots and duped by this bastard." Emma told the cowering Lows folk, who had watched in horror as I dealt with their Lord. All his promises shown to be false, his lies exposed.

They didn't need to be told twice, scurrying and scrabbling over the bodies of their fallen kin in their hurry to flee.

"We need to get topside and find out if that bastard was telling the truth." I told Emma, as Pippa stepped up to look at the frozen Rat God. "If he was …"

"Then there's a real chance things have just gotten more fucked up." She agreed, as she Changed back to her mortal suit. "You head back up. Maybe we beat them too quickly, got ahead of whatever they wanted you out of the picture for. We'll wrap things up here."

I didn't even bother Changing, just tossed my blood-stained swords back into my bag and started running for the way back, and the nearest entrance to London Upper.

All the while, with Rous's snickering laughter echoing in my ears.

Chapter 49

I was too late.

News travelled fast in the Lows, and I was met by a small guard of gnolls as I hit the marketplace at full pelt. Soaked with silver blood, still Changed, I snarled at the gnolls to get out of my way, but they simply told me Molly had ordered them to show me to the nearest Way back up to London.

The guard who spoke to me managed to get most of that out without stuttering too much or looking like he was going to pee himself, so I reigned in my anger and motioned for him to lead the way. Meanwhile Changing to my mortal suit.

The stairs they took me to led back up to the Egyptian obelisk on Embankment, called Cleopatra's Needle. This monument had nothing to do with the famous woman of the same name, but instead originated from Alexandria, the royal city of Cleopatra. It was about three and a half thousand years old, and was brought over sometime in 1878 by the British to commemorate their victory over Napoleon. Which, of course, an Egyptian stone needle with matching Sphinxes patiently watching over it totally does.

Under the stony stare of the guardian statues, I slipped from the portal, reaching for my mobile even as the door slid silently shut behind me.

The clock on my phone told me we'd lost all of the morning and were starting into the afternoon. The time disparity between the Lows and the rest of London playing havoc as always.

I had over a dozen missed calls from Felix, one from Jessica and a text message that I popped open straight away.

Jacob broken out. Felicity informs me Sarah gone too. Injuries sustained. Call as soon as you get this.

"Fuck!" I snarled to the open air, earning some worried looks from a few mortals as they hurriedly walked past me.

I dialled Felix first, knowing I should call my Alpha but this was personal.

"Morgan! Thank fuck!" She picked up on the first ring, and I read from her tones just how upset she was. She didn't sound in pain, which was one good thing in all this mess. "I've been trying to call you for ages!"

In between her haranguing me, Felix managed to tell me what had happened. It was as bad as I feared.

Things had been fine at the apartment after I left. Sarah had curled up with the journal and a coffee, hunting for more clues, whilst Felix texted as many of her witch contacts as she could to check on them. Goldspur was out of her tree, thoroughly delighted at finding not just Bear but also Albert now as companions to play with, and the three of them had raided the trollhound's toy stash and were occupied in a three-way tug of war around the living room.

"It all happened so fast!" Felix told me, voice still shaking. "One moment the dogs were play fighting with Goldspur, and I was checking my phone for any replies to my texts. Then Bear just suddenly stopped and started growling. I mean, properly snarling, all angry like. I went to calm him down, but Goldspur stopped me, telling me we weren't alone. That something had gotten past the wards somehow."

"Then Sarah looked up at us, and, oh Morgan, her eyes! They were bright yellow, slitted and just so pissed looking." She took a moment, drawing a breath to calm herself. "Bear was facing her, and he'd started to get real big, snarling and barking. Albert was whining, shit scared of whatever it was, and Goldspur got in between me and Sarah, drawing those knives of hers."

"All Sarah said was ... *where's my knife?* ... but in a weird, fucking freaky voice. Then Bear went for her, and Goldspur too."

I gripped the phone, seeing how it had played out in my head as Felix spoke.

It was my fault. I'd invited Sarah into my home before I knew she was a host for Lykaois. Bear had reacted to her that first time, so the bastard *must* have been linked to her still, just enough so the invite included it too. Thus negating the wards and protection I'd vouchsafed and assured her would keep her from the bastard's reach.

I can be *so* fucking stupid at times.

Lykaois, since that was who had gotten into my home, had Changed Sarah even as Bear and Goldspur attacked. It had simply swatted the trollhound away, sending him crashing through my sofa and coffee table, leaving him unconscious from the strength of its blow. The dryad, wielding her Shadow-wrought knives, should have presented a bigger problem, but it simply shrugged off her attack, knocking the weapons from her grasp as she tried to use the same trick that had been so successful on the mortal OPS strike squad. In this instance, Lykaois had punished her for thinking it was as weak as any mortal.

"Sarah … what she'd turned into … it just wouldn't stop hitting Goldspur. There was blood everywhere, and she was screaming but it wouldn't stop." Felix told me, and I gritted my teeth, hearing what the bastard had done. "I tried hitting it with everything I had, just to make it stop hurting her. But it just laughed, and nothing I did seemed to affect it."

Eventually it had dumped Goldspur on the floor and gone after Felix, but she'd had enough time to see nothing she did worked. So she had closed herself off in a warding circle, locking it before Lykaois could reach her.

"It was so horrible. It kept snarling and trying to break the circle. It trashed your home and used the broken bits to throw at me, then tried threatening Goldspur unless I let it in." She told me, her voice shaking. "I … I almost did, but I knew it would just hurt me too. I couldn't help her, or Bear. But I wanted to!"

Eventually, Lykaois had calmed, and returned Sarah to her normal form. Wearing that, it had spoken to Felix, leaving me a message before walking out the front door of my home.

"It said to tell you *Bring me my knife. I'll be in touch but if you don't I'll make this one remember what she did. Where I buried the bodies. Whose blood stains her hands.* That was it." Felix fell silent then, but then added before I could speak.

"After it left, I tried my best to see to Goldspur. Bear's ok, just a little dazed, but he seems to be in one piece and Albert is fussing over him anyhow."

"Goldspur?" I prompted, bracing myself for the worst news.

"I … I got one of those *voices* again. The ones I've told you about." She replied, and I nodded, remembering that Felix seemed connected to something in Twilight. Something or someone that guided her when she used her magic. We still had no idea who it might be, which was another reason we were keeping her as far from the mists as possible. "It told me to take her to the tree and lay her in its roots. When I did, they wrapped around her and took her back inside the trunk. I think it was to heal her, keep her safe. Well, I hope."

I'm not all that familiar with dryads and their trees, and the link they share. But the apple tree was her father, and if anything could help her when she had been seriously wounded, I guessed it would be that. So at least she was in the best place possible to get the help she needed, so I could quit worrying about her. I still felt guilty as hell for what had happened, but that was just a simple fact.

It was my fault.

"Stay put. I'll be there as soon as I can." I told her, knowing I had to call Jessica next and find out what had happened at the office. And then I needed to get to the witch's cottage and make sure the knife was still safe. Neither Felix or I had granted permission for anyone else to bypass the wards there, so it should still be out of reach for Sarah or Jacob. Or Jack, if the bastard was back from his little side trip to the Lows.

"We will save her, won't we?" Felix asked, reminding me again she was still only a young woman at heart. A mortal dumped into my world, and still only finding her feet when the rest of us had been through the mill a few times now and knew just to grit our teeth and get on with things. "It wasn't her, it's that bastard who's to blame."

"Trust me, I'm not letting Sarah be another casualty of this fucker." I promised her. "Now, just rest up. I'll be there shortly."

I put a call into Jessica even as I picked up my pace, heading in the direction of Primrose Hill. There was little I could do at the office, what with the shit having already hit the fan, so my plan was to go collect the knife and get back home. I had no idea when Lykaois would get in touch, but I wanted to have a few things sorted before any meeting.

"Ah expect you've spoken tae Felicity already." Jessica told me as the call connected, as ever knowing exactly how I worked. "As such, ah will keep this brief. The first warning we had of any problem with Jacob were the trolls. They came running into the office, screaming about the wolf in the cage going mad. Patrick and Jarthi were with me, so we went tae investigate. We arrived in time tae be met by Jacob in worgen form, but different enough fer me tae realise it was not him, instead the *other* was in control. Ah tried tae warn the other two, but ah was not quick enough, and Patrick got too close. The creature is definitely fae in origin, fer it is far faster than any lycan, far stronger too. Even fer three Alphas, it was beyond our ability tae contain and it escaped the office."

"Who got hurt?" I asked, knowing there was no way Lykaois would have resisted the urge to do some damage and vent its rage.

"Jarthi. It broke her back like it was snapping twigs." Jessica answered with a sigh, and I knew from that there was more bad news. "She will heal, eventually, but fer now she is resting in mah bed."

"Patrick?" I prompted, and Jessica sighed again.

"It gutted him, Morgan." She finally spoke, and I heard the rage barely contained in her voice, warring against the weakness that ravaged her. "There was nae we could do, the damage it did too great. Ah have told Sean Boseman, and ah expect him here shortly. Patrick was an Alpha of many centuries, Morgan, but it ripped him apart like he was nothing. *Nothing.*"

"How about you?" I queried, knowing Jessica would focus on everyone else first and foremost, having managed her own personal pain and loss from losing Mark for so long now. "You still standing?"

Jessica managed a pained chuckle, immediately telling me she *wasn't* ok.

"Ah'll be fine, but ah won't be running anywhere soon." She eventually admitted. "Mah left leg is pretty much broken from top tae bottom, and the bastard made a fair attempt at pulling mah left arm from its socket. The swelling is … *inconvenient* and more than a little troublesome but ah will recover."

Fuck. Three Alphas, no matter the fact they were afflicted by whatever bad juju Lykaois had sicked the packs with, should have been an unstoppable force. Complete overkill for handling one supernatural entity. But instead, it had wiped the floor with them, fatally for Patrick and disabling both Jarthi and Jessica in the process.

And I was thinking of throwing down with the bastard. Seriously.

"Morgan," Jessica interrupted my bleak thoughts, obviously sensing where the news was taking me. "There is nae use blaming yerself or any other except this creature fer the hurt and damage done. It is still out there, looking fer the one thing you have, the one thing it cannot … it *must nae get*. And it has people we care about, who nae deserve tae be its playthings. Whatever you have planned, whatever it is you think will work against this creature, ah think it is time we tried a little of yer particular brand of insanity. So go do what you need tae do, tae bring them both back safe."

That must have used up all the strength Jessica had to talk, given her wounds, as she simply hung up.

I slipped the phone back into my pocket, stopping on the pavement to let things settle in my head. It was a sign of just how much shit we were in, that Jessica was giving me a green light to do whatever I thought needed doing, whether it followed the rules or not. She trusted me, and right now, she didn't need me to be a law-abiding member of the pack.

No, she needed the *Real* me, whatever the fuck that was.

Standing still wasn't going to get things done, I told myself, and mentally kicked my arse back into gear. First, get the knife. Second, get back home and check on what sort of damage had been done, and how Bear and the others were. Third … third, I was beginning to think I needed that plan B in place, and if so, there was a call I needed to make.

Desperate times, and all that.

Chapter 50

"Morrigan, by blood of my blood. By bond passed from mother to son, from son to me, I call on you." I quietly called out the summoning, this time deciding to keep to the ritual and not risk incurring any more of this particular immortal's ire. "By bond between comrades, through blood spilled on the field of battle, I call on you. By right of Knight to his Herald, both of the Shadow Court, I call on you."

"There now. That was not so hard now was it?" The Morrigan's wintry tones chilled the air even further as I stood on my balcony overlooking the Thames.

It was nearing five, and the sky was darkening towards evening with the moon already shining bright and full as it rose to eventually take its place above us. Full moon, the night when werewolves were supposed to revert to their most bestial, and when Lykaois was going to be at its strongest. Still, it *was* a beautiful sight, the shining orb pinned to the blue-black sky.

"Nope. Not the hardest thing I'll face tonight, by a long shot." I agreed, turning to find the Shadow fae leaning against the balustrade running around the balcony. I had a glass of merlot poured, and handed it across before picking up my own and raising in the universal sign of cheers. "Thanks for coming on short notice."

The Morrigan eyed me for a long moment, then took a sip of the wine. Savouring the bite of the peppery after tones, she looked back towards the apartment, one eyebrow cocked.

"I sense that violence was done here recently, and I would be enfeebled indeed to miss the stink of the creature I warned you was hunting you." She told me with her customary bluntness. "What foolishness has come to pass here, that you bite your tongue and follow protocol as if you mean it?"

It didn't take long for me to explain the circumstances of the morning, as the Shadow fae watched me silently. I finished up with the facts as they were. Lykaois had both Sarah and Jacob, and was probably in league with Morgana somehow. It was the reason the lycans were sick, somehow cursing us through the shared bond it seemed to have with our kin. This was further confirmed given how I, the only one not *really* a lycan like all my other packmates, was unaffected.

I had its knife, the one thing it needed to properly bind itself to a host. Until then, it could only take control of those people who were hurt enough and desperate enough to be weakened. Vulnerable. And it had tasted both my packmate's and my love's blood, strengthening its hold on them. Its other hosts were dead, Miles killed in the museum, and both PC Chambers and Professor Eduardo under the rubble of a church.

And my half-brother was involved. Both Jack and Lykaois were responsible for the death of witches and druids, a direct attack on Tera, the Goddess of the Mortal Realm. That one, I still didn't understand, but Molly's admitting she was weakened whilst Rous had been unaffected had me thinking some very ugly suspicions.

When I finished, the Morrigan eyed me with those bottomless black eyes of hers, pale skin shining under the light of the full moon. She took a long sip of her wine, before setting the glass down on the balustrade beside her.

"What is it you wish of me, pup?" She asked quietly, but held up a hand to stop me answering immediately. "Before you speak, know that I am bound by the Accords as to what I may or may not do. Given my role as Herald to the Shadow Court, even more so than others of *our* kin. So best you think on your words carefully before you ask, and I have to deny you."

I took a moment, having lined things up in my head.

Felix was asleep in one of the guest rooms, exhausted and overwrought by what had happened with Sarah. Goldspur had not emerged from her father's trunk, but I had to hope she was healing her wounds and safe now. Bear was snoring amongst the tree roots, Albert a quieter counterpart to the huge trollhound, who seemed to have had no lasting ill effects from being hurled across the living room and knocked unconscious by Lykaois.

My home was trashed. Far worse than when OPS had stormed the place and shot it full of holes whilst being thoroughly ass-kicked by my resident dryad. None of my furniture had escaped in one piece, and the walls bore the brutal marks of claws and magical fire. The apple tree had been itself damaged, several limbs broken and its bark rent, but I figured it would heal that eventually. The bastard had thrown a complete fit of rage it seemed when it wasn't able to hurt Felix, and vented on both floors of my home. Kitchens had been trashed, anything looking even remotely fragile shattered and broken.

Despite time ticking away in my head, I had spent a solid hour with Felix, cleaning up the worst of the mess. Making sure all the glass and shattered fragments were cleared away, so Bear and Albert weren't risking injury. Then I'd just piled the most intact cushions of the floor as a place to sit, and turned off the water to the apartment before it flooded from the broken pipes.

Now I was alone, outside, with the Morrigan. With no-one to overhear what I said next.

After a moment's thought, I made my request.

The Morrigan eyed me for a long moment, head cocked and expression frozen.

"It's possible. Mark Walker did it. Jessica's told us all the story enough times." I prompted her, sure in my knowledge. "I just need to know *how*. In case, well, just in case."

"Mark Walker was a lycan Alpha almost eight hundred years of age." She replied after a moment, narrowing her eyes and pursing her lips in thought. "You have seen, what forty-five *summers*, and still war with yourself as to your own nature. You are a virtual stranger to yourself, yet you wish to do this thing? Some might say what you ask is impossible."

"Some. Not you." I replied, seeing her smile coldly as I read her right.

"Mayhap there *is* some hope for you … *Morgan*." She spoke, and I almost fell on my arse, hearing her use my actual name rather than the derogatory *pup* I was so familiar with. "But this thing, it will not be easy. Nor can I promise you will not suffer. In fact, I am fairly certain it will be the most painful thing you have ever endured. Or ever will."

I shrugged. Pain was pain. I wasn't being brave, wasn't using false bravado to make me look cool or heroic. I just knew that, after everything that had happened and where the blame lay at my feet, I'd suffer whatever I needed to if I made things right again.

"And what of them?" The Morrigan waved a slim, pale hand to the large glass door leading into my apartment, beyond which Bear, Albert and Felix all slept. "This thing you ask, do they know? Have you considered what it will mean if you succeed, to those you protect? To the one you *love*."

"I'm doing it *for* them." I countered, certain in my mind, having done an awful lot of thinking on that very subject whilst cleaning up the wreckage of my home. "They deserve to have things put right, to be able to move on with their lives and not be hounded by this bastard. I've made provisions, and I'm pretty sure everyone will be cared for."

"Even *her*?" The Morrigan pressed, and I took a breath, feeling the one stab of uncertainty, the one point of pain.

"If I don't sort this out, she's fucked anyhow. Leastways this way, she has a chance to get back to normal." I finally admitted, shrugging once more.

My fae grandmother was silent for a long breath, until she finally nodded, once. Stepping up close, she placed her palms on my cheeks and gently but firmly pulled my head down. Then she planted a single kiss on my forehead.

The touch of her lips was like ice burning through me, as *something* passed between us. A sliver of magic, a bond. Something, that whispered in the corners of my mind before slipping down into the darkness of my Shadow brand.

"There." She told me, stepping back from me but looking me in the eye. "I have given you the knowledge and strength to do what you wish. But I can guarantee with even that, you may not succeed. That depends on you, on your desire and will alone."

"Thanks." I told her, honestly and simply. What I had asked for, she had every right to refuse me. To tell me I was being stupid, idiotic and every bad way of heroic possible. But she had read the truth in me, and knew why I was asking.

"Do not thank me." She shook her head, her braids clattering in the cold October air. "This gift, this thing? It is not something one is thankful for. Ever."

"Now, I must begone, as there are matters for our Queen that I must attend to. As well as pass on word of what you have found out, what you suspect." The fae told me, once again reading me so well that I hadn't even needed to voice my concerns, for her to know them. "Madb will wish to know of her sister, and any plays which might be being made. Even on the foolish mortals."

Coldness swirled in the air on the balcony, chips of ice forming on the ironwork. Beside the Morrigan, her glass frosted and froze, the remaining dregs of red wine looking like droplets of blood. Gleaming in the light.

Before she vanished into the swirling maelstrom, the fae fixed me with her cold, dark eyes.

"Two things I would say before I leave." She whispered, as her form fragmented into whirling crow feathers. "Firstly, *remember who you are, where you come from*. At the end, that will aid you more than magic words or heroic deeds."

"And the second?" I asked, knowing it wouldn't be the Morrigan if she didn't leave me some cryptic comment to thoroughly confuse me. It was just her way.

"Secondly? I sense the approach of your half-brother, and sense he comes bearing words from your hunter. Best prepare, pup, for there is no more time."

With that, she vanished, leaving only a single black feather drifting through the air, frosted with ice, to fall to the balcony at my feet.

I rolled my shoulders, feeling my anger surge like magma inside. In that moment I too sensed Jack's approach, and grinned savagely.

"Time's up, indeed. Now, I want to go hurt someone. And looky who's just shown up?" I told the empty air, and headed for the door.

Chapter 51

"Back off!" Jack snarled as I stormed out of my side entrance, fully intent on smashing that ugly face of his into a bloody pulp. "I mean it! Stop, or we'll hurt the mortal and your packmate in ways you can't possibly imagine."

I slowed my pace, settling on the balls of my feet, crossing my arms and fixing my half-brother with a cold, pissed off stare.

"Oh, I'm imagining a lot right now. Looking at *you*." I growled at Jack.

The Wyld fae was not in good shape. The last time I'd faced him, he had been cocksure and confident, strong in himself and a powerful adversary. Clad in his faux Victorian clothes, no glamour hiding his yellow-fevered eyes and lamprey-like mouth with its circles of needle-like teeth. Fingers ending in sharpened blades of fae-steel, grown to provide him with scalpels on both hands to help dissect his victims with consummate skill.

Now, his face was mottled and patchy, showing the burns from Felix's fire and the ravages of the Thames on his inhuman nature. Running water could be like battery acid on a fae, and it had certainly wreaked its ruin on him. He was clad in an oversized coat, patched and stained with filth, and he wore a wide brimmed bowler hat on his head, brim pulled down to shield his eyes. He stood hunched, oddly contorted to the right-hand side, and I remembered Gregory Allen punching my borrowed cold iron and silver sword into the fae's armpit, jamming the blade deep to rupture the heart and internal organs within.

Unfortunately, I was guessing, Jack didn't have a mortal's physiology, so the blow which would have been fatal for a man or woman, was simply agonising to the fae. But the way he held himself, I reckoned the wound was still open, maybe even a fragment of the weapon broken off inside and stopping it from properly healing. Poisoning the bastard slowly. He deserved it.

"First Knox, now Lykaois." I smiled coldly at him, not caring now as I named the bastard. Let him hear me. "You *really* can't help being someone else's puppet, can you bro? Always someone else pulling your strings, telling you what to do. Oh, how the mighty have fallen. The Terror of Whitechapel, now just a witless lackey. A petty thug for his betters."

Jack snarled, hands flexing and those knives glinting in the streetlamp light. I braced myself, remembering that the fucker was fast, inhumanly so, and had shrugged off blows before like they were gnat bites. The condition he was in now, however, made me think he wasn't so tough, so confident. Otherwise, I reckon he'd have been at my throat by now.

"Go on. Try it." I snarled, uncrossing my arms and showing my hands. "I'm unarmed. Give me your best shot, and then I'll happily beat whatever message you came with out of you. C'mon."

I was lying, of course. I had one of my Rambo-style knives stashed at my back, ready to slip free and ram somewhere particularly painful if Jack went for me. Reckon I might hamstring the bastard first, crippling him before I took off those blade-fingers of his, and started doing more permanent damage.

Sadly, he seemed to hear a voice, cocking his head as *something* spoke to him. Lykaois, or maybe the puppeteer *behind* the fucker who had plagued me these past few days. Whichever, he snarled a curse but backed up a step, lowering his hands and breathing to calm himself.

"You're to bring the knife. Yourself, no-one else." Jack told me, expression twisted with rage at being called to heel, but obeying all the same. "Stroke of midnight tonight, bring it to …"

"No." I growled, cutting him off as I shook my head.

"No? NO?" Jack snarled, yellow eyes blazing. "Do you *know* what we'll do to the bitch you bedded? The ways we'll make her scream? And as for that mutt, that packmate of yours? I'll gut him just like …"

"Shut. The. Fuck. Up." I grounded out, as I locked my eyes on him. "You or that little shit you're shacked up with won't do a fucking *thing* to either of them. Period. And I'm not bringing the knife anywhere it wants. You know why?"

Jack remained silent, but I got a sense he was not the only one listening. Good, I wanted the bastard to hear the next bit.

"Because if you do, if you as much as *look* at either of them in the wrong way, I'll take the bloody knife." I explained slowly, clearly. "And I'll lock it away in a box of silver, salt and iron before I get on a boat out of here. To take me to somewhere in the middle of the *fucking ocean*, where I will dump the box, the knife and everything, over the side. Weighted down, and with a shitload of hexes attached to misdirect any attempts Lykaois might make to find the fucker. He will *never* see that fucking knife again, you hear me?"

Jack hissed a curse, obviously seeing the truth in my face, tasting it in my words. I let my threat sink in, before I continued as I'd planned.

"So, here's how it's going to go. I'm not taking the knife anywhere. Lykaois is going to bring both Sarah and Jacob *here*. To my home. The bastard's been here, so it knows the address." I slowly explained, making sure things were clear. "It fucked up the wards on the place, using a guest to spill blood inside my home, so it's basically neutral ground now. So this will be where we do the exchange. It agrees to release the pair of them, no memories of what they did, no bond to keep them linked to the fucker. And it gets its knife. Midnight suits me, so let's do it then. But that's all I'm agreeing to."

Jack went to snarl a reply, but I cut him off with a growl of my own.

"That's the deal. Either you or it try to make changes, I toss the knife. Any attempt to keep Sarah or Jacob linked, I toss the knife. Basically, you do *anything* to piss me off, I toss the knife." I told him with a happy smile plastered on my face. "And then, when I've done that, I will spend every living breath I have, hunting both you and it down. And when I find you, I won't bother with the Furies, or the Courts or anything. No. I'll just take you both and disappear, and spend every waking moment torturing you to the limit of your immortal lives. Then start over again. Again and again."

I let my smile broaden as if a thought had struck me.

"Oh, and I might just invite one of the Sisters of the Arch to come stay. Seeing how you both have their blood on your hands. They know how to reach beyond the grave, and pull back a spirit that thought it might have escaped *eternal* punishment. I reckon they can show me a thing or two, and get some justice themselves."

I took two quick steps forward, closing the space between Jack and me. Up close, the fae stank of rot and illness, the suppurating wound in his side obviously crippling him and I guessed I'd been right about there being still some of my sword stuck in him. Good.

"You *hear* me, bro? Take that message, and *fuck off*."

Jack snarled, hands twitching with the desire to rend my flesh, carve the smile from my face and dance on my desecrated corpse. But he was on a leash, and after a moment, he nodded and then turned, melting back into the darkness of the night from one breath to the next.

I waited, counting under my breath until one hundred, to make sure the fucker had actually left and was not hanging around under a glamour. But the air was clear, free of the stink of the fae or any trace of Lykaois.

When I was finally sure we were alone, I let loose a breath and talked to the open air.

"You got all that?"

The air shimmered off to my right, and the Veil dropped from where it had been held. Felix looked across at me, her expression pale but her chin set, eyes wide with both fear and anticipation.

"Fuck, Morgan. Who taught you to act?" She laughed a little, repeating back in a mock attempt at my voice. *"You or the little shit you're shacked up with won't do a fucking thing to either of them. Period. And I'm not bringing the knife anywhere it wants. You know why?.* Talk about laying it on thick."

"I didn't want the bastard distracted and *maybe* sensing you listening in." I replied before shrugging. "Anyhow, I meant every word."

"I got that impression." She replied, before stepping close and laying a hand on my arm, looking up at me. "You think they'll come?"

"They'll come. And we'll be waiting." I replied, nodding back to the apartment block. "Midnight's not that far off, and we've got some work to do. You sure you're up for this?"

Felix narrowed her eyes, and sparks of Twilight fury burned at the end of her fingers.

"The bastard got the best of me once," She replied, as magic crackled around her like a second skin. "This time, I'll be ready."

"Just remember, I'd rather the apartment remained standing." I shot at her, and she stuck her tongue out at me before starting to walk back to the side door. Where I'd had her follow me out under her Veil whilst I kept Jack's attention fully on me with all my arrogant and violent threats.

Immortals might have had a long time to play the game, but they can still be fooled, still be beaten. That's what I repeated to myself as I followed Felix back inside, and set about getting my wrecked home ready for what I had planned, and whatever fuck ups were almost guaranteed to happen.

Chapter 52

Strength in numbers

Certain supernatural creatures imbue mortals who form a cult or following with strength and vitality, but at the expense of their own. These normally then rely on their followers to provide for all their needs, much like the Queen ant in a colony. However if the followers are hurt or killed, the creature is equally weakened and suffers pain, diminishing it as those it has bound to itself as slain.

In these instances, such supernatural creatures normally bind at least one mortal to them that is never put in harm's way, to ensure they never lose all their followers and suffer a complete diminishment of themselves.

Midnight found me waiting in my living room, the door to my home open, the worst of my destroyed furniture cleared out of the way.

The rest of the apartment block had been cleared with the use of the alarm system, signalling a major gas leak in the building. This fiction was supported by the careful use of some of my Redcloak accessories. Anointing the central air conditioning system with a mixture of the extracts taken from skunk, green wood hoopoe and bombardier beetles, then mixed with the musk of the corpse flower and a watered-down tincture taken from our old friends the Grimalkin. The resulting stench drove everyone in the floors below me outside and as far from the building as possible, having witnessed greenish vapour billowing from their vents and slipping down the stairs after them.

When handling mortals, it always pays to add a little theatrical element. To keep them from getting underfoot and out of danger's reach.

My tenants were kept outside, if the smell was not enough to deter any return attempts, by OPS agents dressed in suitable 'Mains Gas' uniforms. I'd called Cormac and walked him through the bits of my plan he needed to know, and after soundly berating me for leaving this to the *very* last minute, he agreed firstly to have manpower in place to keep the area around my home free of civilians. I'd hoped to stage this somewhere other than in my backyard initially, but my home having been trashed meant it was a fitting place for things to go down.

I just had to keep Goldspur's tree from being damaged, so she did not suffer any more at the hand of the fucker.

The second part of the plan, Cormac had advised me, would be in place. The team on standby, waiting for my signal whatever that was. I'd replied that they'd know it when they saw it, and had best come running.

With the mortals cleared out, and the OPS agents cautioned to keep their distance and not approach if a certain three or four people whose description I had given them, broke the perimeter, all I had to do was wait. I'd found an unbroken bottle of '98 Merlot, and was taking the opportunity to savour its bold and peppery flavours, as I waited for my guests.

I smelt the stench of Wyld fae and corrupt sickness, the burned spices strong in the air, before I heard footsteps on my stairs.

"Up here." I called out, topping up my glass then filling a second before moving to the far window which overlooked the Thames and a portion of the path running along it. "Please remember to wipe your feet, we've got the decorators in!"

Jack appeared at the top of the stairs, yellow eyes narrowed as he looked around the cleared living room. With most of the broken furniture piled on the floor below, the actual space in the room was apparent. I'd thrown some rugs on the floor to cover up the scorch marks and silver bloodstains where Goldspur had been hurt, but otherwise there was nothing for anyone to be hiding behind or underneath.

Just me, my wine glass, and a whole lot of empty floor.

The Wyld fae sniffed, obviously searching the place for whatever trap I had planned, ambush my half-brother must suspect I had waiting for them. The apple tree was the only element in the room I hadn't been able to move, but there had been no sign of life from it since I'd returned, not even a shake of its branches to acknowledge there was anything going on within the gnarled trunk. Goldspur was not going to be appearing anytime soon.

Apparently satisfied that things were as they seemed, Jack stalked out of the stairwell. Behind, Jacob slowly and stiffly walked into sight. He wore the clothing I'd last seen him wearing, and was in his mortal suit. But his expression was blank, eyes unfocused. Like he was asleep, or unconscious. But still moving.

Behind him, Sarah appeared, and I bit down hard on the stab of pain at seeing her. She was in my baggy t-shirt still, and her casual leggings she had thrown on after waking this morning. But both were stiff and coated with the dryad's blood, splashed in enough quantities for me to realise just how badly Goldspur had been hurt. Sarah too was unfocused, vacant, as she stiffly followed Jacob.

That was it. Just the three of them. The stench of Lykaois was strong around all of them, but no other hosts appeared. I watched carefully as Jacob and Sarah walked to the opposite side of the room to me, stopping like statues as they faced me across my living room. Jack prowled around one last time, opening the bedroom door and checking I had no-one hiding in there either, before stopping by the pair of hostages.

"No one else joining us?" I asked politely, nodding to my wine glass. "It's just that a host needs to know how many guests are coming if they are to be fed and watered properly. Hearth rules, 101."

Jack shook his head, then those yellow eyes of his burned brighter, glowing with an amber hue that was savagely animalistic, bestial. Wholly not his own.

Lykaois.

"Well, Morgan Black. We meet once more." It spoke, Jack's voice rasping and thickening to match its own tones. "Are you ready to name me God, and bow down and serve me?"

"Let's park that for a moment." I replied, reigning in the surge of anger I felt at hearing its mocking tone, that supercilious and arrogant edge that all immortals seemed to use when speaking to *inferior beings*. Which, to them, was pretty much everyone. "Got a couple of questions before we get down to business. Shouldn't take long, if you don't mind?"

Lykaois flicked its eyes around the now sparsely decorated living room, but Jack had found no sign of a trap, so neither did it. I nodded to the glass sitting on the side, full of wine.

"I'd be a shit host if I didn't offer refreshments." I watched as it slowly picked up the glass, its glowing eyes narrowing as it sniffed at the liquid it held. "Oh, and it's not poisoned, if that's what you're worried about. I leave that trick to the mortal authorities. Besides, I wouldn't ruin a decent Merlot that way."

It eyed me for a long moment, then took a sip from the glass. Jack's features were changing, gaining a more brutal and bestial aspect as Lykaois's spirit dominated him. Moulding him like putty into a more fitting form.

"Decent enough, I suppose." It replied after swallowing. "Though nothing truly compares to the taste of freshly spilled blood, hot from a body. So speak on, unless you wish me to appease my thirst with these two."

It waved its hand, holding the wine glass, at Sarah and Jacob, who remained enthralled somehow despite the creature being inside Jack. Its strength had indeed grown, this being its night, its time of worship. And sacrifice.

"Fine." I marshalled my thoughts, going over how I'd planned this. What I needed to find out from the smug, arrogant fucker. "First one. How the hell did you jinx my packmates? My Alpha? It's you making them sick, I'm sure of it. I just can't figure out how."

"Pfffw. You bore me with your lack of imagination." Lykaois yawned, its mouth stretching wide. Where before had been rows of needle-like teeth, impressive canines like those of a massive predatory cat now showed. "I, who have lived for countless millennia, hunted upon every continent where mortals dared dwell. I who have been worshipped and feared this side of the Veil and beyond, have seen so much and yet all you can think of asking is how I weakened the *lesser creatures*. Those only fit to serve as I see fit, who will never know greatness …"

"If you don't know, just say." I cut it off, seeing the anger flare in those amber eyes as I shrugged. "It's ok, sometimes I do things I have *no* idea how, they just sort of happen. Gods know why."

Lykaois snarled, slopping wine over its hand as it shoved the material of its coat up. Revealed, the flesh underneath was scaled and rivered with blackened veins, running from the hidden wound the body bore in its left side. But over this, it wore a twisted bracelet, knotted material wrapped about with what looked like hair and bone.

"A gift. From the one who called to me." It snarled, an evil smile splitting that lipless mouth. "Bone and hair taken from a fallen Alpha, who lost his life to his own greed and stupidity. Bound with coffin cloth stolen from a mortal lost to a wasting illness, apparel worn by one afflicted by the deadliest of disease. Fuelled by my energies, sacrificed to overcome the natural resistance to such tokens. Thrice-cursed, the hex is bound to the mortal remains of your pack, and through that all those you call kin. Crafted by one who has reason to be angered at you and your own, who saw fitting retribution in bringing down the afeared Redcloaks. One who has knowledge in such matters, of the manipulation of genetics. The secrets of *life*."

Fuck. We'd been hexed alright, something that should not be possible. I fought to keep my face calm, whilst inside I raged. A fallen Alpha, lost to stupidity and greed? That had to be Talen Orben, his body lost when he and a bunch of gnolls were devoured by the Harrowing in the Lows. I'd assumed he had been completely destroyed, reduced to ash, but some of his body must have remained. To be used in a bound-curse. Linked to items taken from sick and dying mortals, and then three times cursed to make the bloody thing stick.

The fucker was dead, and *still* proving to be an utter bastard.

And crafted by someone who had solid reason to be pissed at the lycans. At me, possibly, most of all. Someone to whom hexes and curses were like breathing air, but who had branched out into genetic manipulation. Until Jacob and I had pretty much fucked up that line of work, for her and her mortal patsies.

"*Cerce.*" I growled out her name. "That *bitch*."

"You should be wary of crossing witches. They *always* seek payback." Lykaois laughed harshly, shoving the band back under its coat as my brain tried to connect the dots.

Cerce had dealt in knowledge, sharing secrets with Robert Knox when he sought her out to understand how to bring his dead daughter back from beyond the grave. Or so he thought. Morgana had been behind that, she and those idiots from DOPA who had shared forbidden knowledge with the man in the hopes of finding a permanent counter to the threat of the Real, of keeping the Courts at check.

Cerce had also just happened to own one of the artefacts Robert Knox needed to summon Morgana, but he had chosen to steal that from her rather than risk her finding out his true purpose. But that had been it, the sum total of her connection to Morgana. And she was supposed to have done a runner back to the Real when she found out who she had been caught up helping, even if unknowingly.

Or so I had thought.

Now Lykaois, who was somehow linked to the new Queen of Twilight, was wearing a cursed hex-band made of remains that only Robert Knox could have had access to, and crafted by Cerce. A *gift*, it'd said, from the one who had called the bastard from across the seas. Gods, had all the fuckers we'd pissed off recently bandied together to royally mess us up?

It was looking like it.

"Fine. I'll take it under advisement, and quit pissing witches off." I replied as I pulled my brain back onto track. I still needed to understand one final thing. "But this whole schtick of you being the God of lycans. What's up with that? What're you doing here, fucking around with us when you could already be just about *anywhere* else, dealing with mortals who would bend over backwards to serve you. Sacrifice to you. You've *chosen* the one bunch of stubborn bastards guaranteed *not* to do what you want. So why are you *here*? C'mon, you can't be this stupid?"

This time, Lykaois made no effort to contain its rage. The wine glass flew across the room and shattered against the window beside me, its contents running down and soaking the floorboards underfoot. Across from me, Sarah crumpled to her knees, hands wrapping around her head and muted screams coming from underneath. Beside her, Jacob rocked on his feet, eyes still unfocused but breath coming out in short pants as he struggled with whatever pain the bastard was lashing them with.

"Never call me *stupid*!" Lykaois snarled, stalking across the floor until it stood almost face to face with me. "You, who could be so much more than what you are now, yet blunder around like some new-born brat with no wit nor knowledge of how to use what has been gifted him? Even this baseborn-kin that I command, poisoned and weakened to a shadow of the creature he once was, he at least has the drive and desire to prove himself better than the mortal muck you try to protect. And fail."

I stood my ground, wine glass held in one hand, at ease as the other raged. I needed it angry, enraged, not thinking clearly. And if there was one thing I was good at, it was pissing people off. Definitely a talent I knew I had, and used a lot.

"I am *here* for my knife. My sacrificial totem, by which those who serve me are bound to my will and receive my sacrament." It snarled, reaching up to rip at the shirt Jack wore over his chest. The material tore, revealing a scaled chest of grey skin, marred by black veins similar to those already seen at the wrist, but thicker and more twisted. And also, over the heart, a bloody gash that still seeped fouled silver gore, unhealed.

The bond between Jack and Lykaois.

"This pathetic thing, it is no substitute for the bond forged between my chosen and I by my knife." It hissed, dragging a finger over the wound and licking the blood that flowed. "It is enough to control pitiful mortals, and those weakened and made vulnerable for a short while, but unless the chosen one willingly accepts me into them then I must make do with the little I can enforce through the gifting of their vital fluid. And I still require freshly spilled blood to feed me strength, to appease my hunger. Hence my need for my hosts to feast on wild animals and foolish mortals and their pets, so I might sustain myself."

Well, that answered why the bastard had been using my packmate, my love and her colleague to butcher whatever creatures they could lay their hands on. Too late to use that knowledge now, and I had no way of knowing how quickly it might weaken if I'd managed to cut it off from a ready source of blood. But at least now I understood it a little more.

It waved a hand, and Sarah and Jacob settled, she rising once more to stand beside him.

"But do not think to trick me, for the blood bond is strong enough still for me to end their lives with a single command." It told me, amber eyes narrowing. "You ask why I am here, in this sprawling, stinking pit of mortal refuse?

I caught a scent from the being opposite me, a smug hunger that had nothing to do with my half-brother. This was all Lykaois.

"I came to reclaim what is mine. What was taken from me, and used to chain me in the darkness, to force me to do the bidding of those pitiful mortals who thought to rule me. My reliquary, my totem. My *knife*." It snarled, then smiled wickedly. "And claim one other thing."

It pointed one bladed finger at me, its lips curling up with hunger.

"You."

Chapter 53

"Me?" I queried, though I had suspected that was its goal for a while now. The scrawling of my name in blood at the museum, its words when I first met it on the house-boat. The clues hadn't been particularly subtle. "I'm flattered, but seriously. Why me?"

"You have angered someone of great power, and even greater wrath." Lykaois told me, running its worm-like tongue over its lips as if savouring a taste. "She called to me, guided me to this place once She was aware of my release. And then asked only that I do one thing for a chance to restore my former glory."

"To make you suffer."

It waved a hand at the other two again, but this time not inflicting any pain. Just a simple gesture to include them.

"Your packmate. A close friend and ally, shown to be a bloodthirsty monster. Rending the life from defenceless innocents, his own nightmares made real. The betrayal of promises made to the companion he had lost, that he loved." It mocked, before pointing at Sarah. "And the mortal you love, already wounded by the actions of another of your kind. Forced to see the truth, the damage running deep and only just healing before she fell into my grasp. Now blood stains her hands, lives ripped asunder to feed me at first, to staunch the savage hunger. Then the taking of another's life, the ending of all that he was, or ever could be. Staining her with the act of brutal slaying."

"Neither remember their actions, neither are aware fully what they have done." It smiled grimly, eyes locked on mine. Gloating. "It is within my power to release them, unbind them and remove those memories from their minds. Or I can unlock them, letting them see the truth, feel the harm they have done. Reveal where your mortal love hid the remains of the animals she slew, where her clothes stained in their blood lie. I can make them relive the actions they have taken at my bidding. It will destroy her, and, I think, maybe him too."

"I was tasked with *destroying* you, Morgan Black." Lykaois told me bluntly, eyes flickering with the strength of its hunger. "To make you pay, feel pain unlike any other. To leave you broken and grovelling on the ground. A ruin, whose only worth would have been in your spilled blood, your life taken at the very last."

"But then this *host* came to me. Ordered to serve, so that its own retribution might be served in time." It gestured down at Jack's body, stroking a finger over the hidden wound in its side. "And I learned your *true* nature. What you are really worth. And what a *waste* it would be, to simply end you."

"You know, as much as I appreciate the sentiment." I drawled, rolling my eyes in sardonic despair. "And the fact you decided simply killing me was the wrong thing to do, I really think you're overpricing me. I'm probably not even worth selling for glue these days … and the mortals take *anything* to put in that shit."

"Idiot!" Lykaois hissed at me, like a cat that had been sprayed with water. "Son of Herne, brother and heir to the Wyld. Beast in form, Wyld in duality. Knight of Shadow, Errant of Ivory. You are unique, and when I have my knife, I will take you as my chosen and claim all that you squander in wanton idleness. You who protect the mortals when you could *rule* them. You who serve the Courts when they should kneel to *you!*"

"But enough of this!" It snarled, facing me and I guessed we'd reached the end of our discussion. "I came to claim that which is mine, which was stolen from me and used to chain me. Where is my knife!"

"You'll get your knife when you free those two." I pointed at Sarah and Jacob, knowing what I had to do. What was at stake here. "Take your fucking bond off them, remove any memory of what you made them do. Make it so you cannot fucking touch them ever again. That first, before you get your little chopper."

"And what if I just take it, here and now?" It snarled in reply, close enough that it could reach me in its next breath. "You think to bargain with me, but it must be here, hidden from me somehow. What if I tear this place down around us, and take it anyway?"

"Then, before you do anything so monumentally stupid," I explained with a hard smile. "I'll just make one little sign, to the nice person standing at the side of the river down there. You know, the Thames. If you want, chat to your host about how it feels to take a dip in there."

I casually gestured down to where a figure stood illuminated by streetlighting, at the Thames path wall. They remained still, unmoving, but their attention was definitely fixed on the windows of my apartment.

"Who is that?" Lykaois hissed, anger contorting its bestial features into an ugly scowl.

"No-one special. Just someone I gave a small package to." I replied, shrugging as I held out my hands. "About oh so big, a nice little box of silver and cold forged iron. Weighted to sink, but not completely settle, if they toss it into the river. Just the right size for your knife I'd say."

Lykaois stilled, eyes now mere slits.

"I see you get it." I told the creature, pushing myself away from the window, one hand raised and placed against the glass. "Your knife will go over the edge, and be carried by the very fast-moving water out to sea. Where it will disappear into the depths, and no matter of scrying or whatever the fuck you use to sense the thing will help you find it."

"I did some research, you see. It's handy knowing a witch who has access to a *lot* of books on pretty much every subject." I continued, keeping its attention on me as I quickly worked out where we all were in the room. "Your little knife is basically a 'cursed artefact of parasitical nature'. You use it to forge the link between your *chosen* and you, and steal their strength, their willpower to resist you. But to do that, you've had to invest a *shitload* of yourself into it. Like Sauron and his ring. Lugh and his spear. Donald Trump and his hair piece. You're *connected*, and unless you keep those sacrifices coming, I think it drains you instead. Little by little, you're getting weaker and weaker from not using it. So what do you think would happen if I put it out of your reach for ever? Huh?"

Lykaois stared at me, its amber eyes narrowed but I could *feel* the fury pouring from it anyway. The pure and simple desire to tear me apart for my audacity, my keeping it from claiming what was rightfully its own. Warring with its plans to use me, the need to keep me alive for its own nefarious purpose.

I was *really* fucking with this thing's head, which was exactly how I wanted it.

"So again, here's the only deal you're going to get today." I repeated slowly, as I stepped away from the window. Lykaois slowly backed up, as I moved just a little way into the room. Not enough that I was out of sight of the window, just placing myself where I wanted to be. Where I wanted *him* to be too. "You undo whatever juju you've done to Jacob and Sarah. Unbind them, heal that fucking cut you made and remove any memories of what you made them do. Forever. Then, when I've spoken to them and confirmed they are free of your influence, then I'll stop my friend downstairs dumping your precious knife in the Thames, and you can take it and fuck off wherever you like. Just not here. Not in my backyard. You take it, you go."

I knew I was pushing it, and I hadn't even demanded it destroy the hexed item gifted to it that was weakening the other lycan. We'd just have to deal with that ourselves somehow. But right here and now, all I could do was get those two free of the bastard, make it so they were safe from ever being taken back over. Then … well, we'd see.

It eyed me as I stood, wine glass held loosely in one hand, the other poised, ready to signal my contact outside to do as we had agreed. I had no weapon, wasn't in my Changed form. Just facing the bastard with the simple knowledge that I was calling the shots here.

"Seriously, you have the whole fucking *world* to choose from." I sighed, counting off facts on my fingers. "You've been *Ba'alche'* something or other in South America. *Niǒ-Garmr* in Norway and Scandinavia, *Nīp-Gyflin* across all of bloody Germany and some parts of Europe. Gods know whatever when you played with the Romans in Italy and wherever they went. And *Lykaois* in Greece, the cursed King who tried to trick Zeus and got his arse turned into a wolf monster for being such a fucking moron. The point is, you've been *tons* of places, so pick somewhere else and *go fuck off*."

"Someone has done their homework." It growled a snarling laugh, as I shrugged. "But my legacy spans much further than that story, as if I could ever have sprung from the idiocies of one foolish mortal. I have stalked the shadows since they crawled from their caves, taken their blood and their sacrifices to appease my hunger. I have run with the Wyld, before it became a simple puppet of Shadow. I have brought fear to those that thought themselves too powerful to touch, too strong to be bested. I am the terror in the night, the cry that tells those cowering in fear that I have claimed another soul ..."

"Yada yada yada." I made the puppet shape with my free hand and mimed talking. "Heard it all before, by things bigger and scarier than you. Also, hairier but I'm not judging. Now, choose. Free my friends or lose your knife forever."

Lykaois snarled, its amber eyes blazing with fury. But finally, after a moment it turned its back on me and walked over to where Sarah and Jacob stood, somehow held by its will. At some unspoken command, both lifted their arms, Jacob slipping the plaster free from his hand whilst Sarah undid the bracelet and bandage she wore over her wound.

Lykaois growled words I couldn't hear, or possibly understand given it probably knew a few languages I had never come across. Then it leant forward, and that noisome tongue curled out of its mouth, running over both wounds.

Sarah and Jacob shuddered, she falling to the floor in convulsions whilst my packmate locked rigid, muscles straining against something invisible, some other force I could not see. I knew I had to stay put, but it was a battle not to barge past the bastard and check on Sarah, whatever the fucker was doing to them both.

The next breath, *something* rose from both their forms. It was like a smog or thick mist, writhing with unnatural vigour. Shot through with streaks of amber, the same hue as the creature's eyes. This surged up and out of the two, and writhed through the air until it soaked into Lykaois's outstretched hand. Its essence reclaimed, or something like that.

Jacob was the first to rouse, rocking on the balls of his feet and groaning as he shook his head. He took in the state of my home, the lack of any familiar furniture and the scars of the damage done. And then who stood close to him.

"Jacob, no!" I shouted, attracting his attention as my packmate instinctively started to Change, fists already swinging to pound the bastard standing in front of him. "Don't hurt him. Can you check Sarah? Show me her wrist. The right one."

Lykaois snarled, stalking back to where it had been standing when I gave it my ultimatum. Which was fine, as it meant it was away from Sarah, as her shakes slowly stilled. Jacob bit back the hundred or so questions that had to be filling his head, and instead knelt by the mortal woman. He quickly checked her pulse, then gently held up her arm for me to see.

Where before had been a puckered wound, red and weeping, now there was just unmarked skin. Not even a scar, nothing to show that Lykaois had marked her, bonded her in any way.

"And you? Your hand?" I asked him, and Jacob shot me one of those *'what the fuck about my hand?'* looks but I shook my head. "It's important!"

He sighed, but settled Sarah's arm back down and then held up both his hands, for my inspection. Both free of any mark, any wound.

"Now what the fuck is this all about? And what the fuck is *he* doing here?" Jacob growled, and I guessed Lykaois had done a little more than simply removing the memories of the killings it had made them do. When immortals mess with the insides of people's heads, lycan, mortals or whomever, there's always the chance they overdid the whitewash and removed more than they should. But that was something to worry about later.

"I have kept my end of the bargain." It told me from where it stood. "Now, signal your mortal and return to me my knife. Now."

I took a breath, remaining calm as I casually crossed my arms, my hands dipping from its sight. Just for a moment, since I knew I didn't have much time. This was the risky bit, given of all the people involved in my plan, there was one I *hadn't* been able to talk to about their role.

Namely the hulking mountain of muscle I'd just freed from Lykaois's control.

In some stories, you can have an entire conversation with a few simple twists of one's fingers. *Thieves Cant'*, or some such name, for sign language that could convey a whole array of information with minimal effort. Useful when one is being watched and needs their partner to know the whole plan, the reasons behind some of the crazier actions and what not to do. Usually as the last part will ruin everything.

In reality, all I could manage were just a couple of key words for Jacob to pick up on. Made quickly, hoping to fuck he understood.

Wait. Hit. Him. My. Mark.

My packmate gave no sign he even got the message, but then him nodding would have been a dead giveaway. Instead, he knelt down and gently helped Sarah sit up, as I watched for any sign of a trick. Anything to show that Lykaois still had control of her. But she just shook her head, gazing around at the room, then at us, confusion writ all over her tired features.

"Morgan, what's going on? I don't … remember?" She started to say, but I just smiled and motioned for Jacob to deal with her. Right then, I had matters to settle.

"Morgan Walker. My knife." Lykaois hissed, glaring at me but pointing one finger back at the pair. "Or I will undo what has been done, and make them *suffer*."

"Yeah, about that." I smiled at it, shrugging my shoulders. "See, I might have fibbed just a *little*. You see that person down by the river? They don't have your knife. Never did. I couldn't trust you wouldn't have another host or friend lurking around ready to jump whomever I gave it to."

I slipped my arms free, letting my hand brush my waist, as I brought to mind the cursed knife as I'd seen it in Sister Spite's hands. Its green-black blade, smooth and scalloped, and the double grip handle and hooked guard. Simple, effective but ugly all the same.

"So, I kept it on me. Its been here all this time." I deftly drew it from the bag of holding I had strapped to my belt, knowing that as soon as I freed the weapon, Lykaois would sense it. The bond between them reformed, one calling to the other. "That's the only way I could get you here, to do what I wanted. And so I could do … this."

And before the other could move, I slashed a cut across my left palm. Blood spurted instantly, splashing the blade and soaking into the stone like it was drinking the warm fluid down, and I felt a sudden weight on me. A presence, bearing down on me as that thick fog shot through with amber streaks surged out of Jack's body. Unstoppable, unyielding, as it writhed through the air to its newly chosen form, to the wound binding me to it.

Just before it engulfed me, I shouted out.

"Now!"

Felix appeared from under the Veil where she had hidden, the crafting so strong that I could neither sense her nor those waiting there with her. In her hands, a solid looking pump action gun pointed directly at me, her finger already depressing the trigger.

Across the room, Jacob sprang up from where he had waited, cradling Sarah, and powered across the floor, snarling with rage. He hit Jack like a sledgehammer, the Wyld fae still reeling from having its possessor yanked out of it so suddenly, and the pair of them disappeared into the wreckage of the kitchen amidst much snarls and howls of rage and pain.

I looked Felix in the eyes, and nodded, feeling Lykaois soaking into me. My vision tunnelled, the smell of mustard and burned spices filling my nose, choking me as I struggled not to move, not to fall under the onslaught.

And the witch nodded back at me.

Then she shot me.

Chapter 54

The impact almost knocked me off my feet.

We used the heavy gauge weapons as crowd control, for when we faced a large number of critters that needed knocking back. Of simple enough design so that the supernatural didn't mess with their mechanisms, they usually shot cartridges of pure salt and iron filings, sometimes with blessed holy water if the beasties we were hunting were particularly resistant. Think of the sandbag shot that mortal law enforcement often use to take down their targets with non-lethal force. This was like that, just suited more to the sorts of creatures we faced.

But they were adaptable, and on some hunts we used them not to knock our intended prey on its arse, but to knock it out inside.

I'd made sure Felix had suitable ammo to handle the task I'd assigned her.

"What, you think you can *shoot* me?" Lykaois's voice mocked me from all around, filling my head as my sight darkened. I could still feel a dull ache in my chest, where she had shot me dead centre, but it was like someone had thrown a switch and turned off all the lights. "I am *you*, foolish lycan. Mortal weapons will have as little effect on me, as they would you!"

"Yeah, I kinda had the same thought." I spoke the words though I wasn't sure if I was just thinking them rather than saying them. Lykaois was flooding through my body, taking control, pushing me back further and further into the darkness. I doubted I was in charge of a lot of things right now. "That's why I figured I might as well use something that works on me, because you're me too. Like you said."

Felix had dropped the shotgun, and run from where she had hidden. Behind her, Bear and Albert remained in the circle she had drawn and then covered with a Veil, kept still by her whilst everything happened around them. I'd carefully manoeuvred Jack and Lykaois around the room so they didn't accidentally stumble over the witch as she hid, waiting for my signal.

She stopped almost within arm's reach of me, and knelt. It took just a moment, a single breath and a pulse of magic, and the warding sprang to life. It had been set inert, carefully hidden by Felix to keep it unseen. She definitely had a knack for hiding shit, but then I guessed it was something all witches learned early on. A survival trait when they knew their neighbours tended to be paranoid and all too ready to burn, drown, hang or in every other way discomfort a practitioner if they were found out. Even today.

Now, the warding closed, locking us in. Felix was good at either wards to lock things out, or stop things from getting free. She'd used the former to stave off Lykaois the last time he was here in my home, wrecking the place like a bull on steroids in a china shop. This one, the one I'd asked her to craft for me, secured anything inside from getting out. Namely me, and my parasitic arse hole of a God.

Even as she did this, my hands fumbled at the heavy-duty dart sticking out of my chest. Despite being pushed further and further out of the way, I could also feel the numbness and sickness spreading from that wound, the contents of the dart having been injected into me on impact.

"Wolfsbane." I snarled at the creature riding me, as I slowly sank to my knees under the onslaught of the poison. "Jacob was dosing himself with just enough to knock himself out, but I reckon a triple dosage should put even something as fucked up as you out for a bit. And someone as *special* as me. Just enough time for OPS to come and 'contain' us. They'll know a way of getting you the fuck out of me with a proverbial crowbar or something, and then you are going straight back to prison. Do not collect two hundred pounds, pass Go or hurt anyone else, you *bastard*."

"I *beat* you." I snarled, hearing it howl and rage with fury as it realised how it had been tricked, and laughing with purest delight at the sound.

Felix was already on my mobile, calling up Cormac to tell him that the OPS containment team could head on up, to collect both me and Lykaois. It was worth the arse-kicking I'd get for lending the phone to a non-approved contact, if I got this bastard squared away. A small voice in my head *did* wonder how OPS would go about extracting the supernatural entity, and whether they'd bother taking care of the container ... i.e. me ... it was currently inhabiting. But hell, I could handle whatever they put me through to unstick the thing from my being, and I could do with the downtime anyhow. After the last couple of days, I was feeling particularly rough.

I also hoped she'd remember to mention that we had Jack with us, although I had my money on Jacob handling my half-brother in his much-weakened state. I reckoned my packmate had much venting to do, and a fucked up Wyld psycho was the perfect punching bag for him.

And finally, there was Sarah. Felix knew that as soon as she placed the call, her job was to get my mortal love into the safety of the warding with her, Bear and Albert. Get her there and keep her there until OPS arrived and I was safely detained, or it looked like they needed to vacate my home fast. In which case she was just going to do some structural damage and knock holes where she needed to, to get to the stairs down and safety.

All in all, things were wrapped up fairly nicely in my head, as darkness closed around me. The Wolfsbane was coursing through my veins, filling me with weakness and nausea so bad I was surprised I wasn't puking already. Three times the dose I'd ever received, enough to knock out an Alpha even. All for little ol' me. I was *so* going to regret this later.

"No!" Lykaois snarled in my head, its voice raging, and I swear I could feel the spit from its breath, it was that pissed. "I will *not* be taken advantage of so easily! I, who have slain thousands, and feasted upon the ruins of countless more. I will not be caged again!"

"Not much you can do about it, matey." I jovially told it, feeling its presence press down around me on every side. "You're trapped in me, thanks to your knife. And I'm poisoned. Best get used to being back in the box."

Lykaois went silent, and I felt a spike of coldness somewhere that, if I had control over my body, I'd have said was my stomach. Silence was not good, silence meant the bastard was thinking and I wanted it acting stupid and angry. Not smart.

Before I could think up some more insults to wind the creature up, I felt a change come over it. Like it had reached a decision.

Uh oh.

"Poisoned. Yes." It hissed, as I tried to think what it might have worked out, what option I'd missed. "Were I some simple lycan, I might indeed be trapped as you say. But you know so little about yourself, thinking in terms of those simpletons you spend your life protecting. You know *so* little of your potential. So let me teach you a little something."

I felt it happening, as my body convulsed, and pain blazed all around me. Lykaois seemed to rage through my blood and muscles, igniting my very cells as it then savaged any trace of the poison that I'd been injected with. I felt the Wolfsbane burning me like acid, but Lykaois smothered it, soaking into the poison and thinning it. As I tried to fight whatever the fuck it was doing, the creature entwined itself with every trace of the Wolfsbane, then drew it together like a vicious, evil nucleus. Held deep inside me, surrounded and shot through by the creature's essence.

"If you only accepted the truth of what you *are*," Lykaois snarled a laugh, full of mockery. "Then you would have known your little trick was doomed to fail. Neither you nor I are shackled by the weaknesses of those lesser creatures you call kin and pack, but the difference is you are ignorant of this. And thus, still weak, and *not* my equal."

It clenched a metaphysical fist and the poison burned away, all trace removed from my body. I could still feel how weak I was, the aftereffects of the poison still suckering me with nausea and the shakes. But I was conscious, not knocked out. Aware, when I'd planned to have both me and my hitch hiker to be shackled and unconscious, unable to act.

Lykaois had just *royally* fucked my plan.

"What, no clever reply? No witty quip to answer me?" It snarled at me, its mockery almost as sickening as the Wolfsbane had been. "You *dared* try and trap me, broke your promise after I freed those you care for. For that, I think you need to be punished so that you understand just how wrong you were to defy me."

I struggled against the creature's grip on me, the blackness that slowly slipped away as Lykaois allowed me to see once again. It still kept me chained, unable to act, but it wanted me to watch what happened next.

Felix had done everything I'd asked of her, having gotten Sarah from where she had lain, still confused as to what was going on, what had happened. The two women were now in the warding circle, along with Bear and Albert.

Beyond, Jack came crashing from out of the kitchen. My half-brother was stained with silver blood, his coat lost and clothes ripped and torn. The wound on his side was revealed, a massive crusted stinking hole with blackened flesh and corrupted blood seeping from it. Jack snarled, his finger knives flashing as he staggered back from where Jacob emerged from the wreckage.

My packmate had Changed, his clothes torn and stretched to fit his massively muscled frame. He was streaked with crimson and silver blood, Jack's and his own, and bore wounds from where the Wyld fae had slashed and bitten him. But as he stalked out of the ruins of my kitchen, Jacob growled throatily, his massive hands and claws splayed and ready to rend the life from his opponent. He was obviously enjoying himself immensely.

I struggled to shout out, to take control of my vocal cords just long enough to tell Felix I'd fucked up. Warn Jacob that shit was about to hit the fan. Anything. But Lykaois kept a stranglehold on my body, and I yelled in vain.

The creature slowly pushed itself up, cradling its knife in my hand. It clasped my wrist with my other hand, blood seeping from the wound I'd made, and let the weapon shake as if I were struggling against it.

"Now, let's see. Who can I make suffer, that will hurt you the deepest?" Lykaois murmured to me as I snarled and threw myself at the insubstantial yet unbreakable bonds binding me. "I *had* thought your idiotic attachment to the mortal would be your undoing, but you seem to be less distracted by her than I thought. So, maybe your friend, the witch? Young, vulnerable? I missed her the last time I was here but now would be as good a time to taste her blood."

"If you hurt anyone, I swear I'll..." I snarled but Lykaois's laughter drowned me out.

"You'll *what?* Stop me? *Kill* me? Don't be so pathetic." It snarled, swirling around me. "You can *do* nothing, that I do not will first. You can *say* nothing, that I do not allow first. Your threats are empty and worthless. No, I think I know *exactly* how to wound you the deepest."

Lykaois turned, using my body, play acting like I was fighting against the knife I held. Blood dripped from my wound, splashing against the boards underfoot, as it called out in my voice, my words.

"Felix! Sarah! Anyone, its gone wrong! He's getting free!" Lykaois cried out, pulling the names from my head with no effort. "You've got to help me! Just get the knife out of my hand, that will do it!"

It let me watch, hearing my shouts of frustration, of warning. Laughing as they went unheard.

Felix cradled Sarah, arms wrapped around her protectively, eyes narrowed as she looked across at me.

"Morgan, this isn't the plan! You made me promise not to help, no matter what!" She reminded me, eyes full of confusion, of doubt. "I can't tell if it's you or that bastard!"

"It's me, Felix! Remember how I came for you, when Gary had you imprisoned in the boat shed? How I forgot to Change afterwards, and you saw me for who I really am? It wouldn't know that." Lykaois plucked truths from my mind, even as I screamed my rage, trying to throw my strength against it. The bonds around me shivered, stretching as I smashed my mind against them again and again … but the creature clamped down hard on me, strengthening its grip even as it kept up the pretence. "Just break the circle, knock the knife out of my hand. Otherwise it's going to escape again! Please!"

Felix wavered, I could see the fact the creature was winning her over. I could do nothing as she went to set Sarah down, unsure but still willing to risk leaving her warding and come to my aid.

She was going to be killed, because I wasn't strong enough to beat this bastard. Her blood, spilled for this thing's hunger and pleasure, because I'd fucked up.

"Felix, no!" I howled, as she slowly pushed herself up, foot already raised to break the warding.

Chapter 55

Bear beat her to it.

The trollhound had remained silent all this time, curled up in the warding as I'd instructed him to. Keeping Felix safe, and making sure Albert didn't give them away by barking at the wrong time. That had been done by simply laying a heavy paw on the bulldog, which effectively squashed the poor mutt to the floor.

There was no way to tell Bear my plan in any way apart from the fact I needed him to guard Felix. To make sure both she and Sarah were safe. He'd watched me bargain with Lykaois without even a growl, watched as I cut myself and Felix had imprisoned me in the warding with only a twitch of his stubby ears.

But now, all he heard was me calling out. All he saw was me struggling against the creature I stank of. And he saw that Felix was about to go help me.

That was too much for him.

Brushing past Felix, throwing her back into the warding, the trollhound bounded into the circle with me. The witch had only been able to craft a ward to contain what was inside it, not stop anything else entering it, which was why I needed Jacob to keep Jack occupied so that my fucked-up half-brother didn't do something stupid and free Lykaois just when I had it where I wanted it.

But instead, Bear slammed into the circle, snarling at me but not attacking. Unsure, unable to actually attack me like he had Sarah when Lykaois had taken control of her, he faced me with a rumbling deep in his chest. Trying to work out how to help me.

"Oh look. The faithful hound has come to aid his master." Lykaois spat, as I shouted for Bear to get away from me. To defend himself. To just do *something*. "Yes, I think this will do *just* nicely. A fitting lesson for you, Morgan Black. Know your place, and know when you are beaten."

Lykaois quit feigning any sort of battle, hefting the knife as it settled on its feet, focused on Bear. The trollhound back up, pressing against the warding that now stopped it from leaving. He cocked his head, growl lessening to a whine, those eyes of his fixed on me. The trust, the fear. Both warring inside my companion of years.

And this bastard was going to kill him, to pay me back.

Lykaois lashed out lightning quick, grabbing hold of Bear and using my own strength to wrestle him down. I had tussled with the hound many times, but never with my full power, as I was always afraid of hurting him. Even though as a trollhound he was built to go against mountain trolls which were basically walking boulders. I just couldn't live with the sound of him in pain, the knowledge I'd done the damage to him.

Bear scrabbled at the floorboards, unwilling to fight back, not shifting to his larger size that he used against Real threats. He still thought it was me, that somehow I'd stop Lykaois from hurting him. Even as the bastard brought the knife round, slowly, deliberately.

"I'm going to start cutting your dog. Just enough to weaken it at first, so it can't resist." It drawled, even as Felix shouted from where she crouched. She couldn't use her magic either, knowing Bear was too close, that I was proof against whatever she could throw at me. "Just to draw the blood, bare the flesh. Let me sink my teeth into him, and watch as he realises *you* are killing him."

The knife gleamed with intent, as it leant on Bear and forced his head to one side, baring his throat and the veins throbbing there. That evil edge, hungry for life, sank down even as I pounded against my prison and screamed my fury at what was going to happen.

At what I couldn't stop the bastard doing to my hound.

The knife sliced down, and howls filled the air.

Chapter 56

Albert hit me like a furry bowling ball.

The bulldog hammered into my arm, snarling and howling like a banshee as he barrelled over the warding and bit down hard on my hand, on the knife.

Lykaois surged back up, snarling a curse as pain savaged it. Albert's teeth dug in deep, his weight momentarily dragging my hand down as Bear scrabbled to his feet, his bulk knocking into me. Unbalanced, in pain, Lykaois couldn't hold me upright and I slammed down to the wooden boards as pain tore up my arm. My head slammed against the bare wood, and for a moment, I felt things weaken. Its hold on me wavering as it tried to deal with everything that was happening to it.

I didn't waste it.

Not knowing what I was doing, I hammered against the prison binding me, feeling it facture, buckle … then shatter as I broke through. Knowing I had seconds, even less, I didn't try to tackle Lykaois for complete control or throw the knife out the window or any of the other clever things anyone else with an ounce of sense would have planned for and done.

No, instead I shot one last look over to Sarah, seeing her watching me with fear and love and a shitload more emotions written plain on her gorgeous face, and mouthed one word.

"Sorry."

Then I slapped my free hand, bloody wound and all, down on me and screamed out one word, with all the strength left in me.

"*Freeze!*"

The Shadow brand ignited as the magic imbued in me flared to life. I triggered the flow of it, feeling the temperature around me plummet, my breath suddenly come out in cold plumes.

"What have you done!" Lykaois hissed, savagely slapping me back down, roaring through me like an inferno. It slammed into the magic as it raced out from my palm, where I could already feel icy tendrils spreading through my body.

"I've fucked us, is what." I snarled back. This had been my gambit, my last chance I'd figured I might need if things went as wrong as they could. What I'd asked my grandmother, the Herald of Shadow, to help me with.

I was going to freeze us both, probably killing me in the process, but stopping the bastard from getting free, or hurting anyone I loved.

"No! NO!" It raged, battering at the summoned craft, siphoning strength from the knife I still held in one hand. The two powers exploded against each other, cold burning inside me then melting away, then shivering strong once more.

Lykaois was horribly powerful, forcing my body to blaze hotter and hotter to fight the coldness filling me. I felt my control over the Shadow brand slipping, snarling as I fought to keep the connection, to keep it filling me with icy death. But I was fighting an immortal, a God, and it would not be denied.

Desperately, I scrabbled inside me, seeking whatever it was the Morrigan had left. What she had gifted me when I asked. The mark on my forehead burned cold, as her voice rang in my ears.

"I have given you the knowledge and strength to do what you wish. But I can guarantee with even that, you may not succeed. That depends on you, on your desire and will alone."

Strength flowed down through that touch, her words channelling me, directing me. Not to end my life, but to aim my focus, shining upon what I needed to win this fight.

The knife.

It was what Lykaois was channelling all its power from, drawing on it like a wellspring. As long as the two were connected, it would be too strong for me. I had to break that connection, separate them.

I hurled everything I had at the weapon clenched in my hand, so that it was engulfed in a maelstrom of ice and crackling power. Lykaois must have realised my intent, as it screamed and tried to overpower me. It lashed me with agonies beyond comprehension, burning my body, setting fire to my nerves and making it feel like every bone was breaking, every muscle wrenched apart under its lash.

I screamed, uncaring, head thrown back and air burning my throat as I sobbed against the agony, the torment. But I kept on pouring the magic into the knife I clenched in my fist, hearing a high-pitched whine fill the air. Felt the metal and stone vibrate in my hand, as cold fury savaged it.

"*Do NOT!*" Lykaois screamed in my head, all of its strength now thrown against me, trying to beat me back, to stop me.

"Fuck you!" I screamed right back at it, and threw everything I had in one last push. One last throw of the dice.

Stone sang …

Shivered …

Broke.

Chapter 57

The explosion hurled me from the warding circle, breaking it as I tumbled across the floor. The air blew out in a maelstrom, bowling Bear and Albert over and over as they scrabbled at the wood beneath them, desperate to latch onto something. The raw magic hammered into Jacob, hurling him off of Jack as the lycan pounded at the Wyld fae, smashing him through my bedroom wall and into the room beyond.

Within her warding, Felix ducked low, shielding Sarah as magic and broken furniture smashed down against the protection surrounding them both. Sparks showered all around them, but the circle held.

Just.

Jack was sent tumbling as well, smears of his silver blood painting the floor as he rolled and crumpled against the far wall, almost beside the apple tree. Which bent and groaned under the onslaught of the magic in the air, but apart from losing a few leaves, seemed to survive ok.

The windows in my apartment, on the other hand, fared less well. Glass exploded out into the night, as icy October air filled the living room. Distant screams and shouts told me those mortals still hanging around the security bollards surrounding my home hadn't appreciated having a half ton of shattered glass dumped onto them, and I just had to hope none of the OPS staff had been injured by the falling debris. If they had, Cormac was going to have my skin.

I groaned, realising that I had control of my body again as waves of pain assaulted me. The hand I had cut was throbbing from the wound I'd inflicted, but I could feel the damage already starting to knit together. The other hand, the one I'd been holding the knife with when I'd shattered it, felt like someone had repeatedly smashed a hammer down on it, and the finger bones all felt crooked and wrong. I was bleeding from Albert's bites, but not enough for me to think I needed to wrap the thing. I'd had worse, after being almost flayed alive by Morgana, and still walked away.

Well, kinda crawled, but it was the act that counted.

"What have you *done?*" A voice snarled, dripping with fury and pain.

I dragged myself up, feeling my vision double a second before it decided to play ball. To find Jack glaring at me from where he was slumped, at least several bones broken by the crooked angle of his legs. Silver blood spilled around him, but the pain wasn't just his. Nor were the amber eyes blazing in their sockets, as Lykaois panted and hissed with fury.

"Fucked you royally, I reckon." I tried to smile, finding even the muscles of my face hurt. Hell, maybe this *was* worse than what Morgana had done to me. "Destroyed your knife, destroyed you. Can't bind anyone now, you bastard."

Lykaois snarled again, then it slowly raised one hand. In it, a large shard of shattered stone, definitely part of the knife's blade. Jagged and broken, but still dangerously sharp.

"Maybe. Maybe … hnh … not." It hissed, the fury in its eyes so hot I almost felt scorched under its lash. "But I can … can do one *last* thing."

Before I could stop it, given it was halfway across the room from me and none of my muscles were working properly just yet, it slammed the shard into its own body through the wound over its heart. Shoving the stone fragment in deep, forcing it into Jack's body. Piercing the Wyld fae's working heart.

"One … hnh … last *sacrifice.*" It hissed, as its body arched and bowed in agony. "And one … last … *chosen.*"

Power flared, the last of whatever had been in the knife flowing into Jack's body as the shard sliced into him. The Wyld fae convulsed, silver blood bursting from his lips, as his body strained and cracked. Bones broke with sickening snaps, reforming stronger, thicker. Muscles burgeoned as Lykaois surged through the body of its host. His crooked and broken legs grated and pulled back together, coarse fur bursting from his scaled skin as his clothing ripped and fell away. The lamprey mouth distended, pushing out from a thick muzzle filled with jagged, predator's teeth whilst that gross tongue flicked at the blood coating his lips.

Felix gasped, seeing the transformation, whilst Sarah cursed several choice phrases in Spanish. Hearing them, Lykaois craned its massive head across at them and let its mouth gape in a wolfish smile, long fangs glistening and tongue testing the air.

Those blades that Jack had attached to his fingers were now transformed into curving claws, like the fingernails of ancient Chinese Emperors. Just a lot sharper and deadlier. These it scratched along the wooden floor, peeling several inches of wood from the boards with a simple brush of its paws.

It levered itself up, body crooked and grossly muscled. It was well over seven feet tall, the breadth of its shoulders more fitting for an ogre than a lycan, and its bestial features was a mix of wolf and cat, those amber eyes blazing with rage and hunger from beneath a jutting, furry brow.

"Hnh. He was growing tired of killing witches and druids anyway." Lykaois hissed, as it rolled its shoulders and spread its claws out in anticipation. "Now, we are one. And one son of Herne is as good as the other to challenge for rule of the Wyld Court, I think."

"That's why you wanted me?!" I drew a breath and pushed myself up, telling my body to shut the fuck up and quit complaining. "You want to challenge Herne, become a Lord of the Court? In your dreams, you psycho weirdo!"

Then a thought struck me.

"And is that why you were killing those witches and druids? Because of their link to the Wyld? You wanted to weaken Herne somehow, so you went off on one butchering a bunch of mortals?" I shook my head, beginning to realise just how many people had died because of this lunatic's ambitions. "Are you fucking serious?"

"I shall enjoy taking that tongue from your mouth." Lykaois snarled, as it took a step forward, flexing its claws. "No. The children of the Goddess died at the whim of She who summoned me. But it suited my purpose, to have your father also diminished by their shed blood. Now, enough talk."

"Couldn't agree more." I snarled, squirrelling away the fact it had let slip. That the death of the witches and druids was orchestrated by Morgana, for whatever mad reason the newly crowned Queen of Twilight had for attacking the Goddess of the Mortal Realm.

I shot a glance to Felix, motioning for her to stay put. She'd only get hurt, trying to take on this hybrid of my half-brother and Lykaois. Plus, I needed her to keep Sarah safe, and maybe help out if it turned out brute force wouldn't put this fucker down.

Jacob pushed through the wreckage of my wall, shaking his head and snarling as he took in what we faced. I nodded to him as he padded to my left, even as Bear lumbered up from where he had fallen, to take my right. The trollhound huffed a query, and I ruffled his thick mane even as I felt him swell, taking on his non-mortal friendly size that he normally reserved for hunting trolls. His claws scratched at the wood as he shook himself, snarling at the one who had fucked with me, and almost hurt him.

Together, my packmate, my trollhound and I faced the immortal. I felt the Change take me, as I raised a hand, and beckoned to it.

"Let's finish this." I snarled.

Chapter 58

We came together in a crash of howls, snarls and savagery, as the three of us hurled ourselves at the Lykaois-Jack meld.

Two lycans, Changed, and a trollhound in Real form were enough to deal with most situations swiftly and decisively, given the sheer amount of hurt we could individually throw down, let alone the mayhem we could cause together.

But this was the God's holy night, with a full moon high overhead, and it was melded with a powerful Wyld fae. Despite his being poisoned by silver and cold iron, the bastard was tough enough to still be breathing after Jacob had pounded on him, and now he was blended with an immortal that might be the actual origin of us lycan. Whatever, it was savage and horrendously strong, and I'd spent the evening pissing it off by refusing to bow down and then destroying its reliquary.

This was by no means going to be an easy fight.

Wary of how the bastard had disappeared and re-appeared in the church, fighting against Cormac, Sister Spite and me, I harried the bastard, trying to keep its attention on me. Which, since it was enraged by everything I had said and done, wasn't as hard as it sounded.

Jacob went high, looking to overpower and overbalance the bastard, even as Bear darted in with his jaws agape, aiming to hamstring and cripple it. I summoned armour through my Ivory brand, encasing my fist and arm in shining facets that glowed and sparked as Lykaois-Jack hacked at me with its razor-sharp claws.

But the creature was monstrously strong, its blows pushing me back even as it shielded itself from my packmate's attack with one arm. His blows drew blood, silver gore shining on its skin, but the wounds knitted over almost immediately. And Bear's snapping jaws closed on thin air as it jerked its leg from reach, kicking out with a foot that grew spike-like claws and almost spitting the trollhound before he scrambled back and away.

With the trollhound circling, looking for another opening, Jacob and I threw ourselves onto the meld, me trusting my Ivory armour to keep me in one piece whilst Jacob blocked the slashing claws as best he could. Blood soon stained my packmate's hide, and he snarled in pain, grabbing hold of the meld's left arm as it sought to gut him, wrenching it to one side. Seeing an opening, I ducked a claw meant to rend my throat, and hammered my left fist into the creature's sternum.

"Freeze!" I snarled, trying to lock the bastard down like I had before. A nice quick win.

But Lykaois-Jack was wise to my gifts now, and even as ice blossomed on its skin, this blackened and dropped free. Discarded, with a glimmer of bone showing underneath before new flesh knitted and covered the wound. The fucker simply discarded anything I froze immediately, blocking my magic. Smart.

Snarling, I dove past, battering at it to try and give Jacob a chance to get close and do more serious damage. But he was thrown aside, the arm he gripped buckling then resetting so that it folded unnaturally, pushing him off his feet and hurling him back across the room as the creature slapped him away.

Bear threw himself at the creature, his own weight enough to stagger Lykaois-Jack as the trollhound's teeth and claws ripped at it. I powered up from where I'd rolled, lashing out with my own claws to catch the attack meant to rip Bear apart, sparks bursting all around us as my Ivory armour took the brunt of the blow. I snarled against the pain, unable to block the second clawed hand that slashed at me instead, feeling flesh rip and blood spurt as it carved into me.

"Fools! You cannot defeat me!" The meld snarled, hurling Bear from it with a solid kick that made the trollhound cry out as he landed badly. The hound staggered and shook his head from the glancing blow, obviously dazed. "You only delay the inevitable. Lay down, offer up your throats and know you died worthily to appease my hunger!"

"You talk too much." Jacob snarled, barrelling back into the fight. He faked an attempt to wrestle the bastard, letting Lykaois-Jack grab at him with its oddly jointed arms, but instead slipped to the side and proceeded to hammer at the creature's torso. Bones snapped under his onslaught, and it screamed as it faltered. I went after it, seeing it distracted, slamming my claws into its weird-ass arm and throwing all my weight plus my Wyld strength behind a sudden jerk and twist.

Muscles ripped, tendons snapped and bones shattered as I tore the forearm free of its socket. I cast the ripped limb to the floor, as Lykaois-Jack screamed. Fouled black-silver blood spurted from the wound, but before I could celebrate, the bastard slapped me with its undamaged hand, claws ripping through the fae-summoned armour as well as my skin and muscle and hurling me from my feet.

Before Jacob knew he was in trouble, the creature lashed out and gripped him by his throat with its remaining hand. With a hissing roar, it lifted him clear of the ground and shook him, even as my packmate hammered his claws at the limb holding him upright. It roared again, and its mouth gaped wide, lower jaw dropping and teeth bristling as it made to drag its captured prey close enough to bite.

Purple fire shattered the air, hammering into the creature and splashing out in flickering shards. I ground my teeth against the pain in my chest and looked over to find Felix standing outside her warding, arm outstretched in the classic *I'm hurling magical fire* pose that you always see wizards, witches and sometimes baseball players use.

"Get back in the warding! Now!" I barked at her, as Lykaois-Jack staggered, momentarily distracted. Her fire had done it no harm, like before when she'd tried to aid Goldspur, but it did leave her vulnerable.

As the witch scrabbled back to safety, Jacob managed to get a grip on the creature as it held him tight. Using leverage, he hammered both feet into its chest then pushed with all his strength, like a parkour expert doing a flip off a wall. He jerked free of its grasp, leaving bleeding wounds around his neck where it had ripped his flesh, and tumbled back out of reach.

Snarling a curse, the meld flickered and disappeared from sight. Just like in the church. I rolled from where I crouched, expecting the bastard to appear on top of me and use those spikes to skewer me. But it had other ideas.

The creature appeared across the room from me and Jacob, crouching down over where its severed limb had been tossed. It grinned at me, showing all its teeth, as it gathered up the forearm and jammed it back against the stump of its elbow. Fur and skin rippled and oozed together, binding and reknitting until it held up the limb and waggled its claws.

"You cannot end me." It snarled with smug, dripping tones. "Why prolong the inevitable?"

The bastard was right, I admitted silently in my head. Jack had been weakened by the silver and cold iron still inside him, but now bonded with this thing, he was hitting above lycan Alphas on the scale of indestructible. With Jacob still sick from the hex that Cerce had created, still powered and in place, and me suffering the aftereffects of all the Wolfsbane I'd pumped into my body … even with Bear along, we were getting nowhere.

And there was Felix and Sarah to think about, as until they got out of the apartment, they were relying on the witch's warding to keep the creature out. Sooner or later, it'd smash the crafting and get to them.

I had to try something. Anything. Imprisoning it inside me hadn't worked, nor had my half-baked idea of freezing my ass solid. This thing needed containing, but was way past OPS's ability to handle now that it had melded with my psychotic half-brother.

I felt Felix's eyes on me, Sarah's as well. Both hoping I had a plan, a way out of this where we won, and it lost. I'd tried foolhardy, I'd tried desperate. What the fuck else did I have?

And in that moment, my grandmother's mocking tones came back to me.

"… *Remember who you are. Where you came from. At the end, that will aid you more than magic words or heroic deeds.*"

Who am I? A Redcloak, a lycan. One of the pack. A finder of lost pets. Knight of Ivory, Envoy of Ivory. All of which was proving fucking useless against the bastard.

But that wasn't entirely true. I wasn't a *true* lycan, not born of their kith and kin. I was the child of a witch, a government agent who had been involved in a truly stupid attempt to confine an immortal of the Real as a means to protect the mortals of this Realm, or at least this island we stood on, from monsters such as Lykaois.

And the son of an immortal, the Lord of the Wyld Court. Herne the Hunter. An elemental, a creature of myth and legend, who was the biggest pain in the arse and terror to the lycans whenever we crossed into the Real. Until I came along.

That was when something clicked in my head.

I'd tried foolhardy and desperate, yes. So maybe it was time for one last, very last gamble.

And I try asking *family* for help.

Chapter 59

True Name

Whilst most creatures are not affected by the use of their name, except for it attracting their attention, there are those to whom hearing it uttered causes indescribable pain. They will go to any length to hide their name, creating aliases and whole personas to hide the truth. Changing any written record, destroying any evidence that would lead another to learn its name and be able to use it against it.

However, these creatures often then attempt to trick mortals by forcing them to guess the true name, when they are sure there is no record of it anywhere to be found. This invariably leads to the name's discovery, and the creature to be tormented by its utterance. Much to its chagrin.

There was no time to plan, no time to check with anyone about whether this would work. I'd just have to throw the dice, and hope that *this time*, whatever immortal bastard kept messing with my life let me have a win. Just this once.

I threw myself at Lykaois-Jack as it rose back to its full height, both arms reaching out to snatch at me. But I was faster, ducking under its lashing claws and slamming into it. And as it roared and tried to prise me off it, I punched my hand under its raised left arm, down into the blackened and crusted wound Gregory Allen had caused when he stabbed Jack.

Noisome things squished under my questing fingers, as I felt the creature slam its claws down and pierce my body with bolts of liquid fire. I snarled, forcing myself to ignore the pain as I shoved my arm into the wound, fingers grasping, seeking the one thing I knew had to be in there.

A brush, a touch of coldness against my fingertips that numbed my flesh, telling me I'd found what I was after. And with everything I had left, I jerked the stub of my sword, left there when Jack had managed to rip the weapon out of its body, up and to where I knew its other heart had to be. Where the shard of Lykaois's knife had been thrust.

Cold iron and silver met cursed obsidian, and the creature convulsed as if I'd just pumped electricity through it. Its claws ripped free of my back, forcing a scream from my lips, as I shoved off against its massive chest and freed my gore-soaked arm. Back-pedalling, I scrabbled across the floor as Lykaois-Jack shook, black and silver blood bubbling up from its maw and gushing over its chest. It sank to its knees, claws ripping at its own body to try and reach what I had lodged together inside it before it collapsed.

"Felix!" I croaked, the wounds in my back burning with fresh pain as I rolled and pushed myself up. "I need a containing circle around it. Now!"

"It's not dead?" She asked, as she stumbled from the warding, approaching nervously. "Didn't you kill the bastard?"

"Not even close. Just fucked it up a little." I replied, gesturing at the shivering form. "I just short-circuited the curse that made it into that thing, but it won't last. So, please, a circle if you would be so kind?"

"No need to be sarky." She shot at me, but went about the task in the next breath. I'll give her this, she was quick and efficient, snapping shut the warding almost within a minute from me asking. "There. It's in a circle of containment. Again. Now please don't step on the line and mess things up. Again."

"Ha!" I snarled good naturedly, as she stepped back into her own circle and safety.

Jacob lurched from where he'd landed, one hand at his throat and the raw wounds there. He eyed the creature, as its convulsion slowly stilled, then looked over at me.

"Now what?" He asked, but I was interrupted from replying as Lykaois-Jack slowly rose back to its feet. It swiped at the tainted blood staining its lips, amber eyes narrowed and shot through with fury.

"Yes, now what?" It asked with a snarl, pressing one hand into the air before it. The warding held, flattening the creature's palm as if it met something more solid than thin air. "You have me contained once more, but if you think your mortal allies will be able to secure me now, then you are more of a fool than even I thought. I have been inside your head, remember? Even you know they cannot hold me now."

"I hate to agree with the bastard, but he's right." I answered Jacob, trying to ignore the creature's smug chuckle. "If OPS try and take him now, that'll just be a monumental waste of life and more lives added to its tally. So, I'm not going to risk that."

I turned to look at Lykaois-Jack, folding my arms and taking a slow, calming breath.

"No. This time, I'm going up the food chain and calling in a favour. From a higher power." I smiled thinly, seeing the creature flinch, amber eyes narrowing as it tried to guess my play.

"Herne, Hunter. Lord of the Wyld. By blood of my blood, father to son. I call on you." I spoke slowly, reaching out through the summons. Letting my need be felt, plain and simple. "Herne, by my mother's sacrifice, and her love for you. I call on you. Herne, father. I call on you."

"What are you doing?" Lykaois-Jack snarled, pounding at the walls of its prison, spitting and cursing. "Why are you calling *him*?"

"You said you wanted to face him, to fight him for rule of the Wyld Court." I replied glibly, as the air in the apartment warmed. "Well, here's your chance. Face to face, no backstabbing or ambush like you probably planned."

The cold October air that had been blowing in through my shattered and broken windows lessened, warming as the scents of the forest flowed in and around us. Then it changed, to the taste of the sun-beaten savannah and musk of predator, of prey. Then back, switching and melding as the sense of the Wyld bourgeoned all around us.

"I hope you know what you are doing." Jacob growled, but I just shrugged, knowing I was literally winging it. Herne did not like being summoned, and the last attempt to properly drag him over to the Mortal Realm had ended with a lot of dead DOPA scientists and, eventually, me. The cost, my mother's life.

"Let me loose from here!" Lykaois-Jack hissed, crouching down and searching all around. Seeking the one I'd called. "Let me go free, and I shall leave you and your pitiful companions alive. I shall go from here, and never return."

"Too late for that, mate." I replied, and it snarled with fury, slashing at my floorboards and carving great rivets in the wood.

The air swirled around me, my senses telling me we were no longer alone. Then a familiar voice drawled close to my ear.

"Now what sort of trouble have you been getting into now, pup?"

I turned, as a mouthful of needle-like teeth shimmered into being at about eye level. Above these, two round eyes appeared, alive with dark humour, as the rest of the Bayun Cat slowly blurred into view.

The Wyld fae floated in mid-air, its paws folded beneath it and that spiked tail lashing the air behind. For all intents and purposes, a perfect representation of the Lewis Carroll character, apart from the murderous and psychopathic nature that it barely bothered hiding.

"Bayun Cat." I acknowledged it, feeling my stomach sink a little. "I was kinda hoping for Herne. He around?"

"The Lord heard your summons, and has answered." The Cat told me, as a weight seemed to settle in the room. "I am here, as ever, to deal with the troublesome fact you still rely upon speech as a means of communication. So ... *primitive*."

Herne seeped into being, his massive form settling on my bare boards and making them creak under his weight. He was clad in his furs and leathers, stained in dark tones to further blend into the wilds he normally stalked. His hood was up again, hiding his face except for those burning eyes of his, and the great antlers which arched over his head, the tines scored with runic script and hung with small bones and charms. He leant upon his massive spear, the brutal weapon notched and carved with tiny figurines. Representing each and every soul he had hunted.

Behind me, I heard Felix give a sigh. Just a quiet breath, but one obviously in reaction to the musk and overpowering masculine nature of the Hunter. Another reason for this not to take too long, as I didn't want my friend exposed to the immortal for any longer than necessary. One witch already had fallen for him, and lost her life because of that fact. I wasn't risking anyone else.

Herne had not come alone this time. Beside him, settled on their haunches and sat as still as statues, were two hounds. Coal black, they were built like Rottweiler-Doberman crossbreeds that had been juiced on steroids then streamlined to be as aerodynamic as possible. Whilst still retaining the threatening air of *I can tear you apart with my teeth* that all such hounds possess. It helped that they were only marginally smaller than Bear, and their eyes glowed with hellish fire.

Herne's Hounds were infamous throughout the Real and Mortal Realms, since the bastard tended to take those he thought would make perfect hunters, then change them into shapes more suited for the Hunt. Mortals, immortals, lycan … no-one was safe from his touch when he set his mark on them.

The Morrigan, on my behalf, had managed to agree an amnesty with Herne for all lycans, freeing those he had as his hounds already and stopping him from choosing anyone from the packs for a year and day. It had been a cause of celebration back this side of the Veil, and since it had been down to my efforts in defending the Courts at the Beltane Tourney, I'd managed a few weeks of *not* being the butt of all the pack's jokes and friendly ribbing about my usual clients.

But here he was, with two hounds at his side. Bear eyed them from where he had settled, his ruff bristling, and stubby tail held stiff. Wholly unhappy at their presence, whilst they chose to ignore him completely.

"If you have finished gawping?" The Bayun Cat hissed, sliding through the air to move closer to its Lord. Not too close to the hounds, I noted but didn't comment. Pissing off the Wyld Herald was never a clever idea, especially not when I needed Herne's help right now. "You summoned our Lord. For what reason?"

"For this." I pointed to Lykaois-Jack, as it seethed in the containment circle. "I want my *father* to help deal with this mess."

The Bayun Cat stalked through the air, reaching the edge of the containment warding and peering at the creature trapped inside. Lykaois-Jack snarled at the Wyld fae, amber eyes blazing with fury but also more than a little fear. Its arrogance might be monumental, but it was trapped. Vulnerable. And it knew it.

"Hssst. This is … *interesting*." The Cat smiled, revealing all its teeth as it slowly circled the warding. "I taste the get of our Lord, his son long imprisoned for preying on the foolish mortals and breaking their silly laws. But there is more … I sense one of our Court, long lost to us. Having run to hide in the Mortal Realm after failing in its bid to rule. Oh, this is indeed a merry meeting!"

"So, this thing tried to take over the Court before?" I asked, finding it wholly unsurprising that I wasn't even its first attempt to challenge for the Wyld. "How come it's still alive? I thought losers tended to be dealt with, like, terminally? Hence most sane people not bothering challenging?"

"Indeed." The Cat hissed, rolling in the air with mirth. "*Starrk*, or whatever it calls itself now, thought itself fit to rule and challenged for the Court. It sought to use its mortal sycophants, the creatures you know as *lycan*, to ambush and slay its opponents in deceit and secret. But the crones judged it unfit to rule when it turned on those same servants in a fit of paranoia, slaying them with the belief that they would betray it too."

"The crones sentenced it to be imprisoned in the Verdance. Staked down and restrained, for all the Wyld creatures to feed upon until it learned humility and the wrongs of its own acts. Instead, Starrk ripped free of its own body and fled, hunted all the way to the Mortal Realm where it hid away. Craven and cowardly."

The Cat snarled the last, spitting out its utter disdain for what Lykaois … Starrk … whatever this thing's name was … had done. For its part, the meld of my half-brother and the creature sunk lower on its legs, crouching under the lash of its truth being fully revealed. No angry snarls escaped its maw now, instead a whining hiss that spoke of fear.

I turned from watching it, and faced Herne. My father. Lord of the Wyld. We had clashed wills outside the Beltane Tourney, when he had tested me to see if I was fit for the challenge. Typical father-son bonding … not. Now, those burning eyes of his met mine, and the immortal cocked his head and lowered his spear, pointing to what lurked in the circle.

"Our Lord asks, what is your desire here?" The Bayun Cat asked, its own eyes glowing and that shark smile filling its face. "The crone's punishment still stands, for neither Herne nor I think it has learned any humility in the ages since its escape. Do you wish it, and your half-brother, to be taken back to serve out their time as decreed?"

I shook my head, knowing what I wanted. It was a little twisted, but then I was never going to win any awards for being angelic of thought. And I wanted this bastard to *suffer*.

"It's not enough." I growled, and Herne nodded, once.

"Then, you wish your father to Hunt it? To end his own son, and the creature tied to him?" The Wyld fae asked, one eyebrow quirked as if it had not expected such from me. "You must be clear, pup, as to your wish. And the consequences of what you ask."

I shook my head again, taking a breath before replying.

"I'm not asking Herne to do anything I wouldn't. If I could." I answered, locking my eyes on the immortal. So that it could see the truth in my eyes, understand me. "I don't want Lykaois … Starrk … Jack, either of them to have a chance to get free again. To threaten those I love and care for. Or any defenceless mortals, given both Jack's and this bastard's habit of butchering anything they can reach."

"But I don't want them simply executed. That's too quick." I continued, squaring my shoulders as I saw the fires in my father's eyes flare, with understanding. "I summoned you, Herne, Lord of the Wyld and my father, to *ask* that you take this creature. This thing that was your son, and one of your Court, and you do as you will with any living creature. Turn them into a Hound, make them one of your Hunt. Forever."

Lykaois-Jack snarled and pounded at the invisible wall holding it back, spitting curses and cries against what I asked. The Bayun Cat's eyes widened in surprise, and I relished that single moment of actually getting one up on the sarky fucker.

For his part, Herne remained silent, spear still pointed at the warding circle.

"I want them aware, knowing they are bound and never to be free. Yours to command forever." I added, with the certainty that binding Lykaois this way was the ultimate punishment. Making it serve another, robbing it of its Godhood and followers, denying it the worship it craved. "Can you … *will* you do this?"

The immortal kept my gaze for a long moment, then nodded. Once.

"NO!" Lykaois-Jack screamed, but shut up as Herne stepped up to the warding. The creature cowered away, snarling and spitting, fighting to get away as the immortal slowly extended its spear. The weapon pierced the warding, but somehow did not break the circle since Lykaois-Jack remained imprisoned. The meld pressed hard against the back of the warding, jaws gaping, drool running from between its curved teeth and eyes wide in horror and fear … as the tip carefully, gently, passed the space between them and pressed against the creature's forehead.

I was expecting mystical lights, fireworks, a tornado exploding in the warding. Basically, anything to mark the change from monster to, well, monster dog. All I got was a fading scream, as Lykaois-Jack blurred and shrank, body re-shaping under Herne's will.

There were two dull thuds, and I saw first a jagged stump of silver and cold-iron fall to the floorboards, covered in blackened blood. Then it was joined by the shard of Lykaois's knife, the two fragments expelled as the creature fully changed.

Until, finally, a Hound of white and grey fur crouched in the warding circle. Its eyes were still burning amber, but now it resembled a slightly smaller version of the two black Hounds who waited at Herne's side. No curving talons, no jutting teeth. No blackened wound in its side.

Herne slowly pulled back his spear, then deliberately stepped onto the edge of the warding circle. A shower of sparks erupted, lines of purple fire running around the full warding before it finally died away. The Hound shivered, head cocking as it looked across at me and a deep growl started in its throat. I could see its muscles tensing as it readied itself to spring at me.

The next moment, the two black Hounds were at its side, jaws gaping and bearing it down as they grabbed it by its throat. Snarls erupted from their maws, and both set their paws on the third dog and held it down as its own growls changed to whimpers and whines. Its amber eyes widened with fear, and it convulsed on the floor, as one of the black Hounds shook it hard between its teeth as a warning.

"Sember and Roth will teach this one its place, until it earns its name and rank in the pack." The Bayun Cat spoke up, as Herne stepped away, lowering his spear. "The Lord of the Wyld accepts this new member to his Hunt, but wants it clear this is no breach of the agreement made between the Morrigan and him. *You* asked for this, so the claim is valid and right."

I loosed the breath I had been holding, realising finally we'd done it. We'd beaten the bastard. Then a thought kicked me in the arse, and I stepped up to the Hound as it lay restrained by its packmates.

Crouching, I stared it full in the face, seeing the flickers of anger still burning there, the consciousness that was both Jack and Lykaois. Both doomed to an eternity of serving my father.

"I'll take this, thank you." I reached down and freed the corded band that was still wrapped around the Hound's forelimb. The cursed hex-charm, made by Cerce, that had messed up all my packmates and left us open to the bastard's coercion. "I hope you remember every day what I did here. What I *cursed* you to. And I hope it makes you fucking howl."

I stood, stepping away as Herne moved to join his three Hounds. The Bayun Cat followed, slipping through the air like gravity was something that happened to other creatures, as the Wyld creatures began to fade.

"The Lord of the Wyld wishes you success with your next challenge," It told me, grinning that evil smile. "He thanks you for his new Hound, and thinks you handled this situation … *adequately*. You are learning, *finally*, who you are. And what he sees pleases him."

"Great. I'll get him a *Best Dad Ever* mug next Father's Day." I snarked, and the Cat hissed a laugh. Whether from my father, or itself, I didn't know and didn't really care at this point.

"Now, we are done here. And you had best ready yourself. For I sense your day is not yet done, your life about to get a lot more … *complicated*." The Wyld Herald announced cryptically, but before I could get more answers, or more likely simple abuse and frustration, from it, the Cat, Lord of the Hunt and his three Hounds faded and vanished from my wrecked apartment.

I locked eyes with Jacob as I sank down onto the broken floor, heaving a deep and heavy sigh.

"What the fuck now?" I asked the room.

Chapter 60

Song

Certain supernatural creatures cannot abide the sound of singing, without there needing to be special words or a specific tune sung. Simply the sound will cause them extreme pain, to the point where they will either become enraged and attack the singers to try to stop the noise or flee from the sound.

Creatures with keen hearing especially suffer from this, being incapacitated by the sounds they cannot block out. This is most effective when children sing, forming a circle around the supernatural monster and effectively trapping it in a wall of sound and pain until it passes out. Many of the games played by mortal children now are based on this method of defending against particular monsters.

The next moment, Felix cried out, arms wrapping around herself as she writhed in sudden agony. She crumpled, and I scrabbled across the wood floor to reach her before she hit the ground.

Sarah got there first, shaking off her stunned horror at what had just happened in front of her. She caught the falling woman, cradling her as they both settled to the floor, as Felix cried out again. Purple fire sparked at her fingertips, blazing around her like a throbbing pulse, but Sarah held on and gritted her teeth, keeping her safe as the younger woman convulsed.

I reached their sides just as sounds from below announced the arrival of OPS. I motioned for Jacob to go greet them and give them the good news they'd missed all the fun, as I carefully gripped Felix's hands and gently prised them away from her body. Fire ran over my own skin, but didn't do anything except spark and die, thanks to my own natural immunity.

"Hey! What's wrong?" I asked her, a little stupidly.

Felix cracked open her eyes, as her shakes began to still. Her breathing was coming out like she'd just tried to run a marathon with no training, and sweat stained her skin. She gritted her teeth, fighting against whatever she was feeling, before she answered.

"Feels like ... something ... trying to grab hold inside me. Like something's pulling ..." She gasped, and Sarah exchanged a confused look with me. I shrugged, not knowing what the hell was going on. "It hurts ..."

The next breath, she convulsed again, sending Sarah sprawling and jerking her hands free of my own. Fire blazed up, a roaring inferno that leapt from her fingers to slam into the centre of my wrecked living room. It narrowly missed the apple tree, settling into a blazing pillar that roared up to almost touch the ceiling.

At the same moment, Jacob reappeared with a small surprise. Not the OPS strike team I'd been expecting, but Cormac Smith, looking particularly stressed.

"Morgan." He greeted me, eyes on the burning pillar. "We've got a problem."

"Like I said," I repeated to the world in general. "What the fuck now?"

"The mists." The OPS agent replied, as Felix slumped to the floor, the fire dying from her hands. The pillar continued to rage in the centre of the room, somehow not igniting the wood underneath. Just a roaring, raging conflagration. "They've all come down. Here. America, Europe ... wherever we had eyes on them, my agents and colleagues are telling me they've vanished. But whatever was there before, it's not there now. I'm getting reports of mountains and grass-covered hills, like they've opened up on somewhere entirely different. Possibly Norway, from the descriptions."

"*Twilight.*"

A new voice rasped, as the fire in the centre of the room collapsed in on itself, guttering and dying. Revealing a figure slumped on its knees, bent almost to the floor. Wrapped in a tattered cloak, the hood pulled up to hide its features.

But the scent. I knew this person. And the voice ... it pierced me through.

Elspeth.

"It's Twilight. She's opened the Ways." The witch spoke again, slowly reaching up to drag the hood back from her face. Revealed, she was gaunt and tired-looking, her red hair tangled and knotted. Faint traces of the intricate tattoos she had gained when she took Morgana's hand many months ago, and bound herself to the Twilight Queen, still glimmered like frost before the morning sun on her skin.

But her eyes. They were filled with pain, and anguish. A deep sorrow, weighing so heavily upon her. It cut right through me.

"She? You mean Morgana?" I asked, and swore loudly as she nodded once.

"She tricked me. Never meant to aid Gregory or I." Elspeth half whispered, her voice choked. As she spoke, Felix staggered upright, pushing away from Sarah and making for her. The young witch crashed to her knees, making me wince at the bruises she'd have from that impact, and wrapped her arms around the other. Felix buried her head in her shoulder, and tears seemed to spring from nowhere, wracking her body. "She used the bond between the Goddess and I … my Lady never fully broke it, no matter that I broke my oath to her."

"That's what the other witches were doing. The druids. They were trying to stop Morgana." I worked out, things clicking together in my head. "Fuck, what has she done?"

"She tricked Her. Wounded Her. Drained Her of Her essence." Elspeth whispered, rocking Felix. It seemed the bond between them had reconnected, and the younger woman was getting all of whatever Elspeth was feeling like an emotional rollercoaster. "Morgan. She *used* me to wound my Goddess. Poison Her, and through Her, any of us who connect with Her to use our magic. She's stripped the Mortal Realm of its power."

"Oh, fuckity fuck!" I snarled, but was stopped from any more questions as a disturbance outside caught all our attention.

The air above London boiled and writhed, clouds contorting as if maddened. It grew heavy, like gravity had somehow tripled, and I winced at a sudden thunderous ache behind my eyeballs, a pressure pushing at my brain. Everyone else seemed to suffer the same, even Jacob letting out a grunt of pain as he staggered and caught himself.

Then a shape began to form in mid-air, made up of thickening cloud and vapour, lit by flashes of lightning.

Queen Morgana. Lady of Twilight.

Her head, at least. Massive in size, hovering above the city. It swivelled, slowly casting its gaze to all four corners of the compass, and I saw that not all was the same as when last I faced the fae.

Whilst the right side of her face still resembled the creation Robert Knox had crafted for her from kidnapped and tortured mortal women, albeit thinner, more fae-like and with Twilight tattoos marking the skin, the left-hand side was now covered by a single piece of armour. Polished and smooth, like the curve of an egg, the mask clung to her face covering forehead and cheek, wholly encasing the eye and part of the nose. Only her mouth was free, a slit carved to allow the thin dark lips to be seen.

I had to guess what lay beneath was the ruin left by the Harrowing, unleashed by me when I tried to stop her from taking her new throne. I'd failed, but managed to break a container holding the killer of immortals against her, embedding it in her flesh. It looked like whatever she had tried over the past six months had not freed her completely from its ravages.

"Creatures of the Mortal Realm! Rejoice, for your Queen has returned!" Morgana's voice rang out, magically enhanced. It boomed across the land, reaching us like she stood directly in front of us, and I guessed the same would be for every living person, mortal, immortal and whatever else, that lived on the British Isle.

"Too long have you suffered under the yoke of witless fools, of powerless yattermongers who have not the wit to protect you. To ward you." She continued, her voice strident. "Too long have you lived in blind ignorance of the truth of what your world *really* is, and your place in it. But no more!"

Thunder boomed out, crashing and rolling overhead. I shot a glance at Cormac, who was talking urgently into a phone, and he caught my look. The OPS agent shook his head, the truth of how unprepared we all had been for this new development a solid slap in the face. No-one had even guessed what the fae planned, and any contingencies in place had either failed or been countered. She had done her homework and outmanoeuvred anything that could stop her.

"Mortals. Immortals. I am Queen Morgana. Lady of Twilight, and true heir to the throne of this Realm. Offered to me by the one you know as *King Arthur*, before he and his true master betrayed and imprisoned me. But I have thrown off their yoke, escaped their prison and have returned to take my rightful place above you all."

I growled a curse, feeling more than ever a desire to hunt down Artur and pound the slippery bastard for his stupidity and dumb arse promises made to ensure he got lucky with another fae. The idiot was owed some severe hurting.

"I make this offer once and once only." Morgana's head continued. "Join my Court. Take my pledge and serve me."

Beside her the image of her sigil formed. The upside-down trident, that I had seen painted and crafted on too many idiots and corpses in the Real.

"There is a place for you all, and I will not turn aside any who seek to take my mark. Mortals, know you are as welcome as your betters, and all shall find true meaning in serving me."

"But know this. To those who seek to stand against me, I say beware!" She snarled, looming large in the sky, as lightning flickered in her eyes and within the darkness of her mouth. "I have struck down your Goddess, poisoned the wellspring of your magic and might. Only those who take my mark will be spared, all others will weaken and sicken until you come crawling on your hands and knees to beg forgiveness. Or you die."

"Your protectors? The mortal authorities? They have not the power to stop me, and some even have elected to serve me already." She crowed, eliciting a scowl from Cormac who started speaking even more fervently into the phone. "As for your precious Redcloaks, the packs who so diligently patrol your cities and keep the peace? They are struck down, sickened. Weakened. I say to any and all of you who have been maltreated and mishandled by these wretched lycan. They are vulnerable! Strike them down, crush them for they are your enemies. And mine."

"Even as I speak, my armies enter your cities, your towns. Your homes." She announced, and the image of her head shifted for a moment, revealing scenes of armoured fae and Real creatures spilling out of the opened Ways, bristling with weapons and the desire to maim and kill for their Queen. "Bow down to my knights, my soldiers and you will be spared. Seek to fight, and you will be torn apart and fed to the crows. There will be no mercy granted."

Switching back, the massive head loomed even larger, seeming to focus in on my apartment. It towered in front of my broken, shattered windows. Morgana's eyes narrowed and a vicious, cruel smile carved her face into the appearance of a devil.

"Morgan Black! I know you can hear me." She cried out, fingers appearing to tap the plate covering half her face. "Do not think I have forgotten or forgiven the wrong you did me. Hear me, all you dwellers of this Realm. I will reward with riches and power beyond imagining the one who brings me the head of the lycan Morgan Black. His body need not be attached. His life is forfeit, as are those of any who shelter him or seek to aid him. Find this lycan, *kill* this lycan and bring me the proof of the deed and I shall be generous beyond anything you think possible."

She snarled down at me, victory burning bright in her eyes.

"Now *you* are the one who is hunted, Morgan. Now you shall know fear and pain. See those you care for suffer simply for knowing you" Morgana crowed, her voice booming across the heaves. "I await the news of your death with great anticipation!"

With that, her image shattered, as dark forms burst through. Great wings caught the air, as scaled drakes opened their fanged maws and sent forth a torrent of raging, burning destruction down upon London. Flames erupted as buildings exploded, screams carrying high into the air along with the sudden wailing of an alarm not heard across the city in over half a century.

The drawn-out drone of an air-raid siren, the cry echoing across London as the emergency broadcast was activated. It picked up, rising and falling across the city from archaic and battered speakers. A sound to elicit terror in those old enough to know its meaning, and fear in those that had never heard its wail before.

"He's coming for you too, Morgan." I turned, hearing Elspeth's words. And that's when I realised something.

Only Ellie had appeared.

"Where's Greg, Ellie?" I asked, feeling ice settle in my guts as tears coursed down her cheeks.

"Oh Morgan. He thought he was helping me. She tricked him too." She answered, and I felt the surge of pain and fear rise in her like some vast monster breaching from the depths. "She took his oath, and he is now her Knight. Her Knight of Twilight."

Elspeth met my gaze, hot tears coursing down her cheeks.

"And he's coming to kill you."

Outside, fires raged across the skyline of London. The cries of mortals in terror, in pain, lifted and merged with the wailing siren to fill the air with dread. Dragons screamed their rage as they dove through the night's sky, and beneath them came the howls and roars of Morgana's armies as they spilled out of the Ways and began their slaughter.

And I stood in the ruins of my home, gazing at the friend I'd failed to save. As my elation at beating Lykaois crumbled and fell away like ashes on the wind.

As the reality of what had happened unfolded in front of my eyes.

Gods, we were *Really* fucked.

Morgan's story, and that of the Pack, continues in Book 7 –

Dogs of War

Coming soon.

About the Author

Born the fourth son of the sprawling Cameron Clan, JP Cameron was introduced to the wonder of words and story-telling with the magical tale of The Hobbit, as one of the first books he remembers.

Taking The Lord of the Rings to primary school as his book for class set his feet firmly on a path, an endless road and a love of the fantastical, strange and magical.

Through school, work and into adult life (what little of that he knows), JP continues to expand his library and scope of writing, exploring other genres and inventing strange new worlds. But his love of fantasy remains at the core of his writing. Living with his wife and their hairy behemoth disguised as a Chow Chow in the green rolling hills of West Sussex, he is often found gazing happily at bookshelves groaning with volumes by Sir Terry Pratchett, Terry Goodkind, Terry Brooks and many, many more authors not called Terry.

Otherwise you may meet him up and down the UK coastline, celebrating a rich and happy history of piracy in fine company.

His published works to date include Tales of the Blade, and The Spire set, and now his debut into dark fantasy – The Lycan Files.

Find him at @JPCAuthor for tweets and questions.

Printed in Great Britain
by Amazon